I don't remember actually opening the door. I remember feeling the rain prickling my face as I emerged from the kitchen porch. I remember walking, stumbling through the weeds and the long grass, hurrying faster and faster, afraid to miss whoever it was who was swinging on the swing, and yet even more afraid that I might get there before they ran away.

I came around the apple-tree, right next to the swing, and stopped dead. The rain-wet chair was swinging backwards and forwards, high and steady, all by itself. The chains went *creakkk-squik, creakkk-squik, creakkk-squik,* but the chair was empty.

THE PARIAH

Look for these other TOR books by Graham Masterton

CHARNEL HOUSE

THE DEVILS OF D-DAY

THE DJINN

IKON

THE MANITOU

REVENGE OF THE MANITOU

SOLITAIRE

THE SPHINX

TENGU

THE WELLS OF HELL

THE PARIAH

GRAHAM MASTERTON

TOR

A TOM DOHERTY ASSOCIATES BOOK

THE PARIAH

A TOR Book

Published by Tom Doherty Associates,
8-10 West 36 Street,
New York, N.Y. 10018

Cover design by Carol Russo

First TOR printing: November 1984

ISBN: 0-812-52193-5
CAN. ED.: 0-812-52194-3

Printed in the United States of America

"But there is One Other, whose Name is never spoken, for he is an Outcast both from Heaven and from Helle; a Being shunn'd in every Realm spirituale or temporale. His Name was excis'd from evry Boke and evry Tablette, and his Image was banish'd from evry Place where People sought to worship him. He is a *Pariah* and he is terribly to be Fear'd; for at his Bidding the dead arise, and the Sonne itselfe is extinguish'd from the Skie."

—The so-called "forbidden last
paragraph" from the *Codex Daemonicus*,
1516, itself a "forbidden book" until
reprinted (without the last paragraph)
by the Ibis Press in Paris, 1926. The
only known complete copy of the *Codex*
is now in the Vatican Library's secret case.

CONDO DEVELOPER'S WIFE MISSING IN "NIGHTGOWN BOAT TRIP" MYSTERY

—Granitehead, Tues.

Coastguard helicopters were scouring Massachusetts Bay between Manchester and Nahant early today for Mrs. James Goult III, wife of the Granitehead condo developer, who has been missing from her home since late last night, apparently last seen dressed only in her nightgown.

Mrs. Goult, a 44-year-old brunette, drove to Granitehead Harbor at about 11:30 p.m. and disappeared out to sea in the family's 40-foot yacht *Patricia*.

Mr. Goult said, "My wife is an experienced sailor and I don't have any doubts that she is capable of handling the boat under normal circumstances. But obviously these are not normal circumstances, and I am deeply concerned for her safety."

There had been no quarrel between himself and his wife, Mr. Goult said, and her nightgown-clad disappearance was "a complete mystery."

Lt. George Rogers, of the Salem Coastguard, said, "We are carrying out a systematic search and if the *Patricia* is there to be found, we will find her."

ONE

I opened my eyes, abruptly—unsure if I had been asleep or not. Was I still asleep now, and dreaming? It was so dark that I couldn't tell if my eyes had actually opened. Gradually I was able to make out the luminous hands of my old-fashioned bedside clock; two dim green glows, like the eyes of an ailing but malevolent goblin. Ten after two, on a cold March night on the Massachusetts coast. But nothing at all to suggest what might have awakened me.

I lay tensely where I was, snuggled up alone in that big old colonial bed, holding my breath, listening. There was the wind, of course, rattling and chattering at the window, but out here on the Granitehead peninsula, where your bedroom is separated from the shores of Nova Scotia by nothing but hundreds of miles of dark and ruminative sea, the wind is a fact of life. Persistent and fretful even in spring.

I listened with the acuteness of someone who was still desperately unused to being left alone at night; with the same hypersensitive ears as a wife left at home while her husband goes away on a business trip. And when the wind suddenly rose, and worried around the house, and then just as suddenly died away again, my heartbeats rose and pounded and died away with it.

The window rattled, fell silent, rattled.

Then I heard it, and even though it was almost inaudible, even though I probably perceived it more through my teeth and more through my nerve-endings than I did through my ears, I recognized it at once as the sound that had woken me up, and my senses prickled like static electricity. Plaintive

9

and monotonous, *creakkk-squik, creakkk-squik, creakkk-squik*, the chains of my garden swing.

I stared into the darkness, eyes wide. The goblin-eyes of my clock stared back at me, and the more I stared the less they looked like my bedroom clock. I defied them to move, defied them to wink at me. But outside in the garden, on and on, there was that *creakkk-squik, creakkk-squik, creakkk-squik*. And the eyes refused to wink.

It's only the wind, I thought to myself. It must be. The same wind that's been rattling my window all night. The same wind that's been having such breathy conversations with itself down my bedroom chimney. But I had to admit to myself that I had never known the wind to blow my *swing* before; not even on a gusty night like this, when I could clearly hear the seething, disturbed sleep of the North Atlantic Ocean as it pounded a mile-and-a-half away; and the garden gates of Granitehead Village banged as always in intermittent applause. The swing was too heavy,ʾ a high-backed chair carved out of solid American Hop Hornbeam, suspended by iron chains. The only way that it could possibly creak was if somebody were to swing in it, steady and high.

Creakkk-squik, creakkk-squik, creakkk-squik, over and over; sometimes muffled by the wind, and the background roar of the sea, but continuing without a single break in rhythm while the clock hands moved through five whole minutes and the goblin appeared to incline his head.

This is madness, I told myself. There's nobody out there, at twenty after two in the morning, *swinging*. This must be the depressive neurosis Dr. Rosen was trying to tell me about; a change in perception, a shift in mental balance. It happens to almost everybody when they lose somebody close to them. Dr. Rosen said that I would probably experience it quite often: the unnerving sensation that Jane was still with me; that she was still alive after all. He had gone through similar delusions himself, after his own wife died. He had glimpsed her in supermarkets, just turning around the end of an aisle, and out of sight. He had heard her mixing pastry in the kitchen, and hurried to open the kitchen door, only to find that the room was quite empty, that the bowls and the spoons remained spotless and unused. This must be the same, this creaking I thought I was hearing. Real enough, in its way, but actually a sympathetic hallucination caused by the emotional after-effects of sudden bereavement.

And yet: *creakkk-squik, creakkk-squik, creakkk-squik*, on and on, and somehow the longer it went on the harder it became to believe that it was nothing more than my mind deceiving my ears.

You're a rational adult man, I told myself. Why the hell should you climb out of a warm comfortable bed on a night like this, just to go to the window and watch your own garden-swing blowing backwards and forward in a March gale?

Yet—what if there *is* somebody out there? What if there *is* somebody swinging, the way Jane always used to, hands held high to clasp the chains, head leaning back against the seat, eyes closed? Well, what if there is? That's nothing to be afraid of.

You really think there's somebody out there? You really believe that somebody took the trouble to climb over your backyard palings and stumble their way through eighty feet of unkempt orchard, just to sit on your rusty old garden-swing? On a black windy night, cold as a witch's nipple, with the thermometer down to zero?

It's possible. Admit it, it's possible. Somebody may have been walking back up Quaker Lane from the village, drunk maybe, or even just playful, or maybe pensive, or depressed? And maybe they just caught sight of the swing and maybe they just decided it would be fun to try it, and hang the wind, and the cold, and the chance of getting caught.

The trouble was, I thought to myself, who could that somebody be? There was only one more house on Quaker Lane before it zigzagged downhill to the Salem Harbor shoreline. The track was stony and broken and almost impossible to follow in the daytime, let alone at night. And what was more, that last house was almost empty in the winter, or so we'd been told.

It could have been Thomas Essex, the old hermit in the wide-brimmed caballero hat who lived in that run-down sea-cottage close to Waterside Cemetery. Sometimes he passed this way, singing and hopping; and once he had confided in Jane that he could catch sea-bass just by whistling to them. *Lillibulero,* he said, that's what they liked. He could juggle, too, with clasp knives.

But then I thought: he's eccentric, sure. But he's old, too. Sixty-eight if he's a day. And what's a 68-year-old man doing on my swing, at well past two o'clock in the morning, on a night like this?

I made up my mind to ignore the creaking and go back to sleep. I bundled the soft hand-stitched comforter around my ears, burrowed down into the bed, closed my eyes, and breathed with exaggerated deepness. If Jane had still been here, she probably would have teased me into going to take a look out of the window. But I was tired. I hadn't been able to get more than four or five hours a night since the accident, often less, and tomorrow I had to be up early for a breakfast-time meeting with Jane's father; and then I had to go to Holyoke Square to Endicott's, where they were putting up a collection of maritime prints and paintings, rare ones, worth bidding for.

I managed to keep my eyes closed for something like an entire minute. Then I opened them again and the goblin-eyes were still watching me. And from the garden, no matter how forcefully I muffled my ears, that continual *creakkk-squik, creakkk-squik, creakkk-squik.*

And then . . . God, I could swear it, someone *singing.* Faintly, in a high-pitched voice, blown by the wind; so indistinct that it could have been nothing more than the draft blowing across the top of the chimney-stacks. But singing, all the same. A woman's voice, clear and particularly mournful.

I scrambled out of bed so quickly that I banged my knee on the mahogany bedside table, and sent the clock tumbling and ringing across the floor. I was too scared to get up slowly: it had to be a *kamikaze* charge or nothing at all. I dragged the comforter along with me, wrapping it around my waist, and stumbled to the window breathless and blind.

It was so damned dark out there that I could hardly see anything at all. The very faintest distinction in tone between hills and sky. The shadowy thrashing of the trees as the wind relentlessly bowed them down, and bowed them down again. I stared and listened, feeling ridiculous and heroic at the same time. I pressed the palm of my hand against the window-pane, to stop it from rattling. But the creaking of the garden-swing seemed to have died away, and there was nobody singing, nobody that I could hear.

And yet that tune seemed to echo in my head, that peculiar

mournful tune. It reminded me of the sea-chanty that old Thomas Essex had been singing the very first time we came across him, as he walked up Quaker Lane.

> *"O the men they sailed from Granitehead*
> *To fish the foreign shores.*
> *But the fish they caught were nought but bones*
> *With hearts crush'd in their jaws."*

I had later found it written down in *Sea Songs of Old Salem*, by George Blyth; but unlike almost all the other chanties in the book, there was no explanation of what it meant, or whether it had any foundation in genuine local history. It was simply subtitled "A Curiositie." And yet who had been singing "a curiositie" outside my cottage, so late at night; and why? There couldn't have been more than a dozen people in Granitehead who knew that song.

Jane had always said the song sounded "deliciously sad."

I waited by the window until my shoulders began to feel cold. My eyes became slowly accustomed to the darkness, and I could indistinctly make out the black rocky reaches of Granitehead Neck, limned by the Atlantic surf. I took my hand away from the window-pane, and it was chilled and clammy. My handprint stayed on the glass for a moment, a ghostly greeting, and then faded away.

Groping my way back across the bedroom, I found the wallswitch and turned on the light. The room was the same as always. The big wooden early-American bed, with its puffy duck-down pillows; the carved double-fronted wardrobe; the wooden wedding-chest. On top of the bureau on the other side of the room was a small oval mirror in which I could just see the pale blur of my own face.

I wondered if it would be an admission that I was going to pieces if I went downstairs and poured myself a drink. I picked up the royal blue bathrobe I had dropped on the floor when I went to bed last night, and tugged it on.

The house had been so silent since Jane had gone. I had never realized how much noise, how much *aura*, a living person actually gives off; even when they're asleep. When Jane had been alive, she had filled the house with her warmth and her character and her actual breathing. Now, no matter which room I looked into, there was nothing but coldness and silence. Rocking-chairs which never rocked. Drapes which were never drawn unless I drew them myself. An oven which was never lit unless I went into the kitchen and lit it myself for one of my own solitary meals.

Nobody to talk to: nobody even to smile at when I didn't feel like talking. And the enormous incomprehensible thought that I would never see her again, ever.

It had been a month. A month and two days, and a handful of hours. I was over the self-pity. I *think* I was over the self-pity. I was certainly over the crying, although you can't lose someone like Jane without being susceptible for the rest of your life to unexpected tears. Dr. Rosen had warned me that it would happen from time to time, and it did: I would be sitting at an auction, ready to bid for some special piece of marine memorabilia which I particularly wanted to acquire for the shop; and I would suddenly find that tears were sliding down my cheeks, and I would have to excuse myself and retreat to the men's room and blow my nose a lot.

"Damn spring colds," I would say to the attendant.

And he would look at me and know exactly what was wrong because there is an unadmitted kinship between all the closely-bereaved, a feeling which they can never share with anybody else because it would sound too much as if they were being morbidly sorry for themselves. And yet, damn it, I was.

I went into the low-beamed living-room, opened up the sideboard, and took stock of what liquor I had left. Half a mouthful of Chivas Regal; a teacupful of gin. A bottle of sweet sherry to which Jane had taken a fancy when she was first pregnant. I decided on tea instead. I almost always drank tea when I woke up unexpectedly in the middle of the night. Bohea, without milk or sugar. A taste I had acquired from the people of Salem.

I was turning the key in the sideboard when I heard the kitchen door close. Not slam, as if it had been blown by the wind, but *close*, on its old-fashioned latch. I froze where I was, breath caught, heart banging, and listened. There was no other sound, only the wind blowing; but I was sure that I could sense a *presence*, a feeling that there was somebody else in the house. After a month on my own, a month of complete quiet, I had become alert to every little fidget, every

little squeak, every little scurry of mice; and the larger vibrations of human beings. Human beings *resonate*, like cellos.

I was sure there was somebody there, in the kitchen. There
was somebody there, but strangely there was no warmth, and
none of the usual friendly noises of humanity. I crossed the
brown shag carpet as silently as I could, and went to the
fireplace, still ashy and glowing from yesterday evening's
logs. I picked up the long brass poker, with its heavy seahorse
head, and hefted it in my hand.

In the hallway, my bare feet made a squeaking sound on
the waxed pottery tiles. The long-case Tompion clock which
Jane's parents had given us for a wedding-present ticked
deeply and thoughtfully inside its crotch-mahogany torso. I
reached the kitchen door, and listened for the slightest creak,
the slightest breath, the slightest *frisson* of material against
wood.

Nothing. Just the clock, measuring out the rest of my life.
Just the wind, which would blow across Granitehead Neck
long after I had left there. Even the sea seemed to have been
stilled.

"Is anybody there?" I called, in a voice that started off
loud and ended up strangled. And waited, for somebody or
nobody to answer.

Was that singing? Distant, faraway singing?

> *"O the men they sail'd from Granitehead*
> *To fish the foreign shores . . ."*

Or was it nothing more than the draft, sucking at the
bottom of the garden door?

At last, I eased open the latch which secured the kitchen
door, hesitated, and then pushed the door inwards. No groaning or squeaking—I had oiled the hinges myself. I took one
step, then another, then patted my hand a little too frantically
against the wall, trying to find the light switch. The fluorescent light flickered, paused, then blinked on. I reared up the
poker in front of me in nervous reaction, and then I realized
that the old-style kitchen was empty, and I lowered it again.

The garden door was still locked and bolted, and the key
was still lying where I had left it on top of the softly-
humming icebox. The polished Delft tiles behind the kitchen

range shone as blandly as ever, windmills and Dutch boys and tulips and clogs. The copper saucepans hung in mildly-shining rows; and my soup-bowl from last night's supper was still there, waiting to be washed.

I opened up cupboards, banged doors, made a lot of noise to reassure myself that I was really alone. I stared fiercely out of the window, into the absolute ebony blackness of the night, to frighten off anybody who might be lurking in the garden. But all I saw was the shadowy reflection of my own face, and I think that frightened me more than anything. Fear itself is frightening. To see *yourself* frightened is worse.

I walked out of the kitchen, and back into the hallway, and called out again, "Who's there? Is anybody there?" and again there was silence. But I had a curiously unsettled feeling that something or somebody was *passing through the air*, as if atmospheric molecules were being disturbed by unseen movements. There was a sensation of coldness, too: a sensation of loss and painful unhappiness. The same coldness you feel when you hear your own child crying in the night, an infant's dread of what the dark might bring.

I stood in the hallway, unsure of what to do or even how to feel. It was quite plain that there was nobody here; that apart from me the house was empty. There was no physical evidence of any intrusion. No doors were forced, no windows were broken. And yet it was equally obvious that somehow the perspective of the house had been subtly altered. I felt as if I was now looking at the hallway from a new viewpoint, the right-hand picture of a stereoscopic photograph, instead of the left.

I went into the kitchen, hesitated and then again decided to make myself a cup of tea. Maybe a couple of aspirin would help, too. I went over to the stove where the kettle was standing, and to my alarm there was already a thin curl of steam rising out of the spout.

With the tips of my fingers, I touched the kettle's lid. It was scalding hot. I stepped back from the kettle and frowned at it. My frowning reflection, ridiculously distorted, stared back at me from its stainless-steel sides. I knew that I had been *thinking* of making tea, but had I actually switched on the kettle myself? I couldn't remember doing it. Yet the water had boiled, which usually took two or three minutes.

I must have done it myself. I was tired, that was all. I reached up to the wall-cupboard to take myself down a cup and saucer. And as I did so I could hear it again—I was convinced that I could hear it again—that faintest of singing. I paused, straining my ears, but it was gone. I took out the cup and saucer, and the small Spode teapot.

Maybe Jane's sudden death had affected me more than I had realized. Maybe bereavement found ways of expressing itself in visions, tricks of the mind, and odd sensations. Hadn't Jung talked about a collective unconscious, a pool of dreams in which we all shared? Maybe if one soul was lost to that pool, it set up ripples that everybody could feel, especially those who were closest.

As the kettle continued to boil, slowly, its shiny surface began to mist over, as if the temperature in the kitchen had suddenly dropped. But it was a chilly night, and so it didn't surprise me much. I went across to the other side of the kitchen to fetch the old pewter tea-caddy. When I came back, however, for a few brief seconds, I was sure that I saw *writing* on the misted side of the kettle, as if somebody had quickly scrawled something there with his finger. At that instant, the mist faded away. But I peered at the kettle intently for a sign of what I had seen, and after I had filled up the teapot I turned it on again to see if the writing reappeared. There was a smear which might have been an "S" and another smear which might have been an "e," but that was all. I was probably going quietly bananas. I took my tea into the living-room, and sat down by the still-warm fireplace, and sipped it, and tried to get my mind straight.

That couldn't have been writing. It couldn't have been anything more than greasy marks on the side of the kettle, where the condensation wouldn't cling. I didn't believe in ouija boards or automatic writing, or "presences." I didn't believe in poltergeists and I didn't believe in any of that occult thought-transference stuff, psychokinetics, moving ashtrays around just by thinking about it, any of that. I wasn't saying that people weren't entitled to believe in them if they wanted to. Maybe some people had actually witnessed that kind of thing. But *I* hadn't, and more than anything else I prayed that I wasn't going to.

I very much didn't want to think that Quaker Lane Cottage

might possibly be haunted, especially by anyone I knew. Especially, God forbid, by Jane.

I stayed in the living-room until the long-case clock in the hallway struck five, sleepless and unhappy and deeply disturbed. At last the North Atlantic dawn came austerely through the leaded windows, and dressed the living-room in gray. The wind had died down now, to a chilly breeze, and I went out through the back door and took a barefoot walk in the dewy garden, dressed in nothing but my bathrobe and my old sheepskin jacket, and stood by the garden swing.

It must have been low-tide, because far out over the sands of Granitehead Neck, the terns were already swooping down for clams. Their cries were like the cries of children. Off to the north-west, I could see the Winter Island lighthouse, still winking. A cold photographic morning.

Our swing was more than seventy or eighty years old, constructed like an armchair, with a wide carved splat. On the cresting-rail was chiseled the face of the sun, Old Sol, and the words, *"All, except their sun, is set,"* which Jane had discovered was a quotation from Byron. The chains of the swing were suspended from a kind of gallows; but this was hard to detect because whoever had built the swing all those years ago had planted a small apple-tree beside it, and now much of the swing was obscured with gnarled old fruit-branches, and in the summer the apple-blossoms showered around you when you were swinging, like snow.

Swinging (Jane had said, as she swung and sang) was the pastime of fools and jesters, a kind of medieval madness not unlike the whirling of Dervishes. It reminded her of motley and mummers and pigs'-bladders on sticks, and she said that it had once been a way to conjure up imps and devils and hobgoblins. I remembered laughing at her, and as I stood there that early morning alone, I found my eyes following the arc in which she had once soared, although the swing itself now hung still, beaded with dew, unmoved by the breeze.

I thrust my hands into my jacket pockets. It looked as if it was going to be one of those clear, fresh Atlantic days, cold as hell, but bright. I pushed the swing a little so that the chains complained, but even when I pushed it harder, I couldn't reproduce the noise I had heard last night. To set up that distinctive *creakkk-squik*, you had to sit right up on the swing, right up on that high-backed seat, and push yourself back, and up, and back, and up, until your toes were almost brushing the lower branches of the apple-tree.

I walked down through the orchard, right to the end of my garden, and looked down the twisting slope of Quaker Lane toward Granitehead Village. Two or three chimneys were already smoking, fishermen's houses, and the smoke was leaning off westwards, towards Salem, whose skyline was already becoming clearer across the harbor.

Slowly, I returned to the house, glancing from side to side for any signs of crushed grass, or footprints, any sign that somebody had visited my garden in the night; but there was none. I went back into the kitchen, leaving the door open, and brewed myself another cup of Bohea, and ate three Pepperidge Farm coconut cookies, feeling unreasonably guilty that this was my entire breakfast. Jane had always insisted on cooking me bacon, or waffles, or shirred eggs. I took my cup of tea upstairs with me, and went to the bathroom to shave.

We had fitted out the bathroom with a large Victorian basin we had rescued from a derelict house in Swampscott, and we had adorned it with huge brass faucets. Over the basin was a genuine barbershop mirror, surrounded by an oval frame of inlaid kingwood. I inspected myself in the glass and decided I didn't look too bad for a man who had been awake for most of the night—not only awake, but too scared to sleep. Then I turned on the faucets and filled up the basin with hot water.

It was only when I raised my head to start shaving that I saw the writing scrawled across the mirror. At least, it could have been writing; it might as easily have been nothing more than curving drips of moisture. I stared at it closely, frightened and fascinated, and I was sure that I could make out the letters S, V, E, but with indistinguishable letters in between.

S *something* V *something-something* E? What on earth could that mean? SAVE? SAVE ME?

I was suddenly sure that I caught the reflection of a movement, something white flickering past the open bathroom doorway behind me. I turned around and said, overloudly, "Who's there?" and then I stalked on fright-stiffened legs out on to the landing, and looked down the dark curved staircase towards the hallway. Nobody there. No footsteps, no whispers, no mysteriously closed doors, nothing. Only a small Edward Hicks painting of a matelot, staring back at me in that bovine, placid way that all Edward Hicks people stare at you.

Nobody there. And yet, for the first time since she had died; for the first time in a whole month of loneliness and silent pain, I found myself whispering, *"Jane?"*

TWO

Walter Bedford sat behind his wide leather-topped desk, his face half-obscured by his green-shaded lamp, and said, "I'm taking her mother away next month. A few weeks in Bermuda, maybe, something to settle her mind, help her to come to terms with it. I should have taken her away earlier, I guess; but, you know, what with old Mr. Bibber so sick . . ."

"I'm sorry she's taken it so badly," I said. "If there's anything you want me to do . . ."

Mr. Bedford shook his head. To both himself and his wife Constance, Jane's death had been the fiercest tragedy of their whole lives; even fiercer in some ways than losing their only other child, Jane's brother Philip, at the age of five to polio. Mr. Bedford had told me that he felt when Jane died that he was cursed by God. His wife felt even more bitter, and considered that the agent of the curse was me.

One of Mr. Bedford's younger partners in the Salem law firm of Bedford & Bibber had offered to execute Jane's will, and to arrange for her funeral, and he had insisted on handling all the details himself, with a kind of agonized relish. I understood why. Jane had been such a vivid light in all of our lives that it was difficult to let her go; and harder still to think that one day we wouldn't think about her, even once.

She had been buried at the age of 28 in Waterside Cemetery, Granitehead, on a sharp February afternoon, sharing her coffin with our unborn child, and her headstone read, *"Point me out the way to any one particular beauteous star."*

Mrs. Bedford had refused to look at me throughout the ceremony. I think that in her eyes I was worse than a murderer.

21

I hadn't even had the civility to kill Jane in person, with my bare hands. Instead, I had allowed fate to do my dirty work for me. Fate had been my hired assassin.

I had met Jane by accident less than two years before at a foxhunt, of all places, near Greenwood in South Carolina. My presence at the hunt had been compulsory: it was being run across the 1200-acre estate of one of my employer's most influential clients; whereas Jane was there simply because a gushing girlfriend from Wellesley College had invited her to come for the excitement of being "blooded." There was no blood, the foxes all escaped. But afterwards, in the quiet upstairs gallery of the elegant colonial house, we sat in extraordinary Italian armchairs and drank champagne, and fell in love. Jane quoted Keats to me, and that was why Keats was quoted on her headstone after she was dead.

"I saw pale kings and princes too, pale warriors, death-pale were they all; Who cry'd—'La belle Dame sans merci hath thee in thrall!' "

Ostensibly, we had nothing in common, Jane and I; neither style nor education nor mutual friends. I had been born and raised in St. Louis, Missouri, the son of a shoe-store owner, Trenton's Heel-&-Toe, and although my father had done everything he could to give me a superior schooling—"no son of mine is going to spend the rest of his life looking at the bottom of other people's feet"—I was an irredeemable mid-Westerner. Speak to me of Chillicothe, Columbia, and Sioux Falls; those are the names that move me. I studied business at Washington University, and when I was 24 I found myself a sales job with MidWestern Chemical Bonding, of Ferguson.

I was a 31-year-old business executive who wore gray suits and dark socks and carried copies of *Fortune* in my personalized leather briefcase. Jane, on the other hand, was the only daughter of a venerable but not-so-wealthy family from Salem, Massachusetts, the only daughter and now the only child; brought up in prettiness and grace and old-fashioned ways, but sophisticated, too. What you might describe as the local Vivien Leigh. She liked antique furniture and American primitive paintings and hand-sewn quilts, but she had no time for any sewing of her own, and she very rarely wore any underwear, and whenever she went out into the garden she put on high-heeled French slippers, and sank into the dirt alongside the curly kale.

"Damn it, I *should* have been a good country wife," she always used to tell me, when her bread lay doggedly unrisen in its tin; or her marmalade turned to tar. "But somehow I just don't have that edge."

She tried on New Year's Eve to make Hopping John, a dish of salt pork and black-eyed peas traditional in the South, but it turned out looking like brown marbles and slugs, and when she took the lid off the casserole we laughed until we were weak, and I guess that's what really close marriages are all about. But she said afterwards, as she lay in bed, "The legend is, if you don't serve Hopping John on New Year's Day, you'll have a year's bad luck."

It all ended on Mystic River Bridge, in late January, in blinding snow when she was driving home to Granitehead after visiting her parents' house in Dedham, and slowed up for the tollbooth, a young dark-haired lady six months' pregnant, in a yellow fastback Mustang II; and the air-brakes failed on a Kenworth truck that was following behind her, too close. She and the child she carried were crushed against the steering-wheel by a 17-ton truck and a full load of steel piping for the new sewage project up at Gloucester.

They called me up and I said, "Hel-*lo*" brightly, and then they told me that Jane was dead and that was the end of it.

It was for Jane, less than a year before, that I had handed in my notice at MidWestern Chemical Bonding, and moved to Granitehead. She wanted tranquility, she had told me, a life of tranquility, in old country, old surroundings. She wanted children, and happy Christmases, and the kind of gentle Bing Crosby happiness that modern urban Americans had forgotten about. I argued that I was upwardly motivated, that I needed peer acclaim and dollars, and a jacuzzi, and garage doors that recognized my voice. She said, "You're *kidding*, John. What do you want to tie yourself down with all of *that* stuff for?" and kissed my forehead, although it seemed to me that when we moved out to Granitehead we acquired more material possessions in the way of clocks and rocking-chairs than I'd ever dreamed possible. I felt within me, too, a kind of deep-rooted panic at the prospect of not earning more money this year than I had the year before.

When I handed in my notice I was treated as a suddenly declared closet homosexual. The president read my letter, re-read it, and actually turned it upside-down, to see if it read any different that way. Then he said, "John, I'm going to accept your resignation, but I'm going to take the liberty of quoting to you from Horace. *'Caelum non animum mutant qui trans mare currunt.* They change their skies but not their souls, those who travel across the seas.' "

"Yes, Mr. Kendrick," I said flatly, and drove home to our rented house in Ferguson and finished the best part of a bottle of Chivas Regal before Jane came home.

"You resigned," she said, when she came in, her arms full of parcels that already we couldn't afford.

"I'm home, and I'm drunk, so I must have," I told her.

Within six weeks, we had moved to Granitehead, within a half-hour's driving-distance of Jane's parents; and as summer blossomed we bought Quaker Lane Cottage, on the north-west shore of Granitehead peninsula. The previous owner had grown tired of the wind, the real-estate agent told us; tired of the freezing winters, and had already moved south to a condominium in Fort Lauderdale.

Two weeks later, when the cottage was still in chaos and my bank account was growing frighteningly sparse, we took a lease on a shopfront property right in the center of Old Granitehead Village, overlooking the square in which Granitehead's only witch had been hung by her heels and burned in 1691; and in which in 1775 a detail of British redcoats had shot and killed three Massachusetts fishermen. We called the shop Trenton's Marine Antiques (although Jane's mother had coldly suggested Knautical Knick-Knacks) and we opened it with pride and plenty of ivy-green paint. I wasn't at all confident that we could last very long, selling nothing but windlasses and demi-culverins and clocks made out of flag-staff buttons; but Jane had laughed and said that everybody adored marine antiques, especially people who had never been to sea, and that we'd be rich.

Well—we weren't rich, but we made enough to keep us in logs for the fire, and clam chowder, and Paul Masson red, and to pay the mortgage, and I guess that was all Jane really wanted. She wanted babies, too, of course, but babies are free; at least until they're born.

In the few short months that Jane and I lived and worked

together in Granitehead, I made some of the most important discoveries of my whole life. I discovered, first of all, what love could really be; and it became clear to me that I had never known before. I discovered what loyalty could mean, and self-respect. I also learned tolerance. Jane's father treated me like an anonymous junior clerk he was obliged to amuse at the office Christmas party, and occasionally, though with obvious reluctance, would offer me some of his 1926 brandy. Jane's mother would actually *shudder* whenever I came into the room, and pull faces whenever I spoke in my distinctive St. Louis accent, and treat me with an ice-cold politeness that was even more chilling than bare hostility. She would do anything rather than talk to me directly. "Would he like a cup of tea?" she would ask Jane, right in front of me; but Jane would retaliate by saying, "I don't know, ask him. I'm not psychic."

I wasn't Harvard, you see; I wasn't Hyannisport or Back Bay; or even Kernwood Country Club. They blamed me while Jane was alive for ruining her social prospects; and when she was dead they blamed me for killing her. They didn't blame the truck-driver, who might have swerved; or the mechanic who should have checked the truck's servo-lines, and probably hadn't. They blamed only me.

As if, God help me, I didn't blame myself.

Mr. Bedford was now saying, "I've dealt with all of the tax difficulties now. I've filed form 1040; and claimed for the medical attention that Jane received in hospital, even though of course it was pointless, I'll, er, pass on your accounts to Mr. Rosner from now on, if that's agreeable to you."

I nodded. The Bedford family obviously wanted to wash their hands of me as soon as possible, without appearing to be too boorish, or indecently hasty.

"There's one more small matter," said Mr. Bedford. "Mrs. Bedford thought that you might consider it a suitably sentimental gesture to allow her to keep Jane's diamond-and-pearl necklace."

The request clearly caused Mr. Bedford extreme embarrassment; but it was also clear that he did not dare to return home without having asked me. He drummed his fingertips on his desk, and suddenly looked away, as if somebody else had mentioned the necklace, and not him at all.

"Considering the necklace's value . . ." he put in, abstractedly.

"Jane gave me to understand that it's a family heirloom," I said in the gentlest voice I could manage.

"Well, yes it is. Goes back nearly a hundred-and-fifty years. Always passed from one Bedford wife to the next. But, then, since Jane didn't have any children to pass it on to. . . ."

"And since, after all, she *became* a Trenton . . ." I added, trying not to sound as bitter as I felt.

"Well," said Mr. Bedford, uncomfortably.

"All right, then," I said. "Whatever makes the Bedfords happy."

"I'm obliged," said Mr. Bedford.

I stood up. "Is there anything else I have to sign?"

"No. No, thank you, John. It's all taken care of." He stood up himself. "I want you to know that if we can help in any way at all . . . Well, you only have to call me."

I lowered my head. I suppose it was wrong to feel so antagonistic towards the Bedfords. I might have lost my wife of less than a year and my unborn child; but they had lost their only surviving daughter. Who else could we accuse for such evil luck, but God, and each other?

Mr. Bedford and I shook hands like opposing generals after the signing of an unpopular armistice. I was just turning to leave, however, when I distinctly heard a woman's voice say, in the most natural of tones, *"John?"*

I turned around, my scalp fizzing with fright, and stared at Mr. Bedford. Mr. Bedford stared back at me. "Yes?" he queried. Then he frowned, and said, "Are you all right? You look like you've seen a ghost."

I raised my hand, listening, concentrating. "Did you hear something?" I asked him. "A voice? Somebody saying 'John?' "

"A *voice?*" asked Mr. Bedford.

I hesitated, but there was nothing else to be heard except the traffic outside Mr. Bedford's office window, and the rumbling of typewriters in nearby rooms. "No," I said at last. "I must have been imagining things."

"You're all right? You don't want to see Dr. Rosen again?"

"No, of course not. I mean, no thank you. I'm fine."

"You're sure? You don't look very well. I thought you didn't look too well when you came in here this morning."

"Sleepless night," I told him.

He rested his hand on my back not so much to reassure me that in time we would all get over our grief but rather as if he temporarily needed somewhere to rest his hand.

"Mrs. Bedford will be very appreciative about the necklace," he told me.

THREE

Before lunch, I took a solitary walk across Salem Common, the collar of my coat turned up against the cold, my breath fluttering like smoke. All around the Common, the bare trees stood in the silent chill of winter, like a gaggle of Salem witches, and the grass was silver-faced with dew. I went as far as the bandstand, with its cupola dome, and sat down on the stone steps, while a little way from me, two young children played on the grass, tumbling and running, leaving figure-eight tracks of green across the lawns. Two children like ours might have been: Nathaniel, the boy who had died in his mother's womb. What else could you call a boy who was going to be born within sight of the House of Seven Gables? And Jessica, the girl who was never even conceived.

I was still sitting there when an old woman appeared in a bundled-up Thrift Store coat and a shapeless felt hat, carrying a threadbare carpet-bag and a red umbrella, which she inexplicably opened, and left beside the steps. She sat down only four or five feet away from me.

"Well, now," she said, as she opened a brown paper bag, and took out a liver-sausage sandwich.

I looked at her cautiously. She probably wasn't as old as she had first appeared to be, 50 or 55; but she was so shabbily dressed and her hair was so white and frayed that she could have been mistaken for 70. She began to eat her sandwich, with such neatness and gentility that I couldn't take my eyes off her.

That was how it was, for almost twenty minutes, on the steps of the cupola bandstand on Salem Common, on that cold March morning; the woman eating her sandwich and me covertly watching her, and people passing us by along the radial paths which crossed the Common, some strolling, some intent on business, but every one of them chilly, and every one of them accompanied by their own personal mouth-ghost of frozen breath.

At five before twelve, I decided it was time to leave. But before I went, I reached into my coat pocket and took out four quarters, and held them out to her, and said, "Please. Just do me a favor, will you?"

She stared at the money and then she stared at me. "People in your position shouldn't be giving silver to witches," she smiled.

"You're a *witch*?" I asked her, not very seriously.

"Don't I *look* like a witch?"

"I don't know," I smiled. "I've never seen a witch before. I always thought that witches carried broomsticks, and black cats on their shoulders."

"Oh, superstition," the old woman said. "Well, I'll take your money, if you're not too worried about the consequences."

"What consequences?"

"People in your position always have to suffer consequences."

"What position is that?"

The woman rummaged in her bag and eventually produced an apple, which she polished on the lapel of her coat. "Alone, aren't you?" she asked me, and then bit into it, chewing on one side of her mouth like a Disney chipmunk. "Not long alone, but alone nonetheless."

"Perhaps," I said, evasively. I was beginning to feel that this conversation was heavily laden with unspoken implications; as if this woman and I meeting on Salem Common was predestined, and that the people who walked all around us along the Common's radiating pathways were mere chesspieces. Anonymous, but there for a special reason.

"Well, you know the best of that," the woman told me. She took another bite of apple. "But that's the way *I* see it, and I'm not often wrong. It's a mystic talent, some people say. But I don't see any harm in calling it for what it is, especially here in Salem. Good witch territory, Salem; best in the country. Perhaps not a place to be alone, though."

"What do you mean by that?" I asked her.

She looked up at me. Her eyes were a peculiar pellucid blue, and there was a scar on her forehead like an arrow, or an upside-down crucifix, in the faintest glistening red.

"Everybody has to die sometime, that's what I mean by that," she said. "But it's the *place* you die, not the time, that makes the difference. There are spheres of influence; and sometimes you can die within them, and sometimes you can die without them."

"I'm sorry," I told her. "I don't really understand what you're saying."

"Salem is the root, heart, bowels, and belly. Salem is the witch's boiling-pot. What do you believe those witch-trials were really all about? And why do you think they stopped so sudden? Have you known *anybody* to show such remorse, so quick? Not I. Not as quick as that. The influence came, and then the influence fled; but there are days when I believe that it didn't flee for good and all. It depends."

"Depends on what?" I wanted to know.

She smiled again, and winked, and said, "All kinds of things." She raised her head to the sky, and revealed a neck-band that looked as if it were made of braided hair, fastened with silver and turquoise. "The weather, the price of goose fat. It depends."

I suddenly felt like a complete tourist. Here I was, letting some half-dotty woman string me along with stories about "spheres of influence" and witches, and actually taking her seriously. She was probably going to offer to tell my fortune next, if the price was right. In Salem, where the local Chamber of Commerce enthusiastically exploits the witch-trials of 1692 as a major commercial attraction ("Stop by for a Spell," they entreat you) it was hardly surprising that even the panhandlers should use witchcraft as a selling-angle.

"Listen," I told the woman, "just have a good day, all right?"

"You're going?" she asked me.

"I'm going. It's been nice talking to you. Very interesting."

"Interesting, but not believable?"

"Oh, I believe you," I said. "The weather, the price of goose fat. By the way, what *is* the price of goose fat?"

She ignored my facetious question and stood up, brushing the crumbs off her worn-out coat with a blue-veined hand.

"You think that I'm begging for money?" she demanded. "Is that it? You think I'm a beggar?"

"Not at all. I just have to go, that's all."

A passer-by stopped to watch us as if he could sense that an interesting confrontation was about to develop. Then two more stopped, one of them a woman, her curly hair turned into a strangely radiant halo by the winter sun.

"I will tell you two things," the woman said, in a trembly voice. "I shouldn't tell you either, but I will. You will have to decide for yourself if they are warnings or riddles or nothing but nonsense. You cannot be helped, you know; for the life we lead on this earth is a life without help."

I said nothing, but stood warily watching her, trying to decide if she was a simple lunatic or a not-so-simple con-artist.

"The first thing is," she said, "you are not alone, the way you believe yourself to be, and you will *never* be alone, not ever, although you will pray to God sometimes to release you from your companionship. The second thing is, you must stay away from the place where no birds fly."

The passers-by, seeing that nothing particularly exciting was going to happen, began to disperse. The woman said, "You walk me to Washington Square, if you care to. You are going that way?"

"Yes," I said. Then, "Come on, then."

She gathered up her bag and folded her red umbrella and then walked beside me to the west side of the Common. The Common was enclosed with decorative iron railings, which threw spoked shadows across the grass.

"I'm sorry that you thought I was talking nonsense," the woman said, as we emerged on to the sidewalk of Washington Square West. Across the square stood the Witch Museum, which commemorates the hanging of Salem's twenty witches in 1692, one of the fiercest witch-hunts in all human history. In front of the museum was the statue of Salem's founder, Roger Conant, in his heavy Puritan cloak, his shoulders glittering with dew.

"This is an old city, you know," the woman told me. "Old cities have their own ways of doing things, their own mysteries. Didn't you begin to sense it, just a little, back there on the Common? The feeling that life in Salem is a puzzle of kinds, a witch-puzzle? Full of meanings, but no explanations?"

I looked away from her, across the square. On the opposite sidewalk, among the crowds of tourists and pedestrians, I glimpsed a pretty dark-haired girl in a sheepskin jacket and tight denim jeans, a stack of text books held against her chest. In a moment, she was jumbled up in the crowd, but I felt a funny catch at my heart because the girl had looked so much like Jane. I guess lots of girls did, and always would. I was definitely suffering from Rosen's Syndrome.

The woman said, "I have to go this way. It's been an unusual pleasure to talk to you. It's not often that men will listen, not the way you do."

I gave her a half-hearted smile, and raised my hand.

"You'll want to know my name, of course," she said. I wasn't sure if that was a question or a statement, but I gave her a nod which could have meant yes and could just as easily have meant that I didn't particularly care.

"Mercy Lewis," she said. "Named after Mercy Lewis."

"Well, Mercy," I told her. "Just make sure you take care of yourself."

"You too," she said, and then she walked off at a surprisingly fast pace until she was lost from sight.

For some reason, I found myself thinking of the words that Jane used to read to me from the *Ode to Melancholy*. "She dwells with Beauty—Beauty that must die; and Joy, whose hand is ever at his lips, bidding adieu. . . ."

I turned up my collar against the cold, pushed my hands deep into my pockets, and went to find myself some lunch.

FOUR

I ate a lone corned-beef on rye with mustard at Red's Sandwich Shop on Central Street. Next to me, a black man wearing a brand-new Burberry kept whistling *She'll Be Coming Round The Mountain When She Comes*, over and over, between his teeth. A young dark-haired secretary stared at me in one of the mirrors. She had a strange, pale, pre-Raphaelite face. I felt tired now, and very alone.

About two o'clock, under a clouded sky, I walked to Holyoke Square, to Endicott's Auction Rooms, where they were holding one of their bi-annual sales of antique maritime prints and paintings. The catalog listed three important oils, including Shaw's painting of the Derby ship *John*, but I didn't expect to be able to afford any of them. What I was looking for was antique-shop fodder: engravings and etchings and maps and maybe a watercolor or two, the kind of picture I could have reframed in gilt or walnut and sold at ten times its actual cost. There was one painting listed as Unknown Artist: *A View of Granitehead's Western Shore Late 17th Century* which I was quite interested in buying, simply because it showed the promontory on which I lived.

Inside, the auction-rooms were cold, high-ceilinged, and Victorian, and the weak winter sunlight slanted down on us from high clerestory windows. Most of the buyers kept on their overcoats, and there was a chorus of coughing and nose-blowing and shuffling of feet before the auction began. There were only about a dozen buyers there, unusual for one of Endicott's sales. There weren't even any from the Peabody Museum contingent. The bidding was low, too: the Shaw went for only $18,500, and a rare drawing in a scrimshaw frame fetched only $725. I hoped this wasn't a sign that the recession had at last caught up with the maritime antiques business. On top of everything else that had happened, bankruptcy would just about round off my year.

By the time the auctioneer put up the view of Granitehead, there were only five or six buyers left, apart from myself and an eccentric old man who attended every Endicott auction and outbid everybody for everything, even though he wore no socks and lived in a cardboard box near one of the wharves.

"May I hear $50?" the auctioneer inquired, thrusting his thumb into his dapper gray vest, complete with watch-chain.

I gave him a rabbit-like twitch of my nose.

"Any advances on $50? Come along, gentlemen, this painting is history itself. Granitehead shoreline, in 1690. A real find."

There was no response. The auctioneer gave an exaggerated sigh, banged down his gavel, and said, "Sold to Mr. Trenton for $50. Next item, please."

There was nothing else at the auction I wanted, so I went around to the packaging room. Mrs. Donohue was there today, a motherly Irishwoman with carroty hair, upswept spectacles, and the largest behind I had ever seen in my life. She took the painting, and spread out her wrapping-paper and string, and called sharply to her assistant, "Damien, the scissors, will you?"

"How are you doing, Mrs. Donohue?" I asked her.

"Well, I'm barely alive," said Mrs. Donohue. "What with my feet and my blood-pressure. But I was so sorry to hear about your darling wife. That brought the tears to my eyes, when I heard about it. Such a beautiful girl, Jane Bedford. I used to see her in here when she was tiny."

"Thank you," I nodded.

"Now, is this a view of Salem Harbor?" she said, holding up the picture.

"Granitehead, just north of Quaker Lane. You see that hill there? That's where my house stands now."

"Well, now. And what's that ship?"

"What ship?"

"There, by the farthest shore. That's a ship now, isn't it?"

I peered at the painting. I hadn't noticed it before, but Mrs. Donohue was right. On the opposite side of the harbor there

was a fully-rigged sailing-ship, but painted so darkly that I
had mistaken it for a grove of trees on the shoreline behind it.

"Now, I hope I'm not being interfering, or trying to teach
you your business," said Mrs. Donohue. "But I know you
haven't been buying and selling the old stuff for very long;
and now your darling wife's lost to you . . . But if I were you
I would take a tip and try to find out what ship that might
be."

"You think it's worth it?" I asked her. I wasn't embarrassed about an auction-room packaging lady giving me good
advice. Good advice is good advice, wherever you pick it up.

"Well, it's impossible to say," she told me. "But Mr.
Brasenose once bought a picture here of what was supposed
to be French ships off Salem Sound, but when he took the
trouble to identify the ships by name, he found that what he
had on his hands was the one and only contemporary painting
of the *Great Turk*; and he sold it to the Peabody for $55,000."

I took another close look at the strange dark vessel in the
background of the painting I had just acquired. It didn't look
particularly noteworthy, and the anonymous artist had painted
no name on the prow. It was probably a figment of the
imagination, quickly sketched in to improve the painting's
shaky composition. Still, I would have a shot at identifying it,
particularly if Mrs. Donohue said so. It was she who had told
me to look for the gryphon's-head maker's mark on Rhode
Island lanterns.

"If I make a million out of it," I told her, as she expertly
wrapped it up, "I'll cut you in for five percent."

"Fifty percent or nothing, you rascal," she laughed.

I left the auction-rooms with the painting under my arms.
The remaining pictures I had bought—etchings and aquatints
and a small collection of steel engravings—would be delivered to me later in the week. I only wished I had been able to
afford the Shaw.

Outside, as I crossed the steps in front of Endicott's, the
sun was already eating away at the rooftops of the elegant old
Federal mansions of Chestnut Street, and a low cold wind
rose. Oddly, the same pale-faced secretary I had seen in
Red's Sandwich Shop walked past, in a long black coat and a
gray scarf. She turned and looked at me but she didn't smile.

Down by the curb, I caught sight of Ian Herbert, the
proprietor of one of Salem's most distinctive antique shops,

talking to one of the directors of Endicott's. Ian Herbert's shop was all soft carpeting and hushed discussion and artistically-positioned spot-lights. He didn't even call it a shop: it was a "resource." But he wasn't snobbish when it came to talking trade, and he gave me a casual wave as I approached.

"John," he said, slapping me on the shoulder. "You must know Dan Vokes, sales director of Endicott's."

"How do you do," said Dan Vokes. "Seems like you've been making me marginally richer." He nodded towards the package under my arm.

"It's nothing special," I told him. "Just an old watercolor of the shoreline where I live. I got it for fifty dollars flat."

"As long as you're satisfied with it," smiled Dan Vokes.

"By the way," said Ian, "you might be interested to know that they're selling off some of the old maritime collection up at Newburyport Museum. Interesting artifacts; magical, some of them. For instance, did you know that most of the old Salem ships used to carry a little brass cage on board, with a dish of oats inside, to trap goblins and demons?"

"I could use a couple of those in my accounts department," said Dan Vokes.

"I'm going to have to get back to Granitehead," I told them, and I was about to walk away when my arm was snatched violently from behind, so hard that I was spun around, and almost lost my balance. I found myself face-to-face with a young bearded man in a gray tweed jacket, panting and agitated and wild-haired from running.

"What the hell goes on?" I snapped at him.

"I'm sorry," he gasped. "Really, I'm sorry. I didn't mean to startle you. Are you Mr. Trenton—Mr. John Trenton of Granitehead?"

"That's me. Who the hell are you?"

"Please," the young man said, "I really didn't mean to upset you. But I didn't want you to get away."

"Listen, friend, take a walk," said Dan Vokes, stepping closer. "You're lucky I don't call a cop."

"Mr. Trenton, I have to talk to you privately," the young man urged. "It's very important."

"Are you leaving or do I call a cop?" said Dan Vokes. "This gentleman is a personal friend of mine and I'm telling you to get out of here."

"It's all right, Mr. Vokes," I told him. "I'll talk to him. I'll scream if he tries anything funny."

Ian Herbert laughed, and said, "I'll see you around, John. Drop into the store one day."

"You mean the 'resource,' " I ribbed him.

The young man in the tweed jacket waited for me impatiently while I said my goodbyes. Then, as I tucked my painting more securely under my arm, and started to walk towards the Riley Plaza parking-lot, where I had left my car, he fell into step beside me, occasionally skipping to keep up.

"This is *very* embarrassing," he said.

"What's very embarrassing?" I asked him "*I'm* not embarrased."

"I'd better introduce myself," he told me. "My name's Edward Wardwell. I work for the Peabody Museum, in the archives department."

"Well, how do you do."

Edward Wardwell scratched anxiously at his beard. He was one of those young American men who look like throwbacks to the 1860s; preachers or pioneers or harmonium-players. He wore crumpled corduroy pants and his hair looked as if it hadn't encountered a comb in months. You could see young men like him in the background of almost every frontier photograph ever taken, from Muncie to Black River Falls to Junction City.

He suddenly took my arm again, arresting us both, and leaned so close I could smell the aniseed candy on his breath. "The embarrassing thing is, Mr. Trenton, I was specifically instructed to acquire that painting you just bought for the Peabody archives."

"*This* painting? You mean the view of Granitehead shoreline?"

He nodded. "I lost track of the time. I meant to get to the auction-rooms by three. They told me the painting wouldn't be put up till three. Well, I thought that would give me plenty of time. But I guess I lost track. There's a girl I know who's just opened a new fashion store on East India Square, and I went down to help her out a little, and that's what happened. I lost track."

I started walking again. "So," I said, "you were supposed to acquire the painting for the Peabody Archives."

"That's right. It's *very* unusual."

"Well, I'm glad about that," I told him. "I only bought it because it shows a view of my home. Fifty dollars."

"You bought it for *fifty dollars*?"

"You heard me."

"Don't you know that it's worth a whole lot more? I mean, $50 is a complete steal."

"In that case, I'm even gladder. I'm a dealer, did you know that? I'm in business to make a profit. If I can buy it for $50 and sell it for $250, that's fine by me."

"Mr. Trenton," said Edward Wardwell, as we turned from Holyoke Square into Gedney Street, "that painting has *rarity* value. It really is a very rare painting."

"Good," I told him.

"Mr. Trenton, I'll offer you $275 for that painting. Right here and now. Cash."

I stopped where I was, and stared at him. "Two hundred seventy-five, cash? For this?"

"I'll make it a round three hundred."

"What's so damned important about this painting?" I asked. "It's nothing more than a pretty, inept watercolor of the Granitehead coast. They don't even know who the artist is."

Edward Wardwell propped his hands on his hips and blew out his cheeks, like an exasperated parent trying to explain himself to a particularly obtuse child. "Mr. Trenton," he said, "the painting happens to be rare because it shows a view of Salem Harbor that no other painter recorded at the time. It completes a topographical picture that has been incomplete for centuries; it enables us to pinpoint where certain buildings actually stood; and where certain roads ran, and where specific *trees* grew. I know it's inept, as a work of art, but from what I've seen of it, it's unusually accurate as far as landmarks are concerned. And that's exactly what the Peabody is interested in."

I thought about it for a moment, and then said, "I'm not selling. Not yet. Not until I find out what this is all about."

I crossed Gedney Street and Edward Wardwell tried to follow me, but a passing taxicab gave him an irritated blast on its horn. "Mr. Trenton!" he called, dodging in front of a bus. "Mr. Trenton, wait! I don't think you understand!"

"I don't think I want to understand," I told him.

He caught up with me again, and walked along beside me, short of wind, glancing from time to time at the package under

my arm as if he were actually thinking of snatching it away
from me.

"Mr. Trenton, if I don't go back to the Peabody with that
painting, I may very well be fired."

"So, you may very well be fired. I'm sorry for you. But
the answer to your problem was to turn up at the auction on
time, and put in your bid. If you'd have bid, you would have
got it. But you didn't, so you haven't. Now the painting's
mine and for the time being I don't want to sell it. Especially
not on the corner of Gedney and Margin, on a cold and windy
afternoon, if you don't mind."

Edward Wardwell ran his hand through his tousled hair,
making one side of it stick up like a Red Indian feather. "I'm
sorry," he said. "I didn't mean to come on like that. It's just
that it's really important for the Peabody to have the picture.
It's a really important picture, you know, from the archival
point of view."

I almost felt sorry for him. But Jane had told me over and
over that there is one immutable rule in the antique business;
a rule which must never be broken under any circumstances
for whatever reason. Never sell anything out of pity. Otherwise,
the only person you'll end up pitying is yourself.

"Listen," I said, "it may be possible for the Peabody to
borrow the picture sometime. Perhaps I can make some
arrangement with the Director."

"Well, I don't know about that at all," said Edward
Wardwell. "They really did want to own it, outright. Do you
think I could take a look at it?"

"What?"

"Do you think I could take a look at it?"

I shrugged. "If you want to. Come to my car; it's right
over there on Riley Plaza."

We crossed Margin Street, and then made our way through
the parking-lot to my eight-year-old fawn-colored Toronado.
We climbed inside, and I switched on the dome light so we
could see better. Wardwell closed the door and settled himself
down as if he were about to join me on a twenty-mile trip. I
almost expected him to fasten his seat-belt. As I opened up
the painting's wrapper, he leaned close to me again, and
again I could smell that cough-candy. His hands must have
been damp with anticipation, because he wiped them on the
legs of his corduroy pants.

At last I unwrapped the painting and propped it up on the steering-wheel. Edward Wardwell pressed so close to me as he stared at it that he hurt my shoulder. I could see right inside his left ear, convoluted and hairy.

"Well?" I asked him, at last. "What do you say?"

"Fascinating," he said. "You can just see Wyman Wharf there, on the Granitehead side, and you see how small it is? Nothing but a higgledy-piggledy structure of wooden joists. Nothing as grand as Derby Wharf, on the Salem side. That was all warehouses and counting-houses and moorings for East Indiamen."

"I see," I told him, trying to sound disinterested and dismissive. But he leaned against me even harder as he stared at every minute detail.

"That's Quaker Lane, coming up from the Village there; and that's where the Waterside Cemetery stands today, although in those days they called it The Walking Place, although nobody knows why. Did you know that Granitehead was called Resurrection, up until 1703? Presumably because the settlers felt that they had been resurrected from their lives in the Old World."

"A couple of people *have* told me that," I said, uncomfortably. "Now, if you don't mind . . ."

Edward Wardwell leaned back. "You're really sure you won't accept three hundred? That's what the Peabody gave me to spend on it. Three hundred, cash on the barrel, no questions asked. It's the best price you'll ever get."

"You think so? I think I'll get a better one."

"From whom? Who else is going to pay you three hundred dollars for a nondescript painting of Granitehead beach?"

"Nobody. But then I reckon that if Peabody is prepared to spend $300 on it, they might be prepared to up their offer and spend $400 on it; or even $500. It depends."

"It *depends*? It depends on what?"

"I don't know," I told him, wrapping the painting up again. "The weather, the price of goose fat."

Edward Wardwell twisted one strand of his beard around his finger. Then he said, "Umh-humh. I get it. I see *just* where you're coming from. Well, that's okay. Let's say that it's okay. Nothing to get upset about. But I'll tell you what. I'll call you in a day or two, okay? Do you mind that? And maybe we can talk again. You know, think about the three hundred. Mull it over. Maybe you'll change your mind.''

I laid the painting on the back seat, and then reached out and clasped his hand. "Mr. Orwell," I told him, "I'll make you a promise. I won't sell the picture to anyone else until I've taken my time with it, done some research. And when I *do* sell it, I'll give the Peabody the opportunity to match any price that I'm offered. Now, is that fair?''

"You'll take care of it?''

"Sure I'll take care of it. What makes you think I won't take care of it?''

He shrugged, and shook his head, and said, "No reason. It's just that I wouldn't like to see it lost, or damaged. You know where it comes from, don't you? Who sold it?''

"I haven't the faintest idea.''

"Well, I *think*, although I can't be sure, that it came out of the Evelith collection. You know the Eveliths? Very old family, most of them live up near Tewksbury now, in Dracut County. But there's been Eveliths in Salem ever since the 16th century, of one kind or another. Very inbred, very secretive, the kind of family that H.P. Lovecraft used to write about, you know H.P. Lovecraft? From what I hear, old man Duglass Evelith has a library of Salem history books that makes the Peabody look like a shelfful of paperbacks in somebody's outhouse. And prints, too, and paintings; of which *that* painting is more than likely one. He puts them on the market now and again, who knows why, but always anonymously, and it's always hard to authenticate them because he won't discuss them or even admit that they were his.''

I glanced back at the painting. "Sounds interesting," I admitted. "I suppose it's nice to know that America still has some original eccentrics left.''

Edward Wardwell thought for a moment, his hand pressed against his bearded mouth. Then he said, "You really won't change your mind?''

"No," I told him. "I'm not selling this painting until I know a whole lot more about it; like for instance why the Peabody wants it so badly.''

"I've told you. Very rare topographical interest. That's the only reason.''

"I almost believe you. But you don't mind if I do some checking up of my own? Perhaps I could talk to your Director.''

Edward Wardwell stared at me tight-lipped, and then said, resignedly, "All right. That's your privilege. I just hope I don't lose my job for missing the auction."

He opened the car door and stepped out. "It's been interesting to meet you," he said, and waited, as if he half-expected me to relent and hand over the painting. Then he said, "I knew your wife quite well, before she . . . well, you know, before the accident."

"You knew Jane?"

"Sure," he said, and before I could ask him anything else, he walked off towards Margin Street again, his shoulders hunched up against the cold.

I sat in my car for quite a long time, wondering what the hell I ought to do. I took the painting out of its wrapper again and stared at it. Maybe Edward Wardwell was telling me the truth, and this was the only view of Salem Harbor from the north-west that anybody had ever done. Yet, I was sure I had seen an engraving or a woodcut of a similar view before. It seemed hard to believe that one of the most sketched and painted inlets on the Massachusetts shoreline should only once have been painted from this particular direction.

It had been a strange, unsettling day. I didn't feel at all like going home. A man was watching me from across the street, his face shadowed by an unusually large hat. I started up the engine, and switched on the car radio. It was playing *Love Is The Sweetest Thing*.

FIVE

As I turned off Lafayette Road and drove northwards up the Granitehead peninsula towards Quaker Lane, Atlantic storm clouds, like dark and shaggy beasts, began to rise from the north-east horizon. By the time I reached the cottage, they were almost overhead, and the first drops of rain were beginning to spatter the hood of the car, and pock-mark the garden path.

I hurried up the path with my coat-collar tugged up on one side, and fumbled for my keys. The rain pattered and whispered through the winter-dried creeper beside the porch, and behind me there was the soft applause of the laurel bushes, as the wind rose.

As I slid my key into the front-door lock, I heard a woman's voice whisper, "*John*?" and I froze all over, and turned around, although I was almost too scared to move. The front garden was deserted. Only the bushes, and the overgrown lawn, and the rain-disturbed pond.

"Jane?" I said, clearly.

But there was nothing, and nobody; and plain sanity told me that it couldn't be Jane.

Nevertheless, there was something *different* about the house; whether it was just a feeling or whether somebody had actually been there. I stepped back into the garden, my eyes wincing against the falling rain, trying to see what it could possibly be.

I had loved Quaker Lane Cottage from the first day I saw it. I adored its slightly shabby 1860s Gothic appearance, its diamond-leaded windows, its dressed stone parapets, its creepers.

It had been built on the site of a much earlier cottage, and the old stone hearth in what was now the library was engraved with the numerals 1666. Tonight, however, as the rain dripped from the carved green gables, and one of the upstairs shutters creaked backwards in the unsettling wind, I began to wish that I had chosen to live somewhere more cozy, without this dark sense of disturbed spirits and restless memories.

"*John?*" somebody whispered; or maybe it was nothing but the wind. The black shaggy beasts of the clouds were right overhead now, and the rain grew heavier, and the drainpipes and gutters began to chuckle. I began to feel a sense of deep foreboding; a feeling that chilled the bones in my legs. A feeling that Quaker Lane Cottage was possessed with some spirit that had no earthly right to be there.

I walked back down the garden path, and then around to the back of the house. The rain plastered down my hair and stung my face, but before I went inside, I wanted to make sure that the house was empty; that there were no vandals or housebreakers inside. Well, that's what I *told* myself. I walked through the weedy garden to the leaded living-room window, and peered inside, shading my eyes with my hand so that I could see better.

The room looked empty. The grate was still heaped with cold gray ash. My teacup stood on the floor where I had left it this morning. I walked back round to the front of the cottage again, and listened, while the rain ran straight down the back of my neck. A glimmer of light showed through the clouds, and for a moment the surface of the ornamental pond looked as if it were sprinkled with nickels and dimes.

I was still standing out in the rain when one of our neighbors came churning up the lane in his Chevrolet flatbed. It was George Markham who lived at No. 7 Quaker Lane with his invalid wife Joan and more yipping and yapping dalmations than you could count. He wound down his window and peered out at me. He wore a plastic rain-cover over his hat, and his spectacles were flecked with droplets.

"Anything wrong, neighbor?" he called. "You look like you're taking a shower out there."

"I'm okay," I told him. "I thought I could hear one of the gutters leaking."

"Don't catch your death."

He was just about to wind up his window again when I

stepped across the puddly lane towards him, and said, "George, did you hear anybody walking up the lane last night? Round about two or three o'clock in the morning?"

George pouted thoughtfully, and then shook his head. "I heard the wind last night, for sure. But nothing else. Nobody walking up the lane. Any special reason?"

"I'm not sure."

George looked at me for a moment or two, and then said, "You'd best get yourself inside, get yourself dry. You can't go neglecting yourself, just because Jane isn't here any more. You want to come down later, play some cards? Old Keith Reed might be coming over, if he can get that truck of his started."

"I might do that. Thanks, George."

George drove away, and I was left alone in the rain again. I walked back across the lane, and up the garden path. Well, I thought, I can't stand out here all night. I opened the door, and gave it a push, and it swung back with its usual dour groan. I was greeted by shadows, and the familiar smell of old timber and woodsmoke.

"Anybody home?" I asked. The stupidest question of all time. The only person home was me. Jane was a month dead and I just wished I could stop imagining her accident over and over again, I just wished I could stop replaying the last blurry seconds of her life like one of those auto crashes they show on TV, with helpless dummies being flung through windshields. Except that Jane hadn't been a dummy; and neither had our child.

I stepped inside the house. There was no question about it: there was something different in the air, as if things had been moved around while I had been away. At first I thought: damn it, I was right, I've been robbed. But the long-case clock was still ticking away with weary sedateness in the hallway, the 18th-century painting of foxhounds still hung over the old oak linen-chest. Jane had given me that painting for Christmas, as a kind of affectionate joke about the day we had first met. I had tried to blow the hunting-horn that day, to impress her, and produced nothing more than a loud ripping noise, like a hippopotamus with gas. I could still hear her laughing now.

I closed the door and went upstairs to the bedroom to change out of my wet clothes. I still had this disturbing sensation that somebody had been here apart from me; that things had been *touched*, picked up and put down again. I was sure that I had left my comb on the bureau, instead of the bedside table. And my bedside clock had stopped.

I tugged on a navy-blue rollneck sweater and a pair of jeans. Then I went downstairs and poured myself my last half-mouthful of Chivas Regal. I had meant to buy more liquor while I was in Salem, but what with all that business with Edward Wardwell about the painting, I had completely forgotten to stop by the Liquor Mart. I swallowed the whiskey straight down, and wished I had another. Maybe when the rain eased off I would walk down to the Granitehead Market, and pick up a couple of bottles of wine, and a Gourmet TV dinner, lasagne maybe. I couldn't possibly look another Salisbury steak in the face. Salisbury steak must be the loneliest food in America.

It was then that I heard the whispering again, as if there were two other people in the house who were discussing me under their breath. I stayed where I was for a little while, listening; but every time I listened too hard the whispering seemed to turn into the wind, gusting under the door, or the gurgle of rain down the waterpipes. I stood up, and walked out into the hallway, with my empty glass in my hand, and said, "Hello?"

No answer. Just the steady shudder of loose window-casements. Just the sighing of the wind, and the distant thundering of the sea. "It keeps eternal whispering around desolate shores." Keats again. I almost cursed Jane for her omnipresent Keats.

I went into the library. It was cold in there, and damp. The desk was strewn with letters and bills and last month's auction catalogs, under a huge suspended brass lamp that had once hung in the cabin of Captain Henry Prince, in the *Astrea II*. On the windowsill there were five or six framed photographs: Jane when she was graduating from Wellesley; Jane and I standing outside a roadside diner in New Hampshire; Jane in the front garden of Quaker Lane Cottage; Jane with her mother and father, eyes squinting against the winter sunshine. I picked them up, one by one, and looked at them sadly.

Yet, there was something odd about them. None of them seemed to be quite the same as I remembered them. That day I had photographed Jane standing outside the cottage, I was sure that she had been standing on the path, and not in the front garden itself—especially since she had only just bought herself a new pair of mulberry-colored suede boots, which she wouldn't have wanted to get muddy. There was something else, too. In the dark glass of the crisscross leaded window only four or five feet behind her, I could make out a curious pale *blur*. It could have been a lamp, or a passing reflection; and yet it looked disturbingly like a woman's face, hollow-eyed and distressed, but moving too quickly to have been sharply caught by the camera.

I knew that, apart from Jane and myself, the cottage had been empty that day. I examined the picture as closely as I could, but it was impossible to tell exactly what that pale blur might have been.

I looked through all of the photographs again. In all of them, although it was impossible to be certain, I had the extraordinary feeling that people and things had been *moved*. Subtly, not noticeably. For instance, there was a picture of Jane beside the statue of Jonathan Pope, the founder of Granitehead harbor, and the "father of the tea-trade." I was sure that when I had looked at the photograph last, Jane had been standing on the right side of the statue; and yet here she was on the *left*. The picture hadn't been reprinted in reverse, either, because the inscription on the statue clearly read, "Jonathan Pope" the right way around. I held the photograph close, and then far away, but there was nothing to suggest that anybody had tampered with it. All that disturbed me, apart from Jane's altered position, was a quick, unfocused shape in the background, as if someone had been running past when the photograph was taken, and had suddenly turned around. It looked like a woman in a long brown dress, or a long brown coat. Her face was indistinct, but I could make out the dark sockets of her eyes, and the indistinct smudge of her mouth.

I suddenly began to feel very chilled, and frightened. Either I was reacting to the stress of Jane's death by hallucinating, by going more than quietly mad; or else something unnatural was happening in Quaker Lane Cottage, something powerful and cold and strange.

A door closed quietly somewhere in the house. I thought for a terrible moment that I could hear footsteps coming down the stairs, and I barged my way clumsily into the hall. But there was nobody there. Nobody there but me, and my haunted memories.

I looked back into the library. On the desk, where I had left it, lay the picture of Jane in the front garden. I walked into the room and picked it up again, frowning at it. There was something grotesquely alien about it. Jane was smiling at me quite normally; and apart from the pale reflection in the window behind her, the house seemed unchanged. But the photograph was different, wrong. It looked as if Jane were *propped-up*, rather than standing by herself; like one of those terrible police pictures of murder victims. Holding the photograph in my hand, I went to the library window and looked out into the front garden.

The photograph must have been taken about mid-afternoon, because the sun was low to the west, and all the shadows in it lay exactly horizontal, from one side of the picture to the other. Jane's shadow lay half-way along the path, so that even though she was nine or ten feet off to the left of it, and her legs were concealed by the low hedge of laurel bushes between us, I could work out exactly where in the garden she was standing.

I lifted the photograph again and again, comparing it with the front garden. I felt a desperation rise up inside me that almost made me bang my head against the window. This was impossible. And yet the indisputable evidence was here; in this blandly-smiling photograph.

Jane, in this photograph, was standing in the one place in the garden where it was humanly out of the question for *anyone* to stand, on the surface of the ornamental pond.

SIX

I left the house and walked down the lane between the wind-whipped yew trees to the main Granitehead highway, and then north-east towards Granitehead Market, on the outskirts of the village itself. It was a good three miles' walk, there and back, but it was the only real exercise I ever managed to get, and tonight I wanted the rain in my face and the wind in my eyes and anything that would reassure me that I was sane and that I was real.

A dog barked persistently somewhere off to my right. A sudden burst of dry leaves scurried out of the hedgerow and whirled around in front of me. It was one of those nights when slates are blown off rooftops, and television antennae are brought down, and trees collapse across roadways. It was one of those night when ships go down, and sailors are drowned. Rain and wind. Granitehead people call them "Satan's nights."

I passed my neighbors' cottages: the austere gambreled rooftops of Mrs. Haraden's house; the picturesque huddle of Breadboard Cottages, all shiplap and trellised porches; the Stick Style Gothic of No. 7, where George Markham lived. There were warm lights inside, televisions flickering, people eating supper; each window like a happy memory, brought to mind in the rainy wildness of the night.

I felt loneliness as well as fright, and as I neared the highway I began to have the unnerving sensation that somebody had been following me down the lane. It took all the determination I could muster not to turn around and take a look. Yet—weren't those footsteps? Wasn't that breathing? Wasn't that a stone, chipped up by somebody's hurrying feet?

It was a long, wet and blowy walk all the way along the main road to Granitehead Market. A couple of cars passed by, but they didn't stop to offer me a ride, and I didn't attempt to canvass one. The only other people I saw, apart from car-drivers, were three young men from the Walsh place, all dressed up in oil-skins, lifting a fallen tree from their front fencing. One of them remarked, "Just glad I ain't out at sea, not tonight."

And I thought of that song, that curiosity from Old Salem:
"*But the fish they caught were nought but bones
With hearts crush'd in their jaws.*"

After a while I saw the floodlights shining across the market's parking-lot, and the red illuminated sign saying *Market Open 8–11*. The store window was all misted up, but inside I could see the bright colors of modern reality, and people shopping. I opened the door, stepped inside, and stamped my feet on the mat.

"Been for a swim, Mr. Trenton?" called Charlie Manzi, from behind the counter. Charlie was fat and cheerful, with a thick rug of black curly hair, but he was also surprisingly sharp.

I briskly brushed the rain off my coat, and shook my head like a wet dog. "I'm seriously thinking of trading in my car for a birch-bark canoe," I told him. "This must be the wettest place on God's good earth."

"You think so?" said Charlie, slicing salami. "Well, on Waileale Mountain in Hawaii, it rains 460 inches every year, which is about ten times more than it does here, so don't knock it."

I'd forgotten that Charlie's hobby was records. Weather records, baseball records, altitude records, speed records, fattest-man records, eating canteloupes upside-down records. There was a standing advisory among the residents of Quaker Hill that you didn't mention anything that was either the best or the worst of anything whenever Charlie Manzi was in earshot; Charlie would always prove that you were wrong. The lowest temperature ever recorded on the North American continent was minus 81F, at Snag, in the Yukon, in 1947, so don't try to tell Charlie that "this has got to be the coldest night that America has ever known."

For a general-store owner, Charlie was friendly, loquacious, and enjoyed ribbing his customers. In fact, swapping smart remarks with Charlie was one of the major attractions of the Granitehead Market, apart from the fact that it was the nearest general store to Quaker Lane. Some customers actually rehearsed what they were going to say to Charlie before they went shopping, to see if they could get the better of him; but they rarely did. Charlie had learned his bantering the hard way, from being a fat and unpopular child.

Because of his unhappy childhood and his lonely growing-up years, Charlie's own recent personal tragedy was more poignant than most. By one of those Godsent miracles of circumstances and fate, Charlie had met and married at the age of 31 a handsome and hardworking lady schoolteacher from Beverly; and although she had suffered two anguished years of gynecological complications, she had at last given him a son, Neil. However, the doctors had warned the Manzis that any more pregnancies would kill Mrs. Manzi, and so Neil would have to remain their only child.

They had brought Neil up with a care and a love that, according to Jane, had been the talk of Granitehead. "If they spoil that boy any more, they'll ruin him for good," old Thomas Essex had remarked. And, sure enough, on the brand-new 500 cc motorcycle which his doting parents had bought him for his 18th birthday, Neil had skidded one wet afternoon on Bridge Street, in Salem, and hurtled headfirst into the side of a passing panel van. Massive cranial injuries, dead in fifteen minutes.

Charlie's hard-won paradise had collapsed after that. His wife had left him, unable to cope with his obsessive preoccupation with Neil's death; or with her own inability to give him another child. He had been left with nothing but his store, his customers, and his memories.

Charlie and I talked often about our bereavement. Sometimes, when he thought I was looking particularly down, he would invite me into the small office at the back of his store, hung with lists of wholesale orders and sexy Japanese calendars, and he would pour me a couple of shots of whiskey and give me a lecture on what he had felt like when he had heard that Neil had been killed, telling me how to manage, how to come to terms with it, and how to learn to live my life again. "Don't let anyone tell you that it ain't hard, or miserable, because it is. Don't let anyone tell you that it's easier to forget about someone who's dead rather than someone who's simply left you, because that ain't so, either.'' And I had those very words in mind as I stood wet and chilled in his store that stormy March evening.

"What are you looking for, Mr. Trenton?" he asked me, as he measured out coffee beans for Jack Williams, from the Granitehead Gas Station.

"Liquor, mainly. My outside's drowned, I thought I might as well drown my insides as well."

"Well," said Charlie, pointing down the aisle with his coffee scoop, "you know where it is."

I bought a bottle of Chivas, two bottles of Stonegate Pinot Noir, the very best, and some Perrier. At the freezer, I collected a lasagne dinner, a frozen lobster-tail, and a couple of packs of mixed vegetables. By the counter, I picked up half a pecan pie.

"That's it?" asked Charlie.

"That's it," I nodded.

He began to punch out the prices on the cash register. "You know something," he said, "you should eat better. You're losing weight and it doesn't suit you. You look like Gene Kelly's walking-stick after he'd been singing in the rain."

"How much did *you* lose?" I asked him. I didn't have to say when.

He smiled. "I didn't lose nothing. Not a single pound. In fact, I put twelve pounds on. Whenever I felt low, I cooked myself up a big plate of fettucine and clam sauce."

He shook out two brown-paper sacks, and began to pack away my liquor and groceries. "Fat?" he said. "You should have seen me. Charlie the Great."

I stood there for a while, watching him put everything away. Then I said, "Charlie, do you mind if I ask you a question?"

"Depends what it is."

"Well, let me ask you this. Did you ever get the feeling, after what happened with Neil—"

Charlie looked at me carefully, but he didn't say anything. He waited while I tried to put into words what had happened to me up at Quaker Lane Cottage, while I tried to find some plausible way of asking if I was hallucinating, or if I was going crazy, or if I was simply experiencing the exaggerated effects of withdrawal and loss.

"Let me put it this way," I said. "Do you ever get the feeling that Neil is *still here*?"

He licked his lips, as if they tasted of salt. Then he said, "That's your question?"

"Well, I guess it's half question and half statement. But did you ever feel anything which led you to believe that— well, what I'm trying to say is, did you at any time think that he might not be completely—"

Charlie kept on staring at me for what seemed like a very long time. But at last he lowered his eyes, and then his head, and looked down at his meaty hands resting on the counter.

"You see these hands?" he said, without looking up.

"Sure. I see them. They're good strong hands."

He lifted them up, both of them, big red joints of bacon with callused fingers. "I could cut them off, these fucking hands," he said. It was the first time I had ever heard him swear, and it gave me a prickling feeling at the back of my neck. "Everything these hands ever touched turned to shit. King Midas in reverse."

"They're still good and strong," I repeated. "Capable, too."

"Oh yes, sure. Strong and capable. But not strong enough to bring my wife back to me; and not capable of resurrecting my son."

"No," I said, oddly aware that this was the second time in a single day that "resurrection" had been mentioned. It wasn't, after all, a concept you heard about too frequently except on Sunday morning television.

I was silent for a moment, and then I said to Charlie, "You never feel that—I mean, you never feel that Neil comes *back* to you in any way? Talks to you? I'm only asking because I've had feelings like that myself, and I was just wondering if—"

"Comes *back* to me?" asked Charlie. His voice was very soft. "Well, now. Comes back to me."

"Listen," I said, "I don't know whether I'm going crazy or not, but I keep hearing somebody whispering to me, whispering my name, and it sounds like Jane. There's a kind of a feeling in the house, like there's somebody there. It's hard to explain it. And last night, I could have sworn I heard her singing. Do you think that's normal? I mean, did it happen to you? Did you ever hear Neil?''

Charlie looked at me as if he were about to say something for a moment; his expression seemed to be congested with unexpressed anxieties. But then he suddenly pushed my sacks of groceries towards me, and smiled, and shook his head, and said, "Nobody comes back, Mr. Trenton. That's the really hard lesson you have to learn when you lose someone you love. They just don't come back."

"Sure," I said, nodding. "Thanks for listening, anyway. It always helps to have people to talk to."

"You're tired, that's all," said Charlie. "You're imagining things. Why don't I sell you some Nytol, just to get you off to sleep?"

"I still have the Nembutal tablets that Dr. Rosen gave me."

"Well, take them, and make sure you eat good. Any more of these TV dinners and your skin is going to start breaking out in separate compartments."

"Come on, Charlie, you're not his mother," said Lenny Danarts, from the Granitehead gift store, impatient to be served.

I picked up the new TV Guide from the rack, paid for it and waved Charlie goodnight, pushing my way out of the store with my arms full. It was still windy outside, but the rain seemed to have eased off, and there was a fresh smell of ocean and wet stony soil. The walk back to Quaker Lane and up the hill between the elm trees suddenly seemed like a very long way, but I hefted my packages and started off across the parking-lot.

I was only halfway across, however, when a cream-colored Buick drew alongside and the driver tooted the horn. I bent down and saw that it was old Mrs. Edgar Simons, a frail and rather dotty old widow who lived just beyond Quaker Lane in a large Samuel McIntire house that I had always envied. She put down the passenger window and called, "May I offer you a ride, Mr. Trenton? It's an awfully stormy night to be walking home with your arms full of groceries."

"I appreciate it," I said, and I did. She opened the trunk for me, and I stored my packages away next to the spare tire, and then joined her inside the car. It smelled of leather and lavender, an old woman's perfume, but not unpleasant.

"Walking to the store is the only exercise I get," I told her. "I always seem to be too busy for squash these days. In fact, I always seem to be too busy for anything but work and sleep."

"Maybe that's a good thing, keeping busy," said Mrs. Edgar Simons, peering out over the long rain-beaded hood of her car. "Now, is it clear your way? Can I pull out? Edgar used to give me such a hard time for pulling out without looking. I went straight into a horse once. A horse!"

I looked northwards, up the highway. "You're okay," I told her, and she pulled away from the parking-lot with a screech of wet tires. It was always an interesting and slightly peppery experience, accepting a ride from Mrs. Edgar Simons. You never quite knew if you were going to arrive at the place you wanted to go, on time, or at all.

"You're going to think me a frightful old busybody," she said, as she drove. "But I couldn't help overhearing what you were saying to Charlie in the store. I don't have many people to talk to these days, and I do tend to eavesdrop more than I ought to. You don't mind, do you? Say if you do."

"Why should I mind? We weren't discussing any State secrets."

"You asked Charlie about his son coming back," said Mrs. Edgar Simons. "And the funny thing is, I knew exactly what you meant by coming back. When my Edgar died—that was six years ago next July 10—I had the same kind of experience. I used to hear him walking around in the attic, for nights on end. Can you believe that? And sometimes I would hear him coughing. You never met dear Edgar of course, but he had a distinctive little cough, clearing his throat, *ahem*."

"Do you still hear him?" I asked her.

"I do from time to time. Once or twice a month maybe, sometimes more frequently. And I still have the feeling when I walk into certain rooms in the house that Edgar has only just been there, that only a moment ago he walked out of another door. Once, you know, I even thought that I saw him, not in the house but in Granitehead Square, wearing a peculiar brown coat. I stopped the car and tried to go after him, but he disappeared into the crowds."

"So—after six years—you still have these feelings? Have you told anybody?"

"I talked to my doctor, of course, but he wasn't very

helpful at all. He gave me pills and told me to stop being hysterical. The funny thing is, the feelings vary in strength, and they also vary in frequency. I don't know why. Sometimes I can hear Edgar clearly; at other times he sounds so faint it's like a radio station you can't quite pick up. And the feelings seem to be *seasonal*, too. I hear less of Edgar in the winter than I do in the summer. Sometimes, on summer nights, when it's very mild, I can hear him sitting outside on the garden-wall, humming or talking to himself.''

''Mrs. Simons,'' I said, ''do you really believe that it's Edgar?''

''I used not to. I used to try to persuade myself that it was all my silly imagination. Oh—look at that foolish girl, walking in the road with her back to the traffic. She'll end up dead if she's not careful.''

I looked up, and glimpsed in the light from our headlamp a brown-haired girl in a long windblown cloak, walking by the side of the highway. We were approaching a sharp bend and so we passed the girl comparatively slowly. As we passed I twisted around in my seat to look at her. It was beginning to rain again, and it was very dark, and I suppose I could easily have been mistaken. But in the fractions of a second in which I could see her through the tinted rear window of Mrs. Simons' car, I was sure that I saw a face that I recognized.

White, with dark eye sockets. A face like the blurry face at the cottage window; a face like the girl who had unexpectedly turned around when I was photographing Jane by the statue of Jonathan Pope. A face like the staring woman in the Salem sandwich shop.

I felt a prickle of shock, and incomprehension. Could it be her? But if it was, how? and why?

''No consideration, these pedestrians,'' complained Mrs. Simons. ''They stroll around as if the roads were theirs. And who do they blame if they get struck by a car? Even if they're almost invisible, it's the driver who gets the blame.''

I kept on staring back at the girl until she had disappeared from sight around the curve. Then I turned around in my seat, and said, ''What? I'm sorry? I didn't catch what you said.''

''I'm just grumbling, that's all,'' said Mrs. Edgar Simons. ''Edgar always said that I was a terrible fussbudget.''

''Yes,'' I said. ''Edgar.''

''Well, that's the strange thing,'' Mrs. Edgar Simons told

me, abruptly resuming our conversation about ghostly visitations. "You see, I've heard Edgar, and I even believe that I've seen him; and now you seem to think that your Jane may be trying to come back to you. Well, you do, don't you? And yet all *Charlie* could say was that you must be imagining things."

"You don't blame him, do you?" I asked her. "It must be pretty hard for anyone to swallow, anyone who hasn't actually felt anything like it."

"But for *Charlie* to dismiss it, of all people," she said.

"What do you mean?" I asked her, frowning.

"I mean nothing less than that Charlie has had the same feelings about Neil, ever since the poor boy died. He's been hearing him walking about his bedroom; he's even heard his motorcycle starting up. And seen him, too, from what I gather. I was quite surprised when he didn't tell you about it. After all, it's nothing to be ashamed of. How can it be?"

"Charlie's seen Neil?" I said, in disbelief.

"Quite so. Over and over again. That was the principal reason why Mrs. Manzi left Granitehead. Charlie always says that it was something to do with her not being able to give him any more children, but the truth was that she couldn't bear to feel that her dead son was still walking around the home. She hoped that if she moved away, he wouldn't follow her."

"Does Charlie still hear Neil now?" I asked.

"As far as I know. He's been much less forthcoming of late. I think he's worried that if too many people start taking an interest in Neil's reappearance, they might frighten him away. He loved Neil, you know, more than his own life."

I thought about all this for a little while, and then I asked, slightly skeptical, "Charlie really told you that?"

"Charlie did indeed."

"Then why didn't he tell *me*?"

"I don't know. He probably had his reasons. He only discussed it with me because he was so upset about Mrs. Manzi leaving him. He hasn't mentioned it very much since. Only edged around it."

"Mrs. Simons," I said, "this is beginning to frighten me. Can I tell you that? I don't understand it. I don't understand what's going on. I'm frightened."

Mrs. Simons stared at me again, and narrowly missed colliding with the rear end of a parked and unlit truck.

"I wish you'd please keep your eyes on the road," I told her.

"Well, you listen," she said, "you don't have any cause at all to be frightened, not the way I see it. Why should you be frightened? Jane loved you when she was alive, why shouldn't she still love you now?"

"But she's *haunting* me. Just like Edgar is haunting you. And Neil is haunting Charlie. Mrs. Simons, we're talking about *ghosts*."

"Ghosts? You sound like a tabloid reporter."

"I don't mean ghosts in the sense that—"

"They're lingering feelings, that's all, pervasive memories," said Mrs. Simons. "They're not phantoms, or anything like that. As far as I can see, they're nothing more at all than the stored-up joys of our past relationships—echoing, as it were, beyond the passing of the people we loved."

We had almost reached the foot of Quaker Lane. I pointed up ahead and said to Mrs. Edgar Simons, "Do you think you could pull up here? Don't bother to drive all the way up the lane. It's too dark, and you'll probably wreck your shocks."

Mrs. Edgar Simons smiled, almost beatifically, and drew the Buick into the side of the road. I opened the door, and a gust of wet wind blew in.

"Thanks for the ride," I told her. "Maybe we should talk some more. You know, about Edgar. And, I don't know, Jane."

Her face was illuminated green in the light from the instruments on her dash. She looked very old and very prophetic: a little old witch.

"The dead wish us nothing but sweetness, you know," she told me, and nodded, and smiled. "The people we used to love are as benign to us in death as they were in life. I know. And you will find out, too."

I hesitated for a moment or two, and then I said, "Goodnight, Mrs. Simons," and closed the door. I lifted my groceries out of the trunk, slammed it shut, and slapped the vinyl roof of the car to tell her that she could go. She drove off silently, her rear lights reflected on the wet tarmac in six wide scarlet tracks.

The dead wish us nothing but sweetness, I thought. Jesus.

The wind sighed in the wires. I turned my face towards the darkness of Quaker Lane, where the elm trees thrashed, and began the long uncertain walk uphill.

SEVEN

I was tempted, as I walked up Quaker Lane, to stop off at George Markham's house and play a few hands of cards with him and old Keith Reed. I had been neglecting my neighbors ever since Jane was killed, and if I was going to continue to live here, well, I ought to visit more often.

But even as I approached George's front fence, I knew that I was only making excuses for myself. Visiting George would be nothing more than a way of deferring my return to Quaker Lane Cottage, and to whatever fears were concealed behind its doors. Visiting George would be cowardice: letting the whispers and the voices and the strange movements scare me away from my own home.

I hesitated, though, and looked in at George's parlor window, where I could just see the back of Keith Reed's head as he dealt out the cards, and the lamplit table, and the beer-bottles, and a sudden blue drift of smoke from George's cigar. I hoisted my sacks of groceries a little higher, and took in a deep breath, and carried on up the hill.

Quaker Lane cottage was in complete darkness when I approached, even though I was sure that I had left the front porch light on to guide me home. The gale blew around the house and rustled its creepers like hair, and the two shuttered upstairs windows looked like tightly-closed eyes. A house that was keeping its secrets to itself. In the far distance I could hear the endless dejected grumbling of the North Atlantic surf.

I put down my sacks of groceries, took out my keys, and opened the front door. Inside, it was warm, and calm, and I could see the dancing light from the living-room fire reflected on the ceiling. I brought in my bags and closed the door behind me. Perhaps the house wasn't really haunted after all. Perhaps the creaking of that swing last night had simply put me on edge, and given me a temporary attack of mild hysteria.

Nevertheless, once I had stacked away the groceries and the liquor, and switched on the oven for my lasagne dinner, I went all the way around the house, upstairs and down, looking into every room, opening up every closet, kneeling down and peering under every bed. I just wanted to know when I sat down and ate my meal tonight that there wasn't anything hiding in the cottage that might come down and catch me unawares.

Ridiculous; but, what would *you* have done?

I watched television for an hour or so, although reception was blurry because of the weather. I watched *Sanford* and *M•A•S•H* and even *Trapper John, M.D*. Then I cleared up the remains of my meal, poured myself a large whiskey, and went into the library. I wanted to take a look at that painting that Edward Wardwell had made such a fuss about in Salem, and see if perhaps I couldn't identify the ship in it.

It was strikingly cold in the library. Usually it was one of the warmest rooms in the house. It wasn't worth laying a fresh log fire; but I switched on the electric heater fan. After only a few seconds, though, the heater abruptly short-circuited, crackled sparks, whirred, and died. There was a smell of burned plastic and electricity. Outside, creepers tapped against the window; a soft and complicated pattern, like unremembered spirits seeking access.

I picked up the painting, still in its wrapper, and selected one or two books from the shelves that I thought might help me discover what the ship might be. Osborne's *Salem Marine*; Walcott's *Massachusetts Merchant Vessels 1650–1850*; and, just out of inspiration, *Great Men of Salem*, by Douglass. I remembered that many of the leading commercial and political figures in Old Salem used to own private ships, and Douglass' book might contain some clues about the one in the picture.

By the time I was ready to leave the library, it was so cold in there that I could actually see my breath. The barometer must be dropping like a stone, I thought to myself. Yet, in the hallway, it was as warm as it had been before, and the barometer pointed to the optimistic side of Unsettled. I looked back at the library, wondering if there was something wrong with it. Rising damp, perhaps. A freak draft down the chimney. And again I thought I could hear—what was it, breathing? Whispering? I froze where I was, unsure if I ought to go back and face whatever might be in there; or if I ought to carry on with what I was doing with as much apparent unconcern as I could. Maybe if you believed in ghosts, that gave them even more strength to manifest themselves. Maybe if you didn't believe in them, they'd get weak, and dispirited, and eventually leave you alone.

Whispering. Cold, soft, persistent whispering; like someone relating a very long and very unpleasant story.

"All right!" I said aloud. "All right, that's it!" and hurtled open the library door. It shuddered on its hinges, and then creaked to rest. The library, of course, was deserted. Only the creepers tapping at the windows. Only the wind, and the occasional spatter of rain. My breath smoked, and I couldn't help thinking of all those creepy movies like *The Exorcist* where the presence of an evil demon is betrayed by a steep and sudden drop in temperature.

"Okay," I said, trying to sound like a tough guy who's decided to be generous and not pulverize the sarcastic barfly who's been making comments about his wife. I reached out for the library door handle and firmly closed the room behind me. Back in the hallway, I said to myself, "It's nothing. Nothing whatsoever. No ghosts. No spirits. No demons. Nothing."

I picked up the watercolor and the books once more, and carried them through to the living-room, where I spread them all out on the rug in front of the fire. I unwrapped the painting, and held it up so that I could examine it closely. The firelight played patterns across it, so that it almost appeared as if the painted sea were moving.

It was strange to think that this same sheet of handmade paper had been pinned to an easel over 290 years ago, only a quarter-mile or so away from here, and that an unknown artist had recreated in paints a day that had really passed; a day when men in frock coats had walked on beside the harbor, and Salem had been alive with horses and carts and people in Puritan clothes. I touched the surface of it with my fingertips. It was a crude painting, in many ways. The perspective and

the coloring were strictly amateur. Yet there was some quality
about it which seemed to bring it to life, as if it had been
painted for a heartfelt *reason*. As if the artist had wanted
more than anything to bring that long-lost day to life, and to
show the people who were to be his descendants what Salem
Bay had actually looked like, in every detail.

I could now understand why the Peabody Museum people
were so interested in it. Every tree had been carefully recorded;
it was even possible to make out the winding curve of Quaker
Lane, and one or two small cottages there. One cottage could
very well have been the forebear of Quaker Lane Cottage; a
tiny lopsided dwelling with a tall chimney and weather-boarded
sides.

Now I examined the ship on the other side of the bay. It
was a three-master, conventionally-rigged, although there was
one distinctive feature which I hadn't noticed when I had
looked at the picture earlier. There were *two* large flags flying
from the stern-castle, one above the other, one of which
appeared to be a red cross on a black background, and the
other one of which was obviously meant to be the colors of
the ship's owner.

Pouring myself some more whiskey, I looked into Walcott's
book on merchant vessels, and discovered that "it was the
custom of some Salem dignitaries to fly on their ships two
flags; one to denote their ownership and the other to celebrate
the voyage on which they were engaged, particularly if it was
expected to be especially significant or profitable."

At the back of the book, I found a chart of owner's flags,
although they were printed in black-and-white, and it was
hard to distinguish between the various designs of stripes and
crosses and stars. There were two which appeared to be
vaguely similar to the owner's flag on the ship in my picture,
and so I cross-referred to Osborne's *Salem Marine*.

One of them was obviously hopeless: the flag of Joseph
Winterton, Esq., who was said to have run one of the first
ferries from Salem to Granitehead Neck. But the other belonged to Esau Hasket, a wealthy merchant who had escaped
from England in 1670 because of his extreme religious views,
and who had quickly established in Salem one of the largest
fleets of merchantmen and fishing-vessels on the east coast of
the colonies.

The text said, "Little is known today about Hasket's fleet,

although it probably numbered four 100-ft. merchantmen and numerous smaller vessels. Although tiny by modern standards, a 100-ft. ship was the largest that Salem's harbor could comfortably accommodate, since it had a 9-ft. tidal range, and ships which had sailed quite easily into harbor when the tide was high would settle into the mud when the tide ebbed again. The names of only two of Hasket's vessels have survived to the present day: the *Hosannah* and the *David Dark*. A scrimshaw rendition of the *Hosannah* made in about 1712 by one of her retired crewmen shows her as a three-masted vessel flying a palm-tree flag to indicate that she usually traded in the West Indies. No known illustration of the *David Dark* exists, although it can fairly be assumed that she was a similar vessel.''

I turned to *Great Men of Salem* and read all that I could about Esau Hasket. A vigorous and firebreathing forerunner to Elias Derby, Hasket had obviously been feared and respected as much for his Puritanical religious fervor as he was for his sea-trading. Hasket had apparently shaken the community's souls as well as their pockets. One contemporary account said that ''Mr. Haskette firmlie believes in the existence on Earth bothe of Angelles & deamones, and is forthright in so saying; for if a manne is to believe in the Lord & His hostes, sayes Haskette, so must he believe with equalle certaintie in Satan and his miniones.'' Derby had subsequently made Salem into one of the busiest and wealthiest seaports on the eastern seaboard, and earned himself the distinction of being America's first-ever millionaire.

I was about to put the books away, satisfied at least that I could now sell the painting either to the Peabody or to one of our regular customers with the catch-all caption, ''Thought to be a rare depiction of one of the merchant ships of Esau Hasket,'' when it occurred to me to look up the name of David Dark. It was a curious name, but there was something about it which rang very distinct bells. Maybe it was something that Jane had once said, or one of our customers. I thumbed through *Great Men of Salem* again until I found it.

The entry was tantalizingly short. Twelve lines altogether.

''*David Ittai Dark*, 1610 (?)–1691. Fundamentalist preacher of Mill Pond, Salem, who enjoyed brief local celebrity in 1682 when he claimed to have had several face-to-face conversations with Satan, who had provided him with a list of all those souls in the Salem district who were surely damned, and to whose 'inevitable incineration' Satan was looking forward to with 'relishe.' David Dark was a protégé and adviser to the wealthy Salem merchant *Esau Hasket* (ibid.) and for some years was engaged with Hasket in trying to establish extreme fundamentalist principles in Salem's religious community. He died in mysterious circumstances in the spring of 1691, some say by the phenomenon of 'spontaneous explosion.' In Dark's honor, Hasket named his finest merchant-vessel the *David Dark*, although it is interesting to note that all contemporary records of this ship were excised from every logbook, chart, account-ledger and broadsheet of the period, supposedly on Hasket's instruction.''

It was then that I found what I had been looking for. I traced the words with my finger as I read them silently. I felt that heady surge of excitement that every antique dealer experiences when he discovers for certain that the goods he has bought are unique and valuable.

''David Dark's insignia was that of a red cross on a black field, to indicate the triumph of the Lord over the powers of darkness. Contrarily, however, this insignia was adopted intermittently for several decades after his death by secret covens of 'witches' and practitioners in the black arts. The insignia was declared illegal in 1731 by Deputy Governor William Clark, presiding officer of the Court of Oyer and Terminer.''

I laid the book flat on the floor and picked up the painting again. So this ship was the *David Dark*, a ship which had been named for a man who had claimed to have conversations with the Devil, and whose name had been expunged from every possible local record.

Damn it, no wonder Edward Wardwell had been so desperate to acquire the painting for the Peabody. This could, quite simply, be the only pictorial record ever made of the *David Dark*. Or at least the only pictorial record which had survived through 290 years and a purge against knowledge of what she had looked like or where she had sailed.

The *David Dark*, with her forbidden banner of black and red, sailing out of Salem Harbor. I examined her closely, and realized that the artist had painted her in quite considerable detail, especially for a vessel that was so far away, and especially since dozens of ships must have sailed in and out of Salem every day.

Perhaps the artist had never intended to paint a straightforward landscape of the Granitehead shoreline at all. Perhaps he
had meant to paint nothing less than an historical record
of the *David Dark* sailing away on a voyage of great
importance. But where was she going? And why?

The log fire suddenly dropped, making my head jerk up in
frightened reaction, and my heart pump blood violently. The
wind had stilled, and I could hear the rain falling more
steadily now, rustling through the orchard and through the
trees. I knelt on the rug, with my books all around me,
listening, daring the house not to whisper, daring the doors
not to open and close, daring the ghosts of three hundred
years not to flow through the corridors and down the stairs.

And in front of me, on its gray painted sea, the *David Dark*
sailed on its unknown voyage, mysterious and indistinct against
the Massachusetts treeline. I stared at it as I listened, and I
heard myself whispering its name.

"*David Dark . . .*"

Silence for a while, except for the ashy crackling of the
fire, and the soft sound of the rain. Then, scarcely audible, a
noise which I was so frightened to hear that I actually let out
a peculiar grunt; the sort of mortally-despairing exclamation
you sometimes hear from airplane passengers when their
plane drops into an unexpected dive. I felt tingling cold, and I
wasn't even sure that I would be able to run if I had to.

It was the garden-swing. Regular and rhythmic, that same
creakkk-squik, creakkk-squik, creakkk-squik that I had heard
the night before. There was no mistaking it.

I stood up and made my way jerkily across to the hallway.
I had closed the library door and now it was open. *The latch
hadn't caught?* No. I had closed it, and now it was open.
Someone, or something, had opened it. *The wind?* Impossible.
Stop blaming the damned wind. The wind can rattle and
shake and whisper and howl, but the wind can't open a
latched door, and the wind can't change people's places in
photographs, and the wind alone can't make that garden-
swing go backwards and forwards. There's somebody out
there, swinging. Face up to the damned fact that things are
happening in this house and somebody's making them happen,
human or inhuman. There's somebody out there swinging, for
God's sake, so go and look. Go and see for yourself what it is
that's making you so frightened. Face up to it.

I limped across the kitchen as if I was injured, but it was only a combination of fright and pins-and-needles from kneeling on the living-room floor. I reached the back door. Locked. I fumbled for the key on top of the icebox and dropped it on the floor. *Purposely? You dropped that purposely. The real point is, you don't want to go out there. The real point is that you're scared shitless, just because some mischievous kid has trespassed into your orchard and swung on your stupid swing.*

On hands and knees, I found the key. Stood up again, jostled it into the lock, unlocked it, turned the doorhandle.

Supposing it's her?

And waves of deadly cold went through me, as if buckets of ice-water were being poured over me in slow-motion, one after the other.

Supposing it's Jane?

I don't remember actually opening the door. I remember feeling the rain prickling my face as I emerged from the kitchen porch. I remember walking, stumbling through the weeds and the long grass, hurrying faster and faster, afraid to miss whoever it was who was swinging on the swing, and yet even more afraid that I might get there before they ran away.

I came around the apple-tree, right next to the swing, and stopped dead. The rain-wet chair was swinging backwards and forwards, high and steady, all by itself. The chains went *creakkk-squik, creakkk-squik, creakkk-squik*, but the chair was empty.

I stared at it, breathing harshly. Alarmed, but oddly relieved. It's a natural phenomenon, I thought. Thank God for that. Science, not ghosts. Some kind of magnetic disturbance. Maybe the moon pulls the chains at certain times of the year, the way it pulls the tide, and the momentum kind of builds up, like in Newton's Law—some kind of inertia or whatever. Maybe there's a magnetic lode underneath the soil here, and certain weather conditions charge it up, like electricity from thunderclouds. Or maybe some sort of highly localized wind starts it off, a katabatic wind down the side of the house that—

Then I saw it. A brief, blueish flicker of light, in the seat of the swing. No more than a half-seen flash of distant lightning, but enough to make me stare even harder at the swing-seat as it squeaked backwards and forwards. Then another flicker, a little brighter than the first. I took a step away from the swing, two steps. The light flickered again and I could finally make something out—but I didn't like it.

What I saw on the seat of the swing was like an image illuminated by camera flashbulbs, an image that was dazzling one instant and nothing but a retinal after-image the next. Half-formed, blurry, as if it were a hologram transmitted from somewhere years ago and far away.

It was Jane, and whenever the light flickered and I could see her, she was looking back at me. Her face was unmarked but odd, thinner somehow, as if her skull were elongated. She wasn't smiling. Her hair crackled as if it were blown by an electrical discharge rather than by the wind. She was wearing a white dress of some kind, a long white dress with wide sleeves, and sometimes she was there and sometimes she wasn't, but the swing kept on swinging, and the light flickered, and the chains went *creakkk-squik, creakkk-squik, creakkk-squik*. And, God almighty, she was dead. She was dead and I could see her.

I opened my mouth. I couldn't even speak at first. My face was wet with rain but my throat was dry and constricted. Jane stared at me, unsmiling, and the flickers began to fade. Soon I could barely see her; only the glimpse of a pale white hand on the chain of the swing, the blur of a shoulder, the outline of flying hair.

"Jane," I whispered. God, I was frightened. The swing began to lose momentum. The chains suddenly stopped squeaking.

"*Jane!*" I shouted. And somehow for a moment, the fright of losing her again overcame the fright of seeing her. If she was really there, if by some unholy miracle she was actually trapped somewhere in purgatory, or the spirit world, if she hadn't yet died forever, then perhaps—

I didn't shout to Jane again. I was about to, but something stopped me. The swing swung three or four more times, then came to a standstill. I stood looking at it, and then slowly approached it, and laid my hand on the wet wooden arm of the chair. There was nothing there, no sign that anybody had been sitting here at all. The two carved depressions in the seat were filled with rainwater.

"Jane," I said, under my breath, but I no longer felt as if she were close. And I was no longer sure that I really *wanted* to call her. If she came back, what could she possibly come *back to?* Her body was crushed beyond repair, and a month decayed. There was no way that she could occupy her earthly self again. And did I really want her to occupy the cottage, and the garden, and me? She had lived, but she was dead now; and there is no one more unwelcome in the world of the living than the dead.

There was another reason I didn't call her. I remembered what Edward Wardwell had said to me today, in Salem. *"Did you know that Granitehead was called Resurrection, up until 1703?"*

Resurrection.

Drenched, and deeply disturbed, I walked back to the cottage. Before I went in, I looked up at the eyes of the bedroom windows. I thought I might have glimpsed a flicker of blue-white light there, but I was probably mistaken. Even nightmares have to end sometime.

The trouble was, I began to feel that my nightmare was just starting.

EIGHT

George opened the door and looked at me in surprise. "You're kind of late for a game of cards, John. We were just about to finish up for the evening. Still, if you'd care to join us for a nightcap . . ."

I stepped into the hallway and stood there, wet and shaking, feeling like the victim of a road accident. George said, "Are you okay? You didn't catch a chill, did you, standing out there in the rain? And where's your raincoat?"

I turned and looked at him but I didn't know what to say. How could I explain to him that I had run down Quaker Lane through the blinding darkness, skidding and stumbling on the wet road, as if I were being hotly pursued by all the demons of hell? And that I had waited outside his house, trying to catch my breath, trying to convince myself that there was nothing after me, no ghosts, no apparitions, no flickering white pictures from beyond the grave?

George took my arm and led me down the hallway to the living-room. The hall was decorated with trellis-patterned wallpaper, and proudly hung with George's fishing certificates and photographs of George and Keith and a few of the other old Granitehead boys holding up cod and giant sunfish and flounder. In the living-room, Keith Reed was sitting by the open fire, finishing a last glass of beer, while Mrs. Markham's wheelchair stood empty in a far corner, with her knitting on the seat.

"Gladys went off to bed," said George. "She tires easily when there's company. Specially a live-wire like Keith."

Keith, a white-haired retired boat-captain, gave a grunt of

amusement. "*Used* to be a live wire, wunst upon a time," he grinned, showing a row of square tobacco-stained teeth. "Used to be a time, no lady within kissing distance was safe from Keith Reed. You ask Cap'n Ray, down at the Pier Transit Company, he'll tell you."

"You want a drink, John?" asked George. "Whiskey, maybe? You're sure looking white in the face."

"Too much clean living, that's your trouble," said Keith.

I reached out for the arm of the chintz-and-oak chair by the fire, and unsteadily sat down.

"I don't know what to tell you," I said. My voice sounded shaky, and congested by phlegm. Keith glanced across at George, but George shrugged to show that he didn't know what the matter was.

"I, um, I ran down the hill," I told them.

"You ran down the hill?" repeated Keith.

I suddenly realized that I was close to tears. Tears brought on by fright, relief, the effects of seeing Jane, and the unexpected concern for my wellbeing that was being shown to me by two grizzled old Granitehead boys who normally treated strangers with a contemptuous spit on the sidewalk.

"It's okay now, John, you sup down some of this whiskey and tell us what's wrong," said George. He handed me a tumbler with a transfer-picture of a sailing-ship on it, and I took a large swallow. The liquor burned down my throat and into my stomach, and made me cough; but it steadied my nerves, and slowed down my heartbeats, and quelled some of the jangling hysteria that had suddenly gripped me.

"I ran all the way from the cottage," I said.

"Now, why did you do a thing like that?" asked Keith. "Cottage isn't on *fire*, is it?" He pronounced it "fye-uh," with a marked Granitehead accent. "Isn't burning down?"

I looked from Keith to George and back again. The normality of the living-room almost made me feel that I had been imagining everything. The brass clock on the mantelpiece, the ship's wheel on the wall, the flowery-patterned furnishings. A tortoiseshell cat, with its paws tucked in, sleeping with its nose toward the fire. A pipe-rack, hung with burned-down briars. Upstairs, I could hear the sudden blur of laughter, as Mrs. Markham sat in bed watching television.

"I've seen Jane," I said, quietly.

George sat down. Then he got up again, brought over his

glass of beer, and sat down for a second time, staring at me
closely. Keith said nothing, but didn't stop grinning, although
his grin seemed to have been drained of some of its humor.

"Where did you see her?" asked George, as gently as he
could manage. "Up there, at the cottage?"

"In the garden. She was swinging on the garden-swing.
This is the second night she's done it. She did it yesterday
only I didn't see her then."

"But you saw her tonight?"

"Only for a very short while. She wasn't very clear. She
was like a television picture that's on the fritz. But it was her
all right. I know it. And the swing—the swing was going
backwards and forwards by itself. Well, with her on it. But if
she was a ghost, she was making that swing go backwards
and forwards just as hard as if she was real."

George puckered up his lips thoughtfully, and frowned at
me. Keith raised his eyebrows, and rubbed his chin.

"You don't believe me," I told them.

"Didn't say that," returned Keith. "Didn't say that at
all."

"It's just that, well, it's something of a shock, isn't it?" put
in George. "Seeing a real ghost? You don't think it could
have been some trick of the light? Sometimes the light plays
strange old tricks at night, especially off the ocean."

"She was sitting on the swing, George. Lit up, like a blue
flickering light. Blue-and-white, like flashbulbs."

Keith took a long drink of beer and then wiped his mouth
with the back of his hand. Then he stood up, and pressed his
hands to the small of his back, rubbing it to ease the stiffness,
and walked slowly across to the window. He parted the
drapes and stood there for a long time with his back to us,
staring out at the weather.

"You know what you've just been a witness to, don't
you?" he said.

"I've seen my wife, that's all I know. She's a month dead,
and I've seen her."

Keith turned around, slowly shaking his head. "You didn't
see your wife, John. Maybe your imagination painted a picture for you, turned what you actually saw into something
you thought was Jane. But no sir. I've seen what you saw
tonight a hundred times. Used to frighten sailors to death
back in the old days. St. Elmo's Fire, they call it."

"St. Elmo's Fire? What the hell is that?"

"It's a discharge of natural electricity. You see it mostly on the masts of ships, or radio antennae, or the wings of airplanes. *Corposant*, they usually call it, in Salem. Flickers, like a burning brush. That's what you saw, wasn't it? Kind of a flickering light?"

I glanced at George. "Keith's right," said George. "I've seen it myself, out on fishing trips. Looks real eerie, the first time you see it."

"I saw her face, George," I told him. "There wasn't any mistake about it. I saw her face."

George leaned forward and laid his hand on my knee. "John," he said, "I believe you saw what you said you saw. I truly believe you saw Jane, in your mind's eye. But you know and I know that there isn't any such thing as a ghost. You know and I know that people don't come back from the dead. We may believe in the immortal soul, the life everlasting, amen, but we don't believe that it takes place here on earth, because if it did, this world would be pretty damned crowded with wandering spirits, don't you think?"

He reached behind him for the bottle of Four Roses and poured me another large glassful. Then he said, "You've been bearing up to this pretty well, all things considered. I was saying that very thing to Keith only this evening, that you were bearing up well. But it's bound to break out, now and again, that grief you're feeling deep inside of you. Nobody blames you for it. It's just one of those things. I lost my brother Harry, drowned off the Neck one night, what, eighteen years ago now; and believe you me it took me many a long month to get over that feeling of sadness, and loss."

"Mrs. Edgar Simons told me tonight that she'd seen her late husband, too."

George smiled, and turned to smile back at Keith. Keith, who was pouring himself another Michelob, smiled in return, and shook his head.

"Don't you go taking no notice of what the Simons widow tells you. Everybody knows what *her* problem is." He tapped his forehead to suggest that her brain was 78 cents in the dollar.

"She didn't give old man Simons too much of a life when he was alive," put in Keith. "He told me wunst that she locked him out of the house all night in his long-johns, because he felt like exercising his conjugal rights and she sure as hell didn't. Now, a man wouldn't go back to a widow like that, even if he was a ghost, now would he?''

"I don't know," I replied. I was feeling confused now. I was even beginning to doubt what I had actually seen in the garden of Quaker Lane Cottage. Had it really been Jane? It seemed difficult to believe; and even more difficult to recall exactly what her face had looked like. Elongated, like a saint by El Greco, with crackling hair. But couldn't that crackling hair have been nothing more than the electrical discharge that Keith called corposant, St. Elmo's Fire? It flickers, he had said, like a burning brush.

I finished my second drink, and declined a third. "I won't be able to crawl back up that hill, let alone walk up it."

"You want me to come up there with you?" asked Keith. But I shook my head.

"If there's anything up there, Keith, I think I'd better face it alone. If there is a ghost, then it's *my* ghost, and that's all there is to it."

"You should take yourself a vacation," said George.

"Jane's father told me that."

"Well, he was right. There's no use in sitting alone in an old cottage like that, brooding about what might have been, and what's past. Now, you're sure you're going to be okay?"

"You bet. And thank you for listening. You really calmed me down."

George nodded towards the whiskey bottle. "Nothing better for jingling nerves than the Old Four Roses."

I shook hands with both men and went towards the door. But as I reached the hallway, I turned and said, "One thing more. Do either of you know why Granitehead used to be called Resurrection?"

Keith looked at George and George looked at Keith. Then George said, "Nobody knows why for sure. Some folks say that it was named for the new life that folks here were going to lead, when they first landed from Europe. Others say that it was just a name. But I personally prefer the story that it was named on the third day after Easter, when Christ rose out of the tomb."

"You don't think it was named for anything else?"

"Like what?" asked George.

"Well . . . the kind of thing that I think I saw tonight. The kind of thing that Mrs. Edgar Simons says she's been hearing. And Charlie Manzi, too, down at the market.''

"Charlie Manzi? What are you talking about?''

"Mrs. Edgar Simons says that Charlie Manzi keeps seeing his son.''

"You mean *Neil*?''

"He only had one son, didn't he?''

George blew out his cheeks in exaggerated astonishment, and Keith Reed let out a long whistle. "That woman," said Keith, "she sure has a whole bunch of bearings loose. You shouldn't take any mind of her, John; not any mind at all. No wonder you thought you saw something, if you'd been talking to her. Wheweee, Charlie Manzi, that's something. Seeing Neil, you say?''

"That's right,'' I nodded. I felt embarrassed now, for believing everything that Mrs. Edgar Simons had told me. I couldn't even think why I had listened to her, the way she had babbled on. I must have been overtired, or half-drunk, or just plain stupid.

"Listen,'' I told George and Keith, "I have to go now. But if you don't mind, I'll stop by when I come past here on my way to the shop tomorrow. You don't mind that, do you?''

"You're welcome, John. You can stay for breakfast, if you want. Mrs. Markham and I whip up some fair old buckwheat cakes between us. She does the mixing and I do the baking. You stop by.''

"Thanks, George. Thanks, Keith.''

"You mind how you go, you hear?''

NINE

I left No. 7 and walked out into the drizzling night again. I turned right, to make my way back up Quaker Lane; but then I stopped, and hesitated, and looked downhill, towards the main highway, and the house where Mrs. Edgar Simons lived. It was only a little before 10 o'clock, and I doubted if she would mind if I paid her a visit. She couldn't have too many friends these days; and there were few neighbors on the main Granitehead-Salem highway. Most of the big old houses had been sold now, and demolished, to make way for gas stations and food markets and shops selling live bait and tacky souvenirs. The old Granitehead people had gone with them, too old and too tired and not nearly wealthy enough to be able to relocate themselves to one of the fashionable waterfront houses that bordered Salem Bay.

It was a good ten minutes' walk, but I reached the house at last—a large Federal mansion, foursquare but graceful, with rows of shuttered windows and a curved porch with Doric pillars. The gardens which surrounded it had once been formal and well-kept, but now they were wild and hideously overgrown. The trees which surrounded the mansion itself had remained unpruned for nearly five years, and they clung around the house like spidery creatures trying to consume a brave and exquisite princess. This princess, however, had long ago faded: as I walked up the weedy shingle path, I saw that the decorative balconies had corroded, the brickwork had cracked in long diagonal zigzags, and even the decorative basket of fruit over the front porch, a design especially favored by Samuel McIntire, was chipped and stained with bird droppings.

The Atlantic wind whined across the gardens, and around the corners of the house, and chilled my already-soaking back.

I went up the stone steps into the porch. The marble flooring was broken, and the paint was flaking from the front door as if the woodwork were suffering from a leprous disease. I pulled the bell-handle, and I heard a muffled jangling somewhere within the house. I rubbed my hands briskly together to try to keep myself warm, but with that wind whipping around the corner it wasn't easy.

There was no answer, so I rang again, and knocked, too. The knocker was fashioned in the shape of a gargoyle's head, with curved horns and a glaring face. Enough to scare off anybody, even in daylight. What was more, it made a dead, flat, sepulchral sound, like nails being driven into the lids of solid mahogany caskets.

"Come on, Mrs. Simons," I urged her, under my breath. "I'm not standing out here all night."

I decided to give it one last try. I slammed the knocker and jangled the bell, and even shouted out, "Mrs. Simons? Mrs. Edgar Simons? You there, Mrs. Simons?"

There was no reply. I stepped away from the door, and back down the porch steps. Maybe she had gone out visiting, although I couldn't think who she would want to visit at this time of night, in the middle of a furious gale. Still, there didn't appear to be any lights in the house, and although it was hard to to tell in the darkness, the upstairs drapes didn't appear to be drawn. So she wasn't downstairs, watching television or anything; and it didn't look as if she were upstairs, asleep.

I walked around the side of the house just to make sure there were no lights on in back. It was then that I saw Mrs. Edgar Simons' Buick, parked just outside her open garage doors. The garage doors were trembling and rattling in the wind, but there was nobody around, no lights, no sounds, nothing but the rain sprinkling against the car's hood.

Well, I thought, uncertainly—maybe somebody's called by and taken her out. It's none of my business anyway. I turned around to retrace my steps around the house, but suddenly, out of the corner of my eye, I thought I saw a white light flash in one of the upstairs rooms.

I stopped, and squinted up against the rain. There was nothing for a while, then the light flashed again, so briefly that it could have been anything at all—the reflected headlights from some faraway car, a distant flash of lightning, mirrored in the glass. Then it flashed again, for a long sustained flicker, and I could have sworn that I caught sight of a man's face, looking down at me as I stood in the garden.

My first inclination was to run like hell. I had tried to be calm and collected after I had seen that flickering hallucination of Jane, but after I had got back to the cottage, I had immediately been seized by a terrified panic, and I had wrenched open the front door and cantered down Quaker Lane as fast I could go.

Now, however, I was a little braver. Maybe Keith and George had been right and all that I had been witnessing around Quaker Hill tonight was St. Elmo's Fire, or some other kind of scientific phenomenon. Keith had said that he had witnessed it hundreds of times, so what was so unusual about my seeing it twice?

There was another, deeper reason why I didn't run away, a reason tied up with the sad and complicated feelings I had about Jane. If Jane had really appeared to me as an electrical phenomenon, then I wanted to know as much about these manifestations as I possibly could. Even if she couldn't be brought back physically, maybe there was a way of communicating with her, even talking to her. Maybe all this sèance stuff was true after all; maybe people's souls were nothing more extraordinary than all the electrical impulses which had made up their brain-pattern in life, released from their fleshy body but still integrated, still functioning as a human spirit. And since the brain contained the sensory matrix for the body as well, wouldn't it make sense if occasionally the body was able to appear as a flickering illusion of electrical discharges?

All these kind of thoughts had been teeming around in my brain during my walk down to Mrs. Edgar Simons' place, and that was why I didn't run off when I saw the face at the upstairs window. If ghosts were nothing more than formations of electricity, then how could they hurt me? The worst I could suffer would be a mild shock.

I went back to the front door to see if I could force it open.

I even tried wangling my Bank AmeriCard into the latch, the
way that thieves do in the movies, but I couldn't make it
budge. Early 19th-century locks were probably impervious to
late 20th-century plastic. I walked around to the other side of
the house, skirting the twisted and briar-infested trunks of the
trees which clung around the brickwork, until I found a small
cellar window. It had once been screened by mesh, but the
salt ocean air had corroded the wire, and it took only two or
three hard tugs to pull the meshing loose.

Close by, on the overgrown garden path, lay the blind and
broken head of a stone cupid. I picked it up, carried it quickly
over to the window, and tossed it like a bowling-ball through
the glass. There was a splintering smash, and then a heavy
thud as the head hit the floor down below. I kicked out the
remaining splinters, and then put my own head through to see
what was inside.

It was utterly black, and it smelled of damp, and mold, and
the peculiar fustiness of hundred-year-old buildings, as if the
accumulated experiences of all those decades of time had
permeated the timbers and dried out, leaving a saltpeter of
sadness, and passion, and evaporated joys.

I withdrew my head, and reentered the cellar window feet
first. I tore the knee of my pants on a glazier's nail on the
window-frame, and said, ''Shit,'' in the stuffy stillness of the
cellar; but it turned out to be quite easy to lower myself down
to the floor. There was a sudden scurrying noise in the far
corner of the cellar, and a flurry of squeaks. Rats, and vicious
ones, too, if they ran true to the tradition of Granitehead
rodents, most of whom had jumped from ships. I groped my
way across the floor, hands out in front of me, feeling like a
blind man for the cellar steps.

I went around three walls before I eventually found the
wooden banister rail, and the first stone step, and everywhere
I shuffled the rats would squeak and scamper and jump.

Inch by inch, I worked my way up the cellar steps to the
cellar door itself, and turned the knob. Mercifully, the door
was unlocked. I eased it open, and stepped out into the hall.

Mrs. Simons' house had been built when Salem was the
fifth most prosperous seaport in the world, and the sixth city
in the United States, collecting one-twentieth of the entire
Federal revenue in import duties. Its hallway ran all the way
from the front door to the back garden door, and a magnifi-

cent suspended staircase came curving down one wall. Even though I was wearing soft-soled shoes, my footsteps set up a murmuring of echoes as I walked across the black-and-white marble floor, echoes that came back to me from the darkened living-room, the empty kitchen, and the galleried landing upstairs.

"Mrs. Edgar Simons?" I called; too quietly for anyone to have heard. And my voice whispered back to me, from quite close by, "Mrs. Edgar Simons?"

I walked into the main living-room. It was high-ceilinged, and smelled of lavender and dust. The furniture was old-fashioned but not antique, the kind of traditional furniture that had been popular in the middle of the 1950s, clumsy and expensive, Jacobite by way of Grand Rapids. I saw my own pale face across the room in the looking-glass over the fireplace, and I looked quickly away before I started getting hysterical again.

Mrs. Simons was nowhere to be found, not downstairs. I went into the dining-room, which smelled of snuffed-out candles and stale pecans; the pantry, which would have been an innovation when this house was first built; the old-fashioned kitchen, with its white marble working surfaces. Then I took a deep breath, and went back out into the hallway, to mount the stairs.

I was halfway up the stairs when I saw the blue-white flickering again, from one of the bedroom doors that led off the landing. I stopped for a moment, with my hand on the banister rail, but I knew that it was no use hesitating. Either I was going to find out what this electrical flickering was, or else I was going to run away and forget about Mrs. Edgar Simons and Neil Manzi and everything, including Jane.

"*John*," said a familiar whisper, close to my ear. I felt that tightness in my scalp again, that prickle of slowly-rising fear. The light flashed again, from under the bedroom door. It was quite silent, unlike the buzzing, crackling flash you usually get from a heavy electrical discharge; and there was a coldness about it which unnerved me.

"John," whispered the voice again, but this time as if it were two voices whispering in chorus.

I reached the top of the stairs. The landing was covered in carpet, once thick but now threadbare. There were very few pictures on the walls, and it was so dark in the house that it was impossible to tell what they were. An occasional wan face peered out of the blackness of the oil paint but that was all; and I didn't want to turn on the lights in case I frightened away whatever it was that flickered and flashed in the bedroom.

I stood outside that bedroom door for a very long time. What are you frightened of? I asked myself. Electricity? Is that it? You're frightened of electricity? Come on, you've just invented a really neat explanation for the appearance of ghosts, electrical matrices and discharge impulses and all that garbage, and now you're scared to open the door and take a look at a few sparks going off? Do you believe your own theory or not? Because if you don't, you shouldn't be here at all, you should be high-tailing it down that highway to the nearest Ramada Inn, which is the only place where you certainly won't be disturbed by ghosts.

I grasped the bedroom doorhandle, and, as I did so, I heard the singing. Faint, fainter than faint, but clear enough to freeze me where I stood.

"O the men they sailed from Granitehead
To fish the foreign shores . . ."

I closed my eyes, and then immediately opened them again in case something or somebody appeared when I wasn't looking.

"But the fish they caught were nought but bones
With hearts crus'd in their jaws."

I found myself clearing my throat, as if I were about to propose a toast. Then I turned the doorhandle, and cautiously started to push open the door.

There was a fierce crackle, and a blinding flash of light, and the door was banged wide open, the knob wrenched right out of my grasp. I stood in the doorway terrified, staring into the room, and the sight that I encountered left me open-mouthed, unable to speak, unable to move.

It was one of the huge master bedrooms, with a wide curtained window and a draped four-poster bed. In the far corner, dazzling and flickering, stood a figure of a man, his arms spread wide. All around him, in the air, there was a living, crawling aura of electrical power, rising up from the floor with a jerking motion that put me horribly in mind of incandescent maggots. The man's face was long and thin, strangely distorted, and his eyes were impenetrable sockets. But I could see that his eyes were raised towards the ceiling, and with an inexplicable feeling of dread I raised my own eyes towards the ceiling, too.

A vast glass chandelier was suspended there, with tier upon tier of crystal droplets, and a dozen gilded candle-holders. To my alarm, the chandelier was swaying from side to side, and as the crackling of electricity died down, I could hear the crystal pendants tinkling and ringing, not musically, but frantically, as if someone were trying to shake them down like apples from a tree.

There was something spreadeagled in the chandelier. No, worse than that, *there was somebody impaled on it*. I took two or three mechanical steps into the bedroom, and stared up at the chandelier in complete horror, unable to believe what was suspended in front of my eyes.

It was Mrs. Edgar Simons. Somehow, unbelievably, the chain which held up the chandelier had penetrated right through her stomach, and now she was lying face down on top of its twelve spreading branches, writhing and shuddering like a hooked fish, clutching at the candle-holders and the crystal droplets, twisting herself in the agonizing torment of her impossible situation.

"God, God, God," she babbled, and strings of blood and saliva dangled from her mouth. "God, get me free, God, get me free, God, God, God, get me free."

I stared wide-eyed at the flickering apparition which stood on the opposite side of the room, his arms raised. There was no smile on his face, no scowl, just dark and incomprehensible concentration.

"Let her down!" I screamed at him. *"For Christ's sake, let her down!"*

But the apparition only flared and crackled, and ignored me, if he could even hear me at all.

I looked up again at Mrs. Edgar Simons, who stared back down at me with bulging eyes through the sparkling crystal pendants. Blood began to drip on to the carpet, a few patters at first, then more quickly, and then there was a sudden gush of it. She clutched at the crystal and it shattered in her hands, so that shards of it penetrated the flesh of her fingers and sliced through her palms.

I took two or three steps back, and then rushed forward and jumped up to catch hold of the chandelier's branches, in an effort to pull it down from the ceiling. At the first try, I only managed to catch hold of the chandelier with one hand, dangled for a moment, and then had to let go. At the second try, I managed to get a better grip, and swung grimly backwards and forwards, while Mrs. Edgar Simons shuddered and bled and wept for God to save her.

There was a cracking noise, and the chandelier dropped a few inches. Then, with a hideous jingling sound, the chandelier collapsed to the floor, bringing Mrs. Edgar Simons down with it. The whole bedroom was spattered with blood and broken glass.

I got off my knees, where I had awkwardly fallen. On the other side of the room, the apparition had flickered away almost to nothing now, a dim and fitful flame. I crunched through the glass to Mrs. Edgar Simons, and crouched down beside her, resting my hand on her head. She felt death cold, although her eyes were still open, and she was murmuring under her breath.

"*Help me*," she appealed, but there was no hope in her voice at all.

"Mrs. Simons," I told her, "I'll call for an ambulance."

She tried to lift her head a little, so that she could look at me. "Too late for that," she murmured. "Just . . . take out this chain."

"Mrs. Simons, I'm not a qualified medic. I couldn't even begin to——"

"It's so cold," she said. Her head dropped back against the broken glass. "Oh, God, Mr. Trenton, it's so cold. Don't leave me."

I didn't know what to say to her. I held her hand for a moment, but she didn't seem to be able to feel it, so I let her go. "Listen," I insisted, "I'm going to call an ambulance. Tell me where the phone is. Is there a phone upstairs?"

"Don't leave me. Please, whatever you do. He might come back."

"Who might come back? Who was it, Mrs. Simons?"

"Don't leave me," she repeated. Her eyelids were beginning to flutter now. I could see the whites of her eyes in the darkness of the room, sending a few last hopeless signals to a dimming world. "Don't leave me. Don't let him hurt me again."

"Who was it, Mrs. Simons?" I asked her. "You have to

tell me. It's important. Was it Edgar? Was it your husband. Will you nod if it was Edgar?"

Her eyes closed. Her breath rattled in her throat, slowly and laboriously. I knew that I ought to go call for the ambulance, but I also knew that it was useless, and that it was far too late.

I bent down close to her ear. There was drying blood in it, and blood on her diamond earring, too. "Mrs. Simons, you have to tell me. Was it Edgar?"

She died without saying anything more. The last breath came out of her lungs like a long regretful sigh. I stayed beside her for a while, and then stood up, my feet crunching on the broken glass.

It hadn't really been necessary for her to tell me whether it was Edgar who had appeared in this room tonight or not. I knew it had to be him. The same way that the apparition which had appeared on my swing had inevitably been Jane. The dead had returned to haunt the living who had once loved them.

I now knew something else, though, something terrifying. And that was that, far from being harmless flickers of cerebral electricity, these apparitions had the power to do strange and horrifying things. Not only the power, but the will.

I found a telephone on the hall table downstairs. I picked it up, and said stonily, "Get me the police department, please. Yes, it's an emergency."

TEN

The police sergeant unlocked the cell and Walter Bedford came in at a pace that was far too fast for the size of the room. He pulled up abruptly, and looked at me, and gave his head a little shake, and said, "John?" as if he were amazed that it was actually me.

"Thank you for coming, Walter," I told him. "I appreciate it."

"They say you *killed* this woman?" asked Walter. He didn't put down his briefcase.

"She was killed, yes. But not by me."

Walter turned around to the sergeant who had let him in. "Do you have someplace more comfortable where we can talk?"

The sergeant looked doubtful for a moment, and then he said, "There's an interviewing room across the corridor. But you understand that I'll have to leave the door open."

"That's all right," said Mr. Bedford. "Just lead the way."

We were ushered into a pale-green painted room with a scratched table and two steel-and-canvas chairs. There was an overcrowded ashtray on the table and the whole room smelled of stale cigarette smoke.

"You can open the window if you like," Mr. Bedford told the sergeant, but the sergeant only smiled and shook his head.

We sat down facing each other. Mr. Bedford opened up his briefcase and took out a yellow legal pad; then unscrewed an expensive lacquered fountain-pen. At the top he wrote the date, underlined it, then *J. Trenton, Homicide*. Outside the door, the police sergeant loudly blew his nose.

85

"Can you tell me what you were doing in this woman's house?" Mr. Bedford asked me.

"I was attempting to pay her a visit. I wanted to talk to her."

"But according to the police you entered the house through the cellar window. Is that the normal way you visit people?"

"I went to the door but I couldn't get any answer."

"If you don't get any answer at the door, don't you usually assume that there's nobody in, and go away?"

"I was going to, but then I saw somebody's face at an upstairs window. A man's face."

Walter Bedford jotted this down and then asked, "Was it a man you knew."

"It was a man I knew *of*."

"I don't understand."

"Well," I said, "earlier in the evening, Mrs. Edgar Simons had given me a ride back from Granitehead Market, and she had mentioned him to me."

"Had she described him?"

"No."

"Then how did you know that the man you saw at the window was the same man?"

"Because it had to be. Because he wasn't the normal kind of man."

"What do you mean not 'the normal kind of man'?"

I raised my hands. "Walter," I said, "the way you're questioning me now, I'm finding it very difficult to explain to you exactly what happened."

"John," said Mr. Bedford, "I'm questioning you now the way you're going to be questioned by the district attorney. If you can't find a way of explaining what happened when I ask you direct questions like these; then I warn you here and now that you're going to find yourself in a great deal of difficulty when it comes to court."

"Walter," I told him, "I understand that. But right now I need your help, and the only way that I can give you the means to help me is if I tell you in a different way. You're getting the *facts* out of me, but you're not getting the story."

Mr. Bedford made a face, but then shrugged, and put down his pen, and folded his arms. "All right, then," he said. "Tell me the story. But just remember that it will have to be adapted to fit the conventional methods of court questioning;

otherwise, whether you're guilty or not, you'll lose. It's as simple as that."

"You think I'm guilty?"

There was a slight but visible twitch at the corner of Mr. Bedford's mouth. "You were found alone in a darkened house with a murdered woman. Several people saw you riding in her car earlier in the evening, and the police have witnesses who say you were in a disturbed state of mind just before you went to her house. One of them says you were rambling and deranged, as if you had something on your mind."

"Good old Keith Reed," I said, bitterly.

"Those are the facts, John. And let's face it, they're pretty cast-iron. Of course, if you tell me you're not guilty, then I believe you, but for the sake of saving yourself quite a few years in the penitentiary, you might find it worthwhile pleading guilty. I can always do a little plea-bargaining with Roger Adams, he's an amenable man. Or, you could plead insanity."

"Walter, I am not guilty and I am not insane. I didn't kill Mrs. Edgar Simons and that's all there is to it."

"You're suggesting this other man did? This other man who wasn't quite the normal kind of man?"

I pushed back my chair and stood up. "Listen, Walter, you have to hear me out. This isn't easy for me to tell; and it won't be any easier for you to believe. But its one saving grace is that it's the truth."

Mr. Bedford sighed. "All right," he said. "Go ahead."

I walked across to the green-painted wall and stood with my back to him. It seemed easier to explain what had happened to a blank wall. The police sergeant poked his head around the door to make sure I hadn't taken a dive out of the window, and then went back to reading the *Salem Evening News*.

"Something's happening in Granitehead this spring, although I don't know why. People are beginning to see things. Ghosts, if you like, if that's the easiest way to understand what they are. But in any case, they're images, flickering brightly-lit images, of people who used to live in Granitehead and have recently died."

Mr. Bedford said nothing. I could imagine what he was thinking, though. A cut-and-dried case of homicide while temporarily insane.

I went on: "Mrs. Edgar Simons told me earlier in the evening that she had heard and seen her dead husband, Edgar. She had heard him walking about the house, seen him in the garden. She told me that Charlie Manzi at the Granitehead Market had experienced similar visitations from his dead son Neil."

"Go on," said Mr. Bedford, in a deathly dry voice.

"Very early yesterday morning, *I* experienced a visitation, too. I heard someone swinging on the old swing in the garden. Then, when I went home in the evening, I heard it again, and I went outside to take a look."

"Naturally enough," said Mr. Bedford. "And what was it?"

"Not *what* was it, Walter. *Who* was it."

"All right, have it your own way. *Who* was it?"

I turned around. I had to face him to say this. "It was your daughter, Walter. It was Jane. She was sitting on the swing right in front of me, about as far away as I'm standing away from you now, and she was looking at me."

I don't know what I had expected Mr. Bedford to do or say. I think I had expected him to lose his temper, call me a scoundrel and a blasphemer, and refuse to take my case. The notion of ghosts was too much for anyone to swallow, even in the most conducive of circumstances. The idea that a ghost might have murdered an old lady in a house on the Granitehead highway—well, that was beyond even the grimmest of jokes.

I sat down, with my hands in my lap, and looked at Mr. Bedford expectantly. The muscles in his cheek were working, and there was no doubt that his forehead had turned extremely red. But I couldn't read what he was thinking by the expression in his eyes. His eyes were turned inwards, into himself, and they were giving nothing away at all.

"If you want me to lay it on the line," I told him, "it wasn't me who killed Mrs. Edgar Simons. It was the spirit of her dead husband. Now, I know you can't go into court and—"

"You saw Jane?" Mr. Bedford suddenly interrupted me, with considerable harshness in his voice.

I nodded, surprised. "I think so. In fact, I'm sure I did. Old Keith Reed tried to tell me it was St. Elmo's Fire or something, but I saw her face, Walter, just as clear as if she were—"

"You're not making this up? You're not trying to taunt me? This isn't some sort of vicious retaliatory joke?"

Very slowly, I shook my head. "I don't have anything to retaliate for, Walter. You may blame me for what happened to Jane, but you haven't been unkind to me."

"When you saw her—" said Mr. Bedford, speaking with difficulty, "—when you saw her—did she—how did she look?"

"A little strange. Thinner, somehow. But it was the same Jane."

Mr. Bedford put his hand up to his mouth and I realized to my astonishment that there were tears glistening in his eyes.

"Did she—speak at all?" he asked, swallowing. "Did she say anything? Anything at all?"

"No. But I think I've heard her singing. And several times, I think I've heard her whispering my name. You remember in the office, yesterday morning?"

Mr. Bedford nodded. He seemed to be so overwhelmed by emotion that he could scarcely speak. "I've heard about it, of course. Well, nobody admits to it. But you can't look after their births and their marriages and their wills without getting an inkling that something's going on, can you?"

"*What's* going on?" I asked him. "I don't understand."

He sniffed, and cleared his throat, and then burrowed into his pocket for his handkerchief. "I don't know very much about it. Only what some of my clients have told me. But many people say that Granitehead is no ordinary community, and never has been. Many people say that if you live in Granitehead, the chances of seeing your loved ones again after they die are remarkably high. You may know that the town once used to be called Resurrection, before it was changed by order of the governor of Massachusetts to Granitehead. Well, the reason it was called Resurrection was because the dead were said to visit the living, until the living, too, reached the end of their lives."

"You believe me," I said, in shock.

"Did you think I wouldn't?"

"Of course I thought you wouldn't. I've murdered an elderly woman, and my alibi is that a ghost did it?"

Mr. Bedford tucked away his handkerchief. "You really saw Jane," he whispered. "My God, I wish I could have

been there. I would have given a year of my life, just to see
her again.''

"I shouldn't make promises like that,'' I told him. ''If
Edgar Simons' ghost is anything to go by, these whatever-
they-are, manifestations, might be extremely malevolent.''

Mr. Bedford smiled and shook his head. ''Can you really
imagine Jane doing anything cruel, or hurtful?''

"Not the Jane I knew when she was alive, but—''

"Jane would never hurt anybody, alive or dead. She was
an angel, you know, John. An angel when she was living;
and now she's gone, an angel still. I'm going to have to tell
her mother, you know.''

"Walter, I hate to come back to brass tacks,'' I told him.
"But I still don't see how you're going to get me off this
homicide charge. Not if ghosts are my only alibi.''

Mr. Bedford paused in silence for a long time. Then he
looked up at me with reddened eyes, and said, ''Mrs. Simons
was killed in a most remarkable way, wasn't she?''

"Not just remarkable. Impossible. At least for me to have
done it. Or anybody human.''

"Well,'' said Mr. Bedford, ''I think I'll go talk to the
district attorney. I'm sure it's going to be possible to come to
some arrangement. He's an old friend of mine, you know.
We both belong to the same golf club.''

"You really think you can swing something?''

"I can only try.''

He stood up, and put away his pad. He couldn't stop
himself from smiling. ''I can't wait to tell Constance,'' he
said. ''She'll be delighted.''

"I don't really see what you've got to be delighted about.''

"John, my dear boy, we have everything to be delighted
about. Well, almost everything. Once you're released, and
back at the cottage, we can visit you, can't we, and see Jane
again for ourselves?''

I couldn't think what to say. I shook his hand, uncertainly,
and then sat down on my chair as abruptly as if somebody
had hit me with a sockful of wet sand. Mr. Bedford left and I
heard his rubber-soled shoes squeaking up the polished police
station corridor.

The police sergeant poked his head around the door again.

"What are you sitting there for?'' he wanted to know.
"It's back in the slammer for you.''

ELEVEN

I was released late in the afternoon on $75,000 bail, put up by an Essex County real-estate corporation of which Mrs. Constance Bedford was a major stockholder. Outside, it was bright, dry and windy, and I was picked up by Tom Watkins, one of Walter Bedford's clerks, and driven back to Quaker Lane Cottage.

Tom Watkins was young and flush-faced, with a fluffy little mustache. He had never been involved with a homicide case before, and I think I quite scared him.

"I read the police report on Mrs. Edgar Simons' death," he told me, as he drove. "That was some way to die."

I nodded. It was impossible to explain to anybody what I felt about the gruesome events of the previous evening. I was still suffering from residual shock, and a kind of persistent nausea. I could actually imagine what that chandelier chain must have felt like, passing right through Mrs. Simons' insides, cold and uncompromising and beyond any human capability to remove. Worst of all, though, I still felt dread. If Mrs. Simons' dearly beloved Edgar had been powerful and cruel enough in his spirit state to impale his widow like that, what would Neil try to do to Charlie Manzi, or Jane try to do to me? And from what Walter Bedford had told me, Charlie and Mrs. Edgar Simons and I weren't the only people in Granitehead who had been visited by flickering visions of their dead relatives.

For some reason, it seemed as if this year the influence of these manifestations was stronger than usual, although I hadn't really been living in Granitehead long enough to know what "usual" might be. Mrs. Simons had said something about the manifestations being seasonal, more frequent and more obvious in the summer months than they were in the winter. Only God knew why that could be: maybe there was more static electricity in the air in the summer, feeding the apparitions with natural power.

Tom Watkins said, "Mr. Bedford will get you off of this rap. You just wait and see. He talked to the district attorney already, and tomorrow he's going to have a meeting with the chief of police. Actually, the police don't really think you did it, either. They don't know how the hell Mrs. Edgar Simons got herself up on that chandelier chain, but they don't really believe that it was you who put her there. They had to arrest you as a matter of procedure; and to satisfy the newspapers."

"It's in the newspapers? I haven't seen one."

Tom Watkins nodded towards the back seat. "There's a couple of the locals there. Help yourself."

I reached over and picked up the *Granitehead Messenger*. The main headline read, WIDOW IMPALED IN GRISLY GRANITEHEAD KILLING, Local antique dealer held. Underneath there was a morgue photograph of Mrs. Edgar Simons taken when she was ten years younger, and a picture of me that had been taken outside Trenton Marine Antiques when it first opened.

"That'll be good for business," I said, folding up the newspaper and tossing it back on to the seat.

Tom Watkins drove up Quaker Lane, turned around in a circle outside my cottage, and parked. "Mr. Bedford said that he'd call you later this evening. Something about making an appointment to drop over."

"Yes," I said.

"Is there anything else you need? Mr. Bedford said I was to go get anything you wanted."

"No, I don't think so, thank you. I want a drink more than anything else."

"You're sure you're going to be okay?"

"I'm sure. Thanks for the ride. And tell Mr. Bedford thanks, too."

Tom Watkins drove off, and once again I was standing alone outside Quaker Lane Cottage, my hands in my pockets, unsure of what lay waiting for me inside, what strange disturbances from a time and a place that I could only guess at.

Was it heaven? Or hell? Or a shifting, displaced limbo; a half-seen world of distorted psychic energy, where the spirits of the dead faded and flickered like those garbled radio messages which you can pick up during the hours of darkness?

The house watched me with its neutral, shuttered eyes. I walked up the garden path, took out my keys, and opened the front door.

Everything was exactly as I had left it yesterday evening. At least I had had the presence of mind to turn off the oven before I ran out, leaving a half-cooked lasagne dinner on the middle shelf. I went into the living-room and the fire was dead, ashes blowing across the rug from the draft which blew down the chimney. My books were laid out on the floor, and propped up against the side of a chair, the painting of the *David Dark*.

I crossed the room and looked out through the diamond-leaded windows into the garden. I could just see the back of the swing seat, and the right-hand side of the orchard. In the distance, silvery-gray rain clouds were building up over Salem Sound. Seagulls turned and fluttered around the Neck like wind-blown newspapers. I pressed my forehead against the cold window-pane, and for the first time in my life felt unutterably defeated.

Perhaps I ought to leave Granitehead for good. Sell up the business, and go back to St. Louis. There was even a chance that I might be able to get my old job back, at MidWestern Chemical Bonding. I would probably forfeit a few years of promotion, but what was that compared with the extraordinary terror of what was happening here in Granitehead? I was particularly disturbed by the excitement which Walter Bedford had shown when I had told him about the apparition of Jane. There was something grotesquely unhealthy about it, as well as dangerous. The trouble was, I was beholden to the Bedfords not only for bailing me out of jail, but for two-thirds of the finance which had opened up Trenton Marine Antiques and so it was going to be very hard for me to refuse their request to come over to Quaker Lane Cottage and see Jane's apparition for themselves.

I was just about to pour myself a drink when there was a ring at the front doorbell. George Markham, maybe? Or Keith Reed? It had better not be Keith Reed—I'd give him a not-soon-forgotten "thanks" for telling the police that I had been "rambling, and deranged." I called, "All right, I'm coming," and went to answer it.

Standing outside in the evening wind was Edward Wardwell, in a plaid lumberjack coat and a peaked denim cap. "I'm sorry to call on you personally. But I heard what had happened, and I just had to come over from Salem to talk to you."

As a matter of fact, I was oddly relieved to see him. It was better to have *some* company in that unsettled house than none at all. And I did want to talk to him about the painting of the *David Dark*.

"Come on in," I told him. "I haven't lit the fire yet. I've only just been sprung, if that's the word."

"Do you think your attorney can get you off?" Edward Wardwell asked, taking off his cap and stepping into the hallway.

"I hope so. He's my father-in-law. Well, he *was* my father-in-law, before my wife died. Walter Bedford, of Bedford & Bibber. He's pretty well-connected. Plays golf with the district attorney and gin-rummy with the judge."

"I've met him," said Edward Wardwell. "You forgot that I knew your wife. She and I were in a seminar together, to study maritime history. That was, what, three or four years ago now, up at Rockport. She was a very pretty girl, your wife. All the guys there kept trying to date her. She was clever, too. I was sorry to hear that she died."

"Well, thank you for that much," I told him. "Can I get you a drink?"

"I'm a beer man myself."

"There's Heinekin in the icebox."

Edward Wardwell followed me into the kitchen and I opened a bottle of beer for him. He watched me closely as I poured it out.

"You didn't kill that old woman, did you?" he asked me.

I looked up at him; then shook my head. "How did you know?" I queried.

"I have a pretty good idea of what's been going on around here. I don't work for the Peabody for nothing, you know. I know more about the maritime history of Salem and Granitehead than almost anyone, except maybe the Evelith family. But then I don't have their books."

"You *know* what's been going on?"

"Sure," he said, taking the beer-glass out of my hand. He

sipped a little, leaving foam clinging to his mustache. "Granitehead has always had a reputation for ghosts, just like Salem has always had a reputation for witches. Although the town fathers have done everything they can to play it down, there isn't any doubt at all in my mind that Granitehead is a nexus between the spirit world, if I can dare to call it that, and the physical world. More than anyplace else in the whole United States. Perhaps anyplace else on the entire globe."

"So what happened to Mrs. Edgar Simons if you don't think that I was responsible?"

"It's *possible* that you were responsible, but in my opinion not likely. What you obviously don't know is that there have been six or seven deaths of bereaved people in Granitehead over the past ten years, and all of them have been characterized by the extraordinary and inexplicable ways in which they have occurred. One man was found with his head trapped inside a water-pipe, drowned. The newspapers said that he had put his head down through an access hole to discover what had been blocking the pipe up, but the police report reads different. The access hole was tight around the man's neck, so that it would have been impossible for him to have put his head through it. The doctors had to cut off his head to get him out, and then flush his head out of the pipe with a strong jet of water."

I made a face, and Edward Wardwell shrugged. "Mrs. Edgar Simons' death was no different," he said. "A physical impossibility and the police know that, too. They have to prove in court that you killed Mrs. Edgar Simons, and if you can show beyond any question that it was impossible for *any* human being to have impaled her on the chandelier like that, you're home free."

"Come through to the living-room," I said. "I'd like to get the fire going before the temperature starts falling."

We went through to the living-room, where I got down on my knees in front of the hearth and began clearing out the fire. Fortunately, there were plenty of logs and kindling stacked beside the grate, so I didn't have to go out to the woodpile. Edward Wardwell put down his beer, and picked up the watercolor of Granitehead beach. He examined it minutely, and when I turned around from the fire to find some rolled-up copies of *Newsweek* to stuff under the logs, I saw that he was paying particular attention to the ship.

He said, "Out of those six or seven other deaths, only two people were ever charged with homicide, and both of those were released before their cases got to trial. In each case the district attorney said that there was insufficient evidence to proceed. The same will happen to you."

"How come you've made such a study of it?" I asked him, as I struck the first match, and lit the corner of the rolled-up magazines.

"Because the maritime history of Granitehead and the spiritual history of Granitehead are inextricably intertwined. This is a magical place, Mr. Trenton, as you've discovered for yourself, and what's more, the magic is real, and violent. It's not like the Haunted House at Disneyland."

The fire began to catch, and I stood up and brushed my trousers. "I'm beginning to realize that, Mr. Orwell."

"Wardwell. But why don't you call me Edward?"

"All right. I'm John." And for the first time, we shook hands.

I nodded towards the watercolor. "I know now why you were so anxious to lay your hands on that picture. I did a little detective work last night, and I found out what ship that is, in the background."

"Ship?" asked Edward.

"Come on, Edward, don't act so innocent. That ship is the *David Dark*; and this picture must be one of the only surviving illustrations of it. No wonder it's worth more than fifty bucks. I wouldn't take less than a thousand."

Edward tugged at his beard, curling the hair of it around his fingers. He regarded me from behind his circular spectacles with watery eyes; and then let out a long, resigned puff of breath. Licorice and aniseed again.

"I was hoping you wouldn't find out," he said. "I'm afraid I made an idiot of myself yesterday, running after you like that. I should have played it cool."

"You did arouse my interest. Now you've raised my financial expectations too."

"I can't pay more than three hundred."

"Why not?"

"I simply don't *have* more than three hundred, that's why."

"But you said the Peabody was buying this," I told him. "Don't tell me the Peabody only has three hundred."

Edward sat down, still holding the picture. "The truth is,"

he said, "the Peabody doesn't know about this picture. In fact, the Peabody doesn't know about any of the investigations I've been doing into the history of the *David Dark*. In Salem, and especially the Peabody, the *David Dark* is something that people just don't talk about. You say '*David Dark*,' and they say 'Never heard of it,' and they make it pretty damn clear that they don't *want* to hear about it, either.''

I poured myself a whiskey, and sat down opposite him. "But why?" I wanted to know. "David Dark himself was supposed to have had conversations with the devil or something, wasn't he? But I haven't read anything which explains why they cut the ship's name out of all the records, or why people won't talk about it.''

"Well, I'm not sure, either," said Edward. He finished his beer, and put down the glass. "But I first came across the name David Dark the year that I joined the Peabody from college. They gave me a small exhibition to prepare, a special showcase depicting the history of the rescue and salvage operations that had gone on around Salem and Granitehead during the past three hundred years. It was pretty tedious stuff, to tell the truth, apart from one or two spectacular wrecks on Winter Island, and a couple of whalers being overturned by humpbacks. But I was interested in one of the earliest documents I found, which was the log of the salvage vessel *Mimosa*, out of Granitehead. Apparently the captain of the *Mimosa* was a real 18th-century hotshot when it came to bringing up wrecks, and he successfully salvaged one of Elias Derby's Chinamen when it was blown by a storm into the mouth of the Danvers River and sunk in six fathoms of water off Tuck's Point. His name was Pearson Turner, and he kept a really meticulous log for five years, from 1701 to 1706.''

"Go on," I said. I poked the fire to keep it crackling.

"There isn't very much to tell," said Edward, "but one summer there was an unusually low tide in Salem Bay, and even the smaller ships were stranded on the mud. This was 1704, I think, or 1705. The low tide is mentioned in several other diaries and records as well, so it's soundly authenticated. It was during this low tide that a friend of Pearson Turner's spotted in the mud banks to the west of Granitehead Neck a protrusion from the mud which he took to be part of the bow castle of a sunken and half-buried ship. Pearson walked out to

the wreck himself, in wading boots, although he was unable
to get as close as he might have because the ooze was so soft.
He did manage, however, to bring back to the shore a frag-
ment of decorative molding, and Esau Hasket, who owned
the *David Dark*, tentatively identified it as part of his lost
ship.''

''Lost? The *David Dark* was lost?''

''Oh, yes. She sailed out of Salem Harbor on the last day
of October, 1692, and the only reason I know that is because
it happens to be mentioned in the diaries kept by one of the
early Salem wharfingers. He says something like, 'A tempes-
tuous north-westerly gale had been blowing for three days and
showed no sign of letting up, but in spite of the perilous
weather the *David Dark* set sail, the only vessel to do so
during that whole wild week. She vanished into the storm and
was never again seen in Salem.' That's the gist of it, anyway.
I can show you the diary itself, if you like.''

''But what's the connection with apparitions in Granitehead?'' I asked. ''There must be scores of wrecks around
these shores.''

As the fire blazed up, Edward unbuttoned his jacket. ''Let
me get you another beer first,'' I told him.

I went outside to the kitchen. At the foot of the staircase, I
paused for a second or two, listening. I hadn't been upstairs
yet, not since I had seen the flickering light in there last
night. I hoped to God there wasn't anything up there which I
didn't want to see. I hoped to God that Jane wouldn't appear
again, not for her father, not for her mother, and especially
not for me. She was dead but I wanted her to stay dead, for
her own sake, and for the sake of our child who never was.

When I came back with the beer, Edward was leafing
through *Great Men of Salem*. ''Thanks,'' he said. Then,
''You're not having any trouble yourself, are you?''

''Trouble?''

''You haven't seen anything which might suggest that Jane's
trying to get in touch with you? Or maybe *heard* something?
A lot of the Granitehead hauntings have been aural, rather
than visual.''

I sat down, realized my glass was empty, and stood up
again. ''I, er, I—no. No, nothing like that. I guess it only
happens to old Graniteheaders. Not to us strangers.''

Edward nodded, as if he accepted what I was saying, but didn't completely believe me.

"You were telling me about the connection between the *David Dark* and the hauntings," I reminded him.

"Well," he said, "it's only fair to warn you that in strictly scientific terms, it's a pretty tenuous connection. It wouldn't win a history award. But I don't know what sort of a world we're dealing with here: I don't know why these spirits are manifesting themselves, or how. It may just be an unpleasant freak of nature, something to do with weather conditions, or maybe it's something to do with geographical location. Granitehead may be like Easter Island, a spot on the map that for completely incomprehensible reasons happens to be conducive to spiritual apparitions."

"But you think it's the ship."

"I'm *inclined* to think it's the ship. And the reason why is because I've discovered two accounts of the *David Dark* being prepared for her last voyage—one written before she sailed and the other written nearly eighty years later. I found the older account in a boring old book, a late 17th century treatise on maritime shipfitting and metalwork. It was written by a shipbuilder from Boston called Neames, and let me tell you—that man was tedious. But near the end of the book he mentions the Salem coppersmiths of Perly and Fisk, and says what a magnificent job they were making of a 'huge copper vessel' to be fitted inside the *David Dark* for the purpose of 'containing that Great Foulness which has so plagued Salem, that we may look forward to its final removal.'"

"You know this stuff by heart," I remarked, not altogether admiringly.

"I've studied it often enough," said Edward. "But Jane was the one for learning history by heart. She could reel off dates and names like a memory bank."

"Yes," I agreed, remembering the way Jane could memorize telephone numbers and birthdays. I didn't really want to discuss Jane with Edward Wardwell; it was too sensitive a subject, and besides, I felt absurdly but strongly jealous that Edward had known her before me.

"What was the other account?" I asked him.

"The latter one—eighty-two years later, as a matter of fact—was contained in the memoirs of the Rev. George Nourse, who had lived and worked in Granitehead for most of his life. He said that one day in 1752 he attended the death-bed of an old-time Salem bo'sun, and the bo'sun asked him particularly to commend his soul to heaven, since when he was younger he had spied on the secret loading of the *David Dark*'s last cargo, even though he had been warned that all who set eyes on it would be condemned to walk the earth forever, neither alive nor dead. When the Rev. Nourse asked the bo'sun what the cargo might have been, the bo'sun went into convulsions and started screaming about 'Mick the Cutler.' The Rev. Nourse was greatly disturbed by this, and went to speak to all the cutlers in the Salem district to see if he could throw some light on what the bo'sun had said, but without success. But he later said himself that he was sure that he had seen the bo'sun after his death, just turning the corner by Village Street.''

I sat back in my chair and mulled all this over. Under normal circumstances, I would have dismissed it immediately as a fantasy, myth. But I knew now that fairies and goblins and all kinds of other manifestations might actually exist, and if a young man as serious as Edward Wardwell were convinced that the wreck of the *David Dark* was somehow influencing the community of Granitehead, then I was not too far away from taking him seriously.

And what had that old witch-woman said to me on Salem Common? ''It's the *place* you die, not the time, that makes the difference. There are spheres of influence: and sometimes you can die within them, and sometimes you can die without them. The influence came, and then the influence fled; but there are days when I believe that it didn't flee for good and all.''

''Well,'' I said at last, ''I suppose you want this picture because it might give you some clues about what the *David Dark* might have been carrying?''

''More than that,'' said Edward, ''I want to know what she looked like, as exactly as possible. I do have one sketch which is supposed to be the *David Dark*, but it isn't half as detailed as this.''

He looked at me, and took off his spectacles. I knew that he wanted me to say that he could have the picture, that I would drop my thousand-dollar price to $300; but I wasn't going to. There was always the remote possibility that he was a glib and creative con man, and that he had simply invented all these stories about Pearson Turner and the Rev. Nourse and "Mick the Cutler." I didn't really believe that he had, but I still wasn't going to let my picture go.

"The detail in this painting is vitally important," he said. "Although it isn't very artistic, it looks reasonably accurate, and that means I can more or less estimate the size of the *David Dark*, and how many frames her hull was likely to have, and how her superstructure was fashioned. And *that* means that when I do find her, I can be sure I've located the right ship."

"When you *what*?" I asked him.

Edward replaced his spectacles and gave me a small smile of modest pride. "I've been diving off Granitehead Neck for seven months now, trying to locate her. I haven't been able to do too much diving during the winter, but now that spring's here, I intend to start again in earnest."

"What the hell do you want to find her for?" I asked him. "Surely, if she's having this kind of influence on Granitehead, she's better off under the water."

"Under the mud, you mean," said Edward. "She'll be pretty deeply buried by now. We'll be lucky if there's even a few frame-tops showing."

"*We'll* be lucky?"

"There're a couple of other guys from the museum helping me, and Dan Bass from the Granitehead Aqualung Club. And Gilly McCormick's been my unofficial look-out and log-keeper."

"You really believe you can find this wreck?"

"I think so. It's not too deep around that side of the Neck, because of the way the mud builds up. There are dozens of wrecks down there, but almost all of them are yachts and small dinghies, all comparatively recent. We did come across the remains of a fabulous 1920s Dodge motorboat, but that couldn't have sunk more than six months ago. When the summer comes, we intend to scan the seabed with EG & G sub-mud sonar, and see if we can pinpoint the *David Dark* precisely."

"Surely she would have decayed by now. There won't be anything left to pinpoint."

"I think there will be," Edward disagreed. "The mud there is so soft that you can plunge your arm into it right up to the elbow without any trouble at all. Once, I almost sank down to my waist. The *David Dark*, if she sank around there, would have been buried almost up to her original waterline pretty well straight away, and over the next few weeks she would have sunk deeper. All the timber under the mud would have been preserved intact, and as it happens a particularly cold current runs into Salem Bay around Granite-head Neck, and that would have had the effect of inhibiting decay in the timbers that remained exposed. Fungi and bacilli don't like cold water, any more than gribble or *nototeredo norvavica*—that's a woodboring mollusc, to you.''

''Thanks for the marine biology lesson. But what are you hoping to do if you eventually locate the *David Dark*?''

Edward spread his hands in surprise. ''Bring her up, of course,'' he said, as if it had been obvious, all along. ''Bring her up and find out what it is she's carrying in her hold.''

TWELVE

Edward Wardwell drove us down to the West Shore Fishery in his dented blue Jeep, and I bought him a dinner of oyster stew and entrecôte steak. For the first time in two days I discovered that I was really hungry, and I ate two portions of Irish barmbrack with my stew, and a heap of salad with my steak.

The Fishery was decorated in that nets-and-lobsters style ubiquitous in restaurants all along the New England shoreline; but it was dim and relaxing and comfortably normal, and the clams and flounder were better than most. All I wanted was good food and normality, especially after last night.

Edward told me that he had started sub-aqua diving in San Diego, when he was 15 years old. "I'm not especially good at it," he said, buttering another piece of tea-bread, "but it did whet my appetite for underwater archeology."

Contrary to the popular notion that the Pacific and the Caribbean were littered with the wrecks of Spanish treasure-ships, Edward said that the best-preserved vessels were almost always in northern waters. "In the Mediterranean, for example, a timber ship will last about five years under the water. In the Pacific, you'll be lucky if it lasts just over a year. Ironwork, in warm water, will last only thirty or forty years."

He drew circles on the tablecloth with the tip of his finger. "What you grow to understand when you get involved with underwater archeology is that there is no such thing as 'The Ocean.' The conditions under the ocean vary as much from one location to another as they do on land. Take the *Wasa*, which sank in Stockholm harbor in 1628, and was raised almost intact in 1961. She was in amazing condition, simply because the water was too cold for teredo molluscs to survive there, and attack her woodwork. And in the Solent, which is the entry to Southampton and Portsmouth harbors in England, the *Royal George* was still pretty solid after 53 years on the bottom, and the *Edgar* was still an obstruction to shipping after 133 years. The classic example, of course, was the *Mary Rose,* which sank in 1545. That was nearly 150 years before the *David Dark* went down, and yet half of her hull, the half that had been buried in the mud, had survived.''

"It cost hundreds of thousands of dollars to bring up the *Wasa* and the *Mary Rose,*" I reminded him. "How are you going to bring up the *David Dark* when you can't even afford a thousand dollars for a picture?''

"The first step is to locate her, to prove that she's there. Once I've done that, I'll be able to approach the Peabody and the Essex Institute and City Hall, and see what I can do about raising finance.''

"You're pretty confident.''

"I think I have to be. There are two compelling reasons for bringing up that wreck. One is its straightforward historical importance. The other is that it's having this weird effect on the people of Granitehead.''

"Well, I'll go along with that,'' I said. I beckoned to the waiter to bring me another whiskey.

"I have a terrific idea,'' said Edward. "Why don't you come diving with me over the weekend? If the weather's reasonable, we plan to go down on Saturday morning, and maybe Sunday, too.''

"Are you kidding? I never dived in my life. I'm from St. Louis, remember?''

"I'll teach you. It's as easy as breathing. It's pretty murky down there, not like diving off Bermuda or anything like that. But you'll love it, once you get used to it.''

"Well, I don't know,'' I said, reluctantly.

"Just come try it,'' urged Edward. "Listen, you want to find out what happened to Mrs. Edgar Simons, don't you? You want to find out why all these ghosts have been walking in Granitehead?''

"Sure.''

"I'll give you a call then, Saturday morning, if the weather clears. All you need to bring is a warm sweater, a windbreaker, and a pair of swimming shorts. I'll supply the wet suit, and all the sub-aqua gear.''

I drained the last of my drink. ''I hope I haven't let myself in for anything terrifying.''

''I told you, you'll love it. Oh—just remember not to have anything too rich for breakfast. If you vomit underwater, it can be really dangerous, sometimes lethal.''

I gave him a slanted smile. ''Thanks for the warning. Is a bowl of Wheaties overdoing it?''

''Wheaties are fine,'' said Edward, quite seriously. Then he checked his waterproof diver's watch, and said, ''I'd better be going. My sister's coming up from New York tonight, and I don't want to leave her on the doorstep.''

Edward drove me back up to Quaker Lane Cottage. ''Do you know someting interesting?'' he asked me, as he drew the Jeep to a jerking halt. ''I once checked back on the origin of the name 'Quaker Lane' because it always struck me as incongruous that a lane should have been named for the Quakers when there were never any around here. I mean, most of them, as you know, were centered around Pennsylvania; and as far as I could discover there were no records of any Friends in Granitehead, not until the middle of the 19th century.''

''Did you find out why it was named 'Quaker Lane'?'' I asked him.

''Eventually, almost by accident. In the flyleaf of an old book that was sent to the Peabody, someone had written, 'Craquer Lane, Granitehead.''

'' 'Craquer'? That sounds French.''

''It is. It means to crack, or break.''

''So why should anyone have called this Craquer Lane?''

''Don't ask me. I'm only a maritime historian. Maybe the surface of the lane was notoriously broken-up. This was the way they used to carry the coffins up to Waterside Cemetery, remember, so maybe they called it Craquer Lane because they were always dropping the coffins and breaking them. Who knows?''

''That's what I like about historians,'' I told him. ''They always bring up more questions than they answer.''

I climbed down from the Jeep and closed the door. Edward reached over and put down the window. ''Thanks for the dinner,'' he said. "And, you know, good luck with the cops.''

He drove off downhill, the wheels of the Jeep splashing and jolting in the puddles. I went back into the cottage and poured myself another drink, and started to tidy up a little. Mrs. Herron from Breadboard Cottages sent her maid Ethel up to ''do'' for me twice a week, Tuesdays and Fridays, change the bed, vacuum the rugs, clean the windows; but I liked to have the cottage reasonably clean and tidy in any case, and I always liked fresh flowers around. They reminded me of the happy days here with Jane; the best days of my whole damn life.

That evening, I sat in front of the fire and read as much as I could find about sunken ships, and sub-aqua diving, and the old days in Salem and Granitehead. By the time the Tompion clock in the hallway struck midnight, the wind had dropped and the rain had eased off, and I probably knew as much about raising wrecks as anybody, apart from the real experts. I poked the last crumbling log in the dying fire, and stretched and wondered whether I deserved a last drink or not. It was a peculiar thing about drinking on my own: I never quite managed to get drunk. I got the hangovers, though. It was the punishment without the pleasure.

I locked up the cottage and took a last measure of Chivas upstairs with me. I ran a deep, hot tubful of water, and slowly undressed. I hadn't slept properly for two nights now, and I felt exhausted.

Once in the bath, I lay back and closed my eyes and tried to let the tension slowly soak out of me. All I could hear was the steady dripping of the hot faucet, which had never turned off properly, and the crackling of Badedas bubbles.

Now that the weather had quieted down, and the wind had stopped sucking and breathing its way around the house, I felt strangely less afraid. Maybe it was the wind that had brought the spirits, the way that it had brought Mary Poppins; and when it changed or dropped, the spirits left us in peace. I prayed to God that they would. But I also added a codicil that the weather should work itself into a frenzy on Saturday morning, just for a few hours, so that I wouldn't have to go diving.

I was still lying in the tub when I heard a faint whispering. I opened my eyes at once, and listened. There was no mistaking it. It was that same whispering I had heard downstairs in the library, a soft torrent of scarcely audible blasphemy. My shoulders felt chilled, and all of a sudden the bathwater felt uncomfortable and scummy.

There was no question about it. Quaker Lane Cottage was possessed. I could feel the coldness of whatever spirits were passing through it as if all the downstairs doors had silently been opened, and wintry drafts were blowing everywhere. I sat up in the bath and the splashing of the water sounded awkward and flat, like a cheap sound-effect.

It was then that I looked up at the mirror over the wash-basin. It had been misted over by the steam rising up from the bathtub, but now the mist seemed to be condensing in patches, forming itself into the pattern of a hollow-eyed *face*. Dribbles of condensation ran from the darkened eye-sockets like tears, and from the line of the lips like blood; and even though it was probably nothing more than the gradually-cooling vapor, it looked as if the face were alive and moving, as if somehow there was a captive spirit within the silvered surface of the mirror, trying desperately to show itself, trying desperately to speak to the outside world.

I stood up, showering water everywhere, and reached for the washcloth on the side of the basin. With three violent strokes, I wiped the steam off the mirror until it was clear again; and all I could see was my own harassed face. Then I stepped out of the bath, and took down my towel.

It was no use, I told myself, as I went through to the bedroom. If I was going to be visited by whispers and appari-tions every night, then I was going to have to move out. I had read in *Architectural Digest* about an Italian who happily shared his huge palazzo with a noisy poltergeist, but I was neither brave enough nor calm enough to handle the distur-bances at Quaker Lane Cottage. There was a terrible lewdness about the whispering; and a terrible suppressed agony about all the visions I had seen. I felt that I was glimpsing and hearing things from Purgatory, the dreary and painful ante-chamber to hell. The worst part about it was that Jane was there, too, the woman I had loved and married, and still loved.

I toweled myself dry, brushed my teeth, and went to bed with one of the sleeping capsules that Dr. Rosen had given me, and a book about the building of the Panama Canal. It was well past one o'clock now, and the house was silent, all except for the steady ticking of the long-case clock in the hallway, and the occasional chime to mark the quarter-hours.

I don't know when I fell asleep, but I was awakened by the sudden dimming of my bedside lamp, as if the neighborhood were suffering a brown-out. It dimmed until I could see the filament in the light-bulb glowing orange and subdued like an expiring firefly.

Then came the coldness. An abrupt fall in temperature, just the same as the chill I had experienced in the library the night before. My breath began to vaporize, and I wrapped the comforter more tightly around me to keep myself warm.

I heard laughing, whispering. There were people in the cottage! There had to be. I heard shuffling on the stairs, as if four or five people were hurrying up to see me. But the noise died away in a flurry, and the door remained closed, and there was nobody there at all.

I stayed exactly where I was, wound up in that comforter. My elbow ached from supporting my body in the same position, but I was too scared to move a muscle. Yesterday morning, when I had thought back over the way in which I had broken into Mrs. Edgar Simons' house, I had congratulated myself on how courageous I must have been to do it. But now, in the middle of the night, with all these rustlings and murmurings at my bedroom door, I remembered just how blatantly terrified I had actually been.

"*John*," whispered a voice. I glanced around, my teeth clenched rigid with alarm.

"*John*," the voice repeated. There was no mistaking whose voice it was.

Croakily, I answered, "Jane? Is that you?"

She gradually began to appear, standing at the foot of the bed. Not so dazzlingly bright as before, but still flickering like a distant heliograph message. Thin, and sunken-eyed, her hair waving around her in some unfelt, unseen wind, her hands raised as if she were displaying the fact that she was dead but bore no stigmata. What frightened me most of all, though, was how tall she was. In those dim white robes, she stood nearly seven feet, her hair almost touching the ceiling, and she looked down at me with a serious and elongated face that sent dread soaking through me like the cold North Atlantic rain.

"*John?*" she whispered again, although her mouth didn't move. And she began to drift sideways around the end of the bed. My vision of her came and went, as if I were seeing her through a tattered gauze curtain. But the nearer she approached, the colder the temperature became, and the more distinctly I could hear the static crackling of her upraised hair.

"Jane," I said, in a constricted voice, "you're not real. Jane, you're dead! You can't be here, you're dead!"

"*John . . .*" she sighed, and her voice sounded like four or five voices speaking at once. "*John . . . make love to me.*"

For a moment, all vestiges of my courage and my confidence collapsed inside me into that gravitational black hole called panic. I buried my face under the comforter, and squeezed my eyes tight shut, and shouted under the bedclothes, "I'm dreaming this! It's a nightmare! For Christ's sake, tell me I'm dreaming!"

I waited under the comforter with my eyes shut until I could hardly breathe any more. Then I opened my eyes again and stared at the darkness of the quilting, right in front of my nose. The trouble with hiding is that at some point you have to come out again, and face up to what it was that made you hide in the first place. I said a silent prayer to myself that Jane would be gone, that the whispering would have stopped, that the cottage would have warmed and restored itself.

I whipped the comforter away from my face, and looked up. What I saw just above me made me yell out loud. It was Jane's face, only four or five inches away from me, looking directly down at me. She seemed to melt and shift and change constantly; sometimes looking childish and young, at other times looking ravaged and old. Her eyes were impenetrable: there seemed to be no life there at all. And her expression never changed from a dreamless serenity.

"*John,*" she said, somewhere inside my head.

I couldn't speak. I was too frightened. For not only was Jane staring at me closely, she was actually lying, or rather floating, on top of me, toe to toe, five or six inches above the bed. The coldness poured down from her like the vapor from dry ice, and I felt as if frost crystals were forming on my hair and on my eyelashes, but Jane kept floating above me, ethereal and freezing, suspended in some existence where gravity and substance seemed to have no meaning.

"*Make love to me . . .*" she whispered. Her voice echoed,

as if she were speaking in a long empty corridor. *"John . . . make love to me . . ."*

The comforter slipped away from the bed as if it had a life of its own. Now I was lying naked, with this flickering manifestation of Jane hovering horizontally over me, whispering to me, chilling me, and yet begging me for love.

She didn't move her arm, and yet I felt a sensation like a cold hand drawing itself across my forehead, and touching my cheeks, and then my lips. The coldness crept down my bare sides, tingling my nipples, outlining the muscles of my chest, touching the sides of my hips. Then it touched my testicles, making them harden and shrink. But it aroused a curious tingling in my penis which made it rise in spite of my fear and discomfort.

"Make love to me, John . . ." she whispered, voice upon voice, echo upon echo. And the coldness massaged me, up and down, until feelings began to stir inside me that I hadn't felt for over a month now.

"John . . ." she said again.

"This is a dream," I told her. "This cannot be happening. You cannot be real. You're dead, Jane. I've seen you dead and you're dead."

The cold massage continued, on and on, until I began to feel that I was close to a climax. It was like having sex and yet totally unlike having sex: I could feel slipperiness and softness and the wiry stimulation of pubic hair. Yet it was utterly freezing. My penis felt white with cold, and my body was covered with goosebumps.

"Jane," I told her, "this isn't real." And as my body tightened into a climax, I *knew* it wasn't real, I *knew* that it was completely impossible, I *knew* that I couldn't be having sex with my dead wife. As the semen spattered over my bare stomach there was a hideous loud screech and Jane seemed to come hurtling towards me with her face exploding in a welter of blood and shattered glass and for one instant of total terror her skull seemed to collide face-to-face with mine, the cheekbones rawly exposed, the eyes gouged out, the tattered lips spread to bare grinning bloodstained teeth.

I rolled out of bed and across the floor so fast that I collided with the bureau and knocked over a clinking assembly of after-shave bottles, photograph-frames, and ornaments. A vase of porcelain flowers dropped to the floor and shattered.

I stared at the rumpled-up bed, shivering. There was nothing there at all, no blood, no body, nothing. I felt the stickiness of semen sliding down my stomach and I put my hand down there and touched it. A nightmare, it must have been. An erotic nightmare. A mixture of sexual frustration and fear, all tangled up with images of Jane.

I didn't really want to get back into bed, and I was frightened to fall asleep, but it was two o'clock in the morning now, and I was so tired that I couldn't think of anything but crawling under the comforter and closing my eyes. I pressed the heel of my hand against my forehead and tried to calm myself down.

As I did so, gradually, I began to see brown marks appearing on the bedsheet, like scorch marks. Some of them even smoldered slightly as if they were being burned from beneath the sheet by someone with a red-hot poker, or a cigarette-end. I watched them in fearful fascination as letters formed themselves.

They were blurry, difficult to read, but they were definitely letters. SA . . . VA . . . E.

SAVE ME? SAVAGE?

And then it occured to me. It may only have been because I had been talking to Edward Wardwell this evening about that very thing. But it seemed to fit in so well that I could scarcely believe that the letters meant anything else. SALVAGE.

Through the spirit of my dead wife, whatever lay in the hold of the *David Dark* was pleading to be rescued.

THIRTEEN

For the rest of the night, I was undisturbed, and I slept until nearly eleven o'clock in the morning. I drove into Granitehead Village just before lunch, parked in the center of the square, and walked across the brick-laid street to open up Trenton Marine Antiques.

Granitehead was a smaller version of Salem, a collection of 18th- and 19th-century houses and shops gathered around a picturesque marketplace. Three or four narrow streets ran steeply downhill from the square to the curved and picturesque harbor, which these days was always densely forested with yachts.

Right up until the mid-1950s, Granitehead had been a rundown and isolated fishing community. But with the rise of middle-class affluence in the late 1950s and early 1960s, and with it the rise of yachting and deep-sea angling as widespread leisure pursuits, Granitehead had quickly become a desirable place for anyone who wanted a waterfront cottage within driving distance of Boston. An aggressive planning committee had bullied out of state and federal funds enough money to remodel all of Granitehead's most elegant and historic buildings, tear down street after street of slummy old fishermen's cottages, and replace the shabby warehouses and dilapidated wharves with jewelers, boutiques, art galleries, cookie shops, English-style pubs, beef-and-oyster restaurants, and all those fashionable and slightly unreal business ventures that make up the modern American shopping mall.

I often used to wonder where I could go in Granitehead just to buy ordinary food and ordinary household necessities. You don't *always* want to eat Bavarian strudel and buy hand-crafted pottery mobiles for your designer kitchen.

Mind you, Trenton Marine Antiques was just as guilty of shopping-mall *kitsch*, with its green-painted frontage and mock-Georgian windows. Inside, there was an expensive clutter of ships-in-bottles, shiny brass telescopes, sextants, demi-culverins, grappling hooks, navigational dividers, paintings, and prints. The favorite, of course, was always the figurehead, and the more bosomy the better. A genuine figurehead from the early 19th-century, especially if it were a bare-breasted mermaid, would fetch anything up to $35,000, occasionally more. But the demand was so insistent that I employed an old man up at Singing Beach to carve me "authenticated reproductions" of old-time figureheads, using the centerspread from the May, 1982, issue of *Playboy* as his model.

There was a clutch of bills and letters on the doormat, including a note from the post office that they were holding all the prints that I had bought earlier in the week at Endicott's auction. Later on, I would have to go over and collect them.

Although I had managed to catch some sleep, I was feeling depressed and irritable. I didn't really want to leave Granitehead, and yet I knew that I wasn't going to be able to face another night at Quaker Lane Cottage. I was torn by a unique combination of fear and emotional pain. Fear because of the coldness, and the whispering, and the stark fact that I had seen one of these apparitions kill Mrs. Edgar Simons by means of something which I could only describe as black magic; and emotional pain because I loved Jane, and to see her and hear her and feel her, while all the time I knew she was dead—well, that was more than my mind could stand.

A squat middle-aged couple came into the store, in matching maroon quilted jackets. They blinked through matching Coke-bottle spectacles at ships-in-bottles, and whispered between themselves. "Aren't they cute?" asked the wife.

"You know how they *do* that, don't you?" the husband suddenly asked me, in a loud New Jersey accent.

"I have a vague idea," I nodded.

"They cut through the masts, see, so that they fold flat, and they tie them all with thread, and when the ship's inside the bottle, they tug the thread and all the masts stand up."

"Yes," I said.

"You learn something every day," the husband added. "How much for this one? The whaler?"

"That was made in 1871 by a midshipman on the *Venture*," I said. "Two thousand, seven hundred dollars."

"I'm sorry?"

"Two thousand seven hundred. I might go down to two-five."

The husband stared down at the bottle in his hand speech-lessly. Eventually, he said, "Two thousand seven hundred dollars for a model boat in a bottle? I could build it myself for a buck-and-a-half."

"Then you should," I advised him. "There's quite a mar-ket for ships-in-bottles. Even new ones."

"Jesus," the husband said, putting down the bottle as if it were the Holy Grail, and already starting his retreat from the shop. He kept on looking around, so that he wouldn't com-pletely lose face, and I knew that he would ask the price of just one more item before he went, and say "I'll think it over, and come back later," before disappearing forever.

"How much for that hook thing?" he said, right on cue.

"That grappling-hook? That came from one of John Paul Jones' vessels. Eight hundred and fifty. A bargain, as a matter of fact."

"H'm," said the husband. "Let me think about it. Maybe we'll stop by after lunch."

"Thank you," I said, and watched them leave.

They had only just gone, however, when Walter Bedford came into the shop, wearing a broad smile and a black London Fog raincoat that was a size too large for him.

"John, I just had to come by. I had a call from the district attorney this morning. They've decided to be reasonable, under the circumstances, and drop the homicide charges. Insufficient evidence. They've told the newspapers that they're looking for a maniac of considerable strength, just to make it look kosher; but the main thing is that you're free. Right in the clear."

"No money passed hands, I hope," I said, a little sarcastically.

Walter Bedford was in too good a mood to take offense, and clapped me on the back. "The truth is, John, the *modus operandi* was giving the chief of police something of a headache. He had the coroner's report late last night, and the coroner said that the only way in which Mrs. Edgar Simons could *possibly* have been impaled on that chandelier was for the chain to have been forced through her body *before* the chandelier was fixed to the ceiling, and then for the whole caboodle, chandelier and body and all, to be hoisted up, wired, screwed in, and left to dangle. Now—even given that the murderer had a block-and-tackle to lift the chandelier and the body, it would have taken him at least an hour-and-a-half to complete the job, not to mention the time it would have taken to remove the hoisting equipment, of which there was no trace in the house. An hour-and-a-half places you well away from the Simons house, according to Mr. Markham and Mr. Reed, and so your alibi is absolutely solid. Case dismissed.''

"Well," I said, "thank you very much. You'd better send me a bill.''

"Oh, no, no bill. Not for you. Not when you've managed to bring back Jane.''

"Walter, I really don't think—''

Mr. Bedford gripped my upper arm, and looked at me steadily in the eye. He smelled of Jacomo aftershave, $135 a bottle. "John," he said, in his best courtroom voice, "I know how you feel about this. It's scary, and it's also deeply moving. I can understand, too, that you may want to keep these visitations to yourself, particularly after the way in which Constance and I have blamed you so much for what happened. But both of us understand now that it *couldn't* have been your fault. If it had been, Jane wouldn't have wanted to come back to you, and comfort you from the spirit world. Constance, I can tell you, is deeply, deeply, apologetic for the way she's felt about you. She's filled with remorse. And she begs you, John, even though she's not a begging woman—she *begs* you to let her see her only daughter again, even for the briefest moment. I guess I do, too. You don't know what this means to us, John. We lost everything we ever had when we lost Jane. Just to be able to talk to her again, just to see that she's happy in the world to come. Just once, John. That's all I'm asking.''

I lowered my eyes. "Walter," I said, huskily, "I can appreciate your eagerness to see Jane again. But I have to warn you that she isn't exactly the Jane you knew. Nor the Jane *I* knew, either. She's—well, she's very different. For Christ's sake, Walter, she's a ghost.''

Walter stiffened his lower lip, and gave a little shake of his head. "Don't use that word 'ghost,' John. I like 'visitation' so much better."

"We're arguing about what to *call* her? Walter, she's a ghost; a phantom; a restless spirit."

"I know that, John. I'm not trying to evade the truth. But the point is—do you think she's *happy*? Do you think she likes it, where she is?"

"Walter, I don't *know* where she is."

"But is she happy? That's all we want to ask her. And Constance wants to ask if she's managed to locate Philip. You know, Jane's younger brother, who died when he was five."

I simply couldn't answer that question. I tiredly rubbed the back of my neck and tried to think what I could possibly say to put Walter Bedford off. Something that wouldn't antagonize him again, and lose me my most munificent benefactor; not that "munificent" was quite the word that anybody would use in connection with Walter Bedford. "Prudently generous" was probably more accurate.

"I don't really think, Walter, that any of us are going to be able to determine whether she's happy or not. I have to tell you that she appeared again last night, and—"

"You've seen her again? You've actually seen her again?"

"Walter, please. She appeared last night, in my room. The whole experience was very upsetting. She spoke my name a few times, and then—well, she asked me to make love to her."

Walter frowned, and stood suddenly rigid. "John," he said, "my daughter is *dead*."

"I know that, Walter, God preserve me."

"Well, you didn't actually—"

"Didn't actually *what*, Walter? Didn't actually have intercourse with my dead wife? What are you trying to say, that I'm a necrophiliac? There was no corpse there, Walter, only a face, and a feeling, and a voice. It was like freezing electricity, that's all."

Walter Bedford appeared to be shaken. He walked across the shop and stood with his back to me for a while. Then he picked up a brass telescope, and began opening it and closing it, opening and closing it, in nervous distress.

"I think, John, that *we* will be able to discover whether she's happy or not. We are her parents, after all. We've known her all her life. So it's possible that some of the little nuances of expression that you may have missed, not knowing her so well; some of the little give-away words that you may not have recognized . . . it's possible that these may mean something to us that wasn't immediately apparent to you."

"Walter, God damn it," I said, "we're not dealing with a cozy transparent version of Jane here. This isn't a warm and friendly ghost that you can have conversations with. This is a chilly, hostile, frightening manifestation with eyes that look like death itself and hair that crackles like it's running through with fifty thousand volts. Do you really want to face up to that? Do you really want Constance to face up to it?"

Walter Bedford closed up the telescope and put it back on the table. When he looked at me, his eyes were very sorrowful, and he was near to tears.

"John," he said, "I'm prepared for the very worst. I know it won't be easy. But it can't be as bad as that day when they called us up and told us that Jane had been killed. That day was the blackest of all."

"I can't put you off?" I said, quietly.

He shook his head. "I'll have to come anyway, invited or uninvited."

I bit my lip. "All right then. Come tomorrow night, if you want to. I'm not staying at Quaker Lane Cottage tonight, I can't face it. But please do me one favor."

"Anything."

"Warn Constance, over and over, that what she may see may be horrifying, and cold, and even malevolent. Don't let her come to Quaker Lane Cottage thinking that she's going to be meeting the Jane she knew."

"She is her mother, you know, John. The visitation may behave differently when her mother's there."

"Well," I said, not wanting to prolong the argument any further, "I guess that's possible."

Walter Bedford held out his hand, and I didn't have any option but to shake it. He gripped my elbow at the same time, and said, "Thank you, John. You don't know what this means to us, you really don't."

"Okay," I told him. "I'll see you tomorrow night. Make it

late, will you? Eleven o'clock, something like that. And please, don't forget to warn Constance.''

''Oh, I'll warn her,'' said Mr. Bedford, and left the shop like a man who's just learned that he's come into money.

FOURTEEN

I kept the shop open until four o'clock in the afternoon, and considering it was early March, and the weather had been so poor, I was visited by quite a reasonable number of buying customers. I managed to sell a huge and hideous ship's telegraph to a gay couple from Darien, Connecticut, who excitedly took it away in the back of their shiny blue Oldsmobile wagon; and a serious silver-haired man spent nearly an hour going through my engravings and unerringly selected the best.

After I had locked up the shop, I went over to the Crumblin' Cookie (God forgive me) for a cup of black coffee and a doughnut. I liked the girls behind the counter there; one of them, Laura, had been a friend of Jane's, and she knew just how to talk about Jane without upsetting me.

"Good day's business?" she asked me, handing over my coffee.

"Not bad. At least I managed to unload that ship's telegraph that Jane always used to hate."

"Oh, that thing you bought up at Rockport, when you went out buying on your own?"

"That's the one."

"Well," said Laura, "you'd better make sure your taste in acquisitions improves, or she'll come back and haunt you."

I gave an awkward grimace. Laura looked at me, her head tilted to one side, and said, "Not funny? I'm sorry. I didn't mean to—"

"It's all right," I told her. "It wasn't your fault."

"Really, I'm sorry," Laura insisted.

119

"Forget it," I told her. "I'm just having one of my moods."

I finished my coffee, left Laura a dollar tip, and walked across Granitehead Square into the chilly afternoon. I felt like getting into my car and driving all night, as far away from Massachusetts as possible, back to St. Louis, or even further. In spite of the constant wind, in spite of the ocean, I felt that Salem and Granitehead were small and dark and constricting and old. A great suffocating weight of history pressed on me here, layer upon layer of ancient buildings, long-dead people, mysterious events. Layer upon layer of prejudice and argument and pain.

I drove south-west as far as Lafayette Street, and then crossed into Salem, passing the Star of the Sea cemetery. It was unusually sunny; and sharp reflections of light glanced off windows and car windshields and yachts. A distant airplane glittered in the sky like a needle as it circled in to Beverly Airport, five miles away.

On the car radio, WESX was playing *Don't Let Him Steal Your Heart Away*. I drove as far as Charter Street, opposite police headquarters, and then made a right to Liberty Street, where I parked. Then I crossed the road to the Peabody Museum, on East India Square.

Salem had been revitalized in the same way as Granitehead, and East India Square, newly created, was a clean, brick-paved enclave, with a fountain in the center in the shape of a Japanese gate. Running west from East India Square was a long mall of fashionable "shoppes." In contrast, the original 1824 building in which the Peabody Museum had been started, East India Marine Hall, overlooked the square like an elderly relative who had been freshly scrubbed and clean-collared to attend a grandchild's wedding-party.

I found Edward Wardwell in the Maritime History department, sitting in the full-size cabin of the 1819 yacht *Cleopatra's Barge*, reading a sub-aqua manual. I knocked on the woodwork, and said, "Anybody home?"

"Oh, John," said Edward. He put down his book. "I was just thinking about you. Refreshing my mind on diving for absolute beginners. It looks like the weather's going to hold for tomorrow morning."

"Not if the storm-god answers my prayers, it isn't."

"You don't have anything to be afraid of," said Edward.

"In fact, when you're diving, it's very important *not* to be afraid, or at least to try to control your fear. I mean, we all get afraid. We get afraid of not being able to breathe properly; we get afraid of dark water; we get afraid of being tangled up in weeds. Some divers even develop a phobia about surfacing. But if you're reasonably relaxed, there isn't any reason why you shouldn't have the time of your life."

"H'm," I said, unconvinced.

"You don't have to worry," Edward reassured me, taking off his spectacles, and blinking at me. "I'll be right beside you the whole time."

"What time do you finish here?" I asked him. "There's something I want to talk to you about."

"We close at five, but then I'll have about twenty minutes' clearing up to do."

I looked around. Already the light was fading through the museum's arched windows. Another night was approaching; another time when the dead of Granitehead might appear to their loved ones; and another time when Jane might appear to me. I was going to stay in Salem tonight, at the Hawthorne Inn, but I wasn't at all sure that Jane's visitations were restricted to Quaker Lane Cottage.

"Come and have a drink at the Tavern on the Green," I suggested. "I'm going there now. Why don't I see you there about six?"

"I've got a better idea," said Edward. "Go down to Street Mall and introduce yourself to Gilly McCormick. She's going to be keeping log for us tomorrow, so you might as well get to know her now. She runs a fashion shop called Linen & Lace, about the sixth shop down, in the arcade. I'll meet you there when I've finished up here."

I left the Peabody and walked across East India Square to the Mall. It was growing colder now, as well as darker, and I rubbed my hands briskly together to keep myself warm. A small party of tourists wandered past, and one woman said loudly, in a twanging Texas accent, "Isn't it *marvelous*? You can just *feel* that 18th-century atmosphere."

Linen & Lace was a small, elegant, expensive little shop selling high-collared Princess-Diana style dresses with bows and ruffles and muttonchop sleeves. An extremely svelt black girl directed me to the back of the shop with a long blood-red fingernail; and there I found Gilly McCormick, tying up a gift parcel for a tired-looking Boston matron in a moulting mink.

Gilly was tall, with curly brunette hair, and a striking high-cheekboned face. She wore one of her own linen blouses, with a ruffled lace bodice, but it did nothing to conceal the fullness of her breasts, or the slimness of her waist. She wore a charcoal-gray calf-length skirt, and fashionably small black boots. Pixie boots, Jane always used to call them.

"Can I help you?" she said, when the Boston matron had flustered out of the shop.

I held out my hand. "I'm John Trenton. Edward Wardwell told me to come down and introduce myself. Apparently we're diving together tomorrow."

"Oh, well, *hi*," she smiled. She had eyes the color of glacée chestnuts, and a little dimple on her right cheek. I decided that if this was the quality of the company I was going to be keeping when I went diving, then I might very well become something of a sub-aqua enthusiast.

"Edward told me you bought that watercolor of the *D.D.* the other day," said Gilly. "He totally forgot about the auction, you know; he was here, helping me put up one of my displays. He was so mad when he came back here and told me you'd bought it. 'That damn stuffy guy!' he was shouting. 'I offered him three hundred dollars and all he did was tell me I could borrow it.' "

"Edward's very involved with this theory about the *David Dark*, isn't he?" I said.

"You're allowed to say 'obsessed' if you want to," smiled Gilly. "Edward won't mind. He admits he's obsessed, but that's only because he really believes he's right."

"And what do you think?"

"I'm not sure. I *think* I agree with him; although I'm not too sure about all these apparitions in Granitehead. I've never actually met anyone who's ever seen one. I mean, it could be a kind of mass hysteria, couldn't it, like the witch-trials were?"

I looked at her carefully. "You know about me, and the homicide charge they made against me?" I asked her.

Gilly blushed a little, and nodded. "Yes, I read about that in the *Evening News*."

"Well, whatever it says in the *Evening News*, let me tell you one certain fact, apart from the one certain fact that it wasn't me who murdered that woman. The other fact is that one of those apparitions was there that night. I saw it with my own eyes; and it's my belief that it killed her.''

Gilly stared at me for a very long time, obviously trying to decide whether I was a freak or a fruitcake. She probably wasn't aware of it, but her body language clearly revealed her trepidation: she crossed her arms across her breasts.

''Right,'' I said, without smiling. ''Now you think I'm a maniac. Maybe I shouldn't have told you.''

''Oh, no,'' she stammered, ''I mean, that's quite all right. I mean, I don't think you're a maniac at all. I just think that—''

She hesitated, and then she said, ''Well, I just think that the existence of ghosts is kind of hard to accept.''

''I know that. I didn't believe in them either, until I saw one.''

''You really saw a ghost?''

I nodded. ''I really genuinely saw a ghost. It was Mr. Edgar Simons, the dead woman's late husband. He was like—I don't know, electricity. A man made out of high-voltage electricity. It's hard to describe.''

''But why did he kill her?''

''I don't know. I haven't any idea. Perhaps he was getting his revenge for something she'd done to him when he was alive. It's impossible to say.''

''And you actually saw him?''

''I actually saw him.''

Gilly swept back her curls with her hand. ''Edward's always saying that Granitehead is haunted. I don't think that any of the rest of us really believe him; at least we haven't, up until now. Edward's a kind of an odd duck, if you know what I mean. Very deeply into the Salem witch-scare, and Cotton Mather, and all the peculiar occult sects that kept cropping up in Massachusetts during the 18th century.''

I leaned against the counter and folded my arms. ''I'm not the only person in Granitehead who's been seeing ghosts. The guy who runs the Granitehead Market, that's my local store, he's been seeing his dead son. And, if you ask me, a whole lot of people in Granitehead have been seeing their dead relatives for a long time, but not saying anything about it.''

''That's what Edward believes. But why shouldn't they say anything about it?''

"Would *you*, if your dead husband or wife turned up on your doorstep one night? Who would believe you? And if anybody *did* believe you, the first thing you'd know, you'd have newspapers and TV and ghost-hunters and rubberneckers all gathering around your house like a flock of buzzards. That's why it's all been so secret. Granitehead people, the *old* Granitehead people, they've known all about it for years, maybe hundreds of years. That's what I think, at least. But they're purposely keeping it quiet. They want tourists, not psychic hyenas."

"Well, gee," said Gilly, at a loss for words. Then she looked at me, and shook her head, and said, "You've actually seen a ghost. A real live ghost. Or real *dead* ghost, I guess I ought to say."

"Let me tell you this," I said. "I just pray that *you* don't get to see one, too. They're not at all pleasant, not in any way at all."

We chatted for a little while longer. Gilly told me about the shop, and how she had come to open it. She had studied fashion and textiles at Salem State, and then, with a $150,000 legacy from her grandfather, and some extra finance from the Shawmut-Merchants Bank, opened up a small fashion shop out at Hawthorne Square Shopping Center. Business had been so good that when a lease had become available in the center of Salem itself, she had "seized it with all ten claws," as she put it.

"I'm independent," she said. "An independent business lady selling my own designs. What more could I want?"

"You married?" I asked her.

"Are you kidding? I don't even have time for boyfriends. Do you know what I have to do this evening? I have to drive over to Middleton to collect a whole lot of lace day-dresses that are being hand-sewn for me by two old New England spinsters. If I don't do it tonight, they won't be in the shop in time for tomorrow, and tomorrow's Saturday."

"All work and no play," I remarked.

"To me, work *is* play," she retorted. "I love my work. It's my whole life. It completely fulfills me."

"But you *are* coming diving tomorrow."

"Oh, sure. I do like to prove that I'm as good as a man in other areas as well."

"Did I say you weren't as good as a man?"

She blushed. "You know what I mean."

At that moment, Edward came into the shop, carrying an untidy collection of papers and books. "Sorry to keep you," he said, trying to rearrange his papers and scratch his ear at the same time. "The Director wanted to make sure that everything was ready for the Jonathan Haraden exhibition tomorrow. Do you want that drink now?"

"Sure," I said. "How about you, Gilly? Do you want to come?"

"I have to be in Middleton by seven," she said. "Then I have to get back to press all the dresses and price them."

"Drop into the Hawthorne on your way back, then," I asked her. "I'll still be in the Tavern."

"I'll try."

We left Gilly at Linen & Lace and walked over to Liberty Street to collect my car. "She's an interesting girl, Gilly," said Edward. "Underneath that good-looking exterior she's got herself a real tough business brain. That's women's liberation at its best. Can you guess how old she is?"

"I don't know. Twenty-four maybe, twenty-five."

"You didn't look at the skin closely enough, or the figure. She's just turned twenty."

"Are you putting me on?"

"You wait until tomorrow, when she's in a bathing suit. Then you'll see."

"Are you . . . pursuing her?" I asked him.

Edward shrugged. "She's too dynamic for me. Too much of a go-getter. I prefer the dreamy young college-girl types, you know, mulled cider in front of the fire, poetry by Lawrence Ferlinghetti, Led Zeppelin on the stereo."

"Did *you* ever get stuck in your era."

Edward laughed. "Maybe I did, at that."

We managed to arrive at the Tavern on the Green at the Hawthorne Inn just as one of the tables in front of the fireplace was being vacated. The Tavern, a warm oak-paneled room decorated with pictures of ships and maritime chinaware, was crowded with homegoing businessmen and shop people. I ordered Chivas Regal and Edward asked for a beer.

"I have to tell you something," I said. "Something which I omitted to tell you yesterday, for personal reasons, I guess."

Edward sat forward in his chair and laced his hands together.

"If it's going to make it any easier, I think I already know what you're going to say."

"For the past three nights," I told him, "I've been visited by an apparition of Jane. The first night, I didn't see anything, but I heard her swinging on the garden-swing. The next night I actually saw her there. Last night, after you'd left, I saw her again. She came into my bedroom."

Edward looked at me with concern. "I see," he said, thoughtfully. "Well, I can understand why you didn't want to tell me. Not many people do, not at first. Did she *say* anything to you? Did she give you any kind of message? Were you able to communicate with her in any way?"

"She—spoke my name a few times. Then she asked me to make love to her."

"Yes," Edward nodded. "Several people have had that experience. Go on. What else did she do? Did she actually make love to you?"

"I had—well, I don't know what to call it. I had some kind of a sexual experience. It was extremely cold. I'll never forget how cold it was, like in *The Exorcist*. It all ended when I saw her as she must have looked in her car crash. You know—blood, bones—it scared the living hell out of me."

"Is that why you're not going back to Granitehead tonight?"

"Do you blame me?"

"Of course not. I want you calm for tomorrow, anyway, when we dive. Anxiety leads to stress, and stress leads to mistakes. You don't want to drown your first time out."

"I wish you'd stop being so damned optimistic about this dive."

A waitress in a black tuxedo vest and black bow-tie brought us our drinks. While Edward sampled his beer, I took out my ballpen and said, "There's something else. A kind of written message, burned on the sheets of the bed. It was still there this morning."

I wrote on my cocktail napkin the letters that had appeared on my bed, copying them as exactly as I could. SALVAGE. I pushed them over to Edward and he examined them carefully.

"Salvage?" he asked. "You're sure it's not 'savage'?"

"No. It's definitely salvage. It's the second or third time the letters have appeared. Once they were scrawled on my bathroom mirror, and once on the side of my kettle. It's salvage. It's an appeal to me to salvage the *David Dark*."

Edward pouted his lips skeptically. "You really think that?"

"Edward, when you see one of these apparitions, you're aware of feelings and thoughts that you've never had before in your life. It's an intuitive experience, as well as a sensory one. Nobody said, 'This means that you're supposed to salvage the *David Dark*.' They didn't have to. I *knew*."

"Now listen," said Edward, "I know that I'm given to drawing radical historical conclusions, but I really think that you're jumping a whole lot of logical steps here without any substantive reasoning at all. To find and bring up the *David Dark* we have to be analytical, as well as theoretical."

"Do you have anybody close to you who's recently died?" I asked him, in the softest of voices.

"No, I don't."

"In that case, trust what I'm saying. I've seen my own dead wife, right in front of me. I've had sex with her spirit, if that's what it was. I'm already beginning to realize that there's another existence right alongside of ours, and it's crowded with pain and self-doubt and fear and longing. Maybe if we bring up the *David Dark*, like you've always wanted to do, we can find a way to ease that pain, and settle that doubt, and calm all those fears and those longings, for good."

Edward looked down at the table. He puffed out his cheeks. "Well," he said, without any trace of sarcasm, "you sounded almost religious there, for a moment."

"This is religious, isn't it? It's all tangled up with religion?"

Edward looked doubtful. "To tell you the truth, I don't know what it is. If you've actually seen those apparitions, then you know more than I do, at least in terms of practical experience."

I raised my glass. "Here's to tomorrow's dive. I don't want to go, but I think I'm going to have to."

FIFTEEN

Shortly after ten o'clock, I left the Tavern on the Green and went upstairs to my room. Edward had left around nine-thirty to go home to his sister, and there had been no sign of Gilly, so I decided to have a steak and potato on room service, and spend the rest of the evening boning up on the diving manual which Edward had lent me.

I had a corner room on the sixth floor overlooking Salem Common, and through the trees I could just make out the cupola of the bandstand where I had met the old witch-woman the other day. The room was rather too brown for my taste, brown carpet, brown-and-orange drapes, brown-and-white bedspread, but it felt secure and warm and it was a long way away from Quaker Lane Cottage.

As I lay back on the double-bed with my shoes off, waiting for my filet medium-rare, I wondered what was happening at the cottage right now. Would Jane appear there, even if I wasn't there to witness her visitation? How much did the appearance of a ghost depend on the people who were being haunted? I could imagine her flickering image wandering from room to room, searching for me; and the whispering voices everywhere.

I thought of something else, too. Supposing I *did* drown tomorrow, or die in some other way. Would I find myself in that same electrically-charged limbo as Jane? Would I become one of those distorted figures like her, fading from one reality to another, never at rest? Was she conscious of what she was? Was it really her, in the sense that she knew who she once had been?

I was still thinking about Jane when there was a sharp knock at the door, and I involuntarily jumped in fright.

"Right with you," I said, and padded across the carpet on stockinged feet. I unlocked the door, and opened it; but instead of my filet medium-rare and potato, it was Gilly. She was crimson-nosed from the cold, but smiling, and she was carrying a brown-paper bag which looked more than suspiciously like a bottle of wine.

"This is a peace-offering for being late," she said. "May I come in?"

"Of course. Let me take your coat. You look like you're half-frozen."

"Actually, I'm half-thawed. I was totally frozen when I was out at Middleton. Those little old spinsters are dedicated believers in doing things the old-fahioned way. If you can't get your house warm enough with your wood-burning stove, then put on another couple of sweaters. Central-heating is the work of the devil, making people soft and complacent and idle."

"Sit down," I told her. "I'm having some steak sent up in a while. Would you like some?"

"I'm dieting, but I'll nibble at yours."

"What kind of diet are you on?" I asked her.

"I call it my Pricey Diet. I allow myself to eat *anything* as long as it costs more than $7 a pound. That takes in caviar, smoked canvasback duck, salmon, finest aged filet steak. Really expensive food is rarely fattening, and in any case you generally can't eat too much of it."

We talked for a while about antiques, and the tourist trade. I guess after all we were both shopowners. Then the waiter came up with my steak, and we opened the bottle of wine, Fleurie 1977, and drank a toast to each other. I cut up the steak and we shared it, hardly talking at all while we ate.

"You probably think it's very bold of me, coming up to your room like this," said Gilly.

I put down my napkin and smiled at her. "I wondered when you were going to say that."

She blushed. "I guess I *had* to say it at some point. I had to give you your opening for telling me that of *course* I'm not bold, of *course* it's perfectly acceptable for a girl to come up to a strange man's hotel room unescorted, and eat half of his dinner."

I looked at her seriously. "It seems to me that with Linen & Lace you've shown that you're quite mature enough to do what you want, without seeking any justification from me."

She thought about that, and then she said, in a higher voice, "Thank you."

I pushed the dinner trolley outside into the hallway, and then I came back and lay down on the bed, with my hands behind my head. Gilly stayed where she was, kneeling on the floor.

"You know something," I said, "I'm never quite sure how it is that two people meet each other, or how they decide whether they're mutually attracted, or what the ground-rules of their relationship are going to be. All that part of it, the most important part, seems to me to be decided almost instantaneously, and without any discussion at all; and any discussion after that is simply a matter of trimming the sails here and there."

"Well," said Gilly, "you *are* nautical."

"It's living here that does it. I haven't got salt in my blood yet, but I've started sprinkling it on my salad."

She stood up, and looked down at me. Her lips were slightly parted, and there was a thoughtful, erotic look in her eyes which I hadn't seen in a woman since I first met Jane. She said, quietly, "Do you mind turning out the light?"

I reached out and switched off the bedside lamp. The only light in the room now came from the television; and Gilly was outlined against it. Carefully, slowly, she unbuttoned the cuffs of her blouse, then the lace front panel and drew it over her head. She was wide-shouldered, but her breasts were bigger than I had thought, warmly cradled in a lace bra. She unzipped her skirt, and let it fall, and I saw that she was wearing dark gray stockings and a black garter-belt. No panties. The light from the television silhouetted the wayward curls of pubic hair.

She unhooked her bra, and her breasts were freed with a soft, complicated little bounce. I held out my hand to her.

"I'm not an easy person to satisfy," she said, in a husky voice. "I guess that's one of the reasons I always avoid relationships with men. I *need* a very great deal; I ask a lot—emotionally and sexually."

"For what it's worth," I said, "I can give you everything I've got."

I sat up, and stripped off my shirt, and socks, my pants and my shorts. Gilly lay down beside me, still wearing her stockings and garter belt, and I could feel the softness of her hair against my shoulders, and the heaviness of her wide-nippled breasts against my chest, and the warm slipperiness of nylon against my thighs.

We kissed, tentatively at first, then with increasing passion. Her hands tugged at my hair, caressed my shoulders, gripped at my hip. I held her breast in my hand, arousing the nipple between my fingertips until it stood crinkled and stiff. My erection rose against the shiny tightness of her stocking, and she put her hand down and held it tight in her fist, pressing and massaging it against her pubic hair.

Neither of us needed very much foreplay; neither of us could actually stand it. For different reasons, both of us had been deprived of sexual company for longer than was good for us, and the pressure suddenly rose between us until there was nothing that either of us wanted but forceful, urgent, sex.

I thrust myself into her, and she was hot and moist and gasping with every thrust. The inside of my brain felt as if it were expanding; she clutched her legs around me so that I could thrust deeper still, and her fingernails dug into the flesh of my back and her teeth bit deeply into the muscle of my shoulder.

"Oh, God, harder, harder, harder," Gilly urged me, and I grasped her hips in my hands and forced myself into her until she gasped and yelped and thrashed her head from side to side on the pillow.

I could feel the orgasm begin to tighten and ripple inside her like shockwaves just before an earthquake. She spoke words that I couldn't understand; breathy and high-pitched, almost as if she were cursing and pleading at the same time. Her eyes were squeezed tight shut and her face was congested. Her breasts were flushed and her nipples tight and erect.

It was then, right on the brink of climax, that I opened my eyes and looked down at her, and froze. For superimposed on Gilly's face was a coldly-glowing mask of *Jane's* face, hollow-eyed, emotionless, flickering in that threatening electrical way. And for one hideous instant I didn't know if I was making love to Jane, or Gilly, or to nothing at all but my own hallucinating imagination.

Gilly opened her eyes, and they showed through the dark sockets of Jane's electrical mask in fright and surprise.

"John—what's happening? John!"

I opened my mouth but I couldn't speak. Gilly's eyes had brought Jane's deathmask to life, and it was the eeriest vision I had ever seen. It was like a painted portrait, with eyes that moved. And it was so cold. So heartless. So *accusing*.

"John—I'm *freezing!*—John—"

There was a roaring, screeching, mind-shattering crack. Every window in the room imploded, and a devastating gale swept the drapes aside, so that the air was thick with glittering, tumbling, razor-sharp shards of glass. I hunched down over Gilly as much as I could, but even so the frigid gale brought a vicious scattering of glass all over my back, and into the flesh of my buttocks, and into the muscles of my thighs. The bedspread was sliced to shreds, and feathers rose from the glass-slashed pillows like snow.

I kept my eyes closed until the last tinkle of falling glass had subsided. The cold March wind blew steadily in through the windows, and flapped at the cover of the magazine I had left on top of the television. I looked down at Gilly and she was just Gilly, nobody else, not Jane; although she was white-faced with fright and there was a cut on the side of her forehead.

"I want you to slide out from under me," I whispered. "Watch out—there's glass on the bed. There's a whole lot of it sticking out of my back. I don't think it's too serious, but I can't move until you've taken it out."

Tears began to pool in Gilly's eyes; tears of shock and distress. "What *happened?*" she trembled. "I don't understand what *happened*."

"I think I overdid the climax," I told her, trying to be ridiculously nonchalant.

"You're shaking," she said. "Don't move."

She managed to wriggle out naked from beneath me. Then she said, "Lie flat. You've got about twenty pieces in your back. They don't look too deep, though."

She found her shoes, and went to the bathroom to fetch a facecloth and a towel. Then she sat down beside me and plucked the fragments of glass out of my back. There wasn't much blood, but the wounds were sore, and I was glad when she had managed to take out the last piece, on the inside of my right thigh.

There was a knock at the door. A voice said, "Sir? Are you there, sir? Assistant manager, sir."

"What is it?" I called.

"Someone reported a loud noise in your room, sir, and the sound of glass breaking. Is everything all right?"

"Wait a minute," I said. Gilly found my trousers for me, and I shook the glass out of them, pulled them on, and then tiptoed to the door. I opened it on the chain and peered out. The assistant manager was a tall man in a tuxedo with very shiny black hair and very shiny black shoes.

"I bought my cousin a set of collins glasses today," I told him. "A souvenir of Salem. Unfortunately I caught my foot in my bathrobe when I was carrying them across the room. I fell over the table, too."

The assistant manager looked at me beadily. "I hope you're not hurt in any way, sir."

"Hurt? No. Not hurt."

He paused, and then he said, "You won't mind if I just take a look?"

"A look?"

"If you don't mind."

I took a deep breath. There was no point in trying to bluff it out. If the assistant manager wanted to take a look, then there was nothing at all I could do to stop him.

"The thing is," I said, "we had a little trouble with the windows. But, I'll pay for them. As long as you understand that."

SIXTEEN

We drove up to Gilly's apartment on Witch Hill Road, over-looking Gallows Hill Park. The apartment was small but scrupulously neat, with framed fashion designs on white-painted walls, and yuccas in tasteful white Portuguese planters. I was still smarting from all those glass cuts, but all of them had been clean, and only one of them, on my shoulder, was actually bleeding.

"Would you like some wine?" asked Gilly.

I sat down stiffly on the beige corduroy sofa. "I'll have a large Scotch if you've got it."

"Sorry," she said, coming in from the kitchen with a large frosted bottle of Pinot Chardonnay. "Everybody I know is a wine-drinker."

"Don't tell me they're vegetarians, too."

"Some of them," she smiled. She set two tall-stemmed glasses down on the table, and sat down beside me. I took the bottle and poured us both brimful measures. At that moment I felt that if I *had* to drink wine, I might just as well drink a lot of it.

"How much do you think the Hawthorne will charge you?" Gilly asked.

"Couple of thousand, at least. Those plate-glass windows must cost a fortune."

"I still don't really understand what was going on."

I raised my glass in a silent toast and swallowed half of it almost straight away. "Jealous wife," I told her.

She stared at me uncertainly. "You told me your wife was—"

134

"She is," I said, assertively. Then, more quietly, "She is."

"Then you mean to say that what happened tonight—that was *her?* Your wife? She did that?"

"I don't know. It's a possibility. It could have been nothing more than a freak gust of wind. You remember that high-rise in Boston, with the windows that kept falling out? Maybe the same thing happened at the Hawthorne."

Gilly frowned at me in complete non-comprehension. "But if your wife is dead, how could it have been even a *possibility* that it was her? You're telling me that *she's* a ghost, too? Your dead wife is a ghost?"

"I've seen her, yes," I admitted.

"You've seen her," said Gilly. "My God, I can't believe it."

"You don't have to. But it's the truth. I've seen her two or three times now, and tonight, when we were making love, I saw her again. I looked at your face and instead it was *her* face."

Gilly took a drink of wine and then looked at me levelly. "This is getting very hard to play along with, you know that?"

"It isn't any easier for me."

"Do you know how often I've been to bed with a man, almost the moment I've met him, the way I did with you?"

"I wish you'd stop trying to justify yourself," I told her. "I went to bed with you just as quickly. Just because you're the woman and I'm the man, does that make any difference?"

"It's not supposed to," said Gilly, a little defensively.

"In that case, don't let it."

"But now you've put me in a weird position."

"Weird?" I asked, picking up my wine again.

"Well, weird, yes—because the first man I've ever picked to pounce on—the very first man ever—and he turns out to have some obsession with his dead wife. And the windows of his goddamned hotel room blow in."

I stood up, and walked stiffly across the patio doors which overlooked Gilly's narrow third-story balcony. Outside, geraniums trembled in the vibrant night wind. Beyond, I could see the smattering of lights that was Witchcraft Heights. It was past two o'clock in the morning now, and I was tired and shaken beyond argument, beyond reproaches. My ghostly reflection in the dark glass lifted his wine, and drank.

"I wish I *could* say that I'm obsessed with my wife," I said quietly. "I wish I *could* say that I'm suffering from hysteria; that I've never seen her or heard her anywhere else except inside my mind. But she's real, Gilly. She's haunting me. Not just the cottage where we used to live, but me, as a person. That's another reason why I'm going to go diving tomorrow, even though I don't want to. I want my wife to be put to rest."

Gilly said nothing. I came back from the window and sat opposite her, although she wouldn't look at me.

"If you want to forget we ever met, that's all right by me," I told her. "Well—it's not exactly all right. It'll upset me. But I can understand how you feel. Anybody else would feel the same. Even my doctor thinks it's nothing but post-bereavement shock."

I hesitated, and then I said, "You're a very attractive person, Gilly. You do exciting things to me. And I still stand by what I said earlier on—how amazing it is that two people can work up a storm together only minutes after they've met. We could both have a good time; you know that. But I have to tell you that Jane's spirit is still around me, and that there may be danger, the way there was tonight."

Gilly looked at me, and her eyes were glistening. "It's not the danger," she said, with a catch in her voice.

"I know. It's the image of the ex-wife."

"I had that before. I had an affair with a married man when I was seventeen. A bank executive. His wife wasn't dead, of course, but she was always there. Either on the telephone, or in the back of his mind."

"And you definitely don't want to go through it again."

She held out her hand to me. "John," she said, "it's nothing against you. It's just that I'm feeling threatened. And there's one thing that I've always promised myself, ever since I started working on my own. Never to let anyone threaten me, no matter how."

I didn't know what to say to that. She was right, of course. She may have thrown herself at me like a sexually-deprived tigress, and I may have thrown myself back at her like an equally sexually-deprived tiger. But she was under no obligation to accept me as a lover with all of the problems I was carrying with me. All the phantoms, and the fears, and the might-have-beens. Not to mention the unhealed wound of my recently-lost wife and our unborn baby.

"All right," I told her. I let go of her hand. "I don't like what you're saying, but I can understand why you're saying it."

"I'm sorry," she told me. "I don't think you have any idea how much you attract me. You're just my type."

"Nobody with a ghost on his back can possibly be your type. He can't be *anybody's* type. Not until he's been exorcized."

Gilly sat and looked at me for a while in silence, and then got up and went into the kitchen. I followed her, and stood in the doorway, while she took out eggs and muffins and coffee.

"You don't have to cook me anything," I said.

"Breakfast, that's all," she smiled. She broke the eggs into a basin and began to whip them up.

"Have you thought about exorcism?" she asked me. "Getting a priest around to lay your wife to rest?"

I shook my head. "I don't think it would work. I don't know, maybe it might. But I think the only way that any of these apparitions in Granitehead are going to get any peace is if we find out *why* they're so restless, what makes them appear."

"You mean like raising the *David Dark*?"

"Maybe. Edward seems to think that's the answer."

"And what do *you* think?" asked Gilly, taking out a pan and cutting a little sunflower shortening into it.

I rubbed my eyes. "I'm trying to keep an open mind. I don't know. I'm just trying to keep *sane*."

She looked at me kindly. "You're very sane," she said. "You're also a beautiful lover. I hope to God you can give your wife some peace."

There was no need to answer that remark. I watched her scramble eggs and toast muffins and perk coffee, and thought about nothing but sleep, and tomorrow's dive. The cold waters of Granitehead Neck were out there now, restless as the spirits of Granitehead itself, waiting for the dawn.

SEVENTEEN

By nine o'clock, we were out in Salem Sound, on a gray and choppy ocean, balancing on the after-deck of a 35-foot fishing boat, *Alexis*, which Edward and Dan Bass and two of Edward's colleagues from the Peabody Museum had pooled together to rent for the morning.

The day was bright and sharp, and I was surprised how cold it was, but Edward told me that the temperature over the ocean was often as much as 30 degrees lower than the temperature over land. There was a heavy cloudbank off to the north-west, but Dan Bass had estimated that there would be two or three hours' diving time before the weather began to roughen up.

I liked Dan Bass immediately. He was a wry, self-confident 40-year-old with eyes that looked as if they had been bleached by sea-brine to a very pale blue. He spoke with a clipped accent that sounded very Bostonian to me, and there was a Boston-Irish squareness about his face, but as he piloted the boat into position he told me that he had first dived for wrecks off the shores of his native North Carolina, Pamlico Sound and Onslow Bay.

"I dived once on a World War Two torpedo boat, which was sunk in a storm in '44. I shone my flashlight in through the windows, and guess what was staring back at me. This human skull, still wearing a rusty steel helmet. I got the fright of my whole darned life."

Edward was in a very high humor, and so were his colleagues; a serious young student called Jimmy Carlsberg, and a freckled, carrot-top graduate from the Peabody's ethnol-

138

ogy department, Forrest Brough. Both were practiced divers: Jimmy wore a sweatshirt with "See Massachusetts and Dive" lettered on the back. Forrest, three years before, had helped to salvage 18th-century cannon and cooking utensils from a wreck off Mount Hope Point, Rhode Island. Both took time out to explain everything they were doing, and why, so that even if I wasn't going to be much help to them, at least I wouldn't be a disastrous liability.

Gilly, bundled up in a thick quilted parka with a fur-lined hood, sat in the boat's wheelhouse with her notepad and her stopwatch, and hardly talked to me at all. But she caught me looking at her once, and gave me a smile that told me that everything between us was as good as either of us could expect it to be. Her eyes were filled with tears but it was probably the cold wind.

Edward said, "We're going to search a little further along the shore-line than we have up until now. Dan's going to position the boat according to transit bearings we've already worked out—that means we take one fix on the Winter Island lighthouse, and a second fix on the Quaker Hill Episcopalian Church, and where the two transit lines meet, that's where we're going to drop anchor."

Dan Bass brought the *Alexis* a little closer into shore, while Forrest took the bearings. It took a few minutes to nudge the boat into position but at last we put down our anchor, and cut the engine.

"The tide's ebbing at the moment," Edward explained. "In a little while, though, it'll be slack, and that's the safest time for diving. Now, since this is your first time, I don't want you to stay down for longer than five minutes. It's cold down there, and the visibility is pretty shitty, and you'll have quite enough to occupy your time just breathing and finning and getting yourself accustomed to diving."

I felt a tightness in my stomach, and at that moment I would have been quite happy to suggest that I should postpone my aqualung initiation until tomorrow, perhaps, or next week, or even next year. The wind whipped across the deck of the *Alexis* and snapped our diving flag, but I didn't know whether I was shivering from cold or nervous anticipation.

Dan put his arm around my shoulders and said, "Don't you worry about a thing, John. If you can swim, you can aqualung, just provided you keep your head, and follow procedure. Edward's a first-rate diver, in any case. He'll help you."

We changed into snug-fitting Neoprene wetsuits, tugging on tight Neoprene vests underneath to give us extra protection from the cold. The suits were white, with orange hoods, which Edward said would give us maximum visibility in the cloudy water. Dan Bass strapped on my air-cylinder, and showed me how to blow hard into my mouthpiece before breathing in, to dislodge any dust or water; and how to check that the demand valve was functioning correctly. Then I fitted on my weight belt, and Dan adjusted the weights for me so that they were comfortable.

"Check your diving buddy's equipment, too," Dan instructed me. "Make sure you remember how his valve works, how to release his weight-belt, if you need to. And try to remember as much as you can about those emergency procedures."

For my first dive, both Edward and Forrest were going down with me. As we sat on the side of the boat, preparing ourselves, one or the other of them would keep thinking of some piece of advice that he'd forgotten to tell me; and by the time we were ready to drop, my mind was a jumble of signals and procedures and hints on what to do if my facemask fogged, or my air wasn't coming through, or (the most likely emergency, as far as I was concerned) I started to panic.

Gilly came over, clutching her notepad, and stood beside me, the wind ruffling the fur of her parka.

"Good luck," she said. "Stay safe."

"I'll try," I told her, with a dry mouth. "I think I'm more scared now than I was when those windows fell in."

"Windows?" asked Edward. He looked at me, and then at Gilly; but when he saw that neither of us were going to tell him what we were talking about, he shrugged, and said, "Are you ready? Let's drop."

I fitted in my mouthpiece, said a silent prayer inside of my head, and then dropped backwards into the sea.

It was cold and chaotic down there: nothing but foggy water and rushing bubbles. But as I started to sink, I glimpsed the whiteness of Edward's suit right next to me, and then another white blur as Forrest came dropping in after us, and I began to feel that aqualung diving might not be as terrifying as I had thought it was going to be.

All three of us finned into the tidal stream; Edward and Forrest with balance and grace, me with plenty of enthusiasm but not much in the way of style. The ocean wasn't too deep here, especially at low tide, no more than 20 or 30 feet; but it was quite deep enough for me, and it was murky enough for me to stay as close to my buddies as I could.

As we descended towards the bottom, I felt myself becoming progressively less buoyant, until, as we skimmed a few feet over the sloping surface of the Granitehead mud bank, I was in a state of neutral buoyancy, although I tended to rise and sink a little as I breathed in and out. I was a good swimmer. But this chilly underwater exploration of the black ooze on the west shore of Granitehead Neck was something different altogether. I felt like a clumsy, over-excited child, inexperienced and only marginally in control of my body and my movements.

Edward swam into view and made the "okay, all is well," hand signal. I gave him the same signal back, thinking how foreign Edward's eyes looked behind his facemask. I had been told not to make a thumb's up signal because that meant something different altogether. Forrest, ten or fifteen feet away, beckoned us to start searching. If I was only going to be down here for five minutes, I might just as well help the hunt for the *David Dark*.

We were planning to make a systematic circular search of the area around the *Alexis*, swimming in an anti-clockwise spiral and leaving numbered white markers on the bottom to show where we had been. We started off where the boat's anchor was buried in the ooze, and began to fin ourselves around and around, until I had totally lost all sense of direction. As we went, however, Forrest pushed the markers into the mud, one at each completed half-circle, so that we could be sure we weren't covering the same ground twice, or straying way off our search area altogether.

I checked my watch. I had been down for three minutes and I was beginning to feel uncomfortable. Not only cold, and awkward, but claustrophobic as well. Although I had started off by breathing easily, I was finding it difficult to keep up the regular rhythm, and I recognized that even if my mind wasn't panicking, my lungs were beginning to act catchy and nervous.

I tried to remember the signal for "something wrong—not

an emergency.'' A kind of hand-flapping, I think Dan Bass had said, coupled with an indication of what was wrong. How did I explain claustrophobia with a hand-signal? Put my hand around my throat and pretend to be strangling? Squeeze my head in my hands?

Remember not to panic, I told myself. You're perfectly all right. You're swimming without any difficulty; you're still breathing. What's more, you only have a couple of minutes to go and then you'll be back on the surface again. Edward and Forrest will take care of you.

But when I looked around again, I couldn't see either Edward or Forrest anywhere. All I could see was cloudy water, almost as thick as barley-broth, whirling with mud and debris.

I finned around and looked behind me, to see if they were there: but again, all that I could see was water. A stray flounder darted through the murk like a Dickensian character making his way through a London fog, quick and confident. But where were the white wetsuits and orange headpieces that were supposed to make my diving buddies visible through ten feet of submarine darkness?

Don't panic, I repeated. They must be around here someplace. If they're not, then all you have to do is follow the markers back to the anchorline, and fin your way up to the surface again. The problem was, there wasn't a marker in sight, and in turning around to look for my companions, I had completely lost my sense of direction. I could feel the chilly tidal stream flowing gently against me, but when we had started diving the tide had been on the turn, and I couldn't work out which direction it was flowing in, or how far it might have carried me while I was just flapping around here thinking about what to do.

My breath came in short, tense gasps. I tried not to think about all the things that Edward and Dan Bass had warned me to watch out for. If you have to surface, even in an emergency, don't come up too fast. You could end up with an air embolism in your bloodstream that could conceivably kill you. Don't come up any faster than your smallest bubbles, that was what Dan Bass had advised; and, if you can, take a decompression stop on the way.

Burst lung was another danger: overinflating the lungs at

depth, and coming to the surface with too much pressure
inside them, causing them to rupture.

I dog-paddled where I was for a moment or two, calming
myself down. There was still no sign of Edward or Forrest,
and I couldn't locate any of the search markers, so I guessed
that the only thing I could do was to surface. In spite of the
tidal stream, I couldn't be too far away from the *Alexis*.

I was about to start finning my way upwards when I caught
a glimpse of something white through the tumbling murk of
the water. My facemask was slightly misted, and it was
difficult for me to make out exactly how far away it was, but
I remembered that, seen through a facemask, all objects
underwater appear to be three-quarters nearer than they actually are. It could only be Edward or Forrest. There weren't
any other divers in the area, and it looked far too large to be a
fish. I thought momentarily of *Jaws*, but Dan Bass had wryly
assured me that the only Great Whites that had ever been seen
off the coast of New England had belonged to Universal
Pictures.

Swimming steadily, trying to control my breathing so that
it was regular and even, I made my way over the ocean floor
towards the white shape. It was turning in the water, turning
and rolling, as if it were being wafted by the tidal stream;
and, as I swam nearer, I realized that it couldn't be Edward or
Forrest. It looked more like a piece of yacht-sail that had
gotten tangled up in a piece of heavy fishing-equipment, and
sunk to the bottom.

It was only when I came very close, no more than two or
three feet away, when I realized with abject terror and disgust
that it was a drowned woman. She pivoted around, just as I
approached, and I saw a face that was bloated and eyeless, a
mouth that had been half-eaten by fish, hair that rose straight
up from the top of her head like seaweed. She was wearing a
white nightgown, which billowed and waved as the tide came
in and out. Her ankle was loosely wound in a sunken trawl-
net—which had prevented her from rising to the surface or
drifting away but her decomposed body was now so inflated
with gases that she was standing upright, and dancing a
grotesque underwater solo ballet beneath the waves of
Granitehead Neck.

I backed off, trying to suppress my horror and my half-
regurgitated Wheaties. For Christ's sake, I told myself, you

can't be sick. If you're sick, you'll choke, and if you choke, you'll end up like Ophelia here, with your eyeballs eaten out by bluefish. So calm down. Look the other way, forget about Ophelia, there's nothing you can do for her anyway. Calm down. And slowly fin your way up to the surface, and call for help.

I began swimming upwards, watching my bubbles carefully to make sure that I didn't come up too fast. I was only about 30 feet under the water, but it felt like 100. I slowed myself down when I thought I was about halfway up, and exhaled, making sure that my lungs wouldn't burst or anything disastrous like that. The water became lighter, and clearer, and I began to feel the pull of the tide more strongly, and the disturbance of the waves.

"*John*," whispered a woman's voice. I felt a chill go through me that was far more intense than the chill of the seawater. The voice seemed close, and very clear, as if she were speaking right in my ear.

I finned up more quickly, keeping down the first surges of real panic. "*John*," whispered the voice, more loudly now, more urgently, as if she were, pleading. "*Don't leave me, John. Don't leave me. Please, John.*"

I was nearly at the surface. I could see the cross-hatching of the choppy morning waves only a few feet above me. But then something wrapped itself around my left ankle, and as I tried to kick myself free I suddenly found myself turned right over, upside down, and a sharp flood of cold water poured into my ears. I lost my mouthpiece, too, in a blurt of bubbles, and the next thing I knew I was threshing and struggling and trying desperately to twist myself free. I thrust one hand up towards the surface, hoping that I was near enough to make a signal that the *Alexis* might see, but it was useless. I was at least 10 feet below the waves, and whatever had snared my leg was dragging me rapidly deeper.

It was then that I really panicked. I was overwhelmed by the pounding feeling of suffocation, and the realization that unless I struggled free, I was going to drown. I've heard people say that drowning is the most peaceful way to die, far more genteel than burning or crushing or shooting; but who-ever said that hasn't been under the North Atlantic ocean on a cold March morning with a lost mouthpiece and some tena-cious entanglement around his leg. I think I shouted out loud, in a rush of bubbles, and before I could stop myself, I was swallowing water. Freezing, salty, and harsh, pouring into my stomach like liquid fire. I puked some of it back up again, and I was lucky not to choke, because my lungs were almost empty of air.

All I could think of was: don't breathe seawater. Don't breathe seawater. Dan Bass had told me that once you've breathed in seawater, you're dead.

Eyes popping, head thundering, I twisted myself around in a last desperate effort to see what had caught my ankle. To my horror, I saw it was the drowned woman's nightdress, in which the body itself still bobbed and floated in its own hideous jig. When I had first swum past her, my finning movements must have dislodged her from the trawl net, and she must have risen after me, blown up with bacterial gases, like a buoy. Once her gown had entwined itself around my leg, however, and I had kicked and struggled against her, she must have turned so that the gas in her ribcage had bubbled out, leaving her heavier, so that now she was dragging me down.

I bent myself double and tore at the nightgown with my hands, but the sodden fabric refused to rip, and it was wrapped around my foot and my ankle as tightly as wet rawhide. I reached around my belt, and wrestled out my diver's knife, but the body kept rolling and sinking in the tide and it was almost impossible for me to cut the nightgown without cutting my own foot.

Two, three, four slashes, and I knew that I didn't have enough oxygen left in my lungs to do anything but strike out for the surface. But I gave the nightgown one last slice, and like a miracle, the fabric parted. The woman's body sank down again into the darkness, back through the clouds of mud and murky water.

I released my weight-belt, which I should have done earlier, and gave two or three kicks of my fins to get me to the surface. My rise to the top seemed to be agonizingly slow, but I was strangely calm now, my panic had dispersed, and I was quite sure that I was going to survive. At last my head broke through the waves, and there was wind and sunshine and fresh air, and almost a half-mile away, the *Alexis*.

I waved frantically. I didn't know whether I was giving the right signal or not, but the simple fact was that I couldn't keep afloat for very much longer, especially with the waves slapping and swamping me, and I was physically and emotionally exhausted. Dan Bass had been right when he had said that "aqualung diving is just as much a mental sport as it is a physical sport. It's not a pastime for panickers, or latent hysterics."

I heard the *Alexis* starting up her engine with a distant growl, and at last she came circling around toward me, and Dan Bass dived into the sea to hold me up. He towed me in to the side of the boat, and then he and Jimmy together managed to boost me up on to the deck. I lay flat against the planks like a landed shark, coughing and retching and spurting up water through my nose. My sinuses felt as if they had been meticulously scrubbed with a comet.

Gilly knelt beside me. "What *happened?*" she said. "We thought we'd lost you. Edward and Forrest came up and said that you'd disappeared."

I coughed and coughed until I thought I was going to vomit. But at last I managed to control my breathing, and with Dan's help, I sat up.

"Let's get you out of that suit," he said. "Gilly, there's a flask of hot coffee in my rucksack, you want to go get it?"

"I guess it's my responsibility," said Dan, hunkering down beside me and looking at me closely to make sure that I was all right. "You should have practiced in a pool first, before you dived in the open water. I just thought you looked like the kind of guy who could handle himself."

I blew my nose loudly, and nodded. "I lost sight of them, that's all. I don't know how it happened."

"It happens easily," said Dan. "When you're wearing a facemask, you're like a blinkered horse, you can only see forwards. And in water like that, your buddies can disappear in a couple of seconds. It's *their* fault, too, they should have kept an eye on you. Maybe we should have used a buddy-line. I don't particularly like them, they can sometimes be more of a problem than they're worth, but maybe we'll consider it the next time down."

"Don't talk to me about the next time."

"There has to be a next time. If you don't go down again soon, you never will."

"It's not the diving I'm worried about," I said. "I think I can handle the diving. I panicked down there, and I'm not ashamed to admit it, but I think anybody would have lost their nerve if they'd discovered what I discovered."

"You found something?" asked Jimmy. "Something to do with the *David Dark?*"

"I only wish. I found a drowned woman. Not too badly decomposed. Her foot was caught in a fishing-net down there, and she was spinning around in the tide, standing up, like she was alive. Her gown got itself caught around my leg, and nearly drowned me."

"A drowned woman? Where is she now?"

"She sank again, right after I'd managed to cut her loose. But I guess the tide should bring her into the shore, now she's free of the fishing-net."

Dan Bass shaded his eyes against the sunlight, and looked around the boat, but there was nothing to be seen. He said, "I guess we'd better get Edward and Forrest back up here. They're still searching for you." He went to the stern of the boat, where there was an aluminum diving ladder, and banged on it five times with a wrench. That was the signal for Edward and Forrest to surface, a signal that would have carried well over a half-mile underwater.

"Let me take a fix on this position," said Dan Bass. "Just in case the police ask you exactly where the body was located when you found it." He went into the wheelhouse and took a compass bearing, and jotted it down in Gilly's notepad.

Gilly said to me, "What was she like, this woman? God, it must have been awful."

"It's difficult to say what she looked like. Everybody's hair looks the same color underwater, especially in water as thick as that. The fish had been at her, too. Fish aren't particularly fastidious. She still had a face, but I don't suppose even her best friend would have recognized it."

Gilly put her arm around my shoulders, and kissed my forehead. "You don't have any idea how glad I am that you're safe."

"The feeling, my love, is mutual."

She helped me down into the cabin just below the wheelhouse, where there were two narrow bunks, a table, and a tiny galley. She lay me down on one of the bunks, peeled off my wetsuit, and toweled me dry. Then she tucked me into the blankets, kissed me again, and said, "Get warm. Doctor McCormick's orders."

"I hear and I obey," I told her.

A few minutes later, the *Alexis* came about, and Dan Bass shut down the engine. I felt the boat rock and sway as Edward and Forrest clambered aboard, and I heard their wet flippers on the deck. Once he had stripped off his wetsuit, Edward came down into the cabin, and perched himself on the opposite bunk.

"Jesus," he said, breathing on his spectacles, and putting them on. He blinked at me with water-reddened eyes. "I can tell you, I really thought for a moment there that you were gone and lost forever."

Forrest peered into the cabin and called, "How're you feeling?"

"Fine, thanks," I said. "I forgot to keep my eyes on you, that was all."

"Well, I'm sorry, we made the same mistake," said Forrest. "It was unforgivable, and I'm real sorry. You know what they say about diving; the smallest error can escalate in seconds into total disaster, and I'm just glad that it didn't happen this time."

"It was damned close," I replied.

"Yes—Dan said something about a body. You found a body down there."

"That's right. A woman in a nightgown. Floating around like a mermaid. I must have set up some kind of a wave when I finned past her, because she came up after me as if she were alive."

"A woman in a *nightgown?*" asked Edward.

"That's right. She was too badly bloated for me to tell what she looked like; but she couldn't have been in the water all that long."

"Mrs. Goult," said Edward.

"Mrs. who?"

"I read about it in the *Granitehead Messenger*, round about the middle of last week. Mrs. James Goult disappeared from her home in Granitehead in the middle of the night, dressed in a nightgown, taking none of her clothes, but driving off in one of the family cars to Granitehead Harbor, and taking off in her husband's $200,000 yacht. Neither the yacht nor Mrs. Goult have been seen since."

"You think *that* was Mrs. Goult?" I asked him. "That body?"

"It might have been. From what you say, she couldn't have been down there more than a few days; and if she's wearing a nightgown . . ."

"It sure *sounds* like her," put in Forrest.

"There's something else," said Edward. "Mrs. Goult's husband said in the newspaper report that his wife had been upset for quite a while recently. She'd lost her mother from cancer, and apparently she and her mother were very close."

"How come you read all of this?" asked Forrest. He sniffed, and wiped his nose with the back of his hand.

"I used to work for the Goults when I was about fifteen, cleaning Mr. Goult's car. They were friends of my folks. My dad and Mr. Goult were both in real-estate, although Mr. Goult's into waterside condos these days. My dad thinks that waterside condos are immoral, prostituting the character of Salem and Granitehead. That's why they don't see too much of each other any more."

"Your dad thinks that waterside condos are *immoral*?" asked Gilly.

Edward took off his spectacles, and gave them another polish. He looked at Gilly seriously. "My dad lives in the past. He can't understand why they stopped building Federal-style houses, with cellars and shutters and wrought-iron railings."

"Edward," I said, "are you thinking what I think you're thinking?"

Edward glanced at Gilly, and then back at me. "I don't know. Maybe I'm just being tendentious again."

"I don't understand," said Gilly.

I nodded towards Edward. "What I think Edward's thinking is that Mrs. Goult may not have drowned in this particular location by accident. She may have sailed here on purpose, and drowned herself here either by accident or design, in order to be close to the wreck of the *David Dark*."

"That was roughly what was passing through my mind," Edward agreed.

"But why would she do that?" asked Gilly, perplexed.

"She'd lost her mother, remember. Maybe she'd been haunted by her mother, the same way—" Edward paused.

"It's all right, Edward," I told him. "Gilly knows all about Jane."

"Well, the same way you've been haunted by your late

wife, and the same way Mrs. Simons was haunted by her late husband. And maybe, just maybe, she felt like I do, that if she could get to the *source* of the hauntings, the catalyst for all these apparitions, she could lay her mother's spirit to rest.''

''You think she'd drown herself to do that?'' asked Forrest, with obvious incredulity.

''I don't know,'' Edward admitted. ''But the motivation to put dead people to rest is extraordinarily powerful in almost every society in the world. The Chinese burn paper money at funerals, so that the dead will be rich when they get to heaven. In New Guinea, they smear their corpses with mud and ashes to make it easier for the body to return to the soil out of which it originally came. And what do we carve on Christian headstones? 'Rest In Peace.' It's important, Forrest, for reasons we may not even begin to understand. It's *instinctive*. We know that once our loved ones are dead, they're going to be facing an experience totally unlike their life when they were alive, physically and conceptually, and somehow we have this urgent drive to protect them, to see them through it, to make sure that they're safe. Now, why do we feel this way? Logically, it's absurd. But maybe there was once a time when dead people were threatened more openly, when the burial rites were an important and well-understood safeguard against the dangers that dead people were going to have to come up against before they were able to rest for ever.''

Forrest grimaced, and rubbed the back of his neck in something that was very close to exasperation, but as an ethnologist he couldn't deny the fundamental truth of what Edward was saying.

Edward went on, ''It's my belief that there's something in the wreck of the *David Dark* that's been unsettling the usual natural process whereby dead souls are laid naturally to rest. I know you think I'm a fruitcake, but I can't help that. I've been over it again and again, and it's one feasible explanation. I'm not saying it's a *rational* explanation, but then what's been happening in Granitehead isn't rational anyway. In the case of Mrs. Goult, maybe she'd been visited by her dead mother; and maybe she felt that if she could somehow get close to the *David Dark*, she could release her mother's spirit.''

"Do you think it's likely that she even knew about the *David Dark*?" asked Jimmy.

"I don't think so," said Edward. "It's more likely that she just felt drawn here by whatever influences this wreck has been giving out."

Gilly ran her hand through her hair. "We're sailing perilously close to Utter Hogwash here," she said, tiredly.

"No," said Edward. "You're looking at the whole thing with modern eyes, with eyes that have been educated to believe only the rational and the non-magical. When you see David Copperfield on television, you don't believe for one second that any of the tricks he does is actual *magic*, do you? But in the days when the *David Dark* was sunk in these waters, in the days when Salem was right in the middle of all of its witch-trial frenzy, people believed in magic, and they believed in the devil, and they believed in God, and who are you to say that they were wrong? Particularly when you have John's testimony that he has actually been haunted by his dead wife; that he's actually seen her, and heard her, and talked to her."

Forrest and Jimmy evidently hadn't been told about this, because they exchanged glances of surprise and disbelief.

Edward said, "John's diving trouble today may have been a blessing in disguise. If Mrs. Goult drowned herself close to the *David Dark*, then she could have pinpointed a wreck that it might have taken us years to locate, if we ever located it at all. You took the bearings, Dan?"

"Sure," said Dan.

"In that case, we'll carry on diving for the rest of the afternoon, as near to the spot where you came across the body as we can. Dan, Jimmy, you take first search."

"What about me?" I asked.

Edward shook his head. "You've done enough for one day. It was pretty rash of us to let you go down at all. A few weeks' pool training, that's what you need, before you're out in the open water again."

"And what about the body?" asked Gilly. "Aren't you going to tell the Coastguard?"

"We'll report it when we get in," said Edward. "There's not much we can do for Mrs. Goult right now."

EIGHTEEN

During the afternoon, the wind rose again, and the weather steadily worsened, until at three o'clock, with heavy showers spattering against the wheelhouse windows, and the waves beginning to dance, Dan Bass called Edward and Jimmy up from the bottom, and told them to call it a day.

They had searched the area beneath us intensively and systematically, but found nothing, not even a scour-pit which might have told them that a wreck was lying beneath the mud. Dan had told me that any obstruction to the normal tidal stream causes the water to speed up as it flows around it, and that the whirls and eddies which this speeding-up creates leave a natural excavation in the ocean floor. Because of this tidal scouring, even a wreck which has been completely buried by mud leaves an unmistakable trace of its presence: a ghostly image in the ooze.

But today, there was nothing. Only the sloping mud-bank which gradually and smoothly descended into the deeper roads of Salem Harbor. Only fishing-tackle, and nets, and rusted automobiles, and dinghies that had fallen apart into firewood.

Edward came up on deck and peeled off his wetsuit. His lips were blue against his beard, and he was shivering with cold.

"No luck?" I asked him.

He shook his head. "Not a thing. But we can come out again tomorrow. We still have all of this eastern vector to cover."

Forrest, who had given up diving about an hour before, and

152

now sat in the wheelhouse in a polo-neck sweater and jeans, said, "I don't think we're making any progress at all, Edward. I think it's time we did some echo-soundings."

"Echo-soundings aren't going to tell us anything unless we have a rough idea where the wreck is located," said Edward. "Apart from the fact that we can barely afford to rent the equipment, especially if it takes us six or seven months to get any results."

"I could help financially," I told him. "A couple of hundred dollars, if that's any use to you."

"Well, it's a generous thought," said Edward. "But the problem is one of time, more than anything else. We can only dive on weekends, and at this rate it could take us forever to find the *David Dark*. We've been at it for over a year already."

"Is there no record at all of where she might have gone down?"

"You know what happened. Esau Hasket made sure that every single mention of the *David Dark* was cut out of the record books."

"How about the Evelith library? Do you think there might be something in there?"

"The *Evelith* library? You have to be joking. Are you joking?"

"Of course I'm not joking."

"Well, let me tell you something about old man Duglass Evelith. He must be about 80 years old now. I've only seen him once, and these days he never comes out of that house of his. What's more, he won't let anybody else in. He lives with a Narragansett Indian servant, and a girl who may or may not be his granddaughter. They have all their groceries delivered, and left at the lodge at the end of the driveway. It drives me crazy to think of all the incredible historical material that one old man is sitting on, but what can I do about it?"

"You sound like you've tried to get in there," I said.

"Have I tried! I've written, telephoned, and visited up there five or six times. Each time: a polite refusal. Mr. Evelith regrets that his library is private, and not open to inspection."

The *Alexis* was puttering back towards Salem Harbor now, her diving-flag struck and packed away, her stern rising and falling as the tide surged in. Dan was singing a sea-song about *Sally Free And Easy*, who "took a sailor's loving . . . for a nursery game."

I said to Edward, "Maybe you've been approaching Evelith the wrong way. Maybe you should *offer* him something, instead of asking for something."

"What could I possibly offer a man like Evelith?"

"He's a collector, isn't he? Perhaps you could offer him an antique. I've got a portable writing-case in the shop that was supposed to have belonged to one of the members of the jury during the witchcraft trials, Henry Herrick. It's engraved with the initials HH, anyway."

"I think you may have a good point there," put in Jimmy. "It's worth a try, anyway. People like Evelith hide themselves away because they think that everybody wants to lay their hands on their stuff. Look at the way he sells his pictures . . . anonymously, in case anybody finds out where they came from."

Edward seemed a little put out that *he* hadn't thought of tempting old man Evelith with a bribe. But he said, as graciously as he could manage, "Let's go up there this afternoon, shall we? It's only a half-hour's drive. Maybe it *is* a good idea."

"I'm too tired to make it today," I told him. "Besides, I have my parents-in-law coming over to the cottage. How about tomorrow morning, about ten?"

Edward shrugged. "Okay by me. How about you, Gilly? You want to come?" He wouldn't normally have asked her, but I sensed that he was trying to find out just what it was between us, if anything. Gilly looked across at me with a direct expression on her face, and said, "No thanks. I have to work in the shop tomorrow. It's like that for us independent business ladies, you know. Can't relax for a minute."

"Suit yourself," said Edward.

We reached the harbor and tied up. As we stowed the diving gear away in the back of Dan Bass' station wagon, Forrest came over and clapped a friendly hand on my shoulder. "You did well, this morning, for a first dive. If you want to put in some training, come on up to the Sub-Aqua Club Monday evening. When we *find* that son-of-a-bitch, you'll want to be down there to see it."

"We'd better go tell the police and the Coastguard about Mrs. Goult," I reminded him.

"Dan will do that. They know him over at police head-quarters. The diving club is always coming up with suicidal mothers and drowned babies and unwanted dogs in sacks full of rocks."

"Seems like the sea conceals a multitude of sins," I remarked.

"You betcha," said Forrest, and he was serious.

Gilly came over to my car as I was about to leave. She leaned in at the open window, her hair blown about in the breeze, and said, "You're really going back to the cottage tonight?"

"I have to."

She looked at me without saying anything, then raised her face against the wind. "I wish you wouldn't," she said.

"I wish I didn't have to. But there's no point in running away from it. I have to face up to what's going on, and I have to find some way of sorting it out. I'm not going through another night like last night. Sooner or later, one or the other of us, or *both* of us, are going to get hurt. I haven't forgotten what happened to poor old Mrs. Edgar Simons. I don't want anything like that happening to you. Or to me, for that matter."

"Well," she said, with a sad and philosophical smile, "that was a whirlwind romance that whirled itself in and whirled itself out again."

"I hope you don't think that it's over," I told her.

"It isn't, not as far as I'm concerned. Not unless you want it to be."

I held out my hand, and Gilly took it, and squeezed it.

"Can I call you later?" I asked her.

She nodded, and said, "I'd like that," and caressed me with her eyes.

As I drove off, I glanced in my rear-view mirror and saw her standing there on the dock, her hands in the pockets of her parka. She hadn't made me forget Jane. I don't think any girl could have done that. But for the first time since Jane had died, I felt alive again, and that the world might be worth living in, after all. I thought how strange it was that human optimism is rarely invested in hoped-for events, or the fateful course of future history; but rather in other people, each of them as uncertain and confused as we are. There is no stronger courage than the courage of knowing that someone loves you, and that you are not alone.

I drove back to Quaker Lane. At the bottom of the hill, fixing his fence, I saw George Markham, and I pulled the Toronado to a halt and climbed out.

"How are you doing, George?" I asked him.

He stood up, wiping his creosote-stained hands on his Oshkosh overalls. "I heard they dropped the charges against you," he said. He was trying to be direct, but I could tell that he was embarrassed.

"Insufficient evidence," I told him. "Besides which, I didn't do it."

"Well, nobody said you did," said George, hastily.

"Nobody said that I didn't. But somebody said that I was rambling that evening, and not myself."

"You *wasn't* yourself. You have to be fair about that."

I thrust my hands into my pants pockets and looked at him with a grin. "You're right, George. I wasn't myself. But then who would have been, if they'd seen what I'd seen?"

George looked at me narrowly, one eye half-closed, as if he were trying to weigh me up. "You really did see Jane, swinging on the swing?"

"Yes," I said. "And I've seen her again since."

He was silent for a long time, thinking. It was cold out there, in the front garden, and he wiped his nose with his hand. I stayed where I was, hands in my pockets, watching him.

At last he said, "Keith Reed didn't believe you. But then Keith don't like to believe anybody too much when it comes to hauntings."

"Do *you* believe me?"

George, ashamed, nodded.

"You've seen a ghost for yourself, haven't you?" I asked him. I wasn't sure that he had, not at all, but there was something about the way he was looking at me, something scared and uncertain and deeply impressionable, something that told me: this man has seen an apparition with his own eyes.

"I, uh . . . heard my brother Wilf," he said, in a throat-dry voice.

"Did you see him, as well as hear him?"

George lowered his head and looked down at the ground.

Then he raised his head again, and said, "Come on inside. Let me show you something."

I followed him into the house. As I closed the door behind me, the first collision of thunder sounded in the distance, out to sea, and the wind suddenly rose, and banged George's garden gate. George led me into the living-room, and went across to a dark-oak bureau next to the fireplace, which he opened up and rummaged around inside. At last he produced a framed photograph, quite a large one, which he solemnly handed to me, as if he were presenting me with an honorary degree.

I examined the photograph carefully, even turning the frame around and looking at the back of it. It was a black-and-white picture of a highway, somewhere local by the look of it, with trees in the background, and a parked car a little way off by the side of the road. That was all. One of the dullest photographs I think I had ever seen.

"Well?" I asked George. "I don't quite know what I'm supposed to be looking for."

George took off his spectacles and folded them. "You're supposed to be looking for my brother," he said, pointing to the picture.

I peered more closely. "I don't see him. I don't see anyone."

"That's the point," said George. "This used to be a photograph of my brother, standing right in the front. Then, two or three weeks ago, I saw that he'd moved back a ways, no more than six or eight feet, but back. I didn't credit it at first, thought I was making a mistake, but the next week he moved even further back, and last week he disappeared back down the highway altogether. That's why I took the picture down from the shelf. My brother's *gone* from that picture, and that's all there is to it. I don't know how, or why, but he's gone."

I handed the photograph back. "The same thing's been happening to my pictures of Jane," I told him. "They've been moving, and changing. Nearly the same, but not quite."

"What do you think it is?" asked George. He grasped my arm anxiously, and looked at me right in the face. "Do you think it's witchcraft?"

"Of a kind," I said. "It's very hard to tell. But some of the people from the Peabody Museum are looking into it.

They may find a way of putting your brother to rest. Jane, too. And all the other spirits that have been haunting Granitehead. At least, I hope they will.''

George put his spectacles back on again. "I heard Wilf crying," he said, staring sadly at the empty highway in the photograph. "Night after night, in the spare room upstairs, I heard him crying. There was nobody there, nobody that I could see, anyway. But this sobbing and weeping went on and on, like a man in terrible despair. I can't tell you how much that affected me, John.''

I gripped his shoulder as reassuringly as I could. "Try not to let it worry you, George. It may sound like Wilf's unhappy, but maybe he's not. Maybe you're only hearing the most stressful side of what he feels like, now that he's dead. It's possible that people's personalities divide up, when they die, and that somewhere there's a happy Wilf, as well as a sad one.''

George shrugged. "I don't really believe that, John. But thanks for the thought.''

"I don't know what else to tell you," I said. "I don't know anything about it myself, except that these people from the Peabody think that they may have guessed the cause of all these hauntings.''

"What is it? Radiation, something like that?''

"Not exactly. But listen, when I know some more, I'll come down and let you know. I promise. Especially if you give me that game of stud you promised.''

We shook hands, although I wasn't quite sure why. Then I left George to fix up his fence, got back in my car, and drove up the uneven roadway to Quaker Lane Cottage.

I had been dreading coming back to the cottage ever since I drove away from the dock at Salem. I had dawdled along West Shore Drive at less than twenty miles an hour, much to the annoyance of a truck driver behind me. But here it was at last, at the top of the hill, looking gray and old and peculiarly squalid under the threatening sky. I made up my mind as I turned around and parked in front of it that this was going to be the last night I was going to sleep here. The cottage seemed so cold and hostile that there wasn't any reason for me to stay.

I climbed out of the car and approached the cottage with a terrible sense of foreboding. A stray shutter clapped at an upstairs window: the hook had been pulled free from the outside wall during the high winds of the past few days, and unless I wanted it to bang all night, I was going to have to go up on a ladder and fix it. I opened the front door, and went into the house, and it was just the same as when I had left it. Chilly, stale-smelling, without warmth or atmosphere or any sense of contentment.

The first task was to light the living-room fire. When that was blazing, I poured myself a drink, and walked into the kitchen, still wearing my raincoat, to see what I could make myself for supper. There was Salisbury steak; or chicken-in-gravy; or hot tamales in a can. I didn't feel like any of those. What I really had a hankering for was one of Jane's chili-con-carnes, fiery with pepper and thick with beans. I felt very sad for her then, and sad for myself. The flickering apparition of her which had been haunting me these past three nights had half-distorted my real loving memory of her, and when I thought of her now I couldn't help picturing that horrified electrical face.

"Jane," I whispered to myself; maybe a little bit to her, too. Dante had written "*nessun maggior dolore che ricordarsi del tempo felice nella miseria*"—there isn't any greater sorrow than to remember a time of happiness when you're in misery. My old boss at MidWestern Chemical Bonding had taught me that one.

"*John*," a voice whispered back.

She was there, in the cottage. I knew she was there. In the wind that sighed down the chimneys, in the beams and the woodwork and the lath-and-plaster walls. There was no way of exorcising her, because she had *become* the cottage, and in an extraordinary way she had become me, too. I knew intuitively that however far I traveled; even if I went back to St. Louis, or across to the West Coast; Jane would always be there, whispering, cajoling me to make love to her, drawing me deeper and deeper into the half-world of electrical purgatory, and making it impossible for me to continue to lead my life. I had loved her when she died, but if she kept on haunting me I knew that I would end up hating her. Perhaps that was what had happened to Mrs. Edgar Simons. She had refused to submit to her dead husband's demands, and he had killed her. How long would it take before that happened to me?

It seemed to me that the dead were jealously possessive of

the living. Charlie Manzi's marriage had been ruined by the ghostly appearance of his dead son. George Markham was growing increasingly anxious about his brother. My relationship with Gilly was in suspense until I could lay Jane's spirit to rest. And God knows how many other bereaved people in Granitehead and Salem were finding that the overwhelming demands of their dead loved ones were making it impossible for them to give affection and attention to the living.

The other night I had wondered whether I would meet Jane again if I were to die. What had she whispered to me, as I struggled under the water this morning? "Don't leave me," as if she wanted *me* to die, too, so that we could be together again. I wondered if the same thing had happened to Mrs. Goult. Had she been called by her recently-dead mother? Had she felt that the only way in which she could possibly be happy was to commit suicide, and join her mother in that flickering, restless world of ghosts?

Perhaps I was being too dramatic, like Edward. But I began to believe that all of these hauntings had the same purpose: to alienate the people whom the dead had loved from the real and physical world, to encourage them to believe that death would be their only chance of contentment and happiness. It was as if the dead were trying to exorcize the living, instead of the other way around. And whether it had anything to do with the *David Dark* or not, I believed then that Edward was right, and that some powerful and malevolent influence was at work.

I finished my drink and walked back into the living-room to pour myself another. The long-case clock in the hallway whirred, and then struck six. It was later than I had thought: time seemed to have jumped, the way it sometimes does after four p.m. The fire was crackling and popping, and I stacked on another couple of logs.

It was then that I glanced across at the painting of the *David Dark*, which Edward had left propped up against the side of my armchair. It was different, somehow; I couldn't immediately understand why. I picked it up, and examined it under the lamplight. It appeared to be gloomier, in a way, as if the sun had gone in. And I was sure that when I had first looked at it, there hadn't been such a menacing build-up of clouds on the right-hand side of the picture.

Perhaps this painting was like spiritual litmus. When dangerous events were in the air, it darkened, and grew more threatening. Even the painted waves seemed to be rougher, and the painted trees were bending in an unseen wind.

I put the picture down again. I was beginning to think that tonight was going to prove to be something of a showdown: a frightening confrontation between me and the Bedfords and the ghosts of Granitehead. A squall of rain lashed against the leaded window, as if in temper, and I stood where I was, chilled in spite of the fire, and wished to God that I knew how to bring this grotesque and terrifying dream to an end.

NINETEEN

I was praying all evening that the Bedfords wouldn't come, but a few minutes after the half-past eleven chimes had struck, I heard the crunching of tires on the lane outside, and when I went to open the front door, there they were, in their shiny gray limousine, bouncing to an expensive stop behind my used-looking Toronado.

I hooked my golf unbrella out of the forged-iron stand in the hallway, and took it out to the front gate, so that Mrs. Bedford wouldn't get showered on. She was wearing a dark mink jacket and her hair must have been waved that afternoon, for it swept up from her forehead in a blue-gray wing, and her little black hat was perched on top of it precariously. She presented her right cheek to be kissed, and when I duly did so, I smelled her heavy Italian perfume.

Constance Bedford was a handsome woman, there was no question about that. But she could also be suspicious and snobbish and tiresome, and all those characteristics showed in her narrow eyes, and the dragged-down wrinkles at the corners of her mouth. I looked over her shoulder at Walter Bedford, and I could tell by the tight, tense look on his face that he had warned Constance to be on her best behavior. He wanted desperately to see Jane, and he knew that the price of that was for Constance at least to be cordial.

"I see you haven't done very much to the cottage recently," said Constance, as she stepped into the hallway and looked around. She twitched her nose a little, as if she didn't approve of the smell.

"I've been busy," I told her. "Can I take your jacket?"

"I believe I'll keep it on for the moment, thank you. It's not exactly climate-controlled in here, is it?"

"Jane always liked a log fire," I replied.

"*I* like a log fire," put in Walter, trying to keep the party sociable. "A log fire, and a glass of punch. Nothing like it, in the winter. It's the most romantic thing you can think of."

"When was the last time that *we* sat in front of a log fire with a glass of punch?" Constance asked him, sharply. She turned back to me, and pulled a face that showed that even if Walter were actually to offer, she wouldn't be seen *dead* in front of a log fire with a glass of punch. "Walter's idea of romance is halfway between a second-rate ski-lodge in Aspen and the center-spread of the Christmas issue of *Playboy*," she said, stalking ahead of us into the living-room.

"Well," she sniffed. "You haven't done very much in here, either."

Walter said to me, *sotto voce*, "Let her settle down, John. Give her time. She's very up in the air about this; very emotional."

"Do you want a drink?" I asked him, as if he hadn't said anything at all.

"Is that Chivas Regal you're drinking?" he asked. "Sure. I'll have one of those, with a little water."

"Constance," I said, "would you care for a glass of wine?"

"Thank you, but I don't drink before six or after eleven."

After I had fixed Walter's whiskey, we all sat down around the fire and looked at each other. The rain sprinkled against the windows again, and upstairs I could hear that loose shutter banging. Constance tugged down the hem of her dress, and said impatiently, "Aren't we supposed to do something? Like hold hands, or close our eyes, and think of Jane?"

"This isn't a séance, Constance," I said. "In a séance, you call the spirits and with any luck they answer. If Jane's going to appear here tonight, she's going to do it whether we want her to or not."

"But don't you think she's more likely to appear if she knows her mother is here?" asked Constance, earnestly.

I looked at Walter. I could have said that I didn't believe for one moment that Constance's presence was going to make the slightest difference. But the truth isn't always necessary;

and the last thing I wanted was an argument. I was very tired after my aqualung diving experience, and all I really wanted to do was go to bed, and sleep.

"I expect that your being here will increase our chances of seeing Jane quite a lot," I said to Constance, and smiled benignly.

"A girl always goes to her mother in times of trouble," said Constance. "She may have been a father's girl when she was little, but whenever it came to anything serious . . . she always came to me."

I nodded, and kept on smiling.

Walter checked his watch. "Almost midnight," he said. "Do you think she'll appear?"

"I don't know, Walter. I don't have any control over it at all. I don't even know why she appears, or what she wants."

"Does she look *well*?" asked Constance.

I stared at her. "Constance, she's dead. How can she look well, when she's dead?"

"I don't have to be reminded that my daughter's been taken away from me," Constance retorted. "I don't have to be reminded how it happened, either."

"Good. Because that was the last thing I was going to talk about."

"Oh," said Constance. "I suppose you accept no responsibility at all."

"What particular responsibility do you *want* me to accept?" I asked her.

"Come on, now," put in Walter. "Let's not start digging over old graves." He was immediately sorry that he had chosen that particular metaphor, and sat back in his chair, and blushed.

"Jane was pregnant," insisted Constance. "And the whole idea of allowing a pregnant woman to drive all that way in a snowstorm . . . all alone, unprotected, while *you* sat at home and watched some juvenile football game . . . As far as I'm concerned, it amounts to criminal negligence. Manslaughter."

"Constance," said Walter, "forget the recriminations, will you? It's over and done with."

"He murdered them, or as good as," said Constance. "And I'm not supposed to feel bitter about it? My only daughter; my only remaining child. My only chance of a grandson. All wiped out, because of a football game, and a husband who was too lazy and too careless to look after the people who were under his care.''

"Constance," I said, "get out of my house. Walter, take her home.''

"What?" said Walter, as if he hadn't quite heard me.

"I said take Constance home. And don't bother to bring her back. Ever. She's been here five minutes and already she's started. When is she going to realize that there *was* no snowstorm when Jane went out to see you; that if anybody's at fault it's you for letting her drive home when the weather was so bad. And when is she ever going to realize that I lost far more than either of you did. I lost my wife, the girl who was going to be my companion for the rest of my life; and I lost my son. So goodnight, okay? I'm sorry you had a wasted journey, but I'm not going to sit here and listen to Constance slandering me, and that's all.''

"Listen," said Walter, "we're just on edge, that's all.''

"Walter, I am not on edge," I told him. "I just want Constance out of here before I do something irresistible, like pushing her teeth down her throat!''

"How dare you speak about me like that!" snapped Constance, and stood up. Walter stood up too, and then half sat down, and then stood up again. "Constance," he appealed to her, but Constance was too irritated and too tense to be mollified by anything, or anybody.

"Even her *spirit* isn't safe in your custody!" she snapped at me, wagging her long-clawed finger. "Even when she's *dead*, you can't take care of her!''

She stalked to the door. Walter turned to me, and gave me a resigned look which, if I knew anything about Walter, meant partly that he blamed Constance for being so volatile, and partly that he blamed me for setting her off again.

I didn't even bother to get out of my chair. I might have guessed the evening was going to develop into another row. I reached for the Chivas Regal bottle and refilled my glass, almost up to the top. "I drink," I said to myself, in my best barfly slur, "to forget.''

"What do you want to forget?" I asked myself.

"I forget," I slurred.

It was then that I heard a furious rattling at the front door; and Walter came back into the living-room again. "I'm sorry," he said. "The front door's jammed. I can't open it.''

"Don't apologize, Walter, just tell him to open the door!" Constance demanded.

Wearily, I got up, and walked into the hallway. Constance was standing there with her hands planted furiously on her hips, but the first thing I noticed wasn't Constance. It was the cold. The strange, sudden cold. "Walter," I said, "it's colder."

"Colder?" he frowned.

"Can't you feel it? The temperature's dropping."

"Will you please open this door," barked Constance. But I raised my hand to silence her.

"Listen, do you hear something?"

"What's he *talking* about, Walter? For God's sake, make him open the door. I'm upset and I want to go home. I don't want to stay in this horrible dilapidated cottage a moment longer."

Walter said, softly, "I hear whispering."

I nodded. "That's what I hear. Where would you say it's coming from?"

"Upstairs, maybe," said Walter. His eyes were bright now, and he had completely forgotten about Constance. "Is this what happens? Is this the way it starts?"

"Yes," I told him. "Whispering, cold, and then the apparitions."

"If you don't open this front door at *once*, you son-of-a-bitch," screeched Constance, "then by God I'm going to—"

"Constance, shut your mouth!" roared Walter.

Constance stared at him with her mouth wide open. I don't suppose he'd dared to speak to her like that more than once in 35 years of marriage. I looked at her and gave her a sour little smile which meant that she had better keep it shut, too, if she knew what was good for her. She said, "Oh," in utter frustration, and then "Oh!"

The whispering grew no louder, but seemed to circle around us so that sometimes the voices seemed to be coming from upstairs, and sometimes from the library, and sometimes they sounded as if they were right behind us, only a few paces away. All of us strained to make out the words, but it was useless: it was a long, persistent, discursive conversation, in what language we couldn't make out. And yet there was something unmistakably obscene about it; a feeling that the whisperers were relishing some filthy sexual act, or some unspeakably sadistic torture, and discussing it in relentless detail.

The temperature kept on dropping, too, until our breath was visible. Constance tugged her mink jacket around herself, and stared at me as if this was all some kind of barbaric hoax. I don't think that Walter had done what I had told him to do, and warned her what it was going to be like; that it could be frightening, and unpleasant, and even potentially dangerous. Constance had probably walked through the door with the expectation that Jane would be sitting in front of the fire in the pink and natural flesh, knitting baby-bootees, no more harmed by death than if she had spent a month in Miami.

"Who is that *whispering*?" she said, with her eyes wide. "Is that *you*?"

"How can it be me? Do you see my lips moving?"

The whispering went on. Constance came closer, and stared at me even harder. Behind her, the front door had silently opened itself. I reached over and touched Walter's arm, but he had seen the door already, and he said softly, "I know. I know, John. The handle turned by itself."

The door smoothly swung open, without its familiar squeaking noise. We were looking out now into the front garden, into the dark and blustery night. And there, halfway along the garden path, much smaller than she had appeared in my bedroom, only the height of an eleven-year-old child, stood Jane.

"Constance," said Walter gently. "She's here."

Constance turned, slowly, hypnotically, and stared out into the garden. She said nothing at all, but I could tell by the shaking of her shoulders that she was sobbing, and trying to suppress her sobs.

"I didn't realize," she wept, her mouth twisted into a snarl of grief. "Oh my God, Walter, I didn't understand."

Jane appeared to be floating a few inches above the path; a flickering image of her that faded and sparkled in the wind. Her arms were straight down by her sides, her face was hollow-eyed and expressionless, but her hair floated around her head like a electrostatic crown.

"*John*," she whispered. "*John, don't leave me.*"

Constance took two or three uncontrolled steps towards her, lifting one arm. "Jane, it's your mother," she appealed.

"Jane, listen to me, wherever you are, darling, it's your mother."

"*Don't leave me, John,*" Jane begged me.

Constance must have been terrified, but she approached the apparition even more closely, her hands raised like a plump madonna. "Jane, I want to help you," she said. "I'll do anything to help you. Speak to me, Jane, please. Tell me you can see me. Tell me you know that I'm here. Jane, I love you. Please, Jane. Please, I'm pleading with you."

"Constance," warned Walter. "Constance, come back here."

Jane's image shifted and altered, both in size and appearance. She appeared taller now, and her face was different, thinner-cheeked, gaunt, like a starving angel. She raised one arm to shoulder height, leaving in the air for a moment a succession of after-images, so that it looked as if she had five arms instead of one.

"*John,*" she whispered, more affirmatively now. "*You mustn't leave me, John. You mustn't leave me, not here.*"

Constance was down on her knees on the garden path in front of her spectral daughter. Walter choked, "No, Constance!" and shouldered his way past me to bring her back; but just as he did so, Jane turned her head and stared down at her mother with those black and empty eyes.

"Jane, don't you *know* me?" Constance wailed. "Jane, it's your mother! You're all I have left, Jane, don't leave me! Come back to me, Jane! I need you!"

Walter seized Constance's shoulders, and cried, "Constance, don't! This is madness! She's dead, Constance, she *can't* come back!"

Constance turned and struck out at Walter with a flailing arm. "You never cared about her the way I did, did you?" she screamed. "You never cared anything about our children! You never cared about *me*, either! You don't want her back because you're guilty, that's why; just as guilty as John; and because you're afraid."

"Constance, this is a ghost!" shouted Walter.

"He's right, Constance," I told her. "You'd be safer if you kept away."

Jane's blue-white electrical image hovered and flickered, and seemed to grow even taller, until it was taller than Walter. But it never once turned its eyes away from Constance,

as she groveled at its feet on the garden path. Walter stared
up at it in abject dread, and took one or two paces back. He
turned around to me, his face gray with fright, and mutely
appealed to me to do something. *Anything.* He hadn't understood what it was going to be like, either, and now he was
scared out of his mind.

"Jane!" screamed Constance. "Jane!"

And it was then that Jane's death-pale lips curled slowly
back over incandescent teeth, and her mouth stretched wider
and wider until she was as hideous and as horrifying as a
stone gargoyle. Her hair flew up behind her head, and she
raised her other arm so that she was standing as if crucified.
Then she rose slowly into the air until she was floating over
Constance horizontally, her bare feet close together, her white
funeral vestments flapping silently in the midnight wind.

Constance stretched back and screamed and screamed, in
utter hysteria. Walter cried, "Constance! For God's sake!"
and tried to grab her again; but Jane's stretched-apart mouth
suddenly let out a hollow roar that made him stumble back
towards the house in mute terror. It was a roar like nothing I
had ever heard before: the roar of coldly-blazing furnaces, the
roar of enraged demons, the roar of the North Atlantic Ocean,
in a catastrophic storm.

Out of Jane's mouth gushed a fuming stream of freezing
vapor, straight into Constance's face. I could feel how cold it
was, even from ten feet away by the door. Constance cried
out in agony, and collapsed on the path, and as Walter
hurried towards her again, Jane's apparition tumbled slowly
head-over-heels through the night air, over the garden hedge,
and across Quaker Lane, uphill, in the direction of the shore.
Arms stretched wide, a quivering crucifix of blue-white light,
over and over, singing as she went.

"O the men they sailed from Granitehead
To fish the foreign shores . . ."

I knelt down beside Walter and Constance. Constance had
buried her face in her hands, and she was twitching and shuddering. "My eyes," she whimpered. "Oh God, Walter, my
eyes!"

I helped Walter carry her inside the house, and lay her
down on the sofa by the living-room fire. She kept her hands

pressed against her eyes, and shook, and moaned, and I was worried that she might have been severely shocked. She wasn't a young woman any more, and she had a history of heart trouble. "Call an ambulance," I told Walter. "And whatever you do, try to keep her warm."

"Where are you going?" Walter wanted to know.

"I'm going after Jane. I've got to end this, Walter, once and for all."

"What the hell do you think you can possibly do? That's a supernatural being there, John. That's a *ghost*, for Christ's sake. What can you possibly do against a ghost?"

"I don't know. But if I don't go after her, I'll never find out."

"Well, take care. Please. And don't be too long."

I ran back out into the windy night. All around me, the telephone wires were droning, and the trees were whistling, as if everything had come mysteriously alive, and was warning me in chorus. Upstairs, at the cottage window, the loose shutter clapped frantically.

Tugging up my collar, I began to run up Quaker Lane until I ran out of road and found myself jogging across tufted sea-grass. There was no sign of Jane, but the last time I had seen her she had been tumbling through the air in the direction of Waterside Cemetery, where she had been buried, and it seemed reasonable, if frightening, to assume that her ghost had actually come from there.

It was a good three-quarters of a mile to the cemetery gates, and I had to stop jogging after the first few hundred yards, and walk, trying to catch my breath. On my right, in the darkness, I could just distinguish the white breakers of the Salem Harbor shoreline. Somewhere out there, beneath the black and chilly waters, buried in the mud of three hundred years, lay the wreck of the *David Dark*. The sound of the sea was infinitely lonely and alien. Jane had said that it always made her think of the moon, cold and uncompromising. The sea, after all, is the moon's mistress.

Through the night, I glimpsed the white arch of the cemetery gates. Beyond it, as I started to jog again, the headstones appeared, spires and crosses and plaques; frozen cherubs and saddened seraphim. A small city of Granitehead's dead, isolated out on the shoreline. I reached the black-painted wrought-iron gates, and clutched them, peering as hard as I could into the rows of graves, looking slightly to the left, to the place where Jane was buried.

"I saw pale kings and princes too; pale warriors, death-pale were they all."

There was no flickering light, no sign of Jane's manifestation. I turned the knob of the gates, and opened them up, and stepped inside.

Whatever clichés are written about cemeteries at night, there was no question that Granitehead's graveyard that gusty night in March had an unsettling atmosphere all its own. Every headstone seemed to possess an unearthly gleam, and as I walked towards Jane's grave between the silent ranks of tombs, I was frighteningly conscious that I was walking amongst scores of people; people who were dead, and would now be quiet forever, eyes closed or eyeless, robed or in tatters, all lying beneath the blackness of the soil. This was not ordinary ground: this was an enclave of buried memories, a noiseless community of lived-out lives, an acre of human beings who would never speak again.

I approached Jane's headstone, and stood beside it, shivering and uncertain. Jane Elizabeth Trenton, Beloved Wife of John Paul Trenton, Daughter of Mr. and Mrs. Walter K. Bedford. "Point me out the way to any one particular beauteous star."

Now I had come here, I didn't know what to do. Should I talk to her? Call her? Should I wait for her to appear? I looked around, and saw the pale marble sentinels of all the other headstones standing close, and felt hemmed-in, and breathless, in spite of the wind. A marble angel watched me from two rows away, staring with sightless eyeballs.

I swallowed, and then I said unsteadily, "Jane? Can you hear me, Jane?"

It was ridiculous, of course, and I found myself seriously hoping that there wasn't anybody else in the cemetery who could hear me. I know people *do* talk to their lost relatives, but they don't often do it in the middle of the night; and they very rarely expect an answer, like I did.

"Jane?" I said again. "Jane, can you hear me?"

There was no response. Nothing at all but the wind, rustling in the long grass outside the cemetery fence. I stayed where I was for a minute or so, shivering with cold, half-hoping that Jane would appear to me and half-hoping that she wouldn't; and then I turned to leave.

And then I said, "Oh, Christ."

She was standing behind me, no more than two or three feet away, a few inches above the ground. She was her normal height, but she seemed to have become desperately thin and emaciated, as if there were nothing beneath that wind-flapped gown but skin and bones. Her expression was empty and remote, her eyes too dark to read. I couldn't actually see through her, she wasn't spectral in that sense, but she was somehow melting and moving and *insubstantial.* I felt that if I should try to snatch at her, I would end up with nothing more than a handful of cobwebs.

"*You came,*" she said, in a voice which sounded like four Janes speaking at once. "*I knew, in the end, you would come.*"

"What do you want?" I asked her.

"*I want you to make love to me,*" she whispered. "*I want you to make love to me forever.*"

"Jane, you're dead."

"*No, John, not dead.*"

"Then *what*, if you're not dead? And what do you *want*?"

"*I belong now to the others. Join me, John. Come with me. Don't leave me here alone.*"

I held out my hand towards her, very gingerly. "Jane, it's impossible. You're dead, you should rest. I can't stand any more of this, Jane; it frightens me."

"*Did you* want *me to die*?" she whispered.

"Of course not. I miss you. I miss you like hell."

"*But I'm here, John. You can have me. We can be lovers again.*"

"Jane, you're dead, you're not real. Don't you understand that?"

"*Real*?" she asked. "*What is real*?"

And as she spoke, she turned, and raised her right arm.

"*I will show you what is real,*" she said.

"What are you talking about?" I said.

I heard a sound like singing, only it wasn't singing. It was more like the keening of mourners at a funeral, or the high unearthly ululation of native women in the Sudan; one of those weird intense ultra-violet sounds which can make your skin crawl. It was coming from everywhere: out of the sky, out of the ground, sometimes setting up an almost unbearable vibration.

I looked around the cemetery, and to my complete horror,

other apparitions were rising out of the graves. Their heads appeared first, blindeyed, growing out of the ground like grotesque pumpkins. Then their shoulders, and the rest of their bodies, rising up and up until they were hovering like Jane above the windblown grass.

There were hundreds of them, men and women and children, each of them flickering dully in the darkness of the night, the faint electrical charge of lives gone by. And as more of them appeared, so the keening they were making grew louder, until the cemetery was echoing with it.

Jane whispered, somewhere inside of my head, *"This is real. This is real, John, come and see."*

I walked stiffly along one of the aisles of gravestones. The apparitions remained motionless, hovering, staring back at me out of eyes that were like holes in a ragged curtain. Some of the apparitions were badly-decayed. A woman stood with no flesh on her skull at all, just bare shining bone and a few tufts of hair. One man's ribcage was revealed, and inside it wriggled heaps of glowing maggots. There was a teenage boy with no lower jaw, just a puffy and ulcerous tongue hanging down from his open throat like a scarf. Hundreds of them, the dead of Granitehead, some almost perfect, untouched, hardly looking as if they had died at all. Others in ruins, smashed and rotted and barely recognizable as human beings.

I walked all around the perimeter of the cemetery until I reached the gates again. I had an almost irrepressible urge to break out of there, and run, but I also had the fearful suspicion that if I did so, the apparitions would pursue me, in one ghostly rush, and hunt me down.

I stood by the gate, looking out across the city of restless dead; shimmering and decayed. Jane stood a little way off, watching me.

"I cannot come back to you," Jane told me, in that soft, distant voice. *"But you could come to me."*

I turned away from her. I could remember how she had looked the day we were married. I could remember her sitting on the side of the bed, still wearing her bridal veil, her skirts drawn up to her thighs, unfastening her white stockings from her white garter-belt. There had been flowers everywhere, the whole room had been heady with sweet-peas and carnations. And her face had seemed to me magical, outlined as it was with morning sunlight, the face of the girl that I loved.

This apparition wasn't Jane. Or at least, it wasn't the Jane I had loved. It was like all of these grisly manifestations in the Waterside Cemetery, dead and decaying, an erratic electrical impulse from a lost life. There was no point in staying here among these ugly and frightening spirits. They were unable to help me in my search for a way to put them to rest. If they were anything like Jane, or Edgar Simons, all they desired was that their living loved ones should join them in whatever half-world they now inhabited. And I didn't really believe that they wanted even this: they were too emotionless, too absorbed in their own unseen agonies. Rather, it was the influence of some greater force that was using them to recruit the living to the realms of the dead, a force that may be lying beneath the mud of Salem Harbor, in the wreck of the *David Dark*.

I started walking back towards Quaker Hill, away from the cemetery. I heard Jane calling after me, but I didn't listen. She would only beg me not to leave her, to come and join her, to stay with her and be her lover. But no matter how painfully I missed her, no matter what I would have done for a chance to see her again, touch her again, be with her again, I wasn't prepared to kill myself. When you've been among the dead, you understand the value of life.

I was only about a third of the way back to the top of Quaker Lane when I caught sight of two or three of the apparitions from the cemetery, keeping abreast of me on the brow of the hill, about twenty yards away. I looked back, and there were more behind me, twelve or thirteen of them at least. And off to my left, about a half-dozen more were following me along the shoreline.

As they came, they kept up that high keening sound. Sometimes it was shrill and distinct, at other times it was blown away by the wind. But it was all around me, an eerie supernatural warcry, as if the dead of Waterside Cemetery were after my blood.

I began to jog, not too fast at first, to see whether the apparitions could keep up with me. They flickered and flew just as quickly, in a strange pell-mell motion, some of them running, some of them tumbling over in the way that Jane's ghost had, some of them soaring arms-stretched with their burial robes fluttering in the ocean wind, like charnel-house kites. I felt a deep and historical terror within me, the kind of terror that people must have felt in the 17th century when leprous beggars came to town, hopping and skipping and horrendously diseased. And all the time there was that whistling and keening, almost joyous now, as if they knew that they could catch me.

I started running in earnest now. But how fast could they go? Perhaps they could easily outstrip me, and they were simply keeping their distance for the sport of it. Still, I couldn't worry too much about that. The only thing I could do was to get back to Quaker Lane Cottage as fast as I could.

And then what? I thought. Jane's apparition had found it easy enough to get inside. This evening, she had opened the front door without even touching the handle. I heard my breath whining and my trouser-legs jostling against each other as I ran, and I thought to myself: don't even consider the possibility. Just run.

I glanced to my right. The grisly apparitions were keeping well up with me, dancing and turning in the wind. On my left, the shoreline began to narrow and edge in closer, and I could see the apparitions distinctly, running towards me in mesmerizing slow motion, and yet easily catching up. I didn't dare to look over my shoulder, because the keening behind my back had seemed to be closer than ever, and I could have sworn that I heard the sea-grass whispering as the apparitions rushed through it.

I was only two hundred yards away from Quaker Lane Cottage when I realized that I couldn't possibly make it. My legs felt as if they were clumsy prosthetics, carved out of heavy wood. My breath shrieked in and out of my lungs, and I was smothered in ice-cold sweat. And all the while, the blue-white apparitions were rushing after me, with decayed and inhuman urgency, the beggars of the night.

I felt something claw at my hair, like a bat or a half-rotted hand. I frantically beat it off, and started running faster again, forcing my legs to take me up the sloping hill, forcing myself through the barrier of total exhaustion and pain. The rushing noises came nearer, until I knew that the apparitions were almost at my shoulder, keening and crying and whispering to me, *stop, stop, join us, don't leave us, come back*.

I felt myself suddenly lifted up—physically lifted up off the ground—and then tossed and tumbled head over heels on to the rough grassy hillside. I tried to scramble to my feet, but then I was hurled on to my back by some completely invisible force, hurled so forcibly that I heard my vertebrae crack, and the air rush out of my lungs. I tried to get up a second time, but I was slammed back to the ground yet again, and this time I was paralyzed, pinned against the grass and the rocks as if some enormous weight were pressing on me.

The apparitions gathered around me, the fading electrical power that had once been their spirits crawling like glow-worms across their scaly and ulcerated faces. They made a *noise*, like soft old tissue-paper, crumpled and recrumpled over years of use; like the breathing you can hear in an old and deserted attic, when there's no one there. And there was a distinctive odor, too, not so much of fleshly decay, but of burned electricity terminals, and rotting fish.

They surrounded me, but they made no immediate move to touch me. I lay where I was, pinned down, panting for breath, scared out of my mind and yet still wondering what the hell I could do. Even in the throes of a scarlet panic, the human mind still plots and schemes and programs for its own survival.

The apparitions stood back a little, and Jane appeared, very tall now, her face stretched out almost beyond recognition. *"You are mi-i-i-ne,"* she said in a chorus of her own voices. I felt as if time had slowed, as if the atmosphere had thickened, and even my struggles against the unseen weight that was holding me down seemed to take endless minutes.

Jane spread out her long-fingered hands, and electricity crackled from one fingertip to the other, like a Van der Graaf generator. She seemed to have built up more power now, because her body was flickering and flashing, and processions of sparks teemed off her shoulders and out of her hair as if she were infested with them. The smell of burning grew even stronger, and I felt a shudder go through the assembled apparitions, as if they were all sharing in Jane's massive discharge of psychic energy.

It had to be enough to kill me. It had to be enough to release my spirit, and leave my body electrocuted on the hillside, another strange and inexplicable fatality. Then I too would be haunting Granitehead, searching for Gilly perhaps, to bring *her* into the hosts of the dead.

Jane touched me with her fingers, and I felt a numbing

shock of current. My left leg involuntarily jerked, and my left eyelid fluttered uncontrollably.

"*You can join me now,*" whispered Jane. "*It would have been better if you had done it by accident, or of your own free will . . . but I cannot wait for you any longer. I love you, John. I want to make love to you.*"

Her outstretched fingers came closer. I could see the electricity creeping along the lines of her palms, along the lifeline and the heartline and the headline. There were even sparkling charges in her nails, and around her wrists. The human energy of a lifetime was being expended to bring me with her to the grave.

I struggled and fought, but the pressure on my chest remained immovable. All around me, the apparitions began to sing and scream, a terrible high cacophony like a madhouse. Right next to my face stood the fleshless leg of a decaying woman, the bones of her toes glowing phosphorescently. A little further away, a hooded man stood with half his face corroded away, one lidless eye glaring at me ferociously.

"You can't call this love!" I shouted at Jane, my voice high with fear. Some hysterical thought process focused on our unborn child. "This isn't what we got married for! This isn't why we wanted to have our baby! God, if you love me, Jane, let me go!"

Jane stared at me with those impenetrable eyes. Electricity crept around her mouth, and outlined her teeth. "*Baby?*" she said, in a resonant echo.

"Yes," I told her, brokenly. I was so scared that I hardly knew what I was saying, or what I was trying to prove to her. "That baby you were carrying when you were killed. Our baby."

Jane's apparition seemed to consider what I had said with burning deepness. Around us, the graveyard creatures whispered and sang; and above our heads, the midnight clouds raced past as if they were fleeing from the same kind of fate that now awaited me.

"*The baby . . .*" she said. She hesitated for a moment, and then seemed to back away from me; or rather, to shrink away, in both size and distance. "*The baby . . .*" she repeated, in a whisper that was just as close as before. "*But the baby was never born.*"

I looked around me. It appeared as if the other apparitions

were shrinking away from me as well, and by twos and threes
the crowd of them was beginning to disperse. I suddenly felt
the pressure relieved from my chest, and I was able unsteadily to stand up, and brush back my windblown hair. I
watched in awe and indescribable relief as the apparitions
floated and tumbled and hobbled away, descending the grassy
hillside with their heads bowed; until they had vanished into
the gates of the cemetery.

Only Jane's apparition remained, quite a long way away,
duller and dimmer now that she was no longer trying to
electrocute me. Her hair flew around her, and her white gown
rippled around her ankles, but I could scarcely make her out
in the darkness.

*"You are lost to me, John . . . I can never have you
now . . ."*

"Why?" I asked her, not out loud, but inside of my mind.

*"Entry into the region of the dead is by succession . . .
you are always called by the loved one who died immediately
before you . . . that is the power which enables the dead to
summon the living. Our baby died in the hospital, long after I
was already dead, and therefore he and he alone can call you
to join us . . . But he was never born, and therefore his spirit
is still in the higher realm, and still at peace, and he cannot
appear here to guide you into the region of the dead . . ."*

I didn't know what to say to her. I thought of the way she
had once been, and the joy she had felt when she knew that
she was pregnant. If only I had known the day Dr. Rosen had
called me up and said that I was going to be a father that my
baby would one night save my life.

"What will happen to you now?" I asked Jane, out loud
this time.

She diminished even further. *"Now, I will have to stay in
the region of the dead forever . . . now, I will never be able
to rest . . ."*

"Jane, what can I do?" I shouted. "What can I do to help
you?"

There was a lengthy silence. Jane's apparition flickered
even more dimly than before, and then disappeared, except
for a flapping darkness against the darkness of the hillside.

Then, blurry and deep, a parody of Jane's voice said,
"Sallvagge . . ."

"Salvage? Salvage what? The *David Dark*, or what? Tell me! I have to know what it is!"

"*Sallvagge* . . ." the voice repeated, growing slower and deeper until it was almost incomprehensible.

I waited by myself for any more voices, any more apparitions, but it appeared now that they had left me in peace. I walked back towards Quaker Lane Cottage, feeling as weary and as beaten as I had ever felt in my whole life.

As I reached the top of Quaker Lane, I saw an ambulance parked outside the cottage, with its red-and-blue lights flashing. I broke into a tired jog, and reached the front gate just as two paramedics were bringing out Constance Bedford on a stretcher. Walter Bedford was following close behind, looking distraught.

"Walter," I asked him, breathlessly. "What's the matter?"

Walter watched the paramedics lift his wife into the back of the ambulance and then he took my arm and led me around to the front of the vehicle, out of earshot. The blood-red light flashed on and off against his face, as if he were Dr. Jekyll one second and Mr. Hyde the next.

"She's not seriously hurt, is she?" I asked. "Jane just sort of *breathed* on her, that was all."

Walter lowered his head. "I don't know what she breathed, or how she breathed it, but whatever it was, it was colder than liquid nitrogen, they said, minus 200 degrees Centigrade."

"And?" I asked him, frightened even to speculate what might have happened to Constance.

"Her eyes were frozen solid," said Walter, in an unsteady voice. "Absolutely solid; and of course they became brittle. When she clapped her hands against them, to try to stop the pain, they shattered, like china. She's lost both of them, John. She's blind."

I put my arm around his shoulders and held him close. He was trembling all over, and he clutched at me as if he didn't have the strength or the ability to be able to stand up any more. One of the paramedics came over and told me, "It's okay now, sir. We'll take care of him. He's had a pretty bad shock."

"His wife? Is she—?"

The paramedic shrugged. "We've done what we can. But it looks like the septum of the nose and part of the forehead have been frozen as well. It's even possible that parts of the brain are affected; the doctors won't be able to tell until they've run some tests.''

Walter quaked in my arms. The paramedic said, ''You don't have any idea how this happened, sir? I mean, nobody around her has any reason to store liquid gases, do they? Nitrogen, or oxygen? Something like that?''

I shook my head. ''Nobody that I know of. Nothing as cold as that.''

Walter said, ''She was always so loving . . . she always loved her mother so dearly. Cold, never. Never, ever cold.''

''He'll be okay,'' the paramedic repeated, and helped Walter into the back of the ambulance. He closed the doors, and then came up to me and said, ''She's your mother-in-law, right?''

''That's right.''

''Well, keep an eye on the old man. He's going to need your help.''

''You don't think that she's going to die?''

The paramedic raised a hand. ''I'm not saying she will and I'm not saying she won't. But it always helps if the patient has some kind of a will to keep on living, and right at the moment this lady doesn't seem to have that will. Something about her daughter, I don't know. Your wife, I suppose.''

''My late wife. She died about a month ago.''

''I'm sorry,'' said the paramedic. ''It hasn't been your year, has it?''

TWENTY

It was raining in torrents when we drove out to Dracut County to talk to old man Duglass Evelith. The sky was an unrelenting gray, like layers of sodden flannel, and the rain just kept on pouring and pouring until I thought it would never end all year; that Massachusetts would never be dry again.

The three of us went in my car—myself, Edward, and Forrest Brough. Jimmy Carlsberg had wanted to come, but at the last moment his mother had insisted that he go over to Cambridge for Sunday lunch to meet his cousins from Arizona. "Jimmy's mother is one of those ladies who won't take no for an answer," explained Forrest, as we drove through the rain.

"Show me a mother who will," replied Edward; and I thought, with sadness and regret, of Constance Bedford. Walter had called me this morning and told me that she was still in intensive care, and that the doctors at Granitehead Clinic were being extremely reticent about her chances of survival. "Overwhelming psychological and physiological trauma," they had diagnosed.

So far, I hadn't yet told Edward or Forrest about the grisly events of the previous night. I needed to think them all out for myself before I discussed them with anybody, particularly with anybody as opinionated as Edward. I *would* tell them, later today or early tomorrow, but at the moment my mind was still a clamor of rushing apparitions, opening graves and shattered eyeballs. I couldn't make any sense of what had happened, and I didn't want to confuse myself any further by attempting to rationalize it. This had all gone way beyond Dr.

Rosen's "post-bereavement hysteria." This was another world, another existence, more mystical and more powerful than anything that doctors or psychiatrists could handle; and if I was going to be able to do anything at all for Jane or Neil Manzi or any of those hundreds of restless spirits who had pursued me last night, then I was going to have to understand it clearly, without prejudice or easy assumptions.

"*Entry into the region of the dead is by succession . . .*" The way Jane had said that, it was almost as if she had been reading from a book. "*You are always called by the loved one who died immediately before you.*" Those words reinforced my earlier opinion that the deaths that had been taking place in Granitehead were a *summoning*, the dead beckoning the living, a kind of séance in reverse, with tragic and often gruesome consequences.

At least I knew one thing now: that I myself was charmed and protected by my unborn son. Perhaps not against the full strength of the force which lay within the *David Dark*, but certainly against Jane.

I felt bitter, as I drove; bitter and tired. I also had a terrible sense of impotence and defeat, a fear that nothing I was able to do would help to put Jane to rest. Knowing that her spirit was trapped in that hideous limbo with all those rotting and skeletal apparitions was far worse than accepting that she was dead. The pain was greater, my feeling of loss heightened by a feeling of helplessness and despair.

I played Brahms on the car's tapedeck to calm me down, and talked with Edward and Forrest about Gilly McCormick, and music, and the *David Dark*, and Gilly McCormick.

"Is she stuck on you?" asked Edward, as we drove into the outskirts of Burlington.

"Gilly, you mean?"

"Who else?"

"I don't know," I told him. "I suppose we do share a certain vague *rapport*."

"You hear that?" said Forrest. "A certain vague *rapport*. That's educated talk for 'we're just good friends.' "

Edward took off his spectacles and polished them with a scrumpled-up Kleenex. "I have to admire your speed, John. When you want something, you certainly go straight in there and get it."

"She's an attractive girl," I replied.

"Well, sure she is," said Edward, and I thought I detected a hint of jealousy in his voice.

Forrest, leaning forward in the back seat, gripped Edward affably on the shoulder. "Don't you worry about Edward," he said. "Edward's been in love with Gilly McCormick ever since he first set eyes on her."

We took a right at Burlington, turning off 95 and heading north-west on 93. The car splashed through sheets of puddles, and sloughed through roadside floods. The windshield wipers kept up a steady, rubbery protest and raindrops hovered on the side windows like persistent memories that refused to let go.

We reached Tewksbury five or ten minutes after noon. It was only a small community, and Edward was quite sure that he could remember where the Evelith house was, but all the same we spent another ten minutes driving around and around the green, looking for the front gates. An elderly man was standing by the side of the green in a full-length water-proof cape and a fisherman's sou'wester, and he watched us gravely as we passed him for the third time.

I pulled in to the side of the road. "Pardon me, sir. Can you direct me to a house called Billington?"

The elderly man came forward, and stared into the car like a country policeman who suspected us of being beatniks, or radicals, or big-city insurance salesmen.

"The Evelith place. That what you want?"

"That's right, sir. We have an appointment to see Mr. Duglass Evelith at twelve o'clock."

The elderly man reached under his raincape and produced a pocketwatch. He opened the case and peered at it through the lower half of his bifocals. "In that case, you're going to be late. It's thirteen minutes after."

"Could you just direct us, please?" asked Edward.

"Well, it's easy enough," said the elderly man. "Follow this road around to the other side of the green, then take a left by that maple."

"Thank you," I told him.

"Don't thank me," the elderly man said. "I wouldn't go in there if you paid me."

"The Evelith place? Why not?"

"That place is bad fortune, that's what that place is. Bad

fortune, and ill luck; and if I had my way I'd see it burned down to the cellars.''

"Oh, come on, now," said Edward. He was obviously trying to coax the old man to tell us more. "Mr. Evelith's a recluse, that's all. That doesn't mean to say that there's anything spooky about his house."

"Spooky, you call it? Well, let me tell *you* something, son, if you want to see anything spooky, you ought to go past the Evelith place one summer night, that's what you ought to do. And if you don't hear the weirdest noises you ever heard, groanings and roarings and suchlike, and if you don't see the most peculiar lights dancing around on the rooftops, then you can come back to me and I'll give you dinner, free of charge, and your fare back to wherever it is that you come from.''

"Salem," said Forrest.

"Salem, hey?" asked the elderly man. "Well, if you're Salem folks, you'll know what kind of thing it is that I'm talking about.''

"Groanings and roarings?" asked Edward.

"Groanings and roarings," the elderly man affirmed, without explaining any more.

Edward looked at me and I looked back at Edward. "Everybody still game, I hope?" I asked. Edward said, "Sure. Forrest?" And Forrest replied, "I'm game. What's a little groaning and roaring?" Edward said, "You forgot the peculiar lights.''

We thanked the elderly man, put up the car windows again, and drove around the green. Past the spreading maple tree, almost hidden by creepers and unkempt bushes, we found the high wrought-iron gates of Billington, the house in which the Evelith family had lived since 1763. Edward said, "There it is. I don't know how I could have forgotten where it was. I could have sworn it was further along the green the last time I came here.''

"Spookier and spookier," grinned Forrest.

I stopped the car outside the gates and climbed out. Beyond the gates, there was a wide gravel driveway, and then a fine white 18th-century mansion, with a pillared doorway, green-painted shutters, and a gray-shingled mansard roof with three dormer windows. Most of the shutters on the first floor were closed, and I wasn't particularly gratified to see a brindled Doberman standing not far away from the steps which led up to the front door, watching me closely with its ears pricked up.

"The bell-pull's over here," said Edward, and tugged at a black iron handle which protruded from one of the gateposts. We heard a very faint jangling sound inside the house, and the Doberman trotted a little way towards the gates, and then stopped again, and stared at us ferociously.

"Are you good with dogs?" Edward asked me.

"I'm wonderful with dogs," I assured him. "I just lie there and cower and let them devour me. Nobody has ever complained to the American Kennel Club about the way I've treated dogs."

Edward glanced at me acutely. "Something on your mind?" he asked me.

"Does it show?"

"If you're not making flippant remarks, you're totally silent. Did you see your wife again last night?"

"I'll tell you later, okay?"

"It was that bad?" Edward asked me.

"It was worse."

Edward came over and unexpectedly took hold of my hand. "Tell us when you're ready to tell us," he said. "But just remember that you don't have to carry this thing on your own. You've got friends now, people who understand what's going on."

"Thanks," I said, and meant it. "Let's see where we get with old man Evelith first. Then we'll go get drunk, and I'll tell you what happened."

We waited for almost five minutes. Forrest got out of the car, too, and lit a cigarette. Edward rang the bell again, and the Doberman came a little closer, and yelped and yawned all in one breath.

"Maybe they're out," suggested Forrest.

"The guy's a hermit, he never goes out," said Edward. "He's probably peering at us through a crack in one of the shutters, sizing us up."

He was about to ring the bell for the third time when the front door of the house suddenly opened, and a tall broad-shouldered man in gray morning-dress appeared. He whistled sharply to the dog, which turned its head, hesitated, and then loped disconsolately away from the gates, as if it was deeply disappointed that it wouldn't get the chance to sink its teeth into our calf-muscles.

The broad-shouldered man approached the gates with the slightly-rolling walk of a 60-year-old body-builder. The same way that Charles Atlas used to walk. When he came close, I saw that he was an Indian; with a magnificent fleshy nose and a face as coppery and wrinkled as a fallen maple-leaf. Although he wore full morning-dress, with a high white collar and a bow-tie, he also wore a long necklace of painted nuts or beads, from which was suspended a silver medallion and a brush of wild turkey feathers. The shoulders of his jacket sparkled with rain.

"You must leave," the Indian said. "You are not welcome here."

"Well, that's too bad," I told him. "The fact of the matter is, I have a little something that Mr. Evelith may be interested in."

"There is no one of that name here. You must leave," the Indian repeated.

"Would you just tell Mr. Evelith that my name is John Trenton, that I am an antique-dealer from Granitehead, and that I have with me a writing case that used to belong to Henry Herrick, Sr., who was one of the jurors at the Salem Witch Trials."

"There is no-one called Evelith here."

"Come on, pal," I coaxed him. "All you have to do is say 'Henry Herrick's writing case.' If Mr. Evelith still doesn't want to see us after you've said that, well, we'll call it quits. But at least give him the opportunity to take a look at it. It's a very rare antique, and I just knew that Mr. Evelith would be interested."

The Indian thought about this for so long that Edward and I started to look at each other worriedly. But at last he said, "Stay here, please, gentlemen. I will confer with him."

"*Confer*," said Forrest, pretending to be impressed. "They don't pow-wow any more. They *confer*. Next thing we know, they'll be using 'aggressively-oriented cosmetics,' instead of war-paint."

"Can it, Forrest," said Edward.

We waited outside the gates for a further five minutes, maybe longer. The rain had settled down to a fine drizzle by now, but it was still heavy enough to plaster our hair against

our heads, and bedraggle Edward's beard. Every now and
then, the Doberman, which was waiting for us just out of
savaging range, gave itself a brisk and anticipatory shake.

Eventually, the tall Indian came out of the house again, and
without a word, unlocked the gates and opened them up. I
went to the back of the car, and took out the Herrick writing-
case, tucking it under my raincoat so that it wouldn't get wet.
The Indian waited until we were all inside the grounds, and
then locked the gates behind us. The Doberman quivered as
we passed, torn between the command it had been given and
its natural bloodlust. Forrest said, ''Throw it a leg, Edward.
It looks hungry.''

We climbed the stone steps to the front door, and the
Indian ushered us inside. The hallway was paneled in dark
oak; with a dark hand-carved staircase on the right-hand side,
leading to a galleried landing. On the walls were oil paintings
of all the Eveliths, from Josiah Evelith in 1665 to Duglass
Evelith in 1947. They were serious, oval-faced, without a
smile between them.

The Indian said, ''Upstairs. I will take your coats.''

We handed him our raincoats, and after he had hung them
up on a huge and hideous hallstand, we followed him up the
uncarpeted stairs. On the walls of the landing there were
halberds and pikes, fowling-pieces and strange arrangements
of metal that looked like instruments of torture. There was
also a glass case, almost impenetrably dusty, which contained
something that could have been a mummified human head.

Throughout the house, there was a smell of staleness and
closeness, as if the windows hadn't been opened for twenty
years. Yet there were always noises, squeaks and bangings,
as if unseen people were moving from room to room, opening
and closing doors. There was supposedly nobody here but old
man Evelith, his alleged grand-daughter, and his Indian
manservant, but it sounded as if there were a score of other
people around. Once, I even thought I heard a man laughing.

The Indian took us along an uncarpeted corridor, with a
polished boarded floor, and then into an ante-room, sparsely
furnished with English-looking antiques and a broken celestial
globe. Above the empty fireplace was an oddly incompetent
painting of five or six cats, American shorthairs by the look
of them.

"Mr. Evelith will be with you by and by," said the Indian, and left us.

"Well," said Edward, "we're in. That's an achievement in itself."

"It doesn't mean to say that he's going to let us look at his library," I said.

"That Indian's kind of weird," said Forrest. "He looks so *Indian*. I haven't seen a face like that outside of an 1860s' photograph album."

We made nervous smalltalk for a while, and then the ante-room door opened, and a girl came in. We all stood up like hayseeds at a Wyoming wedding, and nodded our heads to her, and chorused, "How do you do, miss."

She stood by the door, one hand on the knob, and looked at us in remote and unfriendly appraisal. She was quite petite, no more than five-feet-two, with a thin, sharply-cut face, large dark eyes, and straight black hair that fell brushed and glossy halfway down her back. She wore a black linen day-dress, simply cut, and yet it appeared from where I was standing that she wore nothing underneath. Her shoes were black and shiny with dagger-like toes and extravagantly high heels.

"Mr. Evelith has asked me to escort you into the library," she said, in a clipped Bostonian accent. Edward raised an eyebrow in my direction. This was definitely class. But what was she doing here, shuttered up in Tewksbury with an eccentric old hermit and an Indian dressed like William Randolph Hearst? Especially if she *wasn't* Evelith's grand-daughter?

The girl disappeared, and we had to hurry to follow her through to the next room. She led us across a hallway, her heels clicking on the hardwood floors, and as she passed one of the unshuttered windows, and the gray afternoon light fell through the fine linen of her dress, I saw that I had been right. I could even see a mole on the right cheek of her bare bottom. I knew that Forrest had noticed, too, because he loudly cleared his throat.

At last we were shown into the library. It was a vast, long room, which must have taken up nearly half of the upper floor of the house. At the far end of it, there was an arched window of stained-glass, and the colored light which strained through its amber-and-green panes illuminated the serried

spines of thousands and thousands of leather-bound books, as
well as huge bound volumes of prints and paintings.

Seated at a wide oak table in the center of the library, with
open books spread all around him, sat a white-haired old
man, with a face that had shrunken like a monkey's from age
and lack of sunlight. It was still possible to recognize him as
an Evelith, however—he had kept in old age the same oval
features as his portrait downstairs, and the downward-drooping
eyelids that had distinguished his forebears.

He had been reading with a magnifying-glass. As we came
in, he laid it down, and took off his spectacles, and examined
us long-sightedly. He was wearing a worn-out white shirt, a
black cardigan, and black fingerless mittens on his hands. I
thought he looked rather like an irascible crow.

"You had better introduce yourselves," he said, dryly. "It
is not often that I allow visitors to interrupt my work, so I had
better know who they are."

"I'm John Trenton; I'm an antique dealer from Granitehead.
This is Edward Wardwell, and Forrest Brough, both from the
Peabody Museum."

Duglass Evelith sniffed in one nostril, and put his spectacles back on his nose. "Does it take three of you to show me
a writing-case?"

I laid the Herrick writing-case down on the table. "It's a
fine piece, Mr. Evelith. I thought you might like to take a
look at it, at least."

"But that isn't why you came? Not the *principal* reason?"

I looked up. The girl in black had stepped away from us,
and was standing with her back to one of the bookshelves,
watching us closely, almost as closely and almost as carnally
as the Doberman had watched us. I couldn't tell whether she
wanted to rape us or bite our necks, but the look in her eyes
was certainly intent, and unswervingly avaricious. In the
shadows, her black dress had become opaque again, but the
thought of her nudity beneath it was curiously erotic; and
somehow dangerous, too.

Edward said, "You're right, Mr. Evelith. We didn't really
come here to show you this case, although it's a very rare
antique, and I hope you take some pleasure out of seeing it.
The real reason we're here is because we very badly need the
use of your library."

Old man Evelith sucked at his dentures, and said nothing.

Edward went on, uncertainly, "The point is, Mr. Evelith, we have a very tricky historical problem, and even though the Peabody has quite a stock of literature and charts and so forth, it doesn't have the relevant material we need to solve this problem. I was hoping—we were all hoping—that we might find it here."

There was a very long silence, and then Duglass Evelith pushed back his chair, and stood up, and walked slowly and thoughtfully around the other side of the table, running his hand along the edge of it to keep his balance.

"You realize what a massive impertinence this is?" he asked us.

"It's not really an impertinence, Mr. Evelith," I put in. "There are hundreds and possibly thousands of lives at stake. There are some souls at stake, too."

Duglass Evelith stiffly raised his head, and stared at me with one keenly-focused eye. "Souls, young man?"

"That's right, sir. Souls."

"Well, now," he said. He approached the writing-case, and touched the initials on the top of it with his chalk-dry fingertips. "Well, now, this is indeed a very fine case. Herrick's, you say?"

"Henry Herrick, Senior. The twelfth juror at the Salem Witch Trials."

"Hm. Appropriate that you should bribe your way into my library with such an item. How much do you want for it?"

"Nothing, sir."

"Nothing? You're not a madman, are you?"

"No, Mr. Evelith, not mad. What I mean is, I don't want money for it. All I want is access to your books."

"I see," said Duglass Evelith. He had opened up the lid of the writing-case a little way, but now he closed it again. "Well, that isn't too easy a request for me to grant you. I'm working here, you see. I'm trying to finish my history of 17th-century religion in Massachusetts. The definitive work. I estimate that it will take me another year to finish, and I daren't waste a minute. I could be writing now, you see, instead of talking to you. Supposing I were ten minutes away from finishing my book when I died? Wouldn't I regret this conversation then!"

"Mr. Evelith, we know exactly what we're looking for," said Edward. "If your library is clearly indexed, we shouldn't have to disturb you for more than a day or two. And we could always come at night, when you're asleep.''

"Hm," said Duglass Evelith. "I never sleep at night. I take three hours during the afternoon; and that I find quite sufficient for my needs.''

"In that case, may we please come here during the afternoons?''

Duglass Evelith touched the writing-case again. "This really belonged to Henry Herrick? You have proof?''

"There are three short letters in it, in Herrick's authenticated handwriting," I told him. "What's more, one of the accounts of the Witch Trials specifically mentions 'Herrick's letter-box.' ''

"I see." Old man Evelith opened the case up again, and let his hand stray over the silver-topped inkpots, the sand-shaker, and the ivory-stemmed pens. There was even a piece of green sealing-wax, which must at the latest have been Victorian. "You certainly tempt me," he said. "I could find considerable inspiration in an item like this.''

The girl in the black dress said, "Perhaps your visitors would like some sherry, Duglass.''

Duglass Evelith looked up at her, surprised; but then nodded. "Yes, Enid. Perhaps they would. Sherry, gentlemen?''

We accepted, rather uncomfortably, but then Duglass Evelith beckoned us down to the far end of the library, by the stained-glass window, and offered us a seat on a large leather-upholstered sofa. When we sat down on it, it made a loud noise of escaping air, and clouds of dust surrounded us, like the clouds of battle. Duglass Evelith eased himself into a brocade armchair, right opposite us. The green light from the stained-glass window illuminated his face and made him look as if he were dead and moldering already. But there was plenty of intelligence and animation in his eyes, and when he spoke he was both novel and alert.

"I should like to know, of course, what it is that you're looking for. I may be able to help. In fact, if you are looking for anything at all that is here, I am certain to be able to help. I have spent the past fifteen years cataloging and indexing this entire collection, as well as adding to it, from time to time, and selling off some of the less worthwhile prints and books. A library is a living thing, gentlemen. It should never be allowed to become complacent, otherwise its usefulness will atrophy; and its information become inaccessible to anyone without a pick or a jackhammer. Of course, you don't really understand what I'm talking about, not at the moment, but when you start to use this library, if I agree to let you, you will discover at once how *human* it is. It lives and breathes, as I do; it is at least as alive as Enid and Quamus.''

"Quamus? That's your Indian manservant? The one who showed us in?"

"Indeed. He used to work for the Billington family, years ago, out at New Dunwich; but when the last of them passed away, he came here. No introduction, you know. Just appeared on the doorstep, with his suitcase. Enid thinks he's a wizard."

"A *wizard*?" laughed Forrest.

Duglass Evelith gave a twisted, unamused smile. "Stranger things have been known, round and about this part of Massachusetts. Magical country, of its kind. At least it used to be, before the old families died out, and the old ways were all but forgotten. The first settlers, you see, had to learn what the Indians already knew, that to survive in this country you had to come to terms with its gods, and with its spirits. They didn't have any trouble, of course, accepting the existence of such things. In those days, in the 17th century, they believed without reservation in God and his angels; and in Satan and his demons. So to believe in a few more supernatural forces wasn't a difficult mental jump for them; not like it would be today. They had to rely on the Indians a very great deal, especially in those first hard winters; and many of them came to know the Narragansett intimately. Some settlers, they say, were more adept at summoning up the Indian spirits than the Indians themselves. It was said that the Billingtons could do it; and one of the Eveliths was supposed to have had a hand in it, too."

"Mr. Evelith," said Edward, very anxious that we shouldn't be sidetracked, "what we're actually trying to discover, not to beat around the bush, is the exact location of the wreck of the *David Dark*."

At that moment, Enid came into the library with a small silver tray of sherry. She came click-clacking over to us, and handed it around. For one strangely tantalizing second, she leaned across in front of me, and I glimpsed her small bare breasts through her dress. I accepted my sherry from her with a smile, but the look she gave me in return was one of pure cold indifference.

When she had gone, and closed the library door behind her, Duglass Evelith said, in a phlegm-thickened voice, "The *David Dark*? What do you know of the *David Dark*?"

"Only that she used to belong to Esau Hasket, who had christened her after David Dark the evangelist preacher," said Edward. "Only that she set sail from Salem in a terrible storm in 1692 and was never seen again. At least, that's what the history books say. But they also say that every single reference to her was cut from every single logbook and broadsheet, and that Esau Hasket forbade anybody ever to mention her again. And the inference is that she foundered, quite soon after leaving Salem, and was driven *back* into Salem Sound by a strong north-easterly wind, and finally went down off Granitehead Neck."

Duglass Evelith sucked in his cheeks, and regarded us thoughtfully. "She sank over 290 years ago," he said, choosing his words with care. "The likeliehood of there being anything salvageable left of her is rather less than slim, wouldn't you say?"

"Not if she really did go down where we think she did," Edward argued. "On the west side of Granitehead peninsula, the bottom is very soft mud, and if the *David Dark* behaved like every other sinking ship of the period, which we have no reason to doubt that she did, she would have plunged into that mud right up to her waterline, maybe higher, and buried herself within a matter of weeks."

"Well?" asked Duglass Evelith.

"If that happened, then the *David Dark* will still be there. Preserved, right up to the orlop deck at least. But that means that whatever she was carrying in her hold will be preserved, too."

"You know what she was carrying?"

"We're not sure," said Forrest. "All we know is that the people of Salem were in a hell of a hurry to get rid of it; and that it was contained in a specially-made copper vessel, or could have been."

Edward added: "We've been diving in the area, looking for the wreck, for over a year now. I'm sure it's there; I'm convinced of it. But unless we can find some documentary evidence of where she might have gone down, it's going to take us the rest of our lives to locate her. It's not even worth doing echo-soundings until we have a pretty exact idea of where she is. There are so many small boats and so many heaps of trawl-nets down there, we'd forever be picking up likely-looking signals, and of course we'd have to dive down and investigate all of them.''

Old man Evelith was sipping his sherry all this time; but when Edward had finished, he set down his glass on the table beside him and gave a dry, thin sniff.

"Why, exactly, do you *want* to find the wreck of the *David Dark*?" he asked us. "What is so desperately urgent about it?"

I looked at him carefully. "You know what's in it, don't you?" I asked him. "You know what's down there, and why they tried to get rid of it?"

Duglass Evelith looked back at me, just as shrewdly, and smiled. "Yes," he admitted. "I know what's in it. And if you can convince me that you have a strong enough reason for salvaging it, and that you know what dangers you may be up against, I'll tell you what it is.''

TWENTY-ONE

I had been guessing, of course, when I suggested to Duglass Evelith that he knew what secret was concealed in the wreck of the *David Dark*; but not guessing too wildly. It was obvious from the books that lined the library shelves around us that he was interested in history and magic, and if he knew so much about the early settlers and the way in which they had conjured up Indian spirits to help them in the wilderness, then the chances that he was acquainted with the sinking of the *David Dark* were high.

Besides that, if Duglass Evelith didn't know where the wreck was located, or how it had sunk, then nobody would. This monkey-shriveled old man was our only possible hope.

"My wife was killed in a road accident just over a month ago," I told him, in a quiet voice. "Recently, she's been visiting me. I mean that her *spirit* has been visiting me. Her ghost, if you like. And talking to other people in Granitehead who have recently lost their relatives, I've discovered that what I've been experiencing is not exactly an uncommon phenomenon here."

"That's all?" asked old man Evelith.

"Isn't it enough?" Edward demanded.

"There is more," I said. "An elderly woman who lived out on West Shore Road was killed two days ago by the spirit of her dead husband, and I understand that several other people have died in very gruesome and peculiar ways. It seems as if the ghosts are not benign, but are culling the living to join them in the region of the dead."

Duglass Evelith raised a white wiry eyebrow. "The region

of the dead?'' he inquired. ''Who mentioned the region of the dead?''

''My wife,'' I said. ''As a matter of fact, I saw her again last night. I saw lots of spirits last night, every dead damned soul in Waterside Cemetery.''

Edward looked across at me, and gave me a nod to show that he understood why my behavior had been so fractured this morning. Duglass Evelith sat back in his armchair, his elbows perched on the arms, his mittened hands hanging like the talons of a dead rook. Forrest cleared his throat, and shifted his backside on the leather-covered sofa so that it squeaked rudely.

''You're telling me the truth,'' said Duglass Evelith, after a while.

''Of course we're telling you the truth,'' Forrest protested. ''You don't think we would have driven all the way out here and given you a valuable antique writing-case for nothing, do you?''

''I am regarded by the local populace with grave suspicion,'' said Duglass Evelith. ''I am thought to be a sorcerer, or a madman, or an incarnation of Satan. That is why the gates are locked, and that is why I keep my guard-dogs, and that is why I treat any attempted incursion into my house with the deepest caution. The last time I allowed a party of gentlemen to come into my house, four years ago, they attempted to beat me up and burn my library. It was only because Quamus was so prompt in intervening that my library and I both survived.''

''How do you *know* we're telling you the truth?'' I asked him.

''Well, there are indications. What you say about Granitehead is quite correct; and for some years now I have associated what has been happening there with the wreck of the *David Dark*. But, certainly, the visitations you describe are far more vivid and far more threatening than they have ever been before. You also mentioned 'the region of the dead,' and unless you have been undertaking some extremely detailed research in order to perpetrate an elaborate and apparently pointless hoax, you would not have known that 'the region of the dead' is *exactly* the phrase which is appropriate to the history of the *David Dark*.''

Edward said, ''Have you any idea why the ghosts should be more threatening now than they ever have been before?''

Duglass Evelith thoughtfully rubbed his white-stubbled chin. "There are many possible explanations. One really won't be able to tell until the contents of the *David Dark*'s hold are raised and inspected. But you are right: the influence which is affecting the dead of Granitehead has been emanating from the large copper vessel which on that voyage was the *David Dark*'s only cargo. Perhaps that vessel has at last corroded to the point where the influence has been able to escape."

"What influence?" asked Forrest.

Old man Evelith raised himself out of his chair, and beckoned us. "What happened at the time was known only to a few; and all of those few were sworn to utter secrecy. After it was all over, as you know, Esau Hasket ordered that every mention of the *David Dark* should be excised from every company logbook, every news-sheet, every poster. The only way that we know today of the *David Dark*'s existence is through shipping records that were kept in Boston and also in Mexico City. There are several drawings and mezzotints of the ship, although all of them appear to be copies of one particular sketch that was made of her in 1689. I believe I sold a rather inferior watercolor of her not too long ago; again, a copy of the one known rendition."

"I bought that watercolor myself, at Endicott's," I put in.

"You did? Ah, well, that's fortunate. How much did you pay for it?"

"Fifty dollars."

"Wasn't worth six. It probably wasn't even contemporary."

"So much for your professional judgment," Forrest ribbed me, and I gave him a look of mock annoyance.

Duglass Evelith shuffled along one of the shelves, and picked out a thin, black-bound book, which he laid flat on the library table. "This isn't an original," he said. "The original was probably lost or burned years ago. But somebody had the foresight to copy the original exactly, complete with drawings, and so here it is. This copy was made in 1825, but we don't know who made it, or why. My great-grandfather Joseph Evelith bought it from a widow out at Dean's Corners, and there's a piece of paper inside it in his own handwriting saying, 'This explains at *last*; I have told Sewall.' Here, here it is. The piece of paper itself. See the date on it? Eighteen thirty-one."

"Does it say who wrote the original?" asked Edward.

"Oh, yes. This was the private diary of Major Nathaniel Saltonstall, of Haverhill, who was one of the presiding judges at the Salem Witch Trials. You may remember that it was Judge Saltonstall who first began to have doubts about the testimony at the trials, and resigned rather than continue to sit. In fact, he was so mortified and angered by the trials that he undertook his own investigation into the 'Great Delusion,' as the witch-hunt came to be known; and this diary of his contains the only full and reasonably accurate account of what went on."

Duglass Evelith turned the diary's pages, and ran his chalky fingernails along the sloping lines of 19th-century writing. "Saltonstall had only settled in Salem during the winter of 1691. Before that, he had lived with his wife and family in Acushnet, New Beford, and so he knew nothing of the events which had *preceded* the Salem witch-scare."

While we listened, Duglass Evelith read through the diary's account of the Salem Witch Trials. The "Great Delusion," as Judge Saltonstall constantly referred to it, was said in most history books to have begun in 1689, when a trader called Samuel Parris arrived in Salem Village with the intention of changing his livelihood to that of holy minister. On November 19, 1689, he was installed as Salem's first pastor.

With him, Parris had brought two slaves from the West Indies, a man called John Indian and his wife Tituba. Both slaves were adept at fortune-telling, card-tricks, and palmistry, and they liked to amuse the local children by telling them tales of witchcraft. The children, however, either began to pretend that they were possessed by witches, or else were gripped by a spasm of childish hysteria. Whatever it was, they would throw terrible fits and spasms, and thrash around on the floor and scream. Dr. Griggs, the local physician, examined the "afflicted" children and pronounced at once that they were bewitched.

Horrified, the Rev. Parris invited neighboring ministers to come to his house for a day of fasting and prayer, and to witness the tortures of the "afflicted" children. When they saw the children writhing and shrieking, the ministers confirmed the doctor's diagnosis: the children were unquestionably possessed.

Now the question was: who had bewitched them? And

under intensive questioning, the children said "Good," "Osburn," and "Tituba."

So it was that on March 1, in front of John Hathorne and Jonathan Corwin, the two leading magistrates in Salem, Sarah Good, Sarah Osburn, and Tituba were all accused of witchcraft. Sarah Good, an unfortunate woman with very few friends, earnestly denied everything; but the children shrieked and writhed when they saw her, and she was promptly declared guilty. Sarah Osburn was dragged into court despite being bedridden, and the children threw themselves into spasms when she appeared, so that none of her denials were believed. Tituba, frightened and superstitious, admitted that she had agreed to serve Satan, and that she and the other accused women had all ridden through the air on a stick. This evidence was enough: all three women were chained and manacled and sent to jail.

The "afflicted" children continued their accusations. Eighty-two-year-old George Jacobs, a white-haired dignified old man, answered charges that he was a wizard by saying, "You tax me for a wizard; you may as well tax me for a buzzard. I have done no harm." He was found guilty, and imprisoned.

The trials went on during the summer of 1692, becoming increasingly heated and hysterical. The whole of Salem Village seemed to be possessed by "witch fever," and over and over again, when the villagers looked back on that summer in future years, they referred to it as "a dream" or "a nightmare," as if they had somehow been asleep.

Thirteen women and six men were hanged on Gallows Hill—the first, Bridget Bishop, on June 10; the last, Mary Parker, on September 22. In fact on September 22, eight witches and wizards were hung and as they swung in the air, the Rev. Mr. Noyes remarked, "What a sad thing it is to see eight firebrands from hell hanging there."

Two days earlier, however, an execution had taken place which was so horrible that it had begun to awaken the people of Salem from their "Great Delusion." Old Giles Corey, of Salem Farms, had denounced the claims of the "afflicted" children, and had been brought to stand trial; but he had refused to speak. Three times he had been brought before the judge and three times he had remained dumb. He had been taken to an open field between Brown Street and Howard Street burial ground, stripped naked, and made to lie flat, while heavy weights were placed on to his body. As more weights were added, Giles Corey's tongue was squeezed out of his mouth, and the sheriff with his cane had pushed it back in again. Corey was the first New-Englander to suffer the old English punishment of pressing to death.

Judge Saltonstall had written, "The storme now seem'd to have spent itselfe, and the people awaken'd. There is in Historie no record of so sudden, so rapid, so complete a revulsione of feeling." There were no more executions, and in May of the following year, all those accused and awaiting trial were released.

But Judge Saltonstall's account did not end here. He said that "I remain'd curious as to how the Delusion had begunne; and why it should have died so quicklie. Had the children trulie been afflicted, or had they beene nothing more than eville pranksters? I sette about discoveringe for myself the truthe of these sorry events; and particularlie with the assistance of Micah Burrough, who had work'd for Esau Hasket as a clerke, I piec'd together an Account as frightening as it is remarkable; yette for whose accuracie and truthe I can solemnlie Vouchsafe."

Duglass Evelith rang a small silver bell, and his Indian manservant Quamus appeared. Quamus regarded us impassively, but from what Evelith had told us, he was probably quite capable of throwing all three of us out of there, or tearing us limb from limb. Evelith said, "Quamus, these gentlemen are to be our guests for luncheon. The cold pie will do. And bring up a bottle of the Pouilly Fumé; no, two bottles; and put them on ice."

"Yes, sir."

"Oh, and Quamus—"

"Yes, sir?"

"These gentlemen are here to discuss the *David Dark*. Their visit may prove to be of considerable importance to us."

"Yes, sir. I understand, sir."

Quamus left us, and old man Evelith dragged over one of the upright chairs, and sat himself down. "Please, sit," he asked us. "The rest of Judge Saltonstall's diary is fascinating, but disorganized, and it would better if I told you the story of what happened myself. You are welcome to make copies of any pages that particularly interest you; but if you tried to work out for yourselves what Judge Saltonstall was actually saying, I'm afraid that it would take you some considerable time, as it did me.''

We all drew up chairs, and Duglass Evelith leaned on the table before us, looking from one to the other as he spoke. I shall never forget that hour in the Evelith library, listening to the secret history of the *David Dark*. I felt as if I was closed off from the real world altogether, as if I was back in the 17th century, when witches and demons and goblins were all considered to be credible realities. Outside, the rain began to die away, and a kind of strangled sunlight came through the stained-glass window and illuminated our discussions in a radiance that looked as old as the story itself.

"What occurred in Salem in the summer of 1692 began not with Mr. Parris, as the modern history-books suggest, but much earlier, with David Ittai Dark, who was a fire-and-brimstone preacher who lived first at New Dunwich, and then nearer Salem Village at Mill Pond.

"By all accounts, David Dark was a tall, saturnine man, with long black hair which reached down to his shoulders. He was so convinced that every man, woman and child had to live a life completely beyond reproach before they would even be *considered* for a place in heaven that he taught his congregation to prepare themselves for the almost certain prospect of spending all eternity in hell. In March of 1682, David Dark announced to his flock that in a field outside of Dean's Corners he had actually met with Satan, and that Satan had given him a scroll on which were scorched the names of all those Salem villagers who were already condemned to burn. This, of course, had a remarkable effect on the behavior of all those listed, and Judge Saltonstall records that 1682 and 1683 were 'highly moral years' in Salem and its surrounding communities.''

"Do you think he *had* met with Satan? Or anything similar?'' asked Edward.

"Judge Saltonstall investigated this claim,'' said Duglass Evelith. "All that he could discover was that David Dark had become friends during the previous year with some Narragansett Indians, and one Indian in particular who was claimed by his tribe to be the greatest worker of magical wonders who had ever lived. The judge wasn't a man to leap to conclusions; he liked his evidence to be cut and dried. But he did cautiously express the opinion that it was conceivable that David Dark and this Indian magician could have summoned up between them one of the ancient and evil Indian deities, and that Dark could have taken this manifestation to be Satan, or one of his cohorts.''

The dark-haired girl called Enid came into the library with a crystal decanter on her silver tray, and asked us if we would care for another glass of sherry. Personally, I was dying for a large whiskey, but I took the sherry and was grateful for it.

Duglass Evelith said, ''Very little was heard about David Dark between 1683 and 1689. Apparently he gave up preaching for several years, and devoted himself to study. Quite *what* he was studying, nobody could ever discover, but Judge Saltonstall says that at night there were lights in the sky above his cottage; and that the local people wouldn't go near the woods where he lived because they had heard the howling of strange beasts.

''In 1689, however, David Dark reappeared and began to preach once more; often in church in the center of Salem. After a particularly fiery sermon, he was approached by the merchant Esau Hasket, who was much impressed with what Dark had been saying, and Hasket, who was something of a religious zealot himself, suggested that between them they should begin a campaign to improve the morals and the minds of everyone in Salem.

''This is where the testimony of Micah Burrough comes into its own. Micah Burrough had worked for Esau Hasket for fifteen years, and was one of his most trusted employees. That was why, when David Dark suggested to Hasket that he should send a ship to Mexico on a very special errand, Micah Burrough was there to record what was said.''

''Mexico?'' asked Edward. ''Where does Mexico come into it?''

''Mexico is crucial and central to the whole story of the *David Dark*,'' said Duglass Evelith. ''For whatever spirits or creatures David Dark had been raising at his cottage at Mill Pond, all of them were subservient to the grimmest of demons on the entire American continent. I am speaking of the living skeleton who was worshiped by the Aztecs on the island of Tenochtitlán, which later became Mexico City. How David Dark came to know of this demon, Judge Saltonstall does not say; but it is quite likely that the Narragansett wonder-worker

told him about it. In any case, David Dark persuaded Esau
Hasket that he should mount an expedition to Mexico City,
discover the remains of this demon, and bring it back to
Salem in order to frighten and discipline the local people.
That, after all, was how the Aztecs had used it—as a way of
encouraging any religious backsliders to renew their worship
of Huitzilopochtli and Quetzalcoatl.''

"Surely the Spanish were in control in Mexico City in
those days,'' said Forrest. "When did Cortès overthrow the
Aztecs? Fifteen-twenty?''

"Fifteen-nineteen,'' Duglass Evelith corrected him. "But
remember that the Aztecs were a remarkably organized people.
Long before Cortès had reached the island of Tenochtitlán,
the living skeleton had been carried away from the city on
one of the causeways which joined it to the mainland, and
secreted on the slopes of the volcano of Ixtacihuatl. Again, it
was impossible for Judge Saltonstall to establish how David
Dark had discovered this, but Dark had traveled several times
during the six years between 1863 and 1869, and it is quite
conceivable that he went to Mexico. He may well have
contacted some of the surviving Aztec magicians whose heredi-
tary task it was to guard the demon from the Spanish invaders,
and made an arrangement with them for the demon to be
shipped secretly out of Mexico to Massachusetts. Conversely,
rather than bothering to deal with them, he may have had
them killed. Judge Saltonstall thinks so.''

"So Esau Hasket sent a ship to bring this demon back to
Salem?'' asked Edward.

"That's exactly what happened. The ship was called the
Arabella, and it was generally considered to be one of the
finest vessels in Salem. David Dark went on the voyage as
commander, and the ship was captained by Charles Fisk, the
older brother of Thomas Fisk, who was later to be a juror at
the witch-trials.

"The *Arabella* was away for nearly a year, and when she
returned the crew refused to speak about their expedition, and
even David Dark himself seemed like a different man. They
had aged, every one of them, Judge Saltonstall reported; and
out of a crew of 70 men, thirty-one of them were dead within
the year, either of disease, or of heart failure, or of stroke.
The *Arabella*'s mysterious cargo was unloaded by six men
who had been specially hired from Boston to do the work,

and paid three times the going rate. Then it was carried by wagon to David Dark's cottage at Mill Pond.

"At first, nothing happened. David Dark visited Esau Hasket at his offices several times, and told him that the demon appeared to be comatose, or dead. Perhaps the Aztec magicians had lied to him, and the demon was no demon at all, but simply the skeleton of an unusually tall man. Hasket, who had been so enthusiastic at first that he had re-christened the *Arabella* the *David Dark*, started to have doubts about the expedition, and about the money he had spent on sending the *Arabella* and her crew to Mexico for a whole year, and most of all he began to have doubts about the sanity of David Dark. Micah Burrough overheard a conversation that Hasket had with Dr. Griggs about the possibility of Dark being 'possess'd, or mad.'

"In the spring of 1691, however, extraordinary events began to occur around Salem. Several people began to report that they had seen or heard their deceased relatives, walking around the streets of the village at the dead of night. One man awoke in his bed to find his dead mother standing beside his bed, and he was so frightened that he jumped out of the skylight, and rolled all the way down the long sloping roof, breaking his ankle, but fortunately doing no other damage."

I leaned forward across the table. "How were these dead people described? Were they like ghosts? Or flickering lights?"

Duglass Evelith thumbed through the book, and then turned it around so that I could see what was written there.

"On the morning of Aprille 2nd, 1691, Wm Sayer had visited the Rev. Noyes and tolde him of his great alarm in having seen in broade daylight his deceas'd brother Henry on St. Peter Street; and how Henry had approached him and begg'd him to come with him or else Henry though dead would find no rest. Wm Sayer had runne off quicklie, greatly affrighted, and had tolde the Rev. Noyes that his brother had appear'd to him as much in the fleshe as if he had still been extant."

I passed the book to Edward. "You see how powerful the influence was then? It could summon the dead by daylight, and they looked as solid as if they were still alive."

"That wasn't all," said Duglass Evelith. "The dead began to prey on the living; and although the official history books record that there was a summer epidemic of diptheria in

Salem in 1691, the truth of the matter was that the people of
the village were being snatched from their beds by the corpses
of their dead relatives and killed in all sorts of extraordinary
and ritualistic ways. The body of Nehemiah Putnam was
found butchered like a pig's, and somehow spreadeagled to
the gable at the end of his house, out of reach of windows or
ladders. John Eastey was discovered impaled on a flagstaff
which used to stand in the village square, although he would
have had to have been lifted seventy feet in the air to drive
him down on to it. Of course, the community began to panic,
although David Dark now made his most dramatic reappearance and told them that they had offended the Lord, and that
this was their punishment.

"Esau Hasket, however, began to feel that enough was
enough. His own sister Audrey had appeared in his garden at
night, and he was terrified that *he* was going to be taken, too.
He ordered Dark to destroy the demon; otherwise he would
expose what had been going on, and Dark would probably
find himself torn to pieces by angry Salemites.

"Dark, however, was unable to control the power that he
had brought back from Tenochtitlán; and when he attempted
to break the demon to pieces with an ax, he was immediately
killed. An eye-witness, an illiterate field-worker, said that she
saw him explode in a cloud of blood and entrails.

"After Dark's death, there was chaos in Salem for a while.
Judge Saltonstall said that there was 'night at noontime' and
that many people were buried at sea for fear they would rise
from their graves and slaughter the friends and relatives who
had survived them. In the fall of 1691, however, the chaos
died away as quickly as it had broken out, and for the rest of
the year there was peace in Salem Village.

"What had happened, as Judge Saltonstall later discovered,
was that the Narragansett wonder-worker who had originally
taught David Dark how to summon evil spirits had visited
David Dark's cottage and had encountered the demon from
Mexico. Although he had been unable to destroy it, he had
bound it with enough powerful Indian ritual to suppress its
malevolence. Apparently he hoped to use it to further his own
influence within his tribe, and over other Indian magicians.
He didn't realize what havoc it had been causing among the
villagers of Salem.

"But, shackles are only as strong as their weakest link, and by the spring of the following year, it seems that the demon had worked out ways in which it could break the ritual bonds that the Narragansett had imposed on it. There was some kind of struggle between the Indian and the demon, a struggle in which the demon was temporarily weakened but in which the Indian was severely crippled. The demon then sought to re-establish its grip on the community of Salem by enticing to its lair three young girls who were out walking near Mill Pond: Anne Putnam, Mercy Lewis, and Mary Walcot.

"The demon must have slaughtered them all, although Judge Saltonstall could never find out how. Their bones were later found in a shallow grave in the woods near David Dark's former home. But their ghosts, if you like, returned to Salem Village and began to throw fits, and scream, and writhe around as if possessed. Because of this, nineteen good people were accused of witchcraft, and hung; and Giles Corey was pressed to death. Twenty souls were claimed by the demon in just a few short weeks; a feast."

"But why did the hysteria stop so suddenly?" asked Edward.

Duglass Evelith finished his sherry, and then twisted the glass around between his fingers as if he were trying to decide whether he ought to have another one or not.

"It stopped because Esau Hasket saw two of the girls, Mercy Lewis and Mary Walcot, walking through Salem Village in the very early hours of the morning. He had been up most of the night, supervising the onloading of a very valuable cargo of indigo. He stopped them, when he saw them, and asked them what they were doing up. But all they did, according to Judge Saltonstall, was 'to glare at him with eyes that glowed blue, and to snarle at him like wolverines, frightening him away.' Hasket now suspected that David Dark's demon was active again, and he made plans to visit the cottage, along with a pastor friend of his, to see what was happening there.

"What they saw in Dark's cottage frightened them beyond all measure. Here, let me read from Saltonstall's diary itself. 'Regardless of the houre, which was onlie three and some minutes past, the skies began to grow dark as Mr. Esau Hasket and the Rev. Roger Cornwall approached the erstwhile residence of David Dark. According to Micah Burrough, to whom Mr. Hasket later related this description, the Rev. Cornwall stopped at the stile which bounded Dark's propertie,

and declined for some time to procede any futher, feigning a
severe sicknesse. Mr. Hasket however persuaded him to
continue, and eventualie the two men reached the cottage.
The windows were obscured in some fashion, and therefore
Mr. Hasket elected to force an entrie, which he achieved with
an ax. What met their eyes inside the cottage Mr. Hasket
refused to relate in anything but the most circumstantialle
manner, but Micah Burrough concluded that the stench of
putrefaction within the building was such that bothe Mr.
Hasket and the Rev. Cornwall were sicke unto vomiting; and
that having recovered they saw in the darkness a huge and
terrifying Skeleton, "bone-white," said Mr. Hasket, "and in
alle natural proportions, except that it was many times the
size of a human, & *alive*." The Skeleton's ribs were hung
like a gamekeeper's gibbet with the intestines of hogs, chickens,
and goats, and the skulles of animals formed caps for each of
its bonie fingers. Worst of all was a copper basin which
rested on the floor beside it, a basin heaped with darke and
bloodie things. Even as Mr. Hasket and the Rev. Cornwall
watched in sicknesse & in feare, the Skeleton plunged one
hand into the basin, and lifted uppe some of the gruesome
contents of the basin for them to see; and it was then that Mr.
Hasket understoode that he was looking at a basin of human
hearts, the hearts of every man and woman who had beene
hung during the Great Delusion.' ''

Duglass Evelith turned over the last few pages of the black
notebook. "Esau Hasket now fully realized what devilry he
had unleashed on Salem, and he was shrewd enough to
understand that the witch-hunts were only the beginning. The
demon presumably took its strength from slaughtered animals
and from human hearts, and used the dead whose hearts it had
already taken to bring it more. The hysteria of the Great
Delusion was increasing; and Hasket foresaw a time when the
skies would be permanently dark, and the walking dead would
overwhelm the living."

"That's why the cemetery beside the Granitehead shoreline
used to be called 'The Walking Place,' '' I put in.

"That's correct," said Duglass Evelith. "But the curse on
Granitehead came later, after Esau Hasket had determined
that he would rid Salem of the demon once and for all."

"How did he do that?" asked Edward. "Surely the demon
was powerful enough to prevent anyone from exorcizing it."

"Hasket went to the Narragansett wonder-worker, and bribed him with promises of huge sums of money if he would help him to contain the demon for long enough to ship him out of Salem and make sure that it never returned. The wonder-worker was extremely reluctant to help at first, because the demon had severely injured him in their last confrontation; but eventually Hasket upped the price to nearly £1,000 in gold, which the wonder-worker found irresistible. Now the wonder-worker knew one thing: and that was that the demon was susceptible to intense cold. It was the lord of the region of the dead, the god of hellfire, with uncontested dominion over the furnaces and grates of everlasting torture. It is said, in fact, that bodies lose their heat so quickly when they die because this particular demon extracts it for his own nourishment; and that all the walking dead could be detected by their utter coldness. Every last ounce of thermal energy had been drained from every last cell, in order to keep the lord of the region of the dead both thriving and powerful.

"The Narragansett wonder-worker therefore suggested to Esau Hasket that the demon could be parayized inside Dark's old cottage by the introduction through the doors and windows of twenty or thirty cartloads of ice; that the demon could then be contained in a large insulated vessel also packed with ice; and sailed as quickly as possible northwards to Baffin Bay, and dropped into the ocean. Hasket could see no other way out, so he agreed.

"The plan was carried out in late October, after the *David Dark* had been hurriedly prepared to carry this one malevolent item of cargo. Despite the bloody loss of two horses as they approached the cottage, and the blinding of three men, the wonder-worker was able to contest the demon with his spells just long enough for the doors and windows to be smashed down with picks and axes, and for the ice to be tipped into the room where the demon presided. At the dead of night, the gigantic skeleton was carried out of the cottage, and laid inside the specially-made copper vessel which Hasket had ordered to be prepared. More ice was packed inside, ice which could constantly be replenished through a special trap, and then the copper lid was welded closed. Micah Burrough was actually there that night: just like anybody else whom Hasket felt he could trust. The capturing of the demon had taken thirty good men and many hundreds of pounds. Within the hour, the copper vessel had secretly been loaded aboard the *David Dark*, and the ship's captain had announced that he was ready to sail.

"As they were rowed away from Salem wharf, however, the adverse wind begin to rise sharply, and even within the harbor the sea began to blow rough. The captain signaled back to the shore that he would rather return to his anchorage, and wait until the storm had died down before he attempted to sail; but Hasket was terrified that the demon would escape from the ship if it had to be kept in harbor overnight, and he ordered the *David Dark* to sail at all costs.

"Well, you know the rest. The *David Dark* was rowed out beyond Granitehead Neck; and then she put up the barest minimum of sail with the intention of sailing as far as possible in the south-easterly direction, in the hope that when the storm died down she would then be able to tack northwards past Nova Scotia and head for Newfoundland and the Labrador Basin. But—whether it was entirely the force of the storm, or whether the will of the demon had anything to do with it—the ship was driven back into Salem Sound, and sunk somewhere off the west shore of the Granitehead Peninsula."

"Were there any witnesses to the sinking?" I asked. "Did anybody see it from the shore?"

"No," said Duglass Evelith, closing the book and resting his mittened hands on it possessively, like a cat with a dead blackbird. "But there may have been one survivor. And it is that one possible survivor who has supplied me with the only reasonable estimate of the spot where the *David Dark* might have gone down."

"Somebody *survived* the wreck?" asked Edward, incredulously.

Duglass Evelith raised one cautionary finger. "I said only that it was possible. But three or four years ago, when I was reading the family diary of the Emerys—you know, the Granitehead marine instrument makers—I came across a curious reference to a 'wild-eyed man' whom Randolph Emery's great-grandfather had found 'half-drowned' on the Granitehead shoreline in the fall of 1692. Now, this particular diary, the Emery diary, was written between 1881 and 1885, so there's no saying how accurate this story might have been. But Randolph Emery's great-grandfather had used what he learned from this 'wild-eyed man' in order to instruct his heirs in the

technique of establishing your position at sea by the use of
nearby landmarks. For the 'wild-eyed man' had said that his
ship had gone down not more than a quarter of a mile
offshore, and that after it had sunk, and he had found himself
tossed on the waves on a length of broken spar, he had been
able to ascertain his position by the landmarks he had seen
through the spray. To his left, to the north, he had seen the
beacon on the easternmost headland of Winter Island lined up
with the beacon on the easternmost shore of Juniper Point. Ahead
of him, as the tidal stream swirled around and took him in
towards the shore, he could see a tall tree which sailors used
to call The Hapless Virgin, on account of the way its trunk
was all twisted around like crossed thighs, and its branches
were all flung out like appealing arms—he could see the top
of this tree lined up with the peak of Quaker Hill. Now, the
Hapless Virgin, of course, has long since gone, but it's
possible to work out almost exactly where it was from the
drawings and paintings of Salem Harbor and the Granitehead
shoreline which were made at the time. So—it's a very
simple matter of basic trigonometry to find out where the
David Dark went down.''

"If you knew all this, why didn't you do something about
it before?" asked Edward.

"My dear sir, do you take me for a fool?" asked Duglass
Evelith. "I personally had neither the money, the equipment,
the youth, nor the inclination to go searching for a wreck that
more than likely had rotted away centuries ago. But, at the
same time, I didn't want to publish my findings, because of
the very arguable nature of the laws regarding historic wrecks.
Once I made it known where the *David Dark* was lying,
divers would be swarming down there in their hundreds,
vandals and enthusiastic amateurs and souvenir-hunters and
plain professional thieves. If there *did* happen to be anything
left worth salvaging, I didn't want to see it pillaged, did I, by
bungling tyros and aquatic muggers?''

"I guess not," smiled Edward. "They did the same thing
in England, didn't they? Pretending to be diving for the *Royal
George*, when in fact they were looking for the *Mary Rose*. It
was the only way they could throw the scrap merchants off
the scent. A scrap merchant would have dynamited the *Mary
Rose* to pieces, just for the sake of her bronze cannon.''

Duglass Evelith beckoned to Enid, and asked her in a

hoarse whisper, "Bring me the charts out of the chart-table. There's a good girl."

"Enid's your grand-daughter?" asked Forrest, as she went off to get the maps.

Duglass Evelith stared at him. "My grand-daughter?" he asked, as if he were mystified by the question.

Forrest actually blushed. "Well, you know," he flustered. "It was just an assumption."

Old man Evelith nodded his head, but offered no clarification as to who Enid might actually be. Maid? Mistress? Companion? It wasn't really our business, but I think all of us would have loved to know.

"Here," said Enid, bringing a large folded chart of the approaches to Salem Harbor, and spreading it out on the table. Again, that dark glimpse of red nipples against sheer black fabric; strangely arousing and yet equally frightening, too. Enid caught me looking at her, and looked straight back at me, without smiling, without any hint of possible friendship. The thin sunlight illuminated her hair like a black coronet.

Duglass Evelith opened a drawer under the table and produced a large sheet of tracing paper, on which co-ordinates and transit bearings were already marked. He laid the tracing paper over the chart; although only *he* knew exactly how it had to be keyed into position, so the chart and the overlay would have been useless to anybody else. One bearing ran through the tip of Juniper Point and the southernmost head of Winter Island; the other bearing ran through Quaker Hill, cleaving a sharp line through Quaker Lane Cottage. About 420 meters off the Granitehead shore an X was marked: the supposed position where the *David Dark* had gone down, over 290 years ago.

Edward looked at me in excitement. The X was no more than 250 meters south-south-west of where we had been searching the seabed yesterday morning, but under the sea, with its currents and debris and whirling mud, 250 meters was as good as a mile away.

Duglass Evelith watched us with mild amusement. Then he folded up the chart, and laid it to one side, and slipped the overlay back in his drawer.

"You can have this information on several conditions," he said. "Firstly, that you never once mention my name in connection with your work. Secondly, that you keep me in touch daily with what you are doing, and that you show me everything, no matter how insignificant, that you bring up from the seabed. Thirdly, and most importantly, that if you locate the copper vessel in which the demon is supposed to be incarcerated, that you do not attempt to open it, but that you pack it at once in ice and bring it here, by refrigerated truck.''

"You want it *here*?"

"Do you .think *you* can handle it?" Duglass Evelith demanded. "If it should actually arise, and begin to wield its terrible powers again, do you think *you* could give it what it craves?"

Forrest said, "I'm not sure I like this at all."

But Edward said, "I don't have any particular objection, provided we can have access to whatever it is, once we've brought it here. We'll want to make all kinds of tests. Normal, as well as paranormal. Bone analysis, carbon dating, ultra-violet scanning, X-Ray. Then we'll want to go through the Paarsman test for kinetic energy, and a hypno-volition test."

Duglass Evelith thought about this, and then shrugged. "As long as you don't turn my home into an experimental laboratory."

Edward said, "I have to be quite straight with you, Mr. Evelith. We still lack finance. First of all we have to locate the wreck; then, when we've done that, we have to clear all the mud out of her, collect and tabulate all the broken bits and pieces, and see just how much of the structure we're going to be able to bring up to the surface intact. Finally, we're going to have to rent several large barges, a couple of pontoons, and a floating sheerlegs crane. We have to be talking $5–$6 million. And that's just for starters."

"You mean it may be some considerable time before you can bring the wreck to the light of day?"

"That's correct. We certainly can't bring it up next week even if we find it."

Duglass Evelith took off his spectacles. "Well," he said, "that's rather a pity. The longer it takes, the less chance I have of seeing it completed."

"You really want to come face-to-face with an Aztec demon?" I asked him.

He sniffed. "The lord of Mictlampa is not any ordinary demon," he told me.

"Mictlampa?"

"That's the Mexican name for the region of the dead."

"And does the demon himself have a name?" asked Edward.

"Of course. The lord of Mictlampa is named in the *Codex Vaticanus A* which was drawn up by Halian monks in the 1500s. There is even an illustration of him, descending out of the night head-first, the way a spider descends his web, to ensnare the souls of the living. He holds sway over all the other Aztec demons of the underworld, including Tezcatlipoca, or 'Smoking Mirror,' and alone with Tonacatecutli, the lord of the sun, is entitled to wear a crown. He is always shown with an owl, a corpse, and a dish of human hearts, which are his chief sustenance. His name is Mictantecutli."

I felt a chill go down my back, and looked at Edward sharply. "Mictantecutli," I repeated.

"Yes," said Edward. " 'Mick the Cutler.' "

TWENTY-TWO

I dropped Edward and Forrest off at Edward's house on Story Street, and then drove directly to Salem Hospital, a gray squarish complex of concrete blocks off Jefferson Avenue, and not far from Mill Pond, where David Dark had once lived. The sky had cleared, and there was a high thin sunset, which was reflected in the puddles of the parking-lot. I walked across to the hospital doors with my hands jammed into the pockets of my jacket, and hoped to hell that Constance Bedford was making a reasonable recovery. I should have *insisted* that she and Walter stay away from Quaker Lane Cottage. A warning hadn't been enough. Now the woman was blind and it was all because of me.

I found Walter sitting in the waiting area on the fourth story, his head bowed, staring at the polished vinyl floor. Behind him there was a lithograph of a pelican by Basil Ede. Walter didn't look up, even when I sat down next to him. A soft chime sounded, and a seductive telephonist's voice called, "Dr. Murray, pick up the white phone please. Dr. Murray."

"Walter?" I said.

He raised his head. His eyes were redrimmed, both from tiredness and from weeping. He looked about a hundred years older, and I was reminded of what Duglass Evelith had said about the man who had sailed on the *Arabella*. He opened his mouth, but somehow his throat seemed too dry to say anything.

"What's the latest?" I asked him. "Is she any better? Have you seen her yet?"

"Yes," he said. "I've seen her."

"And?"

214

"She's better."

I was about to say something encouraging, but then I realized that there was something wrong about the way he had spoken, some flatness in the intonation that didn't quite ring true.

"Walter?" I asked him.

Unexpectedly, he reached over and took hold of my hand, and held it very tight. "You just missed her," he said. "She died about twenty minutes ago. Massive cerebral damage, caused by intense cold. Not to mention shock, and the physical trauma to the eyes and face. She didn't really have much of a hope."

"Oh God, Walter, I'm sorry."

He took a deep, sad breath. "I'm a little giddy, I'm afraid. They gave me something to calm me down. What with that, and the tiredness, and the shock of it all, I guess I'm not much good for anything right now."

"Do you want me to take you home?"

"Home?" he stared at me questioningly, as if he didn't know what "home" was any more. Home was only a building now, filled with unpossessed possessions. Rows of dresses that would never be worn; racks of shoes whose owner would never return. What does a single man do with drawersful of lipsticks and stockings and brassieres? The most painful part of a wife's sudden death, as I had discovered for myself, was clearing out the bathroom. The funeral had been nothing compared to clearing out the bathroom. I had stood there with a wastebasket full of nail varnish and hair conditioner and skin-toner, and cried my eyes out.

"You musn't blame yourself for it," said Walter. "You warned me explicitly enough. I somehow thought—well, I somehow thought that Jane would be *benign*. At least to her mother."

"Walter, I saw her later myself. She tried to kill me, too. She isn't Jane, that's what I was trying to warn you about. Not the Jane that either of us used to know. She's like a kind of addict now, can you understand what I mean? Her spirit can't rest until she claims another life, to help feed the force that's controlling her."

"Force? What are you talking about, force?"

"Walter," I said, "this isn't the time or the place. Let me

drive you home; then you can get some sleep and tomorrow we'll talk it over.''

He glanced around over his shoulder, towards the room where Constance must have been lying. "She's there?" I asked him, and he nodded.

"I shouldn't leave her," he said. "It doesn't seem right."

"You won't be leaving her, Walter. She's gone already."

He was silent for a very long time. Every line in his face seemed to have been etched in gray; he was so numbed by exhaustion and tranquilizers that he could barely stay upright.

"Do you know something, John?" he said. "I don't have anybody now. No son, no daughter, no wife. All that family that I thought I would see growing up around me; all those people I loved. They're all gone, and now there's nobody but me. I don't even have anybody to will my gold watch to."

He drew back his cuff, and unfastened his watch, and held it up. "What's going to happen to this watch when *I* die? Constance had it engraved, you know, with my name; and what she said was, 'Some day, your great-grandson's going to wear this watch, and he's going to look at your name engraved on the back, and he'll know who he is, and where he came from.' And do you know something? That boy will never be."

"Come on, Walter," I told him. "I'll just go check with the doctor, and then I'll drive you home."

"Are you going back to—that place tonight? Quaker Lane Cottage?"

"I'll stay with you if you want me to."

He pursed his lips, and then nodded. "I'd like that. If it isn't any trouble."

"No trouble, Walter. In fact, I'm glad to have an excuse not to go back there."

We left the hospital, and walked across the parking lot to my car. Walter shivered in the evening wind. I helped him to climb into the passenger seat, and then we drove out through the suburbs of Salem, southwards towards Boston and Dedham. Walter said very little as we drove; but stared out of the window at the passing traffic, at the houses and the trees and the darkness of the oncoming night, the first night he had known for 38 years which he couldn't share with Constance. As we approached Boston, the lights of airplanes circling Logan Airport looked as lonely as anything I had ever seen.

The house at Dedham had been passed down by Bedfords for four generations, father to son, and although Walter and his father had both worked in Salem, they had kept up residence in the old Dedham house for tradition's sake. For some years, Walter's father had also rented a small apartment near the center of Salem, but Constance had insisted that Walter should drive the 25 miles home every evening, especially after Walter's mother had discreetly told her at Walter's father's funeral that Walter's father had been seeing "women" at the Salem apartment, and that items of underclothing had been discovered under the bed.

It was a huge colonial house set in seven acres of ground; the original forty-one acres having been parceled up by succeeding generations of Bedfords and sold off for property development. White-painted, with a peaked five-gable roof, it was approached by a curving driveway lined with maple trees, and in the fall it looked so picturesque you could hardly believe it was a real dwelling. I remembered how impressed I had been the first time that Jane had brought me back here: and I thought how much better it would have been for the Bedford family if I had turned around that morning and driven all the way back to St. Louis, non-stop, day and night, anything to save them from the tragedy which had visited them these past few weeks, and from the fear which I knew was still to come.

I parked the car outside the front door and helped Walter to climb out. He gave me the front door key and I let us in. The house was still warm: the Bedfords had left the central heating on last night because they had walked out of the house with every intention of coming back. The first thing I saw when I switched on the hall light was Constance's spectacles, lying on the polished hall-table, just where she had left them only 24 hours ago. I looked up, and saw my distorted face in a circular gilt mirror, and behind me, Walter looking shrunken and strange.

"Number one priority is a large Scotch," I told Walter. "Come on into the sitting-room and take your shoes off. Relax."

Walter fastidiously hung up his coat and scarf, and then followed me into the spacious sitting-room, with its waxed honey-colored floors, its Persian rugs, and its mellow 19th-century furniture. Over the wide fireplace hung an oil-painting

of old Suffolk County, in the days before Century 21 reality
and weekend cottages and the Massachusetts Turnpike. Beneath the painting, on the mantel, there was a collection of
Dresden figures which had obviously belonged to Constance.

"I feel numb," said Walter, easing himself down into his
armchair.

"You're going to feel numb for quite some time to come,"
I cautioned him. I poured two large whiskeys out of his heavy
crystal decanter, and handed him one. "It's your mind, pro-
tecting itself from the shock of what's happened."

Walter shook his head. "I can't believe it, you know. I
can't believe any of it. I keep thinking back on what happened last night, the way that Jane appeared like that, and it
seems like a horror movie, something I saw on television.
Not *real*."

"I guess it depends what you mean by real," I said, sitting
down opposite, and pulling my chair a little closer.

Walter looked at me. "Will she always be there? Jane, I
mean? Will she always be a ghost like that? Won't she ever
rest?"

"Walter," I said, "that's one of the things I want to talk to
you about. But not now. Let's wait until tomorrow."

"No," said Walter. "Let's talk about it now. I want to
think this whole thing out. I want to think about it and think
about it until my mind gets tired of thinking about it, and I
can't think about it any more."

"You're sure that's wise?"

"I don't know, but it's what I want to do. Anyway, who
cares about wisdom? I don't have anybody. Have you thought
about that? I have a ten-bedroomed house, and nobody to live
in it but me."

"Finish your whiskey," I instructed him. "Let's have
another. I need to be partially smashed to tell you about
this."

Walter swallowed, shivered, and then handed me his empty
glass. When I had poured us both a refill, I sat down again
and said, "As far as I know, there's only one way in which
Jane's spirit can be put to rest. Even that isn't certain. I've
been hard put to keep believing in all this myself, because the
more I find out about it, the weirder it gets. I think the only
reason I've kept on believing it is because four or five other

people believe it as well: three guys I know from the Peabody Museum, and a girlfriend of theirs.

"This morning we went up to Tewksbury, and talked to Mr. Duglass Evelith. You know Mr. Evelith? Well, you've *heard* of Mr. Evelith, at least. Mr. Evelith's been making a study of psychic disturbances in Salem and Granitehead, and he agrees with us that the probable cause of all these manifestations like Jane's and Mr. Edgar Simons' is—well, is—something that's submerged in an old wreck off the Granitehead coast. The wreck of a ship called the *David Dark*."

"I don't understand," said Walter.

"Neither do I, completely. But apparently the hold of that wreck contains a thing like a giant skeleton, which was brought to Salem in the late 1680s from Mexico. The skeleton was said to be a demon called . . . just a minute, I have it written down here . . . Mictantecutli. The lord of Mictlampa, the region of the dead. It was supposed to have been Mictanecutli's power that created all the havoc that led to the Salem witch-trials; and even though it's sunk beneath the ocean, and several feet of bottom-mud, it's still affecting the dead of Granitehead, and refusing to let them rest."

Walter stared at me as if I was completely mad; but I knew that the only way in which I could convince both him and myself of the true danger of Mictanecutli was if I kept on, and described what needed to be done as rationally and as calmly as I could.

"The wreck of the *David Dark* is going to have to be located," I said. "Then, when we've located it, it's going to have to be raised, and the copper vessel containing Mictantecutli removed, and taken to Tewksbury for old man Evelith to deal with."

"What can *he* do with it that nobody else can?" Walter wanted to know.

"He won't say. But he strongly advised us not to try to tackle the demon on our own."

"*Demon*," said Walter, skeptically; then looked at me narrowly. "You really believe it's a demon?"

"Demon is kind of an old-fashioned way of putting it," I admitted. "I guess these days we'd call it a psychic artifact. But whatever it is, and whatever we call it, the fact remains that the *David Dark* appears to be the center of some extremely intense supernatural activity; and that the only obvious way of finding out what it is, and how to put a stop to it, is to raise the wreck.''

Walter said nothing, but finished his second glass of whiskey and sat back in his chair, exhausted and tranquilized, now half-bombed. I don't suppose I should have been giving him alcohol on top of sedatives, but for my money he needed all the numbness he could get.

I said, as persuasively as I could, ''Even if the wreck *isn't* what we believe it to be, raising it off the seabed will still be a profitable enterprise. There'll be all kinds of archeological spinoffs, as well as souvenirs, book rights, television rights, that kind of stuff. And once we've raised the wreck, it could be put on public show during restoration, and we could make quite a steady income out of admission fees.''

''You're asking me for money,'' Walter surmised.

''The *David Dark* can't be raised without finance.''

''How much finance?''

''Edward Wardwell—he's one of the guys from the Peabody—he reckons five to six million.''

''Five to six *million*? Where the hell am I going to get five to six million?''

''Come on, Walter, most of your clients are business people. If only twenty or thirty of them could be persuaded to invest in raising the *David Dark*, that would mean only about $150,000 each. It would give them the prestige of being involved in an historic salvaging operation, as well as the opportunity to write it all off tax-wise.''

''I couldn't advise anybody to put their money into raising a three-hundred-year-old wreck that might not even be there.''

''Walter, you *have* to. If you don't, Jane's spirit and the spirits of hundreds of other people are going to be damned and cursed for all eternity; never resting; never finding peace. And if all these recent events have been anything to go by, the power of Mictantecutli is becoming stronger. Duglass Evelith believes that the copper vessel in which it's been lying for all these hundreds of years may be corroding. The plain fact of the matter is that we have to get to Mictantecutli before Mictantecutli gets to us.''

Walter said, ''I'm sorry, John. It can't be done. If any one of my clients gets to hear why I've asked him to invest $150,000 in a salvage operation, if any one of them suspects that I've done it to lay a ghost; well, there won't be any doubt about it. My reputation will be finished and so will the reputation of my partnership. I'm sorry.''

"Walter, I'm asking you this for the sake of your own daughter. Don't you know what she's going through, what she must be feeling?''

"I can't,'' said Walter. Then, "Let me think about it tomorrow. Right now I don't know what the hell I'm doing or thinking.''

"Okay,'' I said, more gently. "Do you want me to help you get to bed?''

"I'll just sit here for a while. But if you want to get some sleep, don't let me stop you. You must be as tired as I am.''

"Tired?'' I asked him. I didn't know whether I was or not. "I think I'm more frightened than tired.''

"Well,'' said Walter. He reached out and gripped my hand; and for the first time since we had met, I felt that there was a bond between us, father and son-in-law, even though we had both lost everything that was supposed to keep us together. "I have to admit it,'' he said, "I'm frightened, too.''

TWENTY-THREE

I spent Monday in the shop, even though there was very little business around. I sold a set of etchings of compass roses designed by Theodore Lawrence in the 1830s, and a ship in a bottle, but I really needed to sell a few figureheads and a couple of cannon to keep my profits up to scratch. At lunchtime I went across to the Crumblin' Cookie and talked to Laura.

"You're looking down today," she remarked. "Anything wrong?"

"My mother-in-law died over the weekend."

"I didn't think you liked her too much anyway."

"I've always admired you for your tact," I retorted, a little too caustically.

"We don't serve tact here," said Laura. "Only coffee and cookies and cold hard facts. Was she ill?"

"Who?"

"Your mother-in-law."

"She, um . . . had a kind of an accident."

Laura stared at me, her head slightly cocked to one side. "You're upset, aren't you?" she asked me. "You're really upset. I'm sorry. The way you used to talk about your mother-in-law before . . . I didn't realize. Look, I'm really sorry."

I managed a smile. "You don't have to be sorry. I'm tired, that's all. A whole lot of bad things have been happening one after the other and on top of that I haven't been getting much sleep."

"I know what to do," said Laura. "Come round to my

222

place this evening and I'll cook you my Italian specialty. You like Italian?''

"Laura, you don't have to. I'm fine, really.''

"Do you want to come or don't you? I expect you to bring some wine.''

I put up my hands. "Okay, thanks, I'd love to. I surrender. What time do you want me?''

"Eight, sharp. I may not get too hungry for dinner at eight, but I *do* get too hungry for dinner at eight-oh-five.''

"Even working here?''

"Brother, when you've eaten one cookie you've eaten them all.''

The afternoon back at the shop went by with unimaginable slowness. The sunlight crawled around the walls, illuminating the marine chronometers, the sailing-ship paintings, the brass cleat-hooks. I tried to telephone Edward at the Peabody, but I was told that he was out at an auction. Then I called Gilly but she was busy in the store and said she would call me back. I even called my mother in St. Louis but there was no reply. I sat back at my desk reading a property magazine that had come through the door that morning and feeling as if I were totally alone on a strange planet.

At five o'clock, after I had closed the shop, I went across to the Harbor Lights Bar and sat by myself in a corner booth and drank two glasses of Scotch. I was just considering the possibility of another one before I hit the road when a girl walked past my booth, a girl in a brown cape, and just before she disappeared she turned and glanced at me and I felt myself jump with an involuntary nervous spasm, the way you do when you're about to fall asleep. I could have sworn that it was the same girl I had seen on the road to Quaker Lane, that night when I had been driving home with Mrs. Edgar Simons; and the same girl who had been watching me in Red's Sandwich Shop in Salem. I struggled out of my seat, banging my thighs on the fixed table, but by the time I had reached the door the girl had disappeared.

"Did you see a girl walk past just then?'' I asked Ned Sanborn, behind the bar. "She was wearing a kind of a brown cape, very pale face, but pretty.''

Ned, shaking up a whiskey sour, pulled a face that meant sorry. But Grace, one of the waitresses, said, "A tall girl, was she? Well, quite tall? Dark eyes and a pale face?''

"You saw her too?"

"Sure I saw her. She came out of the back room and I couldn't work out how she got in there. I didn't see her come in, and she hasn't been drinking here."

"Probably a hippie," remarked Ned. According to Ned, any girl who didn't dress in a sensible skirt-and-blouse and wear flat-heeled court shoes and subscribe to *Redbook* was a hippie. "Summer must be coming. First hippie of the summer."

Normally I would have teased Ned about his use of the word "hippie," but this evening I was too disturbed and too worried. If the influence of the demon beneath Granitehead Neck was steadily growing, then who could tell who was one of its ghostly servants and who wasn't? Maybe that girl was a manifestation, more solid than most. Maybe more people than I realized were actually manifestations; maybe Ned was, and Laura, and George Markham. How was I to tell who was a living human being and who wasn't? Supposing Mictantecutli had already claimed them all? I began to feel like the doctor in *Invasion of the Bodysnatchers*, who couldn't tell which of his friends and associates were aliens and which ones weren't.

I left the Harbor Lights Bar and walked over to my car, which was parked in the middle of the square. There was a torn-off note under one of the windshield wipers, on which was scrawled in lipstick, "Eight sharp, don't forget, L." I climbed into the car and drove out of the village center, heading towards Quaker Hill. I wanted to check that the cottage was all right, and pick up some wine at the Granitehead Market.

At the top of Quaker Lane, the cottage waited for me, old and forbidding and now more neglected-looking than ever. I still hadn't fixed that upstairs shutter, and as I got out of the car it gave a slow shuddering squeak. I walked up to the front door, and took out my key. I almost expected that familiar whisper to say "*John*?" but there was no sound at all, just the frustrated seething of the ocean, and the soft rustle of the laurel hedges.

Inside, the cottage was very cold, and beginning to smell damp. The long-case clock in the hallway had stopped, because I hadn't wound it. I went into the living-room and stood for a long time listening for scurries and whispers and footsteps, but again there was silence. Perhaps Jane had given up haunting the cottage now that she knew she was unable to claim me for the region of the dead. Perhaps I had actually seen the last of her. I went into the kitchen, and opened up the icebox to make sure there was nothing in there which was growing mold on it. I took out a bottle of Perrier water and drank four or five large swallows of it straight from the neck. Afterwards I stood there grimacing at the coldness on the roof of my mouth, and the uncompromising fizz of bubbles which seemed to be stuck in my throat forever.

I was going back into the living-room to light the fire when I thought I heard a single footfall upstairs. I hesitated in the hallway, listening hard. It wasn't repeated, but I was so sure that I had heard somebody in one of the bedrooms that I took my umbrella out of the umbrella-stand and began to climb the dark ornamented stairs to see who was up there. I paused half-way up, gripping the pointed umbrella tightly, breathing tightly and tensely.

I thought to myself: don't panic. You know that Jane has no hold over you now. You've faced up to hordes of apparitions from the Waterside Cemetery, and you're still sane and still alive; so there can't be anything up here that's any worse, or any more likely to harm you.

Yet it was the silence that alarmed me, more than the squeaking of the swing had; more than the whispering and the sudden coldness. This cottage was never silent. Old buildings rarely are; they're always creaking or settling or shifting in their dreamless sleep. They're never *silent*, utterly silent, as Quaker Lane Cottage was at that moment.

I reached the top of the stairs, and walked along the darkened landing until I reached the end bedroom. No sound, no breathing, no whispering, no footsteps. I carefully put my hand into the room and switched on the light, then I eased open the door with my foot. The bedroom was empty. Just a painted pine bureau, a narrow single bed covered with a plain woven coverlet. An embroidered sampler was hung on the far wall, with the legend LOVE THY LORD. I looked around, my umbrella half-raised, and then I switched off the light and closed the door behind me.

She was waiting on the landing, under the harsh light of an old marine lantern I had borrowed from the shop. Jane, in the flesh. Not flickering this time, like a half-seen movie; but in the flesh. Her brushed hair shone in the lantern-light, and her face, though white, looked as solid and as real as it had on the morning before she died. She was wearing a simple calico nightgown, off-white, which trailed on the floor, and her hands were clasped in front of her demurely. Only her eyes betrayed the fact that there was something supernatural about her: they were as black and as deep as pools of oil, pools in which a man and all his convictions could easily drown.

"*John*," she said, somewhere inside of my head, without moving her lips. "*I came back for you, John.*"

I stayed where I was, my skin tingling with the sight of her, with the sound of her voice. She had frightened me enough when she had looked like a distant holographic image; but now she stood here in the flesh, I felt as if I were actually going mad. How could this possibly be an illusion? How could a woman look so alive, and yet be dead? Jane had been crushed and destroyed, and yet here she was, my saddest memory brought to life.

The most horrifying thought of all, though, was that the power of Mictantecutli must be increasing every day, if he could bring Jane back to me in such a solid form. What kind of influence and energy it must have taken to conjure her up as she was now, I could only guess. Sometimes I thought I detected her image waver, as if I were seeing her through water, but she remained as solid as ever, smiling slightly, as if she were thinking of all of those times we had spent together when she was alive, times which we could never spend together again.

She had come back for me. But what she was offering now was not fun and laughter and companionship. What she was offering now was death, in the most grisly form imaginable.

"Jane," I said, in a quavery voice, "Jane, I want you to go away. You mustn't come back here, not ever."

"*But this is my home. I shall always be here.*"

"You're dead, Jane. I want you to go away. Don't come around here any longer. You're not the Jane I once knew."

"*But this is my home.*"

"This is a home for living people, not travesties of living people from the graveyard."

"*John . . .*" she said coaxingly. "*How can you speak to me like that?*"

"I can speak to you like that because you're not Jane and because I want you to go. Get out of here, leave me alone. I loved you when you were alive but I don't like you now."

Gradually, subtly, Jane's features began to change. I saw the face of Mrs. Edgar Simons, contorted with incomprehensible agony, melt and change and then disappear again. I saw other women's faces, and men's faces, too, rippling across her features as if she couldn't make up her mind which character she wanted to be. I saw Constance, and Mrs. Goult, freshly-dead faces whose expressions were still blank and tortured with the trauma of dying.

"They are all here," said a deep, blurting voice. *"All their faces, all their characters. They are all here and they are all mine."*

"Who are you?" I demanded. Then, stepping closer, I shouted at the creature, *"Who are you?"*

The creature laughed, a whole assembly of laughs, and then that soft, familiar voice said, *"It's me, it's Jane. Don't you recognize me?"*

"You're not Jane."

"John, darling, how can you say that? What are you saying to me?"

"Keep away," I warned her. "You're dead, so keep away."

"Dead, John? What do you know of death?"

"I know enough to want you out of this house."

"But I'm your wife, John. I belong here. I belong with you. Look, John"—and here she proudly held her protuberant stomach—*"I'm going to have your baby."*

At that moment, I was close to snapping. I could feel my head expanding as if it refused to believe any of the information which was being fed to it by my eyes and my ears. Your wife and baby son are dead, it insisted. This can't be real. What you're seeing and hearing is a delusion. This can't be real.

"What do you want?" I asked her. "Just tell me what you want, and then go away and leave me alone."

Jane smiled at me, almost lovingly, except for the terrible blankness in her eyes. And when she spoke, her voice was grating and rough, more like the voice of an elderly man than a girl who hadn't even turned 30.

"It's very cold down here . . . cold, and isolated . . . sealed off . . . a kingdom without subjects and without a throne . . ."

"You mean down *there* . . . in the *David Dark*?" I asked her.

She nodded, and when she did so, I thought I caught the faintest glimpse of smoldering blue fire within her eyes. "*I thought you would understand . . .*" she told me. "*I knew from the beginning that I would find an ally in you . . .*"

"I intend to salvage the *David Dark*, if that's what you mean."

"*The ship? The ship is unimportant. It is what the hold contains that you must seek . . . the vessel in which those accursed people imprisoned me . . .*"

"I intend to bring your vessel up, too. But I warn you that I also intend to destroy you."

Jane let out a burst of hissing laughter. "*Destroy me? You cannot destroy me! I am part of the order of the universe, just as the sun is; just as life itself is. The region of the dead stretches forever under dark skies, and I am its chosen lord. You cannot destroy me.*"

"I'm going to try."

"*Then you wll condemn yourself to a death far more terrible than any that you can imagine. And everyone you ever loved or cherished will be cursed by your action; and doomed to wander the region of the dead forever, without rest, without peace, with nothing but eternal torment and misery and ceaseless dissatisfaction.*"

"You can't do that," I asserted.

"*Do you want to see me try?*" blared the demon's voice. "*Look for yourself, if you want to understand how powerful I am!*"

At that moment, a small naked boy of about four or five appeared from my bedroom, and stared up at me. Shyly, slowly, he reached out for Jane's hand, and then clung close to her, staring at me all the time as if he knew me, but was frightened of me. Jane ruffled his dark hair with her hand, and then looked at me with an expression that was like a mask of complete contempt.

"*This boy is your son, as he would have been if he had lived. I have taken his whole life; for if anybody dies before their time, I am rewarded with all the years that are left. All the energy, all the emotion, all the youthfulness; and all the blood. I feed off unused life, John, and believe me if you attempt to cross me in any way, then I will feed off yours.*"

Jane passed her hand over the boy's head, and he vanished as suddenly as he had appeared; but not before he had left me with a heartrending image of the child I had helped Jane to conceive, and then lost. I had tears in my eyes as Jane said to me, "*Salvage the* David Dark*; open the copper vessel; but do not attempt to hurt me, because my power at that moment will be devastating, and invincible. If you assist me, I will reward you the same way that I rewarded David Dark, with his life and with his sanity. I will also reward you one more way: and listen closely. If you assist me, I will return your Jane to you, and your son. I have that power, since I am lord of the region of the dead, and they only pass through this region who have my authority. I can turn them back, and you will be able to live again the life you believed you had lost. Constance Bedford, too, could be returned to you. Had you thought of that? Help me, John, and you could regain your happiness.*"

I stared at Jane speechlessly. The thought of having her back again seemed wild and impossible; yet so many wild and impossible things had happened since I had first heard the garden-swing creaking on that dark and windy night that I could almost believe it. And, God, what a temptation, to have her here again, to have her back in my arms again, to talk to her again!

"I don't believe you can do it," I said. "Nobody can resurrect the dead. And besides, her body is smashed. How can you bring back somebody whose body is smashed?"

Jane smiled. Blandly, artlessly, as if she were dreaming a dream of other existences, other places; as if she already had memories that I would never be able to share. "*Am I smashed now*?" she asked me, hauntingly. "*I have been recreated from the matrix from which I was very first born. You are dealing with one who controls the process of life, as well as death. That ruined body of mine is well-decayed by now; but I can live again, as I was meant to. And so could your child.*"

"I don't believe you," I said; although I half-believed already. God, just to hold Jane's hand again, to kiss her, to feel her hair, to make love to her. There were tears streaming down my cheeks which I didn't feel.

Jane's image began to waver again, and shrink. Soon, she was almost invisible, nothing more than a shadow on the landing, a silhouette without substance.

"*John*," she whispered, as she vanished.

"Wait!" I called her. "Jane, for God's sake, wait!"

"*John*," she murmured, and was gone.

I stood on the landing for a very long time, until my back began to ache, and then I went downstairs. I went into the living-room and poured myself a whiskey from a bottle of Chivas Regal whose level was already quite low. I would stay here tonight, I decided. I would light a fire. Perhaps the warmth would tempt the spirits back here. To think that the time might come when Jane and I could sit down beside this fire together, as we used to, watching the flames and telling each other stories of what we would do with our lives, our long futures. It was almost more than I could endure.

I sat up very late that night, until the fire that I had built had eventually died away to ashes, and the room began to grow distinctly cold. I locked the doors, wound up the clock, and went upstairs, more than ready for sleep. I stared at myself in the mirror as I brushed my teeth, and wondered if I was actually going mad, if at last the supernatural stresses and strains of the past week had tipped me over the edge.

Yet Jane had been here, hadn't she, speaking to me in the voice of Mictantecutli, the lord of Mictlampa, the region of the dead? She had promised me my happiness back, hadn't she? Jane and our unborn son, restored to life; and maybe Constance Bedford, too. I couldn't have imagined anything like that, and if it was only a dream, why did I feel so torn about helping to set Mictantecutli free? Scores of people would die if it were to be released unchecked from its copper vessel; yet what did that matter to me? Scores of people die on the highways every day in road accidents, and there was nothing I could do about it. I would only be assisting destiny to take its natural course; and think of the rewards of it.

I was almost asleep when the telephone rang. I picked it up clumsily and said, "Hello; John Trenton here."

"Oh, you're *there*, are you?" a girl's voice said sharply. "Well, you must be, since you're obviously not here. Thank you for a great evening, John. I'm just scraping your *filetto al barolo* down the sink-disposal."

"Laura?" I said.

"Of course it's Laura. Who else do you know who would be stupid enough to cook you an Italian meal and then wait for you to turn up, thinking that you actually would?"

"Laura, I'm so sorry. Something happened tonight . . . something that totally threw me off."

"What was her name?"

"Laura, please. I'm sorry. I got all caught up in something very emotional and dinner with you got wiped out of my mind."

"I suppose you want to make it up to me."

"You know I will."

"Well, don't bother. And next time you come into the cookie shop, go sit someplace else, where Kathy can serve you."

She put down the phone and I was left with a flat whining tone. I sighed, and cradled my own receiver.

As I did so, I heard the faintest high-pitched singing.

"O the men they sailed from Granitehead
To fish the foreign shores . . ."

And the haunting quality of the voice was made even more chilling now that I knew what the words actually meant.

"But the fish they caught were naught but bones
With hearts crush'd in their jaws."

It wasn't an old sea-chanty after all; and it certainly wasn't a song about fishing. It was a rhyme about Mictantecutli, and how David Dark and the crew of the *Arabella* had sailed to Mexico to bring him back to Salem. It was a song of death and supernatural destruction.

TWENTY-FOUR

The following morning, Tuesday, I was visited at the shop by the local police department, who wanted to ask me a few questions about Constance Bedford. The medical examiner had determined that death had been caused by irreparable damage to the frontal lobes of the brain consistent with sudden freezing. A detective in a badly-fitting double-knit suit asked me if I kept any liquid gases at the cottage, oxygen or nitrogen. It was a ridiculous question, but I suppose he had to ask it for the sake of procedure.

"You don't keep any ice, either? Large quantities of ice?"

"No," I assured him. "No oxygen, no nitrogen, no ice."

"But your mother-in-law died from freezing."

"Freezing or something *like* freezing," I corrected him.

"What's *like* freezing?" he wanted to know. "The M.E. said she was subjected to such intense cold that her eyeballs had actually pulverized. Now, how did that happen?"

"I don't have any idea."

"You were *there*."

"It must have been a freak of the weather. I saw her collapse on to the pathway, that was all."

"Then you went running off along the shoreline. Why did you do that?"

"I was going for help."

"The nearest house to yours was only a hundred yards away, in the opposite direction. Besides, you had a telephone."

"I panicked, that's all," I told him. "Is there a law against panic?"

"Listen," the detective told me, fixing my attention with

232

relentless green eyes, "this is the second unusual death in which your name has come up in a week. Just do me a favor: stay away from trouble. You're under suspicion in both incidents and any more funny business out of you and I'm going to have to haul you in. You understand me?"

"I understand you."

The police interview irritated and depressed me, so half an hour later I closed the shop and drove over to Salem. I parked on Liberty Street and walked over to Street Mall to see Gilly. She was serving a blond-haired girl with a red floor-length gown as I walked in, but she smiled and she was obviously pleased to see me.

"I've been thinking about you," she said, when her customer had left.

"I've been thinking about you, too," I told her.

"Edward said you had an interesting trip up to Tewksbury, and that old man Evelith told you where the wreck might be located."

"That's right. I'm on my way to see Edward now."

"Well, you don't have to bother. Edward and I have a lunchdate at twelve; why don't you join us?"

"Miss McCormick, it would be a pleasure."

We met Edward outside the Peabody Museum and then walked down to Charlie Cheng's restaurant on Pickering Wharf. "I felt a sudden urge to eat Chinese," said Edward. "I was spending the whole morning cataloging Oriental prints, and the more I thought about Macao and Whampoa Anchorage, the more I thought about crispy noodles and butterfly prawns."

We were shown to a corner table, and the waiter brought us hot towels, and then a plate of Chinese hors d'oeuvres.

"Forrest and Jimmy both have their regular free day tomorrow," said Edward, "and I've decided to join them and take a little French leave, so that we can do some preliminary echo-soundings over the spot where old man Evelith thought the wreck might be. Do you want to come?"

"I don't think so, not this time," I said. Much as I wanted to help to locate the *David Dark*, I knew that my presence tomorrow wouldn't particularly help. The *Alexis* would be sailing backwards and forwards for hours in a tedious parallel search, and even if the sea was calm, which it would have to be for an accurate echo-sounding of the sea-bed, the trip would be very much less than enjoyable.

Edward picked up a morsel of paper-wrapped chicken with his chopsticks, and deftly opened it. "There's only one thing that bothers me," he said. "Why is old man Evelith so insistent that only *he* take charge of this giant skeleton thing once we've brought it up to the surface?"

"If it turns out to be as dangerous and as malevolent as he says it is, then how are *we* going to handle it?" I asked. "At least he seems confident that he can keep it in check."

"We only have his word for that. Whatever's inside that copper vessel may be incredibly valuable, and yet all *we're* supposed to do is to deliver it unopened, right to his door, meek and unprotesting."

"What do you suggest?" I asked him. I suddenly found myself interested in keeping Mictantecutli away from old man Evelith, for the simple reason that if I *did* decide to let the demon loose, it would be far easier to do so if it was in our custody.

Edward said, "Why don't you try the aromatic crispy duck? It's especially good here. Do you know how they make it?"

I said, "Yes, I know how they make it, but I think I prefer the chicken in black bean sauce."

"We'll share," said Gilly.

Edward said, "We don't have to take the copper vessel out to Tewksbury straight away. We can always rent a refrigerated truck and have it ready at the wharf when we bring up the wreck of the *David Dark*, and take the copper vessel down to Mason's Cold Storage. Then we can open it ourselves and see exactly what it is we've got."

"You actually believe what Mr. Evelith said, about that Aztec skeleton?" asked Gilly. "I find it incredibly far-fetched, I really do."

"You don't think that what happened to us at the Hawthorne Inn was far-fetched?" I asked her.

"Well, sure, but—I don't know. A *demon*. Who believes in demons?"

"It's just a convenient word to use," Edward explained. "I don't know what the hell else to call it. An occult relic? I don't know. Demon is just a handy word, that's all."

"All right, then, call it a demon," said Gilly. "But I don't think it's going to help anybody to believe in and sympathize with what you're trying to do, do you?"

"Well, we'll see," said Edward. Then, to me, "Did you have any luck with your father-in-law, as far as finance is concerned?"

"Not yet. I've left him to think about it."

"Keep pressing him, won't you? We can just about afford these echo-soundings, but not much else. I've already emptied my investment account at the bank, not that *that* amounted to much. Two thousand, one hundred dollars."

"Have you seen any more manifestations?" Gilly asked me. "Any more spooky apparitions? Edward told me what happened to you on Saturday night; that must have been *so* scary."

"You still don't really believe it, do you?" I asked her.

"I'd *like* to believe it—" she said.

"—but you can't," I added.

"I'm sorry," she said. "I guess I'm too pragmatic, too down-to-earth. I see these girls screaming on horror films whenever they're threatened by a monster or a vampire, and I just *know* that I wouldn't react that way. I'd want to know what the monster *was,* and what it wanted, or maybe if it was somebody dressed up to look like a monster. I'm not denying that what happened at the Hawthorne was scary. It could even have been occult. But I think if it *was* occult it came from inside your own mind; it was you doing it yourself. I've been changing my opinion about once every five minutes for the past few days, do I believe in ghosts or don't I, and I think I've come out on the side of the non-believers. People are seeing them; all right; *you're* seeing them. I believe that. But that doesn't mean to say that they're actually there."

"Well, well, little Miss Sensible," I said. "Here's the beef in ginger, help yourself."

"You think I'm too direct," she said.

"Did I say I think you're too direct?" I asked her.

"Not in so many words."

"Well, then, keep my opinions to yourself."

After lunch, I bought a large bouquet of flowers and drove back to Granitehead to present them to Laura, and tell her how sorry I was for forgetting to show up for dinner. I had looked into the Crumblin' Cookie earlier, but she hadn't been there. It was obvious from the way the rest of the staff had stared at me, however, that she had told them what had happened. As I drove along West Shore Drive, I decided to drop into the Granitehead Market, and pick up a fresh bottle of whiskey and maybe a bottle of wine for Laura, to go with the flowers. It was a bright, springlike afternoon, and lunch with Gilly and Edward had cheered me up. I whistled as I parked the car and walked across the parking-lot to the market door.

Charlie wasn't there, but his part-time assistant Cy was serving behind the counter, a good-humored young teenager with bright red spots and what was probably the last crewcut on the Eastern Seaboard. I went to the liquor shelf and picked out a bottle of Chivas and a bottle of Mouton Cadet red.

"Charlie not here?" I asked Cy, as I took out my wallet.

"He went out," said Cy. "I mean, like, he really *rushed* out."

"Charlie *rushed*? I don't think I've ever seen Charlie rush in the whole time I've been here."

"He surely did this time. He went out of that door like a bat out of hell. He said something about Neil."

I felt that familiar, unsettling prickle. "Neil? You mean his dead son Neil?"

"Well, I don't think so," said Cy. "It couldn't have been. He said he'd seen him. 'I just saw him!' he said, and then he rushed out of that door like crazy."

"Which way?" I demanded.

"Which *way*?" said Cy, surprised. "I don't know which way. Well, maybe kind of up that way, past the parking-lot and up the hill. I was serving, I didn't take too much notice."

I pushed my two bottles to the side of the counter. "Keep these here for me, will you?" I told him, and then wrenched open the market door and ran out into the parking-lot. I shaded my eyes against the afternoon sun and stared up the hill, but I couldn't see any sign of Charlie. However, he was fat, and unfit, and he couldn't have gotten far. I ran across the parking-lot and started climbing the hill as rapidly as I could.

It was a long, hard climb. Up here, the range of hills of which Quaker Hill was the southernmost were steeper and rougher than anywhere else. I had to cling on to the rough grass to keep my balance, and several times my foot slid on the crumbling soil, and I scraped my ankles.

After four or five minutes, panting and sweating, I reached the crest of the hill and looked around. Off to the north-east, I could see Granitehead Village, and beyond it, the glittering North Atlantic. To the west I could see Salem Harbor and Salem itself, strung along the shoreline; to the south I could see Quaker Hill and Quaker Lane Cottage, and off to the south-west, Waterside Cemetery.

It was breezy and cold up here, in spite of the sunshine. My eyes watered as I looked frantically around for any sign of Charlie. I even cupped my hands around my mouth, and shouted, "Charlie! Charlie Manzi! Where are you, Charlie?"

I descended the gentler slope that eventually led down towards the sea. The grass whipped against my legs, and whistled in the wind. I felt chilly and very alone up here, and even the smoke which rose from Shetland Industrial Park, right next to Derby Wharf, didn't seem to assure that there was any human life around here. I could have been alone, in a world suddenly deserted.

Not much further down the slope, however, I caught sight of Charlie. He was jogging through the grass, heading diagonally towards the shoreline, his shoulders hunched, his white apron flapping like a semaphore signal. I shouted out, "Charlie! Wait, Charlie! Charlie!" but either he didn't hear me or he was determined to ignore me.

Although I was already out of breath, I ran as fast as I could down the slope, and at last caught up with him. He didn't even turn to look at me, and I had to keep on running just to stay abreast of him. His cheeks and jowls were white with effort, and his forehead glistened with sweat. As he ran, his breasts joggled up and down under his checkered shirt.

"Charlie!" I shouted at him. "What are you running for?"

"You stay away, Mr. Trenton!" he gasped. "You stay away and leave me alone!"

"Charlie, for Christ's sake, you'll have a heart attack!"

"None of your goddamned business! Stay away!"

I stumbled on a rock, and almost fell, but then I caught up with Charlie again and yelled, "He isn't real, Charlie! He's an illusion!"

"Don't you give me that," puffed Charlie. "He's real and I've seen him. I prayed for God to bring him back and now God's brought him back. And if I get Neil back, then Moira will come back, too. So stay away, you got me? Don't question miracles."

"Charlie, this is a miracle," I panted, "but it's not God's miracle."

"What are you talking about?" Charlie slowed down to a hobbling, jerky walk. "Who else does miracles, apart from God?"

I pointed to the north-west, to the sparkling stretch of water about a half-mile south of Winter Island. "Charlie, under the ocean—right there—where I'm pointing—lies the wreck of a three-hundred-year-old ship. Inside that ship are the remains of a kind of demon, a devil, do you understand me? An evil spirit, like in *The Amityville Horror*, only worse."

"You're trying to tell me it was *that* which raised up my Neil?"

"Not just your Neil, Charlie, but my wife, too, and the wives and husbands and brothers and children of scores of other people in Granitehead. Charlie, Granitehead is cursed because of that demon. The dead of Granitehead are never allowed to rest, and your Neil is the same."

Charlie stopped, and stared at me for a very long time, while he caught his breath. "Why are you telling me this?" he said at last. "Is it true?"

"As far as I know it. I'm working with several other people, including three custodians from the Peabody Museum. We're doing what we can to raise that ship off the bottom, and get rid of the demon forever."

Charlie wiped his mouth with his hand, and narrowed his eyes towards Waterside Cemetery. "I don't know what to say, Mr. Trenton. I saw him, and he was real. Real and alive as I am."

"Charlie, I know. I've seen Jane the same way. But, believe me, it isn't the Neil you used to know when he was alive. He's different, and he's dangerous."

"Dangerous? I used to take my belt to that boy, when he misbehaved himself."

"That was the Neil you knew when he was alive. This Neil is something else altogether. Charlie, he's controlled by that demon, and he's out to kill you."

Charlie sniffed, and then cleared his throat. He looked at me and then looked down towards the cemetery.

"I don't know," he said. "I don't know what to believe. You, or my own eyes."

It was then that we both heard calling. A boy's voice,

carried on the wind. We both strained our eyes to see where it was coming from, and at last Charlie said, "There . . . look, over there!" and when I followed his stubby pointing finger I saw Neil, young Neil Manzi, standing on a small grassy promontory, waving to us as freely and cheerfully as if he were alive.

"Dad . . ." he was calling. "Come on, Dad . . ."

Charlie immediately started jogging again, down the hill.

"Charlie, for God's sake!" I shouted, and ran after him, trying to catch his arm. "Charlie, that isn't Neil!"

"Don't give me that, look at the boy," Charlie puffed at me. "Look at him, the same as always. It's a miracle, that's all. A plain miracle, just like they used to happen in the Bible."

"Charlie! He'll kill you!"

"Well, maybe I deserve it!" Charlie shouted. "Maybe I deserve it, for buying him that motorcycle. Get away, Mr. Trenton, I warn you. Leave me alone."

"Charlie—"

"Mr. Trenton, I can't be any unhappier than I am now, alive or dead."

That last shouted remark stopped me in my tracks. I watched Charlie Manzi galloping fatly down that hill, waving as he ran to the slender boy in denims who stood just a little way away from him, waving back; and I knew that there was nothing I could do. I could have football-tackled Charlie, I suppose, or tried to knock him out. But what was the point of that? I'd never be able to watch over him night and day, to make sure that Neil didn't come back to get him; and besides which, if I did knock him out, he wouldn't even want to talk to me again.

I stood where I was, my hands down by my sides, as Charlie ran further and further away. Soon he was a tiny fat figure in the distance, his white apron blinking at me from almost a quarter of a mile away.

I decided to go back to the market, and pick up my car, and maybe drive around to the cemetery to see if there was anything I could do; but then I saw Neil run down from his promontory, and disappear, only to reappear much nearer the cemetery gates, almost the same distance away as Quaker Lane Cottage. Charlie kept after him, and I knew then that however hopeless it was, I was going to have to chase up behind and see if there was anything I could do to make him change his mind.

I ran down that hillside as fast as I used to run at high school, when I was swimming and running every day and generally considered myself to be a junior edition of Johnny Weissmuller. I was exhausted by the time I was within hailing distance of Charlie, and I could scarcely croak, let alone shout, but I kept on running at a slow, even pace, until there were only twenty yards between us.

"Dad!" came the cry on the south-west wind. "Come on, Dad!" And the sound of it was all the more chilling because it was so young. I saw Charlie reach the cemetery gates, and open them, and disappear inside, somewhere behind the headstones.

I summoned up a last burst of effort, and reached the cemetery gates just in time to see Charlie making his way down the center aisle of tombstones. He was walking now, holding his chest with both hands because he was so deeply out of breath, but not stopping to rest, not even for a moment, not while Neil was waiting for him at the end of the aisle, his arms outstretched, smiling, welcoming his father so warmly, and with such encouragement, that I knew I would never be able to persuade Charlie to turn around.

"Charlie!" I shouted, in a strained voice. "Charlie, for one minute, wait!"

I wrestled with the wrought-iron cemetery gates, but somehow they refused to open. They weren't bolted; and they couldn't be locked, because Charlie had walked through them so easily. But no matter how violently I shook them and kicked at them, I couldn't get them to budge.

"Charlie!" I screeched at him. "For one second, Charlie, just listen! Don't go near him, Charlie! Don't go near! Charlie, it isn't Neil! Don't go near!"

I rammed against the gates with my shoulder, but they weren't going to move. There was nothing I could do but stand there and shout, while Charlie plodded slowly between the gravestones towards the son he thought he had lost.

It was then that I heard a deep, gravely, grating noise. It sounded like a ton of rock being dragged slowly across a cement floor; and I wasn't sure if I was hearing it through my ears or through the soles of my feet. Then there was another noise, grittier than the first, and louder.

Maybe it was an earthquake. Maybe something was shifting, under the ground. I had heard there were caverns underneath parts of Granitehead, where the ocean had eroded the softer subsoil. I peered in the cemetery through the bars of the gates, and tried to see if anything was happening there.

To my horror and astonishment, I saw that one of the tombs, a large white-marble catafalque with an engraved marble coffin on top of it, had somehow slid across the aisle in front of Charlie, and was now separating him from his son. Charlie turned around, bewildered, and I heard him shout, "Neil! Neil, what's going on here? Neil, answer me!"

Before he could walk back towards the gates, another huge tomb began to slide across the aisle behind him, boxing him in. It moved with a slow, grinding sound, and it blocked the aisle completely, a wall of solid Barre granite.

"Charlie!" I yelled. "Charlie, get yourself out of there! For God's sake, Charlie, get out!"

I heard Charlie calling for Neil again; but then I also heard another sound. The steady grating of more tombstones, as they shifted themselves in on both sides, narrowing the aisle in which Charlie was standing by slow but inexorable inches.

"Charlie!" I shouted. "Charlie!"

The tombstones pressed further and further into the space that was left, until I heard above the grinding noise they were making a sudden high-keyed shout for help.

"Mr. Trenton, my sleeve's caught! Mr. Trenton!"

I rattled furiously at the cemetery gates but there was nothing I could do to get in there. I could only watch in horror and disbelief as Charlie tried to claw his way up the polished side of the marble catafalque, desperate to escape the two huge upright gravestones which ground their way in towards him on either side. They must have weighed nearly a ton each, those stones, decorated with stone lilies and sobbing cherubs; and they moved like giant funeral carriages, *des chars funèbres,* gray and grotesque, faceless and unstoppable.

"Oh, God!" shrieked Charlie. "Oh my God! Neil! Help me! Oh God, somebody help me!"

By some unimaginable effort, Charlie managed to heave his bulky body halfway out of the relentlessly closing space. His face was crimson with fear, his eyes starting out of his head. He raised one arm towards me, but then the massive tombstones closed in on him, trapping him between two upright faces of solid granite.

Without hesitation, the tombstones crushed him. I heard the bones in his legs snapping like a fusillade of pistol-fire; and then he soundlessly opened his mouth for a moment in utter agony, before a fountain of blood surged from between his lips and darkly splattered the gravestones all around him. He was pinned upright for a moment, jerking and writhing, and then he mercifully collapsed.

I closed my eyes, still clutching the bars of the wrought-iron gates. I was shivering all over, and I could hear the blood pumping through my veins like the rushing traffic to hell itself. Then, without looking towards Charlie any more, I turned around, and began to walk back up the hillside.

Behind me, there was a shuddering, screeching, scraping sound, as the tombstones moved back into their proper positions. It was a sound that crawled into my bones, as Yiddish people sometimes say. I knew that I would wake up at night for years to come and think that I could hear that grating noise of an impossible and unavoidable death.

I could have reported Charlie's death to the police, I suppose. I could have knelt beside him until somebody came. But I was already involved in enough mysterious fatalities; already tangled up in enough fear and enough complications. How could I possibly explain Charlie's crushing to anybody who hadn't seen it for himself? I couldn't even believe it myself, the way those massive tombs had moved of their own terrifying volition. I kept on walking up the hill, past the end of Quaker Lane, and back at last to the Granitehead Market.

It seemed to take me three times as long to get back to the store as it had to run down to the cemetery, and I was bushed when I walked back in there to collect my liquor.

"Did you find him?" asked Cy.

"Not a sign," I lied.

"You're worried about him?" Cy wanted to know.

"There was something I wanted to tell him, that's all. But I guess it can wait."

"The way you ran out of here, like another bat out of hell . . ."

"Forget it, okay?" I said, more sharply than I meant to. I picked up my wine and my whiskey. "I'm sorry. Thanks for taking care of the booze."

"Any time," said Cy, looking puzzled.

I drove into Granitehead. Somebody had taken my favorite parking spot and so I had to go all the way down to the municipal lot by the harbor. By the time I had trudged back uphill to the square, I wasn't in the best of tempers: shocked, tired, and edgy. I walked into the Crumblin' Cookie with a scowl on my face like Quasimodo with a hunch-ache.

"Well," said Laura, "you've actually dared to show yourself."

By the simple fact that she was speaking to me I knew that I was halfway forgiven. I set the flowers and the bottle of wine on the counter, and said, "The flowers are to say sorry. The wine we should have shared last night. If you want to throw the flowers away and drink the wine on your own, I'll understand."

"You could have *called* me," she said, resentfully.

"Laura, I don't know what else to say. I feel like a total pig."

She took the bottle of wine and examined the label. "All right," she said, "since you have such excellent taste, I forgive you. But only just. And if it happens again, I may un-forgive you very fast."

"Whatever you say, Laura."

"Well, you could *look* as if you're sorry."

"I'm just upset, that's all."

"You don't think *I'm* upset?"

"I didn't say you weren't."

"At least when you're saying 'forgive me' you might look as if you want to be forgiven."

"What do you want me to do?" I demanded. "Sing *I'm Sorry* and pour ashes all over my head?"

"Oh, get out of here. You're about as sorry as . . . I don't *know* what."

"You don't even know what it is I'm as sorry as, and you're telling me to get out?"

"John, for God's sake."

"All right," I told her, "I'm going."

"Take your wine and your flowers with you," she said.

"Keep them. Just because you don't know what it is I'm as sorry as, that doesn't mean to say that I'm *not* sorry."

"You're about as sorry as Gary Gilmore," she snapped.

"Well, you know what his famous last words were, don't you? 'Let's do it.' "

I walked out of the Crumblin' Cookie and left Laura to her justified anger. I liked her, I didn't want to upset her. Maybe I'd call her later this evening and see whether she'd cooled down. I knew that, sure as hell, *I* wouldn't have been very happy if I'd spent all evening preparing an Italian meal for somebody who couldn't be bothered to turn up.

I was crossing the cobblestones of Granitehead Square when I thought I glimpsed the girl in the hooded brown cape on the other side of the street just turning into Village Place. I changed direction, and followed her, determined this time to catch up with her and find out who she was. Maybe she was nobody special at all: maybe her frequent appearances had been coincidence. But after Charlie's death and Constance's death, I was determined that I was going to lay the ghost of the *David Dark,* and that meant I was going to track down anything and everything that could help me.

I turned the corner into Village Place: a little narrow cul-de-sac lined with fashionably chintzy shops. The girl was standing in front of the Granitehead Bookmart, staring into the window, either at the books that were displayed inside, or at her own reflection.

TWENTY-FIVE

I approached the girl cautiously, circling around behind her so that I could see her pale face mirrored in the bookstore window. She must have known I was there, but she stayed where she was, quite still, one hand clasping her hood around her head, the other hanging with almost unnatural stillness by her side.

We both stood there in silence for quite a long time. A man in a woolly ski-hat came out of the store with a package under his arm, saw us, stopped for a moment in surprise, and then went hurrying off.

The girl said, "Why did you follow me?"

"I think I should be asking you that question. Everywhere I've been in the past few days, I've seen you."

She turned around and looked at me. There was something strangely familiar about her, although I couldn't think what it was. She was very pale, but quite pretty, with the darkest of eyes; yet her eyes were liquid and animated, not like the dead and lightless eyes of Jane, or Edgar Simons, or Neil Manzi.

"You're not one of them," I said.

"Them?"

"The manifestations; the ghosts."

"No," she smiled. "I'm not one of them."

"But you do know who I mean?"

"Yes."

I took out my handkerchief and dabbed at my forehead. I felt hot and uncomfortable and I wasn't quite sure what to say. The girl watched me placidly, still smiling; although it was a quiet and friendly smile, not supercilious, or sly, or

245

marked with that coaxing twist of the lip that had characterized Jane's smiles whenever she had appeared.

"I was only watching you," she said. "Just to make sure
that no harm befell you. Just to make sure that you were safe.
Of course, you have always been fairly safe, because of your
unborn son; but you might have unwittingly put yourself into
a dangerous situation without knowing it."

"You were watching me?" I asked her. "Who are you?
And what were you watching me for? You don't have any
right to watch people."

"These days," said the girl, not at all upset by my
aggressiveness, "everybody has a right to watch everybody
else. You never know, after all, who your very best friend
might be."

"I want to know who you are," I insisted.

"You have already met some of us," she said. "Mercy
Lewis you met on Salem Common; Enid Lynch you met at
Mr. Evelith's house. My name is Anne Putnam."

"Mercy Lewis? Anne Putnam?" I asked. "Aren't those
the names of—"

The girl smiled even more broadly, and held out her hand.
Hesitantly, I took it, I'm not sure why. It just seemed impo-
lite to refuse. Her fingers were long and cool, and there was a
silver ring on every one of them, including her thumb.

"You're right," she said. "They are the names of witches.
Not our real names, of course; but names we have adopted.
They have power, those names; and besides, they remind us
of the days when Salem was in the grip of the Fleshless
One."

"You mean Mictantecutli? From what I've seen, Salem is
still in his grip, and Granitehead, too. But you're not seriously telling me that you're a *witch?*"

"You can call us what you like," said Anne. "Listen—
take me back with you to your cottage, and then I can explain
everything to you. Now that you have found me out, I think it
is better that you know."

I looked down at our joined hands. "All right," I said, at
last. "I've always wanted to meet a witch."

We walked out of Village Place and into Granitehead
Square, hand-in-hand; and, just my luck, Laura was stepping
out of Crumblin' Cookie on the far side of the square, and
she stopped and stared at us with her hands planted firmly on

her hips to indicate to me that she had seen us, and that she thought I was more than a pig. In fact, she thought I was a don't-know-what.

As we descended the winding hill to Granitehead Harbor, Anne said, "You are troubled today. I can feel it. Why are you so troubled?"

"You know about Mrs. Edgar Simons? The way she died?"

"I saw you with her that night, when I was out on the road."

"Well, I just witnessed another death; Charlie Manzi, the guy who owns the Granitehead Market."

"Where did it happen?"

"Where? Down at the Waterside Cemetery. He was crushed, somehow I can't even describe it. But it seemed like the tombstones came together and crushed the life out of him."

Anne gave my hand a conciliatory squeeze. "I'm sorry," she said. "But there is great power here. The Fleshless One is about to be free; and all the energy he has been storing for three hundred years is about to strike us."

We reached my car, and I opened the door for Anne and then climbed in myself. "I'm amazed you know so much about this," I told her, as I started the engine. I twisted around in my seat as I backed out into the roadway. "Edward and I and the rest of us, we were all in the dark until we went to talk to Mr. Evelith."

"You forget that all of Salem's witches can trace their ancestry directly back to David Dark," she said. "It was David Dark who brought the power of the Fleshless One to Salem, in his attempts to impose some kind of hellfire morality on the people of Essex County; and the first witches were girls and women whom the Fleshless One had killed and then reincarnated as its handmaidens, to entice their own relatives and friends to one grisly death after another, in order that the Fleshless One could have their hearts."

"That's what old man Evelith told us," I said, turning left on West Shore Drive.

"Not all of the witches were named and caught, though," said Anne. "And many of those who *were* caught were released from jail when Esau Hasket disposed of the Fleshless One. They were very much weakened, because the Fleshless One was trapped in its copper vessel underneath the sea; but they survived for long enough to be able to educate their daughters in the ways of witchcraft, and to pass on the knowledge of what had happened, if not the power.''

''And you're one of those to whom the knowledge was passed down?''

Anne nodded. ''Seven Salem families were witch families— the Putnams, the Lewises, the Lynches, the Billingtons, the Eveliths, the Coreys, and the Proctors. During the 18th and 19th centuries, their descendants met at various times and performed pacifying rituals against Mictantecutli, the Fleshless One, and sacrificed pigs and sheep and, once, they killed a girl who was found wandering at Swampscott suffering from loss of memory. The witch-groups were illegal, and so was the banner of David Dark under which they met; but there is no question that they kept the Fleshless One somnolent for three hundred years, and protected Salem from terrors which you can only imagine.''

''So the witches—who started off as Mictantecutli's minions— have actually become our protectors against it?''

''That's right. As much as we are able. We still meet from time to time, but there are only five of us left now; and many of the older rituals have been lost to us. That is why Enid lives and works with Duglass Evelith, not only to serve him and to look after him, but to research as much as she can into the ancient magic, in order that the Salem witches can be strong again.''

I cleared my throat. ''I thought Enid was old man Evelith's granddaughter.''

''Well, she is, after a fashion.''

''After a fashion? What does that mean?''

''That means that they are related, in a curious way; but nobody quite knows how. You mustn't say that I mentioned it, but I believe there was rather a lot of incest in the Evelith family, back in the early part of the century, when the roads were bad.''

''I see,'' I said, although I didn't quite.

We drove past Granitehead Market, and I saw that there were two police cars parked outside, with their lights flashing.

''That's Charlie Manzi's place,'' I told Anne. ''Somebody must have found him.''

''Aren't you going to stop?''

''Are you kidding? Do you think they'd believe me about the tombstones? I'm already under suspicion for two other deaths. This time, they'd be sure to lock me up. I won't be any good to anybody if I'm shut up in a cell."

Anne looked across at me carefully. She was very attractive, in a thin, poetic kind of way, with long dark hair that had been gathered on each side of her face into three or four narrow braids. Not actually my type: too ethereal and pedantic and inclined to speak as if she were reading from an encyclopedia, but nice to have around, all the same. It was hard to believe that she was actually a witch.

"What does a witch find to do these days?" I asked her. "Can you work spells, stuff like that?"

"I hope you're not laughing at me."

"I'm not, actually. I've seen too much horror in the past few days to laugh at a witch. Do you *call* yourselves witches?"

"No. We call ourselves by the old name, wonder-workers."

"And what wonders can you work?"

"Do you want me to show you?"

"I'd be delighted."

I drove back up Quaker Lane, and parked outside the cottage. Anne got out of the car and stood staring at the cottage in silence. When I walked towards the front door she made no immediate move to follow me.

"Something wrong?" I asked her.

"There is a very strong and evil influence here."

I stayed where I was, halfway down the garden path, jingling my keys in my hand. I looked up at the bedroom windows, shuttered and blind; at the dead fingers of creeper which tapped so persistently against the weatherboard; and at the dank, distressed garden. There was green scum all over the surface of the ornamental pool, unnaturally bright in the leaden afternoon light.

"My wife comes back to me almost every night," I said. "That's what you can feel."

Anne approached the cottage with obvious trepidation. The loose upstairs shutter suddenly banged, and she reached for my hand in fright. I unlocked the front door, and we stepped inside, still holding hands; Anne raising her head slightly as if she were sniffing the darkness for evil and mischievous spirits.

I switched on the light. "I wouldn't have thought that a witch would be afraid."

"On the contrary," she said. "When you're a witch, you're far more sensitive to occult manifestations, and you can sense how malevolent they are, far more acutely than an ordinary person.''

"What do you feel in here? Is it bad?"

She shivered. "It's like a cold draft from hell itself," she told me. "Because your wife used to live here, this cottage has become one of the portals through which the dead have been returning to the world of the living. Can you feel how cold it is? Especially here, where your library is. Do you mind if I go in?''

"Help yourself.''

Anne pushed the library door open a little wider, and stepped inside. As she did so, I felt a chilly wind run through the room, and the papers on my desk began to shift and stir, and one or two of them floated to the floor. Anne stood in the very center of the room, and looked around, and I could see her breath, as if she were standing outside in five degree cold. There was a smell, too: a sour, cold smell, as if something had gone rotten in the icebox. I must have unconsciously noticed it yesterday, and that was why I had checked in the icebox to see if anything had gone bad. But it wasn't that at all: it was freezing and sickly, like chilled vomit, and I felt my stomach tighten into knots of nausea.

Anne whispered, "It knows that I am here. Have you ever felt it as strongly as this before? It knows that I am here, and it's restless.''

"What are you going to do?" I asked her.

"For the moment, nothing. There's nothing I can do. There isn't any point in closing this portal, because the Fleshless One will only find another. There are probably several more around here in any case. Every time someone dies, his home becomes susceptible to visitations not just from him, but from any apparition whom the Fleshless One chooses to send. Have you heard whispering, talking, anything like that?''

I nodded. The way Anne was going on, I was beginning to feel more than a little terrified. I felt that I could cope with Jane's spirit, thanks to our unborn son. But if the cottage was an entrance to the region of the dead, through which any number of apparitions might be rustling and shuffling, then it was time to move, as far as I was concerned. It was like living on the brink of a gaping mass grave, in the bottom of which all the corpses were sightlessly waving and calling.

"I think I need a drink," I said, unsteadily. "Hold on a minute, I left a bottle of Chivas Regal in the car."

I went outside, leaving the front door open, and walked down the garden path to the car. Unlocking it, I took out the bottle of whiskey, and then turned to go back to the house.

I stopped where I was, and almost dropped the bottle on the ground. Standing behind the laurel hedge, smiling at me, was Jane. Just as real, just as solid as she had been last night. Except that she was standing exactly where she had been standing in that altered photograph, on the surface of the ornamental pool. And in the library window, just behind her, I could see Anne's face looking out in horror, just the same as in the photograph.

I took two stiff steps towards the garden path, then another. Jane rotated where she was, without moving her feet. She was smiling at me, coaxing, encouraging. But my own face was set into an oxolyte mask, nerveless and expressionless. As soon as I had passed the laurel hedge I saw that Jane's bare feet were resting on the weedy surface of the water without even breaking the water's green meniscus.

"*John,*" she said. "*Remember that you can have me back. Don't forget, John, you can have me back. And Constance. And our son. You can have us back alive, John, if you set me free.*"

Slowly, still smiling, Jane began to sink into the pool. She didn't even disturb the surface as first her legs disappeared beneath it, then her body, then her face. The green water passed over her wide-open eyes and she didn't close them, or even blink. Then she was gone. And the most disturbing thing was that the pool was only two feet deep.

I walked over to the edge of the water and stared down at it. Then I picked up a dead stick, and cautiously prodded beneath the scum. There was nothing there, only stinking weed, and the white fungous body of a dead goldfish.

Anne was standing in the front porch when I turned around, paler than ever. "I saw her," she said, and gave a sudden and slightly hysterical giggle. "I actually saw her."

"She's becoming stronger," I said. "First of all, she only appeared as a flickering light, and only at night. But then she started to look more solid. Now she's appearing just as frequently in the daylight."

"The Fleshless One must be breaking free from his casket,"

said Anne. "Did Jane say anything to you? I thought I heard a voice, but I couldn't make out what the words were."

"She said that if I—well, she said that I had to be careful."

"Was that all?"

I felt guilty, not telling Anne that Mictantecutli had promised to return my wife and my child to me; but then it was something I wanted to think about. There was no question of my doing anything to prevent Edward and Forrest and Jimmy from taking charge of the living skeleton, and eventually delivering it to old man Evelith; but all the same, I *had* been made an extraordinary offer, and there was no harm in considering it, thinking it through. I thought of all those days and evenings when Jane and I had been driving the length and breadth of the North Shore, looking for likely antiques to put in the shop, and the remembered happiness of those times was almost too sweet to bear.

"Let's have that drink," said Anne, and led the way back into the cottage.

I lit a fire, switched on the television, and poured us each a sizeable whiskey. Then I took my shoes off and warmed my toes by the crackling logs. Anne knelt on the floor beside me, the firelight reflected in her eyes and in her long shiny hair.

"We first began to feel vibrations about you when your wife was killed," she said. "We were having a meeting at Mercy Lewis' house; she's our senior wonder-worker, if you like. It was Enid who sensed that something was in the air. She said that a Granitehead girl had died, she could feel it, and that her spirit had fled back to Granitehead and been ensnared by the Fleshless One. Not all spirits are caught; only those which the Fleshless One believes will bring him more hearts, and more blood, and more years of unlived life.

"Because your wife's spirit was caught, we immediately sought your name."

"By magic?" I asked.

Anne smiled. "I'm afraid not. We looked in the obituary columns of the *Granitehead Messenger*. And there she was, Jane Trenton. We started watching you straight away, or *I* did, mostly, since I don't live too far away. I even went to the funeral."

"That's where I've seen you before," I told her. "I thought your face was familiar."

"Anyway," she said, "the more we watched you, the

more limited we realized our abilities to help you. Our power, what we have of it, comes from the Fleshless One himself, the very one we are determined to keep in check. That is why it will be better for you and your friends from the Peabody to raise the *David Dark*, and extricate Mictantecutli, and then for we witches to pacify it with ritual sacrifices and prayer, before Duglass Evelith and Quamus finally destroy it. It is quite possible, and all of we witches are prepared for this, that when the Fleshless One is brought up from the ocean-bed, we shall be completely in his thrall. But Duglass Evelith and Quamus are satisfied that they can handle this eventuality, and that the only way in which they can bring the Fleshless One to total destruction is by using *us* to serve and exalt him.''

''Where does Quamus come into this?'' I asked her. ''I thought he was the butler.''

''He helps Mr. Evelith to run the house, yes. But he is also the last of the great Narragansett wonder-workers. He was trained from childhood in the higher arts of Indian magic; and I have seen him with my own eyes set fire to pieces of paper by simply looking at them, and making a whole row of chairs fall over backwards one by one.''

''Quite a trickster.''

''Not a trickster, John. Definitely *not* a trickster. Not Quamus. He's been helping Duglass Evelith for years to invoke some ancient Indian spirit that was supposed to have taken the soul of one of his Evelith ancestors, way back in 1624, when the Puritans first came to Salem and it was still called Naumkeag. It's very secret. Neither of them will tell me what they've achieved. Even Enid isn't allowed to know. But she says that they lock themselves in that library for days on end sometimes, and you can hear these terrible shouting and groaning noises, so loud and deep that they make the doors and the windows rattle, and that quite a few Tewksbury people got up a petition because of the strange lights that were appearing in the sky.''

I sat back, cupping my whiskey-glass in my hands. ''Tell me I'm going to wake up in a minute,'' I told her. ''Tell me I fell asleep last week and I'm still dreaming.''

''You're not dreaming, John,'' she insisted. ''The spirits and the demons and the apparitions are all real. Within their own sphere, they're all much more real than you and I appear to be. They've always been here, and they always will be. *They're* the ones who inherited the earth, not us. We're just usurpers, shadowy little beings who have been meddling and trying to manipulate whole realms of power and grandeur that we don't even begin to understand. Mictantecutli is real. It's really down there; and what it can do to us is real.''

"I don't know," I said, tiredly. "I think I've seen enough death and enough pain and enough spiritual torture to last me a lifetime.''

"You're not thinking of quitting?"

"Wouldn't you?"

Anne looked away. "I suppose I might," she said. "If I didn't care about the lives of other people; if I didn't care whether my own dead wife ever found any rest or not. Then I'd quit.''

Upstairs, a bedroom door banged shut. I looked up, and then at Anne. There was a creak right above our heads as *something* stepped on a floorboard. There was a lengthy silence, and then another creak, as if the same something were walking back across the room again. The living-room door suddenly opened by itself, and a cold draft blew in, stirring up the ashes of the fire.

"Close," said Anne, and raised one hand, palm forwards, towards the door. There was a moment's hesitation, and then the door closed, apparently by itself.

"I'm impressed," I said.

"It's a simple enough thing to do if you have the power," she said, but she wasn't smiling. "But the spirits *are* in the house, and they feel unsettled.''

"Is there anything you can do?"

"I can dismiss them for now; just for one night. That's if the Fleshless One hasn't increased his influence very much more than usual.''

"In that case, please dismiss them. It'll be a change to get a night's sleep that isn't disturbed by walking apparitions.''

Anne stood up. "Do you have any candles?" she asked me. "I shall also want a bowl of water.''

"Surely," I said, and went into the kitchen to fetch what she wanted. As I crossed the hallway, I was conscious of the coldness and the restlessness of unhallowed spirits, and even the clock seemed to be ticking differently, almost as if it were ticking *backwards*. There was a dim flickering light under the library door, but the last thing in the world I was going to do was open it.

I brought Anne back two heavy brass candlesticks, complete with bright blue candles, and a copper mixing-bowl half-filled with water. She set them down in front of the fire, one candle on each side and the bowl in between. She made a sign over each of them, not the sign of the cross, but some other, more complicated sign, like a pentacle. She bent her head and whispered a lengthy chant, of which I could hear almost nothing except the repeated chorus,

"Dream not, wake not, say not, hear not;
Weep not, walk not, speak not, fear not."

After the chant was finished, she remained with her head bent for three or four minutes, praying or chanting in silence. Then she turned to me abruptly and said, "I shall have to be naked. You don't mind that, do you?"

"No, of course not. I mean, no, why not? Go ahead."

She tugged off her black sweater, revealing thin arms, a narrow chest, and small dark-nippled breasts. Then she unbuckled her belt and stepped out of her black corduroy jeans. She was very slim, very boyish; her dark hair swung right down to the middle of her back, and when she turned around and faced me I saw that her sex was shaved completely bare. A beautiful but very strange girl. There were silver bands around her ankles and silver rings on every toe. She raised her arms, completely composed and unembarrassed, and said, "Now we shall see who has the greater power. Those poor lost spirits, or me."

She knelt down in front of the candles and the bowl of water, and lit the candles with a sputtering piece of kindling from the fire. "I can't use matches: there mustn't be any sulphur in the flame." I watched in fascination as she bent forward and stared at her own reflection in the bowl of water, holding her hair back with her hands.

"All you who seek to penetrate the mirror here, turn back," she said, in a sing-song tone. "All you who try to cross again the borders of the region of the dead, go back. Tonight you must rest. Tonight you must sleep. There will be other times, other places; but tonight you must think on what you are, and turn away from the mirror which leads to the life you knew."

The cottage became quiet, as quiet as it had been last night.

All I could hear was that odd backward-sounding ticking of the long-case clock, and the fizzing sound of the candles as they burned into their bright blue wax.

Anne remained bent over, her breasts pressed against her thighs, staring into the copper bowl. She wasn't saying anything, but she gave no indication that the working of this particular wonder was over yet; nor that it was going to be successful.

To my amazement, the water in the bowl began to bubble a little, and steam, and then to boil. Anne sat up straight, her arms crossed over her chest, and closed her eyes. "Go back," she whispered. "Do not try to penetrate the mirror tonight. Go back, and rest."

The water in the bowl boiled even more noisily, and I stared at it in disbelief. Anne knelt where she was, her eyes tight closed, and I could see tiny beads of perspiration on her forehead, and on her upper lip. Whatever she was doing, it obviously required enormous effort and intense concentration.

"Go . . . back," she whispered, as if it was a struggle to get the words out. "Do not cross . . . do not cross . . ."

It was then that I began to get the feeling that she was involved in a struggle with something or someone, and that she was losing. I watched her anxiously as she began to quiver and shake, and the sweat ran down her cheeks and runneled between her breasts. Her thighs quaked as if she was being prodded with an electric goad, and she started to give little involuntary spasms and jumps.

The living-room door opened again, just a fraction; and again that coldness began to course through the room. The fire cowered down amongst its ashes and the candles guttered and blew. In the bowl, the water stopped boiling, and as suddenly as it had bubbled, began to form a thin skin of ice on its surface.

"Anne," I said, urgently. "Anne, what's happening? Anne!"

But Anne could not reply. She was losing whatever mental wrestling-match she was involved in; yet obviously she didn't dare to break her concentration or release her hold, in case she would suddenly free the beast with which she was struggling. She was still sweating and shivering, and every now and then she let out a little gasp of strain.

The living-room door opened wider. There, in her funeral robes, stood Jane. Her face was different now, ghastlier, as if decay had begun to set. Her eyes were wide and staring, and her teeth were drawn back in a grisly grin.

"Jane!" I shouted. "Jane, leave her alone, for God's sake! I'll do what you want! You know that I'll do what you want! But leave her alone!"

Jane didn't seem to hear me. She came gliding into the room, her white funeral robes swayed by the chilly wind, and stood only a few feet away from us, her eyes still staring, her grin just as skeletal and horrifying. I prayed to God that she wouldn't do to Anne Putnam what she had done to Constance, her own mother.

"Jane, listen," I said, trying to sound reasonable. "Please, Jane. Just leave her alone and I'll get her out of here. She was only trying to help me. You know that I'll do what you want. I promise you, Jane. But leave her alone, please."

Jane lifted both her arms. As she did so, Anne was lifted up, so that she was standing, her knees slightly bent, her eyes still closed, shaking and trembling as she tried to break free of the influence that gripped her. She looked as if she were being held up by two invisible helpers.

"Leave her, Jane," I begged. "Jane, for God's sake, don't hurt her."

Jane made a circling motion with her hand. Without a sound, Anne rotated in the air until she was upside-down, her feet nearly touching the ceiling, her dark hair spread out on the carpet beneath. I watched in frightened silence. I knew there was nothing I could do to stop whatever was going to happen now. Jane was proving to be a fatally jealous bride; a bride who would take her revenge on any woman who came near me.

The cold wind blew up more ashes from the fire. Jane stretched out her arms, and, in response, Anne's legs were opened wide, so wide that I heard the tendons crack, and her naked sex was exposed. She was suspended there in front of me, in inverted splits, her body slippery with sweat, her eyes tight closed, her teeth grimly clamped together. Jane stretched out her arms again, and Anne's arms stretched out, too. There were two inches of clear space between the top of Anne's head and the floor, although because of the length of the hair, it looked as if she were somehow balancing supernaturally on her braids.

"Jane, please," I said, but Jane didn't even turn and look at me.

Slowly, Jane described a curve in the air with her hands; and equally slowly, Anne's body was bent back in mid-air. Anne grunted with effort and pain, struggling as hard as she could to resist the force that was attempting to snap her spine, but I could tell that it was no use. The power of the Fleshless One was comparatively weak, but it was strong enough to overwhelm one of its own witches.

I heard another crack, as cartilage snapped in Anne's left knee. She said, "*Aach!*" and grimaced, but she was reserving all her energy for fighting against her demonic master.

"Jane!" I shouted. I got to my feet, but instantly I was hurled back by a force as powerful as a truck. I hit my head against the side of the chair, and stumbled over the crashing fire-irons; but then I scrambled up to my feet again and yelled, "Jane!"

Jane ignored me. In utter helplessness, I saw Anne's back being bent over as if she were being forced over a barrel, or the back of a chair. The veins stood out on her narrow hips, and her neck tendons were swollen with effort.

"God, you're going to kill her!" I screamed. "Mictantecutli! Stop it! Mictantecutli!"

There was a strange shimmering sound, like the blade of a saw being wobbled. Jane raised her eyes and stared at me; and her face wasn't Jane's face at all, it was the skeletal face of an ancient demon, the fleshless creature which David Dark had stolen from the Aztec magicians. Mictantecutli, the lord of Mictlampa, the prince of the region of the dead.

"*You called my name,*" Jane said threateningly, in a voice which was blaring and harsh.

"Don't kill her," I said. I could feel the sweat chilling under my armpits. "She was only trying to protect me, that's all."

"*She is my servant. I shall do whatever I wish with her.*"

"I'm asking you not to kill her."

There was a long pause. Jane looked at Anne's naked suspended body, and then reached out with her palm facing downwards. Anne slowly sank to the floor, and lay on the carpet shaking and panting, and holding her hand to her back in an attempt to ease the pain.

I started to kneel down beside her, but Jane said, "*Stay*

where you are. I offer you no guarantees of my handmaiden's life. First, you must promise that you will serve me; and that you will accept the bargain which I proposed to you. Help your friends to raise me from the waters, and then set me free. Your wife and son will be returned to you, and your wife's mother, too; and you shall remain invulnerable from harm."

"How can I be sure that I can trust you?"

"You can never be sure. It is a risk that you will have to accept."

"Suppose I say no?"

"Then I will break this girl's back."

I glanced down at Anne. She was lying flat on her back now, her hands held over her face as she tried to contain the agony she was feeling in her back and her thighs.

The point was, I had already been considering the possibility of letting Mictantecutli free; I had already been tempted by the offer of having Jane restored to me, so what difference would it make if I actually said yes? It would save Anne; it would bring back all the people I loved; and who knew, the consequences might not really be so bad. If Mictantecutli had reigned unchecked before the days of David Dark and Esau Hasket, what difference would it make if it reigned again now? As Mictantecutli itself had told me yesterday, it was part of the order of the universe, just as the sun was and the planets, and God Himself.

Anne whispered, "John . . . don't agree to anything. Please."

Instantly, her arm was twisted right around behind her back, so violently that her wrist was snapped. She screamed out in pain, but the demonic force wouldn't release her, and deliberately pressed her body down so that her own shoulder-blade rubbed against her fractured bones. She screamed and screamed, writhing and thrashing, but Mictantecutli wouldn't let her go.

"Stop!" I yelled at Jane. "Stop, I'll do it!"

Gradually, the pressure on Anne's body was relieved. I knelt down and helped her to ease her arm out from under her back, and rest it gently on her stomach. Her wrist was swollen and misshapen, and I could hear the broken bones grating against each other under the skin. Jane watched over us, smiling malevolently.

"You have made a binding promise," she told me, in her own voice. *"You must keep your promise faithfully, or believe me, you will be cursed forever; and all your heirs will be cursed forever; and anyone who ever knew you will regret the day they first saw you. You will be blighted for all time; you will never know peace. I have my mark on you now; you have freely bargained with me; and whatever rewards and punishments are due, you will surely receive them in the fullest measure."*

I got to my feet. I was exhausted, both physically and emotionally. "Mictantecutli, I want you to go now. Leave us in peace. I've agreed to do what you want, now just get out of here."

Jane smiled, and began to fade. I looked down to make sure that Anne was all right, and when I looked back, Jane had disappeared altogether. The door, however, remained open; and the draft that blew through it was as cold and unrelenting as ever.

Anne said, "You shouldn't have done that. It would have been better for me to die."

"Are you kidding?" I said. "Here, I'll help you up on to the sofa, then I'll call the doctor."

"God, my wrist," she winced.

"God?" I said, wearily. "God doesn't seem to be helping us much."

TWENTY-SIX

Next day, the wind dropped and the sun came out, and I changed my mind about accompanying Edward and Forrest and Jimmy on their search for the wreck of the *David Dark*. We left Pickering Wharf Marina a little after eight-thirty in the morning, on a rather smarter launch than the *Alexis*, which Forrest had persuaded a lawyer friend of his to lend us for the day. Her name was *Diogenes*, which considering she belonged to a lawyer was pretty ironic.

It was cold but calm out in the harbor. I wore a quilted anorak and a peaked denim cap and a pair of orange-tinted sunglasses. Gilly wore a thick red knitted jacket and matching ski-hat, with tight stretch designer jeans, and I think she looked sexier then than at any time since I had met her; and I told her so.

She kissed me on the tip of my cold nose. "Just for that, you can take me out for dinner tonight," she told me. Edward watched us balefully from the other side of the launch.

"You're not scared of ghostly retribution?" I asked her.

"I've been thinking about that. Maybe I let my emotions run away with me. Anyway, a ghost is hardly likely to attack us for *eating* together, is it?"

"That's all you've got in mind?"

"Sure," she grinned. "What have *you* got in mind?"

The advantage of borrowing the *Diogenes* was that she was fitted with a Decca navigation system; and so Dan Bass was able to steer us right on to the spot that Duglass Evelith had pinpointed as the place where the *David Dark*'s sole survivor had found himself swimming in the ocean.

261

Dan said, "It's more than likely that there was quite a time-lapse in between the moment when the ship sank and the moment when the sailor was able to assess his position; so let's assume that the wreck is probably upwind of here; or upwind in relation to the wind that must have been blowing at the time. We'll drop a buoy here, to use as a datum point, but I think we should search in a box towards the north-east, maybe a half-mile square."

So we began the long and tedious business of a parallel search. Dan and Edward had put together an impressive partnership of sonar scanners, similar to the equipment that had been used to locate the wreck of the *Mary Rose*. There was a side-scanner, housed in a torpedo-shaped drogue, which could simultaneously search the surface of the sea-bed for 500 feet both to port and to starboard; and a very powerful and high-quality echo-sounder which not only mapped the ocean floor but the underlying layers of sediment beneath it. Once you knew roughly where to look, this combination of scanners was remarkably effective.

Edward came up and stood beside me as the drogue was trailed overboard. "Any luck with your father-in-law?" he asked me.

"I haven't spoken to him since the weekend," I said.

"We're going to need some money urgently once we locate this wreck."

"Can't we just bring up the copper vessel?" I asked him. "Surely that wouldn't be too expensive."

"The copper vessel is only part of it," said Edward. "Do you realize what's down there? A late 17th-century ship, most of it intact, if the *Mary Rose* experience is anything to go by. It's not just the copper vessel we want, it's the whole thing, the whole environment. There could be all kinds of artifacts down there that will tell us how they intended to dispose of Mictantecutli, and who was on board the ship, and how they managed to keep the demon incarcerated. If we bring up the copper vessel and nothing else, we'll only get a quarter of the story; and, besides, I'm afraid that once the location of the wreck becomes public knowledge, there's a high risk of it being pillaged by souvenir-hunters. But, we'll get Mictantecutli up just as quickly as we possibly can."

He was right about the souvenir-hunters, of course. Even while we were doing nothing more than burbling gently up and down, two or three boats approached us and asked us what we were looking for. "Any treasure down there?" one of the boatmen shouted; and he wasn't joking. Amateur divers would risk their lives to bring up a piece of carving from a sunken schooner; or a rusty fowling-piece; or a few roughly-minted coins. Dan Bass called back that we were looking for a friend's power-boat, which had accidentally flooded and sunk. The boat waited around for a while, until the owners decided that we weren't doing anything particularly interesting, and roared off.

We ate a picnic lunch of spiced chicken and fish enchiladas out on deck, washed down with a couple of bottles of California wine. Then we resumed the search, cruising up and down in 100-foot swathes; up to the line of the datum buoy, and then back again. The wind began to rise a little, and the *Diogenes* began to dip and rise in a way which played unsettling games with my lunch. Gilly said, "This could take days. The bottom of the sea is flat as a pancake around here."

Forrest put in, "We're relying on information supplied by a half-drowned sailor from 290 years ago. Maybe he got it all wrong: maybe the beacons he thought he saw weren't beacons, but house-lights, or flares. I'm beginning to think this damned wreck isn't down here at all."

"Hold it," said Jimmy, who had been sitting in front of the scanner print-outs. He pointed to the smudgy trace from the side-scanner, which had suddenly shown a hiccup. "There's something right there, some kind of interruption in the natural ripple patterns." He turned to the echo-sounder print-out, and, sure enough, there was a noticeable disturbance in the substratum below the surface of the sea-bed.

"Gentlemen, I think we may have something," said Jimmy. He waited until the trace had unrolled a few more inches, then he tore it out of the machine and laid it on our chart-table. "You see this? There's something down there all right, under the mud. And look at the pattern from the side-scanner."

Edward said, "If that isn't a scour-mark caused by a sunken wreck, then I'm a Chinaman."

"The amount of Chinese food you eat, I'm beginning to wonder," said Gilly.

"Gilly, this could be the greatest discovery in modern marine archeology," Edward told her. "Do you understand what this is? A disturbance under the sea-bed that could only have been caused by a buried ship; and a ship of some considerable size, too. What do you think, Dan? A hundred-tonner?"

"Hard to say," remarked Dan Bass. "I don't even want to say that it's a ship until I've gone down and taken a look."

We spent the next hour scanning and re-scanning the ocean floor, right over the spot where we had first discovered the disturbance. Each print-out seemed to confirm our suspicions that we had at last located the wreck of the *David Dark*, and gradually we grew more and more excited. I didn't dare to think about the possible consequences of bringing her up to the surface, or what would happen when we found the copper vessel, so I did my best to push all thoughts of Mictantecutli to the back of my mind, and join in the bustle and self-congratulation with everybody else.

Only Gilly noticed that my enthusiasm was forced. She suddenly looked across at me, and said, "Are you all right, John?"

"Sure. Just a little tired, I guess."

"Something's bothering you."

"You know me so well already?"

"I know you better than anybody else on board." She came over and held my arm, and stared at me seriously.

"You're worried," she said. "I can always tell when somebody's worried."

"Oh, yes?"

"Is it the wreck that's worrying you? Do you really believe they're going to find a demon in it? I mean, a *demon?*"

"There's something down there," I told her. "Believe you me."

"Well," she said, "I'll protect you."

I kissed her forehead. "If only you could."

The tide was on the turn, and Dan Bass had estimated that there was time for one ten-minute dive over the spot where we had located the disturbance. We weighed anchor and raised the diving-flags, while Dan and Edward changed into their white wetsuits, and the rest of us stood around and chafed our hands in the rapidly-cooling wind. Dan and Edward went over the side without a word, and we leaned on the rail and watched their spectral white shapes swimming away under the murky water.

"Are you going to dive again?" Gilly asked me.

"If this is actually the wreck of the *David Dark*, then yes. But first of all I'll get Dan to give me a few lessons in the pool at Forest River Park."

We waited for almost fifteen minutes for Edward and Dan to reappear. Each of them had twenty minutes of air, so we weren't too worried about their safety, but all the same the tidal stream was beginning to flow more strongly now, and the waves were becoming choppier, and if they were tired they were going to find it hard work swimming back to the launch again.

Jimmy brushed back his hair with his hand. "I hope they haven't run into anything weird," he said; and he was expressing the fear that all of us felt. He checked his watch. "If they don't come up in five minutes, I'm going in after them. Forrest, help me get into my suit, will you?"

"I'll come with you," said Forrest.

But Jimmy had only managed to strip off his shirt when two fluorescent orange heads bobbed to the surface only 50 or 60 feet away, and Edward and Dan came swimming methodically back to the diving-lines which trailed all the way around the *Diogenes'* hull. Edward, before we pulled him in, gave us the all-okay signal.

He tugged off his mask, rubbed the water out of his beard, and looked at us all triumphantly. "She's there," he said, "I'm certain of it. There's a scour-pit which looks as if it was caused by a buried wreck, about 130 feet in length. Tomorrow we'll go down with air-hoses, and see if we can blow some of the sediment away."

Dan Bass was less sure of our find; but agreed that it was the most likely trace so far. "The visibility's real bad down there at the moment; you can hardly see your hand in front of your mask. But there's something there, you can make out the shape of the mound that it's made. It's worth taking another look."

We logged the point exactly with landmarks and compass bearings. We didn't want to leave a marker-buoy, in case some nosey treasure-hunter decided to go down and take a look at what we'd been up to.

Edward came up to me, half-dressed in a polo-neck sweater and an athletic supporter, and said, "Do you think you can have another go at your father-in-law? See if you can persuade him to rustle up some money. If this really is the *David Dark,* we're going to need a proper diving-ship, and excavation facilities, and a way of bringing her up once we've dug her out of the mud. We're going to need extra divers, too, professionals."

"I'll try," I said, reluctantly. "He didn't seem too enthusiastic about it the last time I spoke to him."

Edward said, "Come on, John. Give it another try, huh? Ask him. He can only say no."

"All right," I agreed. "Let me take those sonar traces along. Perhaps I'll convince him."

As the sky began to darken, we sailed back into Salem. The first lights began to sparkle in the streets, and there was a strong smell of salt on the wind.

"You know that Salem was named for 'Shalom,' the word for peace," said Edward reflectively.

"Let's hope we can bring it some," I replied, and Gilly, behind me, said, "Amen."

TWENTY-SEVEN

Gilly and I had an early dinner at Le Château, an elegant pink-and-white decorated restaurant that had just opened on Front Street. Gilly had changed into one of her own dresses from Linen & Lace, a simple off-the-shoulder design with a lace bodice and silk-ribbon ties. We ate *moules marinières* and *pintadeau aux raisins*. The candles flickered between us; and if the *David Dark* and all its attendant ghosts hadn't been hanging over us like the relentless menace it was, we would have had a happy, cheerful evening, and probably gone back to Gilly's place and made love.

As it was, we didn't dare. Pragmatic as Gilly was, she nonetheless knew that I was still carrying with me the unexorcized memory of my recently-dead wife; and that any intimacy between us would act as a catalyst for vicious psycho-kinetic forces. Gilly personally believed that the forces came from inside my own mind, that my own guilt was strong enough to make windows shatter and apparitions appear. She simply didn't believe in ghosts, no matter what any of us told her. But however the forces were unleashed, she didn't want to risk a repetition of what had happened at the Hawthorne Inn. Next time, one of us might be seriously hurt, or even killed.

"Do you think you'll ever remarry?" she asked me, as we finished our brandies after dinner.

"It's hard to say," I replied. "I can't envisage it just yet."

"But you're feeling lonely?"

"Not right now."

She reached across the table and traced a line across the

267

knuckles of my left hand with her fingertip. "Don't you sometimes wish you were Superman, and that you could turn the world backwards, and rescue your wife just before the accident?"

"It's no use wishing for the impossible," I said. But at the same time, my mind said slyly, you've done it, John, you've already arranged it; when the *David Dark* comes up from the bottom of the ocean, you'll have your wife back again, just as she was before the crash. Smiling, warm, and loving; pregnant, too, with your first-born child. Only Anne Putnam knew what I had done; what bargains I had made to have my family returned to me from the region of the dead, and to save Anne herself from Mictantecutli's anger. And when I had driven her to Dr. Rosen's clinic late last night, Anne had promised me solemnly that she would tell nobody what I had pledged to the Fleshless One; and that my bargain with the demon would always remain a secret. After all, *her* life depended on it, as much as Jane's.

I felt guilty, of course. I felt that I had betrayed Edward and Forrest, and Gilly, too, in a way. But there are times in your life when you have to make a decision in favor of your own happiness at the possible expense of other people's, and I believed that this was one of them. At least, I had managed to *convince* myself that this was one of them; and that with Anne's life so dangerously at risk, I was powerless to do anything else.

There are always a hundred good excuses for cowardice and selfishness; whereas courage is its own justification.

After dinner, I drove Gilly home to Witch Hill Road, kissed her, and promised to drop into Linen & Lace in the morning. Then I took routes 128 and 1 southwards to Boston, and to Dedham. I thought I would probably be wasting my time, going to talk to Walter Bedford, but Edward had been so insistent that I had to try. I played Grieg on my car stereo and tried to relax, while the lights of Melrose and Malden and Somerville went gliding by me.

When I drew up outside the Bedford house, it was in darkness. Even the coach lamps outside the front door were switched off. Shit, I thought, a 20-mile drive for nothing. It hadn't even occurred to me that Walter wouldn't be home. He *always* went home, every night; or at least he had when Constance was still alive. I should have called him first; he was probably spending a few days with neighbors, to get over the shock.

All the same, I walked up to the front door and rang the bell. I heard it ringing in the hallway; and I stood there for a while, rubbing my hands and shuffling my feet to keep myself warm. A whip-poor-will called somewhere in the tall trees at the back of the house; and then again. I was reminded of the horror stories of H.P. Lovecraft, in which the appearance of grisly primeval monsters like *Yog-Sothoth* was always preceded by the crying of thousands of whip-poor-wills.

I was about to walk around the back of the house, to see if Walter was in his television room, when the front door suddenly opened, and Walter stood there staring out at me.

"Walter?" I said. I stepped closer, and saw that he looked unusually pale, and that his eyes were circled and puffy, as if he hadn't slept. He was wearing blue pajamas and a herringbone sport coat, with the collar turned up.

"Walter," I said, "are you all right? You look terrible."

"John?" he replied. He pronounced my name as if it were his first word in years.

"What happened, Walter? Have you been to the office? You look as if you haven't slept since I last saw you."

"No," he said, "I haven't. I guess you'd better come in."

I followed him into the house. It was chilly and dark in there; and I saw from the thermostat on the wall that he had turned the heat down. As I passed, I turned it up again; and by the time we reached the sitting room, the radiators were beginning to click and clonk as they warmed up. Walter watched me with a curiously stunned expression on his face as I went around switching on the lamps and drawing the drapes.

"Now then," I asked him. "How about a drink?"

He nodded. Then, rather suddenly, he sat down. "Yes," he said, "I guess I will."

I poured us two whiskeys and handed him one. "How long have you been wandering around in the dark?" I asked him.

"I don't know. Ever since—"

I sat down next to him. He looked even worse than I had first thought. He hadn't shaved since the weekend, and his chin was covered in white prickly stubble. His skin was unwashed and greasy. When he lifted the whiskey glass to his lips, his hands trembled almost uncontrollably, probably from hunger and fatigue as much as anything else.

"Listen," I told him, "get yourself cleaned up and then I'll take you down the road to the Pizza Hut. It's not the Four Seasons but you need some hot food inside you."

Walter swallowed his whiskey, coughed, and then looked anxiously all around him. "She's not still here, is she?" he asked. His eyes were haunted and blood-shot.

"What do you mean?" I asked him.

"I've seen her," he told me, clutching hold of my wrist. Close up, he smelled of stale sweat and urine, and his breath was foul. I could hardly believe that this was the same fastidious Walter who had once raised an eyebrow at me because the backs of my shoes weren't polished. "After you left, she came; and she spoke to me. I thought I was dreaming. Then I thought that perhaps it hadn't happened after all, that she wasn't dead, and that I must have been dreaming before. But she was *here,* right here, right in this room, and she spoke to me."

"Who was here? What are you talking about?"

"Constance," he insisted. "Constance was here. I was sitting by the fire and she spoke to me. She was standing right there, just behind that chair. She was smiling at me."

I felt a deep chill of fear. There was no question now that the power of Mictantecutli was spreading, and flourishing. If it could raise Constance's ghost as far away as Dedham, then it wouldn't be long before it could wreak havoc over half the Commonwealth of Massachusetts; and that was while it was still lying on the sea-bed.

"Walter," I said, as comfortingly as I could, "Walter, you don't have any cause to worry."

"But she said she wanted me. She said I should come to join her. She begged me to kill myself, so that we could be together again. She begged me, John. Cut your throat, Walter, she told me. There's a sharp knife in the kitchen, you won't even feel it. Cut your throat as deep as you can, and join me."

Walter was shaking so much that I had to grasp his arms to make him settle down.

"Walter," I said, "that wasn't Constance who was speaking to you. Not the real Constance; any more than it was the real Jane who killed her. You may have seen something that looked like Constance, but it was the spirit that lies inside of the *David Dark* that was controlling it, and making it say things like that. That spirit feeds on human life and human hearts, Walter. It's taken Jane's, and Constance's; now it wants yours.''

Walter didn't seem to understand. He stared at me, his eyes darting from side to side in high anxiety. ''*Not* Constance?'' he asked me. ''What do you mean? She had Constance's face, appearance, voice . . . How could it not have been Constance?''

''Well, if you like, it was a kind of projected image. I mean, when you see Faye Dunaway on the movie screen, the image has Faye Dunaway's face, and voice, and everything, but you know very well that what you're seeing isn't actually Faye Dunaway.''

''Faye Dunaway?'' asked Walter, perplexed. He was obviously in a mild state of shock; and what he needed right now was food, reassurance and rest, not a complex argument about psychic images.

''Come on,'' I said. ''I'll take you out for something to eat. But you ought to get yourself changed first, and showered. Do you think you can manage to do that? It'll make you feel a whole lot better.''

Upstairs, in his large blue-and-white bedroom, I laid out some fresh underwear and slacks for him, as well as a warm sweater and a tweed coat. He looked very thin and frail when he came into the bedroom from the shower, but at least he seemed to have calmed down, and a wash and a shave seemed to have refreshed him. ''To tell you the truth,'' he said, ''I don't much care for pizzas. There's a little restaurant out on the Milton road where they make excellent steak-and-oyster pies; Dickens, it's called. It's like a British pub.''

''If you're feeling like steak-and-oyster pies, you're feeling better,'' I told him. He toweled his hair, and nodded.

Dickens restaurant was just the right place for an intimate dinner: it had small enclosed booths, lit by mock-gaslamps, and scrubbed deal tables. We ordered the London Particular green-pea soup, and one Tower Bridge steak-and-oyster pie, with Guinness to wash it down. Walter ate in silence for almost ten minutes before he put down his soup spoon and looked at me in relief.

"I can't tell you how glad I am that you came," he said. "I think you just about saved my life."

"That's one of the reasons I drove over," I told him. "I wanted to talk to you about saving lives."

Walter tore off some wholemeal bread, and buttered it. "You're still talking about raising money for this salvage operation of yours?"

"Yes, I am."

"Well, I'm sorry, John, I did give it some more thought, but I still can't see my way clear to raising that much money out of people who trust me to keep their capital locked up as safely as possible. They're not looking for large dividends, these people; they're cautious, careful, long-term family investors."

"Hear me out, Walter," I said. "Jane came to visit me a couple of nights ago, and this time she wasn't like a ghost at all. She could have been solid, she could have been real. She said that the influence that's down in this shipwreck, this demon, or whatever it is, is capable of bringing back to life people who have recently died, people who are still wandering in what she called the region of the dead. A kind of purgatory, I guess."

"What are you saying?" asked Walter.

"Simply this: that the demon offered me three lives in exchange for its own freedom. If I help to raise it up off the ocean floor, and then make sure that it isn't handed over to Mr. Evelith, or anybody at the Peabody Museum, I get Jane restored to me; and our unborn son; and Constance, too."

"Constance? Are you serious?"

"Do you think I'd joke about it? Come on, Walter, you know me better than that. The demon is offering me Jane, and the baby, and Constance; back to life just as they were before any of this ever happened. No blindness, no injuries, nothing. Perfect and whole."

"I just can't believe it," said Walter.

"Well, what the hell *can* you believe? You've seen Jane flying through the air like a cartwheel. You've seen your own wife frozen blind right on my front path. You believed before, when I first told you about Jane. Why can't you believe now?"

Walter put down his piece of bread, and chewed his mouthful unhappily. "Because it's too good to be true," he said.

"Miracles like that, they just don't happen. Well, not to me, anyway."

"Think about it," I insisted. "You don't have to come to any decisions tonight. There may be some risk in letting the demon go, judging from how it behaved in the 17th century; but on the other hand, people aren't so superstitious these days, the way they were then, and it's unlikely that the demon is going to be able to exert the same powerful influence that it did then, in 1690. According to Mr. Evelith, it actually made the sky turn dark, so that for days on end it was permanently night. I can't see that happening today."

Walter slowly finished his soup. Then he said, "It actually offered to give Constance back to me? Not blinded? Not hurt in any way?"

"Yes," I said.

"To have her back . . ." he said, slowly shaking his head. "It would seem like none of this nightmare ever happened."

"That's right."

"But how can it *do* that? How can the demon actually *do* that?"

I shrugged. "As far as I can tell, Mictantecutli is the final arbiter of all human death, in the Americas at least. On other continents he probably appears in different forms."

"So what's been happening to the dead while he's been lying beneath the sea?"

"How should I know? I presume they've been going to their ultimate destinations without having to worry about Mictantecutli using them to recruit more blood, more hearts, more restless spirits. According to old man Evelith, Mictantecutli is shunned by every other supernatural creature, good or evil. It's a complete outcast; diseased and utterly malevolent, disregarding any of the protocol of Heaven or of Hell. But its power is such that it can afford to; or at least it *was*, before it was sealed in that copper vessel and sunk to the bottom of Salem Harbor."

"And it can really bring Constance back? And Jane?"

"So it says. From what it's done so far, I don't have any reason to doubt it. Can you imagine how much psychic power it must have taken just to bring Constance's image into your house? There's nothing on earth that can do anything like that, nothing *human*, anyway."

Walter sat there for a long time, thinking. Then he said,

"What do your friends from the Peabody have to say about it? I don't suppose they're particularly happy."

"They don't know. I haven't told them."

"Do you think that's wise?"

"Not particularly. But we're not discussing wisdom here, Walter. We're discussing whether you and I want our dead wives back or not. I'm not saying there isn't a price. It's conceivable that other people may be put at risk, although I doubt if there'll be any *less* risk if the demon is kept in captivity than if we set it free. Both of us have to face up to what we have here: an ancient and incomprehensible influence that controls the very process of death itself. The lord of the region of the dead, that's what they call it. And one way or another, it's going to re-establish its reign, whether we like it or not. If we leave it under the ocean, the copper vessel will eventually corrode to the point where Mictantecutli will be able to escape of its own accord; if we bring it up and keep it at the Peabody, or send it off to old man Evelith, who knows how long *they'll* be able to keep it under control? Even David Dark couldn't, and he was the man who first brought it here. So, from every angle, it looks like a no-win situation—in which case I'm suggesting that at least we rescue Jane and Constance."

I was glad I wasn't somebody else, listening to myself presenting this argument. It was flawed in logic, flawed in fact, and most of all it was flawed in fundamental morality. I didn't know anything about old man Evelith's ability to control Mictantecutli: according to Anne, he already had some kind of plan worked out, a plan involving Quamus and Enid and the rest of the Salem witch-coven. Neither did I know for sure if Mictantecutli's copper vessel was corroding or not. Worst of all, I didn't know what hideous influence Mictantecutli would be able to exert over both the living and the dead once Walter and I had set it free.

I thought of David Dark, literally exploding as he walked towards his house. I thought of Charlie Manzi, and the crushing, grinding noise of those tombstones. I thought of Mrs. Edgar Simons, screaming for help. I thought, too, of Jane: smiling and seductive, a solid form without any reality, a dead wife who walked. All of these images tumbled over in my mind in a confusion of fear, disbelief, depression, nightmare, and unrealized terror. But there was one hope to which I was clinging with fierce and illogical tenacity; one hope which enabled me to disregard the naked fear of Mictantecutli's walking dead, the pariah's children; and the extreme danger of releasing an ancient demon into a modern world. That hope was the hope of seeing Jane alive again, of being able to hold her again, against all the dictates of fate and human destiny, against all accepted logic. It was the one hope which Mictantecutli knew that I could never deny, no matter what the threatened consequences might be; and that was what made Mictantecutli a demon.

Walter said, "I'm not at all sure how I could present this as an investment portfolio."

"It won't be all that difficult," I told him. "Show your clients pictures of the *Wasa,* and the *Mary Rose.* Tell them how much prestige is going to be involved. And then explain how the salvaged ship is going to be displayed to the public, possibly as the central attraction in a recreational theme park. Come on, Walter, five or six million dollars isn't asking for the earth. A cheap movie costs five or six million dollars."

"My clients don't invest in cheap movies," said Walter.

"Listen," I said, earnestly, "do you want Constance back again or don't you?"

The waitress brought him his steak-and-oyster pie. He prodded it with his fork like a man who has suddenly lost his appetite. "You can go back to the salad bar if you want to," the waitress told him. "There's no extra charge."

"Thank you," he said, and then looked across the table with a haunted, tired expression. "Supposing nothing comes of this?" he asked me. "Supposing it's all a dream, all an illusion? I'll have lost my career, as well as Constance."

"Supposing you never try?" I retorted. "What will you think then, for the rest of your life? 'I could have had Constance back, but I was too frightened to make the effort.' "

Walter cut into his pie-crust, and a curl of fragrant steam rose out of it. He ate slowly, and without much obvious relish; but all the same he was still hungry enough to finish most of the pie, and his bread as well. He drained the last of his Guinness, and then drummed his fingers sharply on the deal tabletop.

"Five or six million, is that it?"

"That's the estimate."

"Can you get me an accurate costing?"

"Of course."

He wiped his mouth with his napkin. "I don't know what I'm letting myself in for," he said. "But the least I can do is run it up the flagpole and see if anybody salutes it."

"Think of Constance," I reminded him.

"I am," he said. "That's what worries me."

TWENTY-EIGHT

Dr. Rosen was just parking his Mercedes 350 SL outside of the Derby Clinic when I drew up beside him in my rattling Toronado and gave him a wave of greeting. He stopped on the sidewalk, a neat, immaculately-dressed man with a goatee beard and large California-style spectacles. I often used to think that he would have been happier in Hollywood than he was in Salem: he had a naturally exhibitionist nature and a love of medical jargon that ranged from "sibling shock" to "acceptory neurosis" and back again.

He was very professional, however: thorough and knowledgeable and careful in the finest tradition of New England's country physicians, and his love affair with medical ritz couldn't really be held against him.

"Good morning, John," he said, cheerfully. "Come on in and have some coffee."

"I just came to see Anne," I told him. We walked together up the sun-flecked pathway to the clinic's glass-fronted reception area. Inside, it was calm and air-conditioned, with smooth background music and expensive potted plants, and a discreet waterfall which tinkled into a free-form goldfish pool. Seated at a desk at the far side of the reception area was a stunningly pretty blonde nurse with a white uniform and a white cap and spotless white medical shoes. She probably didn't know the difference between a cyst and a cistern, but who cared. She was all part of Dr. Rosen's "convivial clinic" theme.

"Any calls, Margot?" Dr. Rosen asked her, as he passed her by.

"Mr. Willys, that's all," said Margot, flashing sooty black eyelashes at me. "Oh, and Dr. Kaufman from Beth Israel."

"Call Kaufman back for me in ten minutes, will you?" asked Dr. Rosen. "Forget Willys until he calls back himself. Was it his fibrositis?"

"I guess."

"Come in, John," Dr. Rosen beckoned me. "And, thanks, Margot."

"You're welcome," purred Margot.

"She's new," I commented to Dr. Rosen, walking into his large cream-painted office, and looking around. He still had the large Andrew Stevovich oil painting on the wall, a moon-faced woman and two moon-faced men, a picture which I knew in every detail, every shade, every angle, because I had sat opposite it for hours on end, talking to Dr. Rosen about my depression and my bereavement.

Dr. Rosen sat down at his wide teak desk and sorted briefly through his mail. The desk was bare except for the morning's mail and a small bronze abstract sculpture in a twisted triangle, which Dr. Rosen had once told me was meant to represent the self-curative strength inherent in every human. It always looked more like a serious case of indigestion to me, but I had never said so.

"Anne," he said, as if were continuing a sentence which he had left half-finished, "Anne is suffering from a broken wrist, severe bruising, muscular strain, swollen tendons, and shock. Well, I imagine the shock has probably subsided by now, but the physical damage will take a few days to right itself."

He paused, frowned at a letter from Peter Bent Brigham, and then looked up at me with an expression that wasn't very far away from surprise. "I don't suppose you want to tell me how Anne *got* that way?" he asked me.

"Hasn't Anne told you?"

"Anne said she was jogging, and she fell, but I really find that very hard to believe. Particularly since she must have fallen with her legs stretched wide apart, as if she were a ballerina doing the *splits;* and particularly since the external scratches and lesions on her skin all indicate that she was naked at the time."

I shrugged, and made a face which was supposed to be interpreted as non-committal.

Dr. Rosen watched me for a while, tugging his beard between finger and thumb. At last, he said, "I'm not suggesting for a moment that Anne's injuries are anything to do with you, John. But I'm a physician, remember, and I have to wonder. That's part of my profession. I don't only deal with the effect, I have to do my best to find out the cause in case the effect happens again. I mean, I'm more than a simple mechanic."

"I know that, Dr. Rosen," I nodded. "But, believe me, there's nothing going on here that's—what would you call it?—*untoward,* or anything like that."

Dr. Rosen pursed his lips, obviously dissatisfied.

"Look," I said, "I haven't been beating her up. I hardly know her."

"She was with you the night she got hurt, and at some time during that night she was naked."

"It happens, doctor. People do get naked at night. But, believe me, her nakedness was nothing to do with me. Neither were her injuries. All I did was drive her down here so that you could take care of her."

Dr. Rosen stood up, and walked around his desk with his hands thrust into his pants pockets. "Well," he said, "I have no way of proving you wrong."

"Do you *want* to prove me wrong?"

"I just want to find out what happened, that's all. Listen, John, that girl wasn't injured in any athletics accident. You know it, I know it. I'm not trying to pry, or act like a one-man watch committee. But it would help me medically to know how she got herself bruised and sprained and roughed up so badly. I mean, her injuries aren't consistent with anything but . . . well, if you want to have it straight, s-and-m."

I stared at him. "Are you kidding? S-and-m? You really think that Anne Putnam and I were—"

Dr. Rosen raised his hand, and blushed. "John, please, you don't have to explain yourself."

"I obviously *do* have to explain myself if you think that I was tying Anne Putnam to the bedpost and beating her up."

"Listen, I'm sorry," said Dr. Rosen. "I didn't mean to suggest for a moment that—" He paused, leaving his sentence unfinished. "Well, I'm sorry. It was just that I couldn't think how else she could have come by injuries of this particular nature. Please. It was very tactless of me."

"It would have been even *more* tactless if I actually had been beating her up," I remarked.

"I've said I'm sorry. Now, do you want to see her? She should have finished her medication program by now."

Dr. Rosen led me out of his office and along the corridor, his softsoled shoes squeaking on the highly-waxed floor tiles. He was still embarrassed; I could tell that by the color of his ears. But what else could I do, except deny that Anne and I had been playing torture chamber games? He wasn't going to believe that Jane's ghost had turned Anne upside down and brutalized her by psychokinesis.

Anne was sitting in a white bamboo chair in a corner of her room, watching the *$20,000 Pyramid*. She looked pale and tired, her arm was strapped up, and both her eyes were bruised. She clutched her robe around her as if she were cold.

"Anne, you've got a visitor," said Dr. Rosen.

"Hi," I told her. "How are you feeling?"

"Better, thank you," she said, and switched off the television by remote. "I had a few nightmares last night, but they gave me something to help me sleep."

Dr. Rosen left us and I sat down on the end of the bed. "I feel really guilty about what happened to you," I said. "I shouldn't have let you come up to the cottage."

"It was my fault for tampering," said Anne. "I should have realized that Mictantecutli was far too strong for me."

"You're safe, that's all that matters."

Anne looked up at me. Her left eye was badly bloodshot. "At what price, though? That's the frightening thing."

"No price at all. I was considering that option already."

"You were really considering letting Mictantecutli go free?"

"Of course I was. It was offering me my wife and my child back. What would *you* have done?"

Anne looked away. On the lawn outside, in the sunshine, a meadowlark tentatively hopped, and then flew off. "I suppose I would have done exactly the same thing," she said. "But now I feel that you *had* to make that decision because of me. It's as if my life is being exchanged for all those others."

"All what others?"

"All those others who will die when Mictantecutli gets loose."

"Who says anybody's going to die, just because a three-hundred-year-old demon is set free?"

"Mictantecutli is *far* more than three hundred years old," Anne corrected me. "It was already centuries old when David Dark brought it to Salem. It had been known in Aztec culture since the beginning of recorded time. And always, it has demanded its sacrifices. Human hearts to feed its stomach, unfinished lives to feed its spirit, human affection to keep it warm. It is a parasite without any purpose except to exist; and it was only because the Aztecs used it to threaten any of their people who refused to pay homage to Tonacatecutli the sun-god, and because David Dark tried to use it to frighten the people of Salem into coming to chapel more regularly, that it had any useful function at all. I promise you, John, when Mictantecutli is set free, it will immediately seek more souls."

"Anne," I protested gently, "these are modern times. People don't *believe* in this stuff any more. How can Mictantecutli possibly have any influence if people don't believe in it?"

"It doesn't matter whether they believe in it or not. You didn't believe that Jane could return from the grave until you saw her; but that didn't diminish the power of her manifestation, did it?"

I was silent for a while. Then I looked at her and shrugged. "It's too late now, anyway. I've made Mictantecutli a promise. I'll just have to stick to it and see what happens. I still don't believe that it's going to be *that* much of a danger."

"It will be worse than you can possibly imagine. Why do you think I begged you to let me die? My life is nothing compared with what Mictantecutli will do."

"But I promised," I reminded her.

"Yes, you promised. But what is a promise to a demon worth? If you had once made a promise to Hitler, and broken it, would anybody have held you guilty? Would anybody have said that you were untrustworthy or disloyal?"

"Hitler might have. Just as Mictantecutli might, if I break my promise to set it free."

"John, I want you to break your promise. I want you openly to say to Mictantecutli that you refuse to set it free."

"Anne, I can't. It'll kill you."

"My life doesn't matter. Besides, if you're really so skeptical about Mictantecutli's powers, you shouldn't worry."

"I'm not skeptical about its powers. I just don't think that it's got the strength to survive in a society that doesn't believe in demons any more."

Anne reached up and touched the back of my hand. "And there's Jane, too, isn't there? And your unborn son?"

I looked at her for a moment, and then lowered my eyes. "Yes," I said. "There's Jane."

We sat for a very long time without saying anything to each other. In the end, I got up from the bed, bent forward, and kissed Anne on the forehead. She squeezed my hand for an instant, but didn't speak, not even to say goodbye. I closed the door behind me as silently as if I were closing the door in a house of death.

On the way out, I came around the corner into the reception area and bumped straight into Mr. Duglass Evelith, in a wheelchair. He was being pushed along by Quamus, and Enid Lynch was walking just a little way behind. They looked dressed for an outing: old man Evelith was wearing a black derby and an opera cape, a silver-topped cane held between his knees; Quamus wore an overcoat in gray Prince-of-Wales check; and Enid was dressed in a clinging dress of gray wool, through which her chill-tightened nipples showed with considerable prominence.

"Well met, Mr. Trenton," said Duglass Evelith. He reached out his hand, and I shook it. "Or rather, ill met, under the circumstances. Anne told me on the telephone what had happened."

"She called you?"

"Of course. I am like an uncle to all my witches." He smiled, although there was very little humor in his eyes. His expression instead was suspicious, searching, and critical. I felt there was a magical circle surrounding these people; a psychic bond into which I had unwittingly blundered, setting off alarms within all of their collective minds. If I had hurt Anne in any way, if I had compromised the understanding we had between us to raise the *David Dark* from the sea-bed and deliver Mictantecutli to Duglass Evelith's house without delay— then I felt uneasily sure that all of these people would know about it without even having to ask.

"Anne is . . . very much better," I said. "Dr. Rosen says that she should be able to go home later today, or early tomorrow. He just wants to make sure that she's out of shock."

Duglass Evelith said, "It was your dead wife, she told me. A manifestation of your dead wife."

"Yes," I said. I looked up at Quamus. His face gave nothing away. High-cheeked, impassive, he didn't blink once, or deflect for even a moment that cold, penetrating stare. "Yes, there was some sort of a conflict between them. Anne was trying to give me some temporary peace from ghostly visitations and I think my wife objected."

"You mean that Mictantecutli objected. For it is the demon, you know, which causes your wife to appear in this way."

"I meant—Mictantecutli," I said. I felt ridiculously guilty. All three of them were looking at me as if I had just sold my mother to a white slave-trader. It was obvious that they sensed *something;* although quite what it was they couldn't be sure.

Enid said, "It would probably be better if you were to stay away from your house for the next few weeks. Have you anywhere you can go?"

"I could stay with my father-in-law, I guess, down at Dedham; and, incidentally, talking about my father-in-law, it seems that he may be able to finance the raising of the *David Dark.*"

"Well, that *is* good news," said old man Evelith. "But why stay all the way out at Dedham? If you care to, you can stay with me, at Tewksbury. I have a spare suite of rooms which you are quite welcome to use for as long as you wish. It would be quite convenient, too, wouldn't it, while you and your colleagues are raising the ship? You could keep me in touch on your progress from day to day, and in return you could use my library for any additional research you might need."

I glanced from Enid to Quamus to old man Evelith. It would probably be stuffy and oppressive, living at Billington mansion, but on the other hand it would give me access to all of old man Evelith's papers and books; and I might even be able to discover how he proposed to deal with Mictantecutli once the demon was raised from the bottom of the sea. If I knew what he intended to do, and how he was going to keep the demon in bondage, then I might also be able to find out how to break the bonds, and set the demon free.

Duglass Evelith had probably invited me because he wanted to keep an eye on what *I* was doing, just as much as I wanted to spy on him. But I didn't mind that. The real test of wills would come when Mictantecutli was discovered, and salvaged.

"I'll call you," said old man Evelith. "When you've packed, Quamus will come down and help you to move. Won't you, Quamus?"

Quamus gave no indication that he would or he wouldn't, or even that he had heard. Enid came closer to the wheelchair, and said, "We mustn't be away too long, Mr. Evelith. Let us go visit Anne, and then get back. Mr. Trenton, I'm very glad that you're making progress with the finance."

The three of them went off down the corridor, the wheels of Duglass Evelith's wheelchair making a light purring noise on the tiles.

Outside, a cold wind was rising, and I was beginning to feel that there was something ominous in the air. Something chilly, something threatening, and something that would erupt *soon*.

TWENTY-NINE

It took a week for Edward and Forrest and Dan Bass to prepare a reasonably accurate costing of how much it would take to raise the *David Dark*, and during that week we dived at the location of the wreck eleven times.

We were lucky: on the fourth dive we found protruding from the mud a row of four decayed timbers, which later turned out to be fashion-pieces which outlined the stern transom. This was our first visual confirmation that the *David Dark* was actually there, buried in the ooze, and we celebrated that evening with a dozen bottles of California's best.

During the next few dives, we excavated scores of deck-timbers; and it rapidly became clear that the *David Dark* was lying at an angle of about 30 degrees, with one side of her hull preserved almost up to the spar deck. Edward telephoned a friend of his in Santa Barbara, California, a maritime artist called Peter Gorton, and Peter flew over to help with the preparation of sketch-plans and charts.

Peter dived on the wreck three times himself, groping through the murk to feel the stumpy remains of the stern-post and the black, eroded teeth of the fashion-pieces. Afterwards, silent, absorbed with what he had seen, he sat down in Edward's living-room with a drawing-board and scores of sheets of paper, and created for us a conjectural sheer drawing of what he thought the *David Dark* actually looked like now, as well as dozens of conjectural body-sections.

I went down myself on the twelfth dive. It was a bright, calm day, and visibility was unusually good. Edward swam along with me, a distorted white companion in a soundless

285

world without gravity or wind. We approached the wreck of the *David Dark* from the north-east, and when I first saw her it was hard to understand how Edward had missed her during all that year of diving and searching. Apart from the black timbers which had now been excavated from the sloping ooze, the bulk of the *David Dark* was represented on the sea-bed as a long, oval mound, like an underwater burial-place. During the three cold centuries she had lain here, the tidal streams had scoured around her, creating a natural depression on all sides, and heaping silt onto her upper decks as if they were trying to conceal the evidence of an ancient and unforgiven murder.

I swam right around the wreck, while Edward pointed out the exposed fashion-pieces, and the stern-post, and indicated with a sloping hand just how much the wreck had keeled over when she had sunk to the bottom. I watched Edward cross and re-cross the wreck, flying above the sea-bed at a height of no more than three or four feet, his fins stirring up cauliflower clouds of silt. It was then that I remembered what old Mercy Lewis had told me on Salem Common that day: *"You must stay away from the place where no birds fly."*

This was the place: deep beneath the surface of Salem Harbor. She had warned me, but now it was too late. I was committed to whatever fate was going to bring me; and I was committed to bringing up Mictantecutli, if it was really here.

When we surfaced, Edward shouted across at me, "What do you think? Fantastic, isn't it?"

I waved, panting for breath. Then I swam back to the *Diogenes,* and climbed up the diving-ropes on to the deck. Gilly came over and said, "You've seen it?"

I nodded. "It's amazing that nobody's come across it before."

Dan Bass said, "It isn't really. Most of the time, the visibility is so poor that you could swim within a couple of feet of it and not notice anything unusual."

Edward came aboard and shook himself like a wet seal. "It's really extraordinary," he said, handing his mask to Gilly, and wrestling his head out of his orange Neoprene hood. "You get this creepy sense that you're trespassing on history . . . that men were never supposed to discover this wreck. You know what it reminds me of? Those ancient Celtic barrows, which you can only detect from the air."

"Well," I said, "now that we've found it, how long is it going to take us to bring it up?"

Edward blew water out of his nose. "Dan and I have been talking about this, from a logistical point of view. How many divers and marine archeologists we're going to need, how many diving-boats, how much excavation equipment. We're going to require warehouse space on shore, too, so that we can store equipment and lay out all the loose timbers we find. Everything we find is going to have to be numbered, sketched, and filed away for later restoration. Every timber, every spar, every knife, fork, and spoon; every bone; every shred of fabric. Then we're going to require refrigeration storage to keep the main timbers from eroding, and of course somewhere to store the main hull itself, when we eventually bring it up."

"How eventually is eventually?" I wanted to know.

"It depends on our budget, and the weather. If we have a short diving season this year, and if we can't immediately lay our hands on all the specialized equipment we're going to need, then three or four years."

"Three or four *years?*"

"Well, sure," said Edward. He unwrapped a piece of candy and popped it into his mouth. "And even that's less than a third of the time it took them to bring up the *Mary Rose*. Of course we're benefiting from all of their experience; and there's even a chance that we can borrow some of the lifting equipment they developed. Once we've got the budgeting settled, Forrest and I will probably fly over to England and have some detailed meetings with them on the best way to bring up the *David Dark* with the minimum of damage."

"But, for Christ's sake, Edward, three or four *years?* What about Mictantecutli? What about all those people who are going to be haunted, and possibly killed? What about all those spirits that can't rest?"

"John, I'm sorry, but three or four years is pushing it right to the very limit. If there wasn't this unusual urgency, I'd normally expect to take eight or nine years over an historical salvage job of this magnitude. Do you realize what we've *got* here? An historic wreck of absolutely incalculable value; the only known surviving wreck from the late 17th century which hasn't even been *touched* since it first went down. What's more, it was engaged on a secret and extraordinary mission, and as far as we know it's still bearing its original cargo.''

I roughly toweled my face and then tossed the towel down on the deck. ''You specifically told me that you were going to bring this wreck up quickly. You specifically said that.''

''Sure I did,'' Edward agreed, ''and I will. Three or four years is almost *indecently* quick.''

''Not if your dead wife is haunting you every night. Not if half the people in Granitehead are being terrorized by their deceased relations. Not if one single life is put at risk; that's not quick.''

''John,'' put in Forrest, ''we can't lift that wreck any faster. It's not physically possible. It has to be thoroughly excavated, all the silt and the mud sucked out of it; then it has to be strengthened so that we won't break its back when we winch it out. We have to make endless calculations to determine what kind of stress it's going to stand up to; then we have to construct a custom-built frame to enclose the hull while it's actually raised. You're talking about three years' work there already.''

''All right,'' I said, ''but can't we raise the copper vessel first? Excavate the hold, and lift it out separately? How long will that take? A week or two?''

''John, we can't work it that way. If we go charging into that wreck like John Wayne and the Green Berets, we're going to do a great deal of unwarranted damage to the decks, and maybe destroy the value of the entire excavation.''

''What are you talking about? Edward, what the hell's going on here? You said it would take some time to lift the ship up off the sea-bed; all right, that's admitted. But you never said *years*. I always got the impression that we were talking about weeks, or maybe a couple of months at the outside.''

Edward laid a hand on my shoulder. ''There was never any possibility that we could raise the *David Dark* in a matter of weeks, and I never gave you the impression for one moment that we could. John, this wreck is a fragile historical monument. We can't treat it like it's a sunken speedboat.''

''But we can get that damned Mictantecutli out of there,'' I insisted. ''Edward, we have to. Come on, Edward, they brought up all of the cannon from the *Mary Rose* way before they brought up the hull.''

"Of course they did; and of course we'll bring up Mictantecutli ahead of the main structure. We may be able to lift the copper vessel out of there by the beginning of next season, if we're lucky. But we can't afford to go crashing in there with crowbars and winches before we know how much of the wreck is actually there, and how she's lying, and how we can best preserve her."

"Edward!" I shouted at him. "The goddamned wreck doesn't matter! Not by comparison! It's Mictantecutli we have to go for, regardless of the wreck!"

"Well, I'm sorry, John," said Edward, polishing his spectacles, and lifting them up so that he could squint through them and make sure that they were clean. "Nobody else here feels the same way as you do, and that means that you're outvoted."

"I wasn't aware that we were a committee. I thought we were just a bunch of people with the same interest at heart."

"We are. Well, we are, at least. I don't know whether you are."

Gilly said, "Isn't there some kind of compromise we can reach? Isn't there some way we can make it a top priority, getting that copper vessel out of the hold?"

"It is a top priority," Edward insisted. "God knows, I'd rather excavate it logically, so that we don't lift it before we've annotated and earmarked everything around it, and the deck on which it's lying. But I've already compromised to the point where I'm prepared to winch it up as soon as we've removed the deck immediately above it, as soon as it's accessible, and you can't ask any more of me than that."

"Edward," I said, "I'm asking you to get down there with as many air-lifts as you can lay your hands on, as well as picks and crowbars and whatever else it takes to pull that decking up, and to get in there and find that copper vessel as an absolute priority Number One."

"I won't do it," said Edward.

"In that case, you can forget your financing and you can forget me. You've been stringing me along the whole goddamned time."

"I never once promised that I would smash my way into that wreck like King Kong and drag that demon out of there at the expense of the entire integrity of everything we're trying to do here. John—John, listen to me. We're historians, do you understand me? Not scrap merchants, or salvage engineers, or even antique dealers. I know the pressures. I understand the personal anxiety you've been feeling—''

''You don't understand shit!'' I yelled at him. ''You and Forrest and Jimmy and all the rest of you down at that museum, you spend all your time up to your ears in dust. Dust, and relics, and crumbling old books. Well let me tell you something, there's a real world out here, believe it or not, a world where human values count for a whole lot more than history.''

''History is human values,'' Edward retorted. ''That's what history is all about. What do you think we're doing here, except learning about human perspectives? Why do you think we're going to raise this wreck? We want to find out why some of our human ancestors considered it urgent to set sail in the teeth of a terrible storm carrying the skeletal remains of an Aztec demon. Don't tell me that *that* isn't all about human values. And don't tell me either that we're going to be doing ourselves or humanity any kind of a favor if we tear that wreck apart and destroy the incredible historical evidence that we've found here.''

''Well,'' I said, more quietly now, ''it appears that you historians and I hold diametrically opposed views of what constitutes a favor to humanity and what doesn't. The best thing I can do right now is to sit here, say nothing, and get off this boat just as soon as it gets back to harbor. This is the finish, Edward. I quit.''

Dan Bass glanced at Edward, as if he expected Edward to say that he was sorry. But there is nobody less compromising than a riled-up academic, and Edward was no exception. He stripped off his wetsuit, tossed it over to Gilly, and then said, ''Let's get back. Suddenly this trip isn't a pleasure any more.''

Forrest came forward, holding a mug of hot coffee with both hands. ''What about the finance?'' he wanted to know. ''What are we going to do without John's father-in-law?''

''We'll manage—all right?'' snapped Edward. ''I'll go talk to Gerry at the Massachusetts Capital Resource Company. He's been showing some interest in setting the *David Dark* up as a tourist attraction.''

''Well . . . if you think you can drum up $6 million,'' said Forrest, uncertainly.

"I can drum up $6 million, all right?" said Edward. "Now, let's get this boat back to Salem before I say something I'm going to regret."

We turned about, and Dan Bass headed us back towards the harbor. None of us spoke, and even Gilly kept her distance. After we had tied up at Pickering Wharf, I climbed out of the *Diogenes* straight away, flung my kitbag over my shoulder, and started to walk back to the parking lot.

"John!" somebody called. I stopped, and turned around. It was Forrest Brough.

"What is it?" I asked him.

"I just wanted to say that I'm sorry it turned out this way," he told me.

I stood looking back at the *Diogenes,* and at Gilly folding up the Neoprene wetsuits and dusting them with talcum. She didn't even look up, or turn around to wave goodbye.

"Thanks, Forrest," I said. "I feel exactly the same way."

THIRTY

I had, however, misjudged Gilly. I was back at Quaker Lane Cottage, packing together a few shirts and sweaters in preparation for my move to old man Evelith's place, when the telephone rang.

"John? It's Gilly."

"Gilly? I thought you were ignoring me, just like the rest of the Peabody archeological club."

She laughed. "I didn't want to upset them. Come on, John, I've been logkeeping for them for months now, they depend on me. But I think Edward's being very stuffy about this copper vessel you're supposed to bring up from the hold. I mean, if it *really* has anything to do with all of these hauntings, then I think they should winch it up straight away."

"You and me both," I told her. "But you heard what Edward's reaction to *that* was. And he was the guy who said he would always be my friend. I think I'd rather have Mictantecutli for a friend. At least with Mictantecutli, you know where you are."

"Did Edward really promise you that he would bring up the copper vessel especially quickly?"

"He implied as much. As soon as humanly possible, that's what he said. I knew it couldn't be raised in two minutes flat, even when the wreck was located. But there was never any suggestion of *years*. It's too urgent for years. One way or another, that demon has to be brought up out of there, and quick."

Gilly was silent for a while. Then she said, "You're going over to Tewksbury tonight, aren't you?"

"That's right."

"Well, if you can wait until nine or ten o'clock, I'll come over and see you. But I have to finish inventory first."

"Nine or ten o'clock is fine. Make it as late as you like."

I finished packing: then I took a look around the cottage. The bedrooms were empty and silent; and there was a strange *closed* atmosphere about them, as if they actually knew that I was leaving. I walked along the upstairs corridor to the bathroom, and collected my toothbrush, and stood for a moment and examined myself in the mirror over the basin. I looked very tired. There were purple smudges under my eyes, and my face looked oddly sly, as if the decision I had made to free Mictantecutli had somehow affected me physically, like the portrait of Dorian Gray had been altered by the corrupt and profligate life he had led.

I took my suitcase and went downstairs. I made sure that the water was turned off, and the empty icebox left to defrost with the door open. Then I went into the sitting-room and checked that I hadn't left anything behind. I was even going to take the painting of the *David Dark* with me, in case there was anything in it which old man Evelith might have overlooked before he sold it.

I still wanted to go to stay with Duglass Evelith at Tewksbury, in spite of the fact that I had resigned from Edward's diving team. In fact, it was more critical than ever before that I should learn as much as I could about Mictantecutli and the *David Dark*, because I was now determined that if Edward was going to refuse to bring up the copper vessel, then I would have to bring it up myself. Regardless of my inexperience as a diver; and regardless of the laws of salvage and wrecks.

I made sure that the log fire was out, and then I switched off the sitting-room light, and prepared to leave. But I was just about to close the door when I heard that whispering again, that soft, obscene whispering. I hesitated, listening. Then I stared into the darkness of the sitting-room, trying to make out if there was anything or anybody there. The whispering went on: coaxing and salacious, the whispering of a pederast or a voyeur, the whispering of a sexual killer. I looked towards the fireplace, and I was sure that I could see two dim scarlet glows among the logs, like the eyes of a devil.

Graham Masterton

I hesitated, then I switched on the light. There was nobody there. The fire was dead and cold; without cinders or sparks. I glanced around the room quickly, then I turned off the light again and closed the door. I knew then that as long as the cottage was haunted this way, I could never go back. There was too much evil here, too much cold commotion. I may not have been at any physical risk, but if I stayed here much longer I would very likely go mad.

I went through the hallway and picked up my suitcase. As I did so, a familiar voice said, *"John."*

I turned around. Jane was standing at the top of the stairs, her bare feet floating just a few inches above the second tread. She was still dressed in her white funeral robes, which silently fluttered as if they were being blown by an updraft. She was smiling at me, but there was something about her face which was even more skeletal than ever.

I turned away. I was determined not to look, not to listen. But Jane whispered, *"Don't forget me, John. Whatever you do, don't forget me."*

For a moment or two, I stood where I was, wondering whether I ought to speak to her: whether I ought to encourage her, or reassure her that I was going to save her, or whether I ought to tell her to go back to hell. But it probably wasn't her at all. It was probably nothing more than another of Mictantecutli's evil apparitions; and there was no point in speaking to that.

I went out, closed the door behind me, and locked it. Then I walked away from Quaker Lane Cottage with as much determination as I could; promising myself that I wouldn't go back there until Mictantecutli had been raised from the harbor, and fulfilled for me *its* side of the bargain we had made.

But I couldn't resist one last look at the blind and shuttered face of the house that had once been our home, Jane's and mine. It looked so derelict and abandoned, as if the malevolence that now infested it had begun to rot the very structure of the roof-beams, the very substance of the plaster and the brick. I turned on the car engine, and drove off down Quaker Lane, my wheels bouncing in the potholes and ruts.

I was only halfway down the lane when I saw Keith Reed, beating at the bushes along the left-hand side of the lane with a walking-cane. I drew up beside him, and put down my window.

"Keith? How are you doing?"

Keith glanced at me, and carried on thrashing at the bushes. "I thought you wasn't speaking to me," he said, crossly.

"I forgave you," I told him. "Did you lose something?"

"Lose something? Haven't you heard?"

"Heard what?"

Keith came over to the car, and leaned on the roof. He looked as tired and anxious as I did, and his nose was running. I passed him a Kleenex from the glove-box, and he noisily blew. Then he said, "We lost George."

"You lost George? What do you mean, you lost George?"

"Just that. We lost him. He went out yesterday afternoon; said he was off to see his brother Wilf. Well, that's crazy, of course, because Wilf is dead. But we ain't seen George since then, and everybody's out searching for him."

I sat behind the wheel of my car, and thoughtfully bit my lip. So Mictantecutli had claimed George Markham as well. I knew it. And although I wasn't going to tell Keith as much, because I didn't want to discourage him from searching, I knew in my heart of hearts that George was already dead, in the same way that Mrs. Edgar Simons was dead, and Charlie Manzi, too.

"I'll keep my eyes open," I said. "I'm going over to Tewksbury for a while, but I'll be back."

"Okay," said Keith; and as I drove away he went back across to the hedgerow, and carried on beating at the branches in his attempt to find his old stud-poker partner, dead or alive. I felt deeply depressed as I reached the highway, and turned south on to West Shore Drive. The power of the demon was hanging over Granitehead like an Atlantic thunderstorm, dark and threatening.

It was dark by the time I reached Tewksbury, and drew up outside the wrought-iron gates of old man Evelith's house. I rang the bell and waited for Quamus to open up for me, watched as before by the ever-attentive Doberman pinscher. If I've ever seen a dog with a relish for human flesh, that dog was one. I could hear its claws clicking on the shingle driveway in carnivorous impatience.

As it was, it was Enid Lynch who called the dog off and came to open the gates for me. She was wearing an ankle-length satin dressing-gown in electric blue, with a white boa collar. Her hair was pinned back and fastened with diamante combs. She looked like Jean Harlow in *Dinner At Eight*. The only trouble was, I didn't feel very much like Wallace Beery.

"You decided to take Mr. Evelith up on his offer?" she said, lifting one of her thinly-plucked eyebrows, and locking the gates behind me.

"Are you surprised?"

"I'm not sure. I would have thought you were the kind of man who would have preferred to stay at a Howard Johnson's."

I followed her up the steps to the front door. "I'm not sure whether I ought to take that as a compliment or not."

She showed me upstairs to my suite of rooms. There was a large drawing-room, furnished with comfortable but stuffy old sofas and chairs, and carpeted in dark brown. On the walls were oil paintings of the Dracut County forests and the Miskatonic River; and next to the fireplace there were shelves packed with leather-bound books on geology and physics. There was a decent-sized bedroom, with a brass bed, and a huge gilt-framed mirror on the wall; and next to the bedroom there was an old-fashioned bathroom, with a shower that had obviously been dripping steadily for years, judging by the green stain on the tiles.

"I will tell Mr. Evelith that you have arrived when he has finished his afternoon sleep."

"It's evening already. Does he usually sleep this long?"

"It depends on his dreams. Sometimes he will fall asleep during the afternoon, and not wake up until early the following morning. He says he does as much work in dreams as he does when he is awake."

"I see," I said, setting down my suitcase.

Enid said, "You may call me if there is anything that you need."

"I'm fine for the moment. There's just one thing, though: a friend of mine is visiting me later this evening. Miss Gilly McCormick. I hope that's going to be all right."

"Perfectly. Quamus will let her in."

"Quamus isn't here right now?"

Enid stared at me oddly, as if the question wasn't even worth a reply. I snapped open the latches of my case, and tried to look as if I was engrossed in taking out my slippers. Enid said, "We usually eat at nine o'clock. You like beef?"

"Certainly. That'll be marvelous."

"Good. In the meantime, please make yourself at home. Mr. Evelith said you were to have free access to the library."

"Thank you. I'll, uh . . . see you later."

I unpacked my shirts and my underwear and put them away in the deep sour-smelling drawers of the bureau in my bedroom. Then I wandered around my rooms, picking up books and statuettes, and peering out of the windows. My drawing-room had a view of the back garden, which was almost a forest in itself. It was too dark to see it properly, but I could make out the distant shapes of hundred-foot pines, and, closer to the house, a huge Osage orange. There was no television in the room, and I made a mental note to myself to bring in a portable set tomorrow.

Just as the clock on my mantelpiece chimed eight-thirty, and I was sitting with my feet up on one of the sofas trying to get myself engrossed in *Stresses In The Mohorovicic Discontinuity,* my door opened and old man Evelith walked in. He was fully dressed for dinner in a tuxedo and black tie, and his thinning gray hair was combed back with what smelled like lavender oil. He came up to me, and shook my hand, and then sat down next to me, smiling rather distantly, and turned over the cover of my book with his long chalk-nailed finger, to see what it was I was reading. "Mmh," he said. "Do you know anything at all about Moho?"

"Moho?"

"Geological slang. If you *did* know anything about Moho, you'd know what it was. Still, I suppose we all have to start our studies somewhere. You could have picked a better place. That book *Understanding Geology* is probably more up your street."

"Thank you," I said. "I'll . . . dip into it."

Duglass Evelith looked at me fixedly. Then he said, "I wasn't sure that you would come. Well, not *entirely* sure. I told Enid that it would depend on how violently your dead wife has been haunting you."

"Why should it have depended on that?"

"Let me put it this way," said Duglass Evelith. "You're not involved in this search for the *David Dark* for archeological motives; neither are you involved in it for profit. You have been haunted by your dead wife, as many people in Granitehead have been haunted before you; and you want to get to the cause of that haunting, and root it out."

"That's right," I nodded. "My sole interest in the *David Dark* begins and ends with Mictantecutli."

Duglass Evelith took off his half-glasses and folded them up, tucking them into the breast pocket of his tuxedo. "Because of that, Mr. Trenton, you and I have an interest in common. Oh, of course I'm fascinated by the archeological possibilities of the *David Dark*. It's going to be one of the most important finds in American maritime history. But the copper vessel that lies within its hold is a hundred times more important to me than the rotten wood which surrounds it. It is Mictantecutli that I want."

"Any special reason?" I asked him. I knew it was an impertinent question, but if our interests in the raising of the *David Dark* were so closely aligned, then I believed that it was important for me to know why he wanted to lay his hands on Mictantecutli. It might also give me some idea of what Evelith intended to do with the demon once he'd gotten hold of it, and how I could possibly set it free.

"The reason is simple to explain but difficult to believe," said old man Evelith. "During the Salem witch-trials, it was my ancestor Joseph Evelith who was among the most fervent of all the jurors; and it was he who alone believed that the witches were truly possessed, even after the hysteria was over, and the *David Dark* had been sent away from Salem and sunk. After the trials, Joseph attempted in vain to have all the remaining suspects executed, pleading with everybody in Salem that the witch-trials had *not* been a mistake; that in fact they had helped to purge Salem of a terrible evil, and to save the souls who had been hung from a fate far worse than the gallows. The only person who really believed him, of course, was Esau Hasket, and Hasket tried to help him leave Massachusetts to escape the anger of those who had once been his friends and co-prosecutors. But a party of burghers caught him as he was leaving Salem on the Swampscott Road, dressed as a woman, and he was imprisoned. His fate was to be secret and terrible. He was to be taken to the forest and there given as a sacrifice to the Naumkeag Indians, who for some years had been suffering poor harvests and blighted crops. A Naumkeag wonder-worker gave Joseph Evelith to the Spirit of the Future, a servant of Mictantecutli who in Aztec society was called Tezcatlipoca, the Smoking Mirror. My ancestor did not 'die' at the hands of Tezcatlipoca, in the

accepted sense of the word. He became its slave for all
eternity, suffering agonies of humiliation and torture. Tezcatlipoca is thoroughly evil: it wears a snake's-head dangling
from one nostril, so the Aztecs say, and its conjuring wand is
the amputated arm of a woman who died in childbirth.''

I said nothing: I had seen enough hideous magic to believe
that what Duglass Evelith was telling me was wholly or partly
true. Hadn't the wreck of the *David Dark* been located just
where he said it was?

He went on, "Tezcatlipoca has run riot since Mictantecutli
has been lying powerless on the bed of the ocean. It is the
devil of disease and pestilence; and you can lay every major
epidemic that has swept the United States squarely at its door.
Legionnaire's disease, cancer, every type of influenza, and its
latest little joke, herpes.''

Evelith was silent for a while. Then he said, "With Enid's
help—Enid and Anne Putnam and the rest of the wonder-
workers who are descended from the original witches of
Salem—with their help, I have been able to communicate
with Joseph Evelith through séances and signs. Until I can
release him from Tezcatlipoca's service, my family will remain outcast and doomed, forever shadowed by disease and
ruin. My own wife . . . and both my children . . . all of them
were taken by hepatitis. I myself have been sick with angina
for years.''

"So where does Mictantecutli come into it?'' I asked him.
"Surely another demon is only going to make things worse.''

He shook his head. "Tezcatlipoca is Mictantecutli's servant,
and must obey it. If I can bring Mictantecutli here, and keep
it imprisoned with the same magical bonds that the Narragansett
wonder-worker used in the days of David Dark, then I can
command it to tell Tezcatlipoca to let my ancestor go. The
blight will be lifted.''

"Why can't you use the magical bonds on Tezcatlipoca? If
it's a servant of Mictantecutli, then surely it's far less
powerful.''

"It is. But only the spells that bound Mictantecutli have
survived through history. Nothing relating to Tezcatlipoca has
been passed down at all. Quamus and I have tried many
different chants and incantations, and scores of different rituals.
Some of them have succeeded in raising the most terrifying
spirits you can imagine. That is what caused all the noise and

the lights that the local people have been complaining about. But none have succeeded in trapping or taming Tezcatlipoca.''

I stood up, and walked around the sofa. Somehow I felt uncomfortable, sitting so close to old man Evelith. There was something dry and unreal about him, as if his tuxedo and his evening trousers were nothing more than propped-up, empty clothes. I said, ''What guarantee do you have that Mictantecutli will do what you ask?''

''No guarantee at all, except that it will believe that releasing my ancestor will be the only way in which it will be given its freedom.''

''You'd release it?''

Duglass Evelith shook his head. ''I'd tempt it with the *prospect* of release. But can you imagine what would happen if a demon like that actually got loose? It has greater power than a 10-megaton bomb. It can influence the weather, the course of history, the very turning of the earth. It can raise corpses from their graves, and cut the most grisly swathe through the living population that you could ever imagine.''

''Are you sure of that?''

''How sure does anybody need to be? Mictantecutli has been lying under Salem Harbor for three hundred years, and so there is no recent history to support what I say. But come down to my library, and I will show you indisputable evidence that Mictantecutli was responsible for the extinction of the entire Toltec people in Mexico; that his European manifestation was responsible for each of the Black Death pandemics, which killed twenty-five million people in Europe alone. Up until the end of the 17th century, when Esau Hasket at last imprisoned it, Mictantecutli was involved in most of the bloodiest wars and the cruelest human deeds in history. Pliny said that Caligula, who was the bloodiest and most licentious of all Roman emperors, had been possessed after only eight months of his reign by a spirit which he called the Man of Bones.''

I said cautiously, ''You don't think that Mictantecutli would find it difficult to survive in a skeptical world like we have today? I mean, some of a demon's strength must come from how strongly people believe in it, surely?''

''Demons are not fairies from *Peter Pan*,'' said old man Evelith, turning around to stare at me. ''They don't acquire more strength because a million people throughout the world say, 'We *do* believe in demons!' ''

"Still," I said. "I can't see a giant skeleton being able to make much impact on a society that's learned to live with the bomb, and the automobile, and put up buildings only just short of a mile high. Can you? Really?''

"What do you want me to say?" asked old man Evelith. "Mictantecutli is the most vengeful and powerful being that ever was, excluding the Lord our God. I don't think it would be very impressed by H-bombs, or Chevrolets, or the Sears building. No, sir.''

At that moment, there was a brief knock at the door, and Quamus came in. "Mr. Evelith, sir, excuse me. There's a visitor for Mr. Trenton. Miss McCormick.''

Duglass Evelith stood up. "Show her in, Quamus. Perhaps she'd like to stay for dinner, Mr. Trenton?''

"If it won't be any trouble.''

"Not at all. This house hasn't seen any guests for years; I think I shall enjoy having some company.''

Gilly came in, and I introduced her to Duglass Evelith. She smiled and nodded, obviously a little overawed by the gates and the dog and the old-fashioned gloom of the halls and the corridors. When Duglass Evelith had gone, she came over and gave me a kiss, and squeezed me affectionately. She wore a natural-colored cotton dress with ties at the shoulders and pockets, and it made her look fresh and young and pretty.

"This is like Castle Dracula," she said. "Have you checked to see if Mr. Evelith's face actually appears in any of the mirrors?''

"Too late if it doesn't," I smiled. "Sit down. I think I can even offer you a drink. Would you like to stay for dinner?''

"I'd adore it. This place is so *creepy*.''

I poured us two small glasses of whiskey from the half-bottle I had brought with me in my suitcase. "How's Edward?" I asked her. "Did he say anything after I'd gone?''

"Edward's funny. You mustn't think too badly of him. He's been searching for this wreck for so long, and now that he's found it I think that he's almost frightened of bringing it up. He's one of these archeologists who love to explore the unknown, but once they've found out what it is, they don't know what to do with it.''

"I think I follow you. But why is he insisting on bringing

up the wreck so slowly, and so scrupulously? He knows how dangerous this demon could be."

"He's afraid of making a mistake, that's all,"—Gilly told me. "If he makes a mess of this wreck, then everybody at the Peabody is going to treat him like a blundering amateur. Apart from that, he's up against a credibility problem, too, just like you are. Nobody believes in demons; not even me. Well, *you* believe in demons, but you're an exception. And the whole point is that if he chops his way into the wreck, and damages it, and then finds out that there's nothing in there, or that the copper vessel doesn't contain anything dangerous after all . . . how's he going to explain it? 'I smashed up this valuable historical monument because I thought there was a devil inside it'? Jesus, John, he'd lose his job. He's on the verge of losing it anyway, because of all the time he's been taking off."

"My heart bleeds," I said, unsympathetically. "Meanwhile, scores of people in Granitehead are being plagued by terrifying apparitions. Do you know that one of my neighbors is missing tonight? He said he was going to meet his dead brother, and now they can't find him. I can tell you, Gilly: I've got a good mind to dive down to that wreck and bring that copper vessel up by myself."

"You'll have to hurry if you're thinking of doing that. Edward's going to register the wreck tomorrow as belonging to the Wardwell-Brough Maritime Archeological Trust, or some such fancy title. He's also going to arrange to have the wreck marked with an official coastguard buoy and protected around the clock by an official coastguard patrol. He'll be making an announcement to the newspapers and the television, too."

"I thought he was going to keep it quiet for a while."

"He was. But now *you've* quit, and taken your father-in-law's money with you, he needs all the donations he can get. Mind you, he was thinking of going to your father-in-law behind your back, to see if he's still interested."

"Oh, was he?" I was angry and upset. If there's anything worse than having a bitter row with somebody you hate, it's having a bitter row with somebody you like. I liked Edward, very much; but I knew now that the *David Dark* had broken up our friendship forever. I was going to have to salvage that copper vessel, no matter how much damage I did to the ship's historic hull, and I was going to have to do it quickly. Tomorrow morning, if possible. I would have to talk to Duglass Evelith about it. Maybe he could help.

Gilly said, "No ghosts around here?"

"Not one," I told her.

"Would Mr. Evelith object too much if I stayed the night?"

I looked at her narrowly. "I don't think so. He seems to be an understanding old buffer."

"And you?" she asked. "Would *you* object?"

"I wouldn't object. *Object?* Why would I possibly object?"

She shrugged, and then she came closer and kissed me. "Some men don't like to be pounced on."

I kissed her back, and felt her breast through her cotton dress. "Some men are crazy," I told her.

THIRTY-ONE

After dinner, when Gilly had gone upstairs, and Enid and Quamus had retired to the kitchen with the dishes, I sat by candlelight with Duglass Evelith in his library. He showed me book after book, document after document, until the table was heaped high with them. Each related to Mictantecutli, and the demon's terrible power. By the time midnight struck, I was quite convinced that we were up against a force so cold and so malevolent that by comparison it made Satan seem positively cozy.

I said to him, "Bringing Mictantecutli up to the surface seems quite urgent now, doesn't it?"

The old man sniffed, and shrugged. "It's difficult to say. This present activity may be caused by nothing more than exceptionally warm currents, flowing over the wreck. Mictantecutli responds to warmth, remember, and is rendered immobile by intense cold. Perhaps when winter comes, the manifestations will die down again. But personally I would rather not take the risk; quite apart from the desire that I have to free my ancestor from Tezcatlipoca. The interest that you and your friends have shown in locating the *David Dark* will prove to be a Godsend, I believe."

"Mr. Evelith," I said, uncomfortably, "I'm afraid to say that my friends and I have had a falling out."

"Oh? This won't affect the salvage, I hope?"

"Well, I'm sorry to say that it might. You see, my friends, being professional museum archivists, are anxious to preserve the wreck itself in the exact condition in which it has been found. I know that's understandable, and probably admirable, too; or at least it would be if we were dealing with nothing more than an ordinary wreck. The problem is that if the wreck is going to be properly preserved, the process of bringing up the copper vessel is going to take considerably longer than I first believed. It might not even be brought up this diving season.''

"You mean Mictantecutli may be left lying down there for another year?''

"More than likely. I argued against it, but the rest of them wouldn't budge. None of *them* have been haunted by dead wives, or ghostly brothers. They believe in Mictantecutli, for sure, but they don't really understand what they're up against. Their attitude is too academic. They can't see the urgency.''

Old man Evelith looked down at the heaps of books and papers. "Perhaps they ought to come see these,'' he said. "Maybe *then* they'd understand.''

"Mr. Evelith, I don't think there's time. Miss McCormick told me this evening that Mr. Wardwell proposes to register ownership of the wreck tomorrow, which would make it an offense for anybody else to damage it or exploit it; and that the coastguard are likely to start patrolling. Remember that Mr. Wardwell works for the Peabody, which is heavy Salem establishment; and that the Salem authorities will give him all the protection and encouragement he needs. After all, the *David Dark* is going to be a big tourist attraction, once she's raised.''

"Not if they don't make every effort to control Mictantecutli,'' said Mr. Evelith, darkly.

"That's another point. Mr. Wardwell isn't going to deliver Mictantecutli to you straight away, like he promised. He's decided to take a good look at it first, to see what it is that you want so badly.''

"Is he *mad?*'' said Mr. Evelith. "He'll be torn to pieces! Doesn't he know what Mictantecutli *is,* even now? You must stop him! Mr. Trenton, you must do everything you can to stop him!''

I shook my head. "I've already tried, Mr. Evelith. He's made up his mind. Wreck first, Mictantecutli second, open the copper vessel third. Gilly—that's Miss McCormick—Gilly says he won't be swayed.''

Duglass Evelith was extremely agitated. He walked around the table, and then back again, and then he closed all the books he had opened, one after the other, in a succession of snaps. At last he looked up at me and said, "You must dive on the *David Dark* very first thing tomorrow morning. You must bring up that copper vessel at all costs. Otherwise, my God, the world will see such havoc as has never been seen in nine lifetimes."

"That's what I was going to propose," I told him. "A quick dive, first thing tomorrow, with a couple of crowbars and a winch."

"You think crowbars will be adequate?" Duglass Evelith asked me. "Look here."

He shuffled through his heaps of papers until he found a sketch-map of the *Mary Rose* which he had been studying in an effort to understand the problems that faced us with the *David Dark*. "The copper vessel is in the hold," he said. "That means, even if the ship is lying at an angle of 30 degrees, you will still have to penetrate your way through three decks and God knows how many tons of silt before you reach it. I can understand why Mr. Wardwell is so reluctant to bring it up in a hurry. The only way to reach it in a reasonable length of time is to tear the decks wide apart. The copper vessel in fact is so long that it is quite possible that part of each deck was lifted at the time to accommodate it, and then fastened down again once it was securely stowed."

"Then how the hell am I going to get it out of there in one morning's diving?" I wanted to know.

"Simple," said old man Evelith. "I have an old friend who has a demolition business at Lexington. Quamus will drive over there now and collect two cases of dynamite, and some underwater fuses."

"Dynamite? I've never used dynamite in my life. You mean you want me to blow the *David Dark* to pieces?"

"Can you think of another way to reach Mictantecutli before the wreck is registered, and the coastguard prevents anybody from going near?"

"I—" I began, and then raised my hands in resignation.

"You mustn't worry," said Duglass Evelith. "Quamus is an expert diver, and he will swim with you. He knows Mr. Walcott of the Salem Salvage Company; years ago they used to dive together. Mr. Walcott will let us use his boat and all his equipment. I will ask Quamus to call him as soon as he returns from Lexington."

"Do you think Quamus is up to it?" I asked. "He must be at least 60 years old."

"Quamus has been here at Billington ever since I was a child," said Duglass Evelith. "My father used to talk about the rides that Quamus gave him on his back when *he* was a child."

"Are you serious? That would make him—"

"Well over a hundred years old," Duglass Evelith nodded. "Yes. I have often thought about it myself. But it is not a question which one can put to Quamus. He would never answer; and it is quite likely that he would walk out and I would never see him again. But it is interesting to note that there is a Quamus mentioned in Joseph Evelith's diary of 1689."

I stayed silent. In Duglass Evelith's house, I felt myself to be on strange and almost magical territory. It wasn't altogether a frightening sensation, but I felt that I had to conduct myself with caution. There was great influence here that couldn't be explained in scientific terms, and as long as I behaved wisely, I would probably be able to use it for my own benefit.

"It would be sensible for you to get some sleep now," said Duglass Evelith. "I will have Quamus wake you at six o'clock. Over breakfast, I will explain how you will use the dynamite on the *David Dark*."

I got up. "Goodnight, then," I said. "And thank you again for putting me up here."

"A question of mutual interests," said old man Evelith, and went back to reading one of his books before I could say anything else. It was only when I was halfway up the dark staircase, on the way to bed, that I realized what I had actually let myself in for. An illegal underwater demolition job, despite the fact that I had scarcely any experience of diving, and no experience whatsoever with dynamite.

Gilly was sitting up in bed when I came in; and there was a warm fragrance of perfume around. She was reading *A History of Oceanic Geology*. I sat down on the end of the bed, and stripped off my necktie. "Good?" I asked her, nodding towards the book.

"Riveting," she said. "What kept you so long?"

"Old man Evelith and his moldy old documents. No, I shouldn't say that. He's fascinating, especially when it comes to the occult history of Salem and Granitehead. Do you know what he told me about Quamus?''

"Quamus gives me the creeps.''

"Quamus gives *you* the creeps? I found out tonight that Quamus is possibly three hundred years old.''

"How much of that brandy did you have?''

"Not enough.''

I undressed, brushed my teeth, and then climbed into bed. I had already showered once that evening, and the noise of the pipework had been enough to frighten me off showers for ever. Rattling, and groaning, and letting out echoing shrieks.

Gilly lay back, and reached out for me, gently parting her thighs. I climbed astride her, kissing her forehead and her eyes and her neck, and then her shoulders, and her soft pink nipples. We made love silently, as if it were a midnight ritual; prolonging each moment until it was impossible to prolong it any further. I looked down, and saw my hardness enclosed by her tight and succulent lips, and fear and anxiety and grisly manifestations seemed very far away, like an offkey orchestra playing in another part of the house.

"Maybe I ought to talk to Edward again," I said, when the lights were switched off, and we lay in the unfamiliar darkness. "Maybe he won't be so pigheaded after all.''

"You could try. Do you want me to mention it to him?''

I was quiet for a moment, as if I was thinking about it. The truth was, I was trying to allay any possible fears that Edward might have that I would dive on the wreck before he registered it, and if Gilly were to go back to him and suggest that he and I should have a friendly discussion about the raising of the copper vessel, say in a day or so, then he would hardly be likely to suspect that I would try to sneak down there tomorrow.

Quamus woke me at 5:55, when Gilly was still asleep. She lay with her hair spread out on the pillow, one breast bare, and I discreetly covered her up before I tiptoed out. My clothes were already laid out for me in the drawing-room, and Quamus whispered, "Breakfast right away, Mr. Trenton.''

When I went downstairs to the oak-paneled dining-room, the sunlight was already penetrating the French doors at the far end, and sparkling on the silverware and the Spode plates. There were muffins and coffee. Mr. Evelith had ordered that I should not be served the full breakfast today because I was swimming.

I ate on my own for five or ten minutes, until Duglass Evelith came into the room in a bronze quilted dressing-gown, smoking a small cigar. He sat down opposite me and watched as I buttered my muffin, and then he waved the blue cigar smoke away, and said, ''I hope this doesn't bother you. It's a repulsive old habit of mine; six o'clock every morning. How do you feel?''

''Nervous.''

''Well, good. If you're nervous, then you'll be alert. I'll tell you what we've managed to arrange during the night. Quamus has obtained two cases of dynamite, as well as all the necessary fuses; and all that has been loaded on to the station wagon ready to go. Mr. Walcott will be ready for you by the time you reach Salem Harbor, and will sail you out to the *David Dark*. When you dive, you will take down with you an airlift, and you will use this to excavate a narrow crevice in the silt, right beside the *David Dark*'s hull. Into this crevice you will pack both cases of dynamite, and you will then swim back to the surface, paying out fuse as you go. The fuse is largely made of magnesium, so it will burn underwater. You will light it, and then retreat from the area as quickly as possible, while the dynamite detonates. According to the preparatory work I have done during the night, the explosion should completely shatter the hull of the *David Dark*, and blow most of the silt out of the area where the ship has been buried. Now comes the difficult part: you will have to search the sea-bed, almost blind, for a great deal of silt will be clouding the water, and you will have to locate the copper vessel within a matter of minutes. Fortunately, Mr. Walcott has metal-detecting equipment, and that should help you find it reasonably speedily. We will be keeping the coastguard away from the area by putting out a false emergency call from further up the coast, off Singing Beach, and we will just have to hope that nobody else gets too inquisitive before we are able to winch the copper vessel up to the surface.''

''What are we going to do with Mictantecutli; once we get him ashore?'' I wanted to know.

''That is all arranged, too. A refrigerated truck will be waiting by the harbor, and the copper vessel will immediately be put into cold storage, and driven here. Enid will be preparing all the necessary rituals to keep Mictantecutli under our control; and she should be ready by the time we get back here.''

"If this doesn't work," I asked old man Evelith, "what's the worst that can happen? A $500 fine for setting off explosives? A couple of months in jail?"

Duglass Evelith pursed his lips. "Those will be nothing, compared with the fury of Mictantecutli. The worst that can happen, Mr. Trenton, is that every grave in Salem and Granitehead will open, and that the dead will rise to massacre the living."

At that moment, Gilly came into the room, blinking at the sunlight. "I woke up and you were gone," she said. "Does everybody get up this early around here?"

"I have to go to Boston to pick up some research material," I lied. "I thought I might as well make an early start."

Gilly sat down, and Quamus came in to pour her some fresh coffee. He looked across the table at me as he did so, and by the expression on his face he seemed to be asking me whether I was ready to go. I wiped my mouth, put down my napkin, and stood up. Gilly looked at me in surprise.

"You're not even going to have breakfast with me?"

I leaned across and kissed her. "I'm sorry. I really have to go."

"Are you all *right?*" she asked, glancing at old man Evelith as if she suspected him of executing some menacing influence over me.

"I'm fine," I reassured her. "All you have to do is finish your breakfast and leave when you feel like it. I'll call you later in the day. Maybe I'll even drop in and see you. And don't forget to tell Edward that I'd like to talk."

"I won't," said Gilly distractedly, as I left the dining-room, and followed Quamus across the hallway and out to the garage. In the gloom of the garage, Duglass Evelith's LTD wagon was waiting, black and polished, with two large packing-cases stowed in the back, both of them unmarked. Quamus opened the passenger door for me, and I climbed in, turning around to stare at the crates in trepidation.

"How much dynamite do we have there?" I asked him.

He pressed the remote button which opened the garage door. He looked across at me and almost smiled. "Enough to blow this car to Lynnfield, no driving necessary."

"Very reassuring," I told him.

We were circling the shingle driveway when Enid came down the front steps of the house and waved to us. Quamus drew the wagon to a halt and put down the window. Enid looked pale and distraught, and her hair was flying loose.

"What's wrong?" I asked her. "Did we forget something?"

"It's Anne," she said. "Your doctor just called, Dr. Rosen?"

"That's right, Dr. Rosen. What's the matter?"

"It's terrible. I sensed that something was wrong during the night. A feeling of sudden loss. A feeling that part of us had suddenly vanished. A very cold feeling."

"What's happened?" I demanded. "For Christ's sake, tell me what's happened."

"She was found hanging in her room this morning. They had kept her in for one more day of observation. Then, when they went in this morning, they found her hanging. Her own belt, from the light."

"Oh, God," I said, and I felt the coffee curdle in my stomach. Quamus touched his forehead in a sign which I assumed to be the Indian symbol for "bless me," or "rest in peace."

"She left a message," said Enid. "I can't remember what it said exactly, but it was addressed to you, Mr. Trenton. It said something like, 'Don't feel you have to keep your promise, just for me.' She didn't say what promise, though, or why you didn't have to keep it."

I closed my eyes, and then opened them again. The day looked very gray, like a harsh black-and-white photograph. "I know what promise," I said, quietly.

THIRTY-TWO

The cooperative Mr. Walcott of the Salem Salvage Company turned out to be a short, broad-shouldered, Slavic-looking man with shaggy gray eyebrows and a vocabulary that consisted chiefly of "C'd be" and "Likely that's so," two forms of non-committal agreement that after an hour of sailing I began to find extremely irksome and frustrating. He helped Quamus to load the dynamite boxes on to the deck of his diving-boat, a greasy 90-foot lugger; then he started up the diesels, and we left the quayside without any delay.

It was a chilly morning, but the sea was calm, and I was confident that I would be able to cope with the diving conditions. I wasn't at all sure about the dynamite, but I kept telling myself that it was all for Jane; and that if I played my part in this carefully and wisely, I would soon have her restored to me. It was an extraordinary thought, but if Mictantecutli kept his promise, it was possible that I might even have her back by tonight.

Quamus touched my shoulder, and beckoned me back to the lugger's after-deck, where our diving-gear was all laid out. A young girl with short-cropped blonde hair and a smudge of oil on her nose was checking the regulator valves on the oxygen cylinders. She wore identical denim overalls to Mr. Walcott, and her eyes were the same sharp blue, and from her stocky, busty build I took her at once to be Mr. Walcott's daughter. She said, "Hi," and looked at us skeptically, a gray-haired Indian of anything between 60 and 300 years old; and a nervous antique dealer in a dark blue business coat.

"You guys want to get ready?" she asked. "I'm Laurie Walcott. Either of you guys ever dive before?"

"Of course," I told her, trying to be sharp.

"I just asked," she said, and threw me a Neoprene wetsuit. It wasn't like the pristine white wetsuit that Edward and Forrest had lent me: it was gray and smelly, like a discarded walrus-skin, and its wrinkles were clogged with damp talcum powder. The oxygen cylinders, too, were battered and well-worn, as if they had been used to beat off marauding sharks. I guess I had to remember that Walcott was a professional salvage diver, not one of your weekend tyros.

Quamus said, "If you wish, you can change your mind. It is not good to dive if you are full of fear. Mr. Evelith will understand."

"Do I look *that* frightened?" I asked him.

"I would choose the word 'apprehensive,' " said Quamus, with the hint of an ironic smile.

"You must try a career in diplomacy," I quipped, trying to fight down my unease.

When Dan Bass had piloted us out to the *David Dark,* he fiddled around for almost five minutes, positioning the *Diogenes* over the site of the wreck. But Mr. Walcott, with his deeply-bitten pipe clenched between his teeth, and his oily cap pulled well down over his eyes, swung his lugger around as if it were a Harley-Davidson, right on the datum point, and lowered his anchor so accurately that when we dived we found it caught between the *David Dark*'s upright fashion-pieces.

Now Walcott came back to the after-deck, and started up the one-ton Atlas-Copco compressor. This huge machine rattled and coughed and sent up blurts of black smoke, but Walcott assured it was the best in the business. It would release a jet of compressed air down a 100-foot hose, and this would hopefully excavate a trench alongside the sunken hull of the *David Dark* large enough and deep enough for our dynamite.

I was surprised that Walcott asked no questions about what we were doing, or why, but presumably Quamus had paid him to keep his curiosity to himself. Laurie sat on the lugger's rail, chewing a huge mouthful of Bazooka Joe, and staring at the distant horizon as if the whole business were too boring for words.

At a few minutes after nine o'clock, Quamus and I rolled

backwards off the lugger's side, and began our dive. Luckily, the water in the harbor was unusually clear, and it only took a few minutes for us to descend to the bottom. We quickly located the wreck, and Quamus tugged on the shot-line to tell Walcott to feed us with compressed air.

I looked at Quamus through my blinkered face-mask. Physically, he was remarkably muscular, and in his wetsuit he looked as if he had been hewn out of solid granite. It was his eyes that interested me the most, though. Framed in his oval face-mask, they looked serious and reflective, as if life's pageant had passed him so many times that nothing could surprise him any longer; as if he were quite ready for death, whenever it eventually came. I wondered whether old man Evelith had been pulling my leg when he had told me that Quamus had been at Billington over a hundred years ago; I knew that some families gave their servants "below-stairs" names, so that butler after butler was *always* called James, no matter what they had actually been christened. The Quamus who had given piggybacks to Duglass Evelith's father had probably been *this* Quamus' father.

The compressed air spurted out of the six-inch hose with a sudden wallop, and for a moment I almost lost my grip on it. There was a compensator on the hose which prevented any diver who was using it from being jet-propelled all around the sea-bed; but all the same it felt as if it had a life of its own, and after two or three minutes of blasting away at the silt on the bottom of the sea, my arms were aching and my back felt as if I had played *The Hunchback of Nôtre Dame*.

We worked almost blind, because of the dense clouds of silt which the airhose blew up all around us. On our second dive, we would use an airlift, which would clear most of the silt away, but on this dive Quamus had to break through the consolidated layer of grit and shell which lay beneath the first thin coating of silt and "anchorage gash"—that assorted refuse wherever boats are moored. To break through, Quamus used a long metal rod with a sharpened end, and once I had blown away the initial mud, he began to hack at the grit with relentless energy.

We were surrounded by whirling debris: shell, mud, startled hermit-crabs, slipper limpets, clams, and grotesque sponges. I felt as if our underwater world had gone mad, an Alice-in-Wonderland turmoil of shellfish, silt, and bobbing Coca-Cola bottles. But after ten minutes' work, Quamus gripped my arm and squeezed it twice, which was our pre-arranged signal that the first dive was over. Quamus thrust his iron rod into the hole he had made, and marked it with a bright orange flag. Then he finned slowly up to the surface, and I followed him.

"How's it going?" asked Walcott, helping us on board. "You're kicking up enough mud down there." He pointed to the surface of the bay, where a wide muddy stain was already spreading above the wreck.

"We're through to the lower layer of silt," said Quamus, impassively, as Laurie helped him out of his oxygen cylinders. "We should be able to start work with the airlift now."

"Anybody asked you what we're up to?" I said.

Walcott shrugged. "A couple of fishermen came past and asked if I knew where they could sink their lines for the best flounder. So I sent them out to Woodbury Point."

"They won't catch much flounder there," said Quamus.

"Exactly," said Walcott.

We rested for fifteen minutes or so, and then Laurie kitted us up with fresh oxygen cylinders and we prepared to go down again. It was almost twenty before ten now, and I was anxious that we should complete this dive as soon as possible. I didn't want the coastguard prowling around; nor did I want Edward or Forrest or Dan Bass to notice that Walcott's lugger was anchored right over the wreck of the *David Dark*. For all I knew, they might be planning to dive on the wreck themselves this morning, to put down markers before they registered it.

For a further half-hour, Quamus and I toiled away on the bottom of the sea, blowing away the silt from the side of the *David Dark*'s hull. At last, we saw dark encrusted timbers, and Quamus made the "okay" sign to indicate that we were making good progress. With only three or four minutes of oxygen left, we completed a twenty-foot-deep scour-pit into the soft silt down beside the hull, which Quamus marked with his flag. Then he made the thumb's-up sign for "surface."

I turned around, giving a first strong kick of my fins, and to my horror I became entangled in something like wet white sheeting. I struggled and kicked against it, and as I did so I felt the soft bumping of swollen flesh inside it. It was the floating corpse of Mrs. Goult, which had somehow been drawn towards the wreck of the *David Dark*, either by the tidal stream, or by the air-suction work we had been doing on it, or by some other inexplicable magnetism.

Don't panic: I told myself. And I tried to remember what Dan Bass had told me in my three lessons at Forest River Park. I reached for my knife, tugged it out, and tried to cut the floating wet shroud away from me. My blood thundered in my ears, and my breathing sounded like a railroad locomotive. I ripped through linen, cut through seams, but the fabric seemed to billow all around me and entangle me even more.

In total fright, I felt the corpse bump against me again, and its arms somehow wrap themselves around my legs, making it impossible for me to kick myself to the surface. At that same moment, with a squeaky sigh, my oxygen ran out, and I realized I had less than two minutes to make it up to the surface before I suffocated.

Thrashing, panicking, I began to sink slowly to the sea-bed, the corpse embracing me like a long-lost lover. Was this what Mictantecutli wanted after all? I thought to myself. Did he just want me, and me alone, because my unborn son had cheated him of the chance to feast on my heart? I sucked desperately at my mouthpiece, but my oxygen was completely exhausted, and my lungs began to feel as if they were going to collapse from lack of air.

It was then that the corpse shuddered, and suddenly whirled away. The shroud was dragged off me, and my arms and legs were disentangled. My face-mask clear, I saw Quamus rolling away from me in the murky water, brandishing his iron shaft. On the end of it, deeply impaled, was the blue-skinned, half-decayed body of Mrs. Goult, chunks of flesh flaking off her like rotting tuna. Quamus gave her one last twist, and then sent her sinking slowly down to the bottom, the shaft still sticking out of her bare-ribbed chest. He swam back a little way, seized my arm, and urgently pointed upwards. I nodded. I needed no second bidding. I was almost blacking out from oxygen starvation.

Back on the lugger, shaken as both of us were, we said nothing to Walcott or his daughter about what we had seen. Laurie made us each a cup of hot black coffee, and we rested for another fifteen minutes while Walcott prepared the dynamite. Each of the two crates was heavily weighted so that it would sink directly to the bottom; and then, once we had maneuvered it into position, it would sink just as quickly into our 20-foot hole.

"Think the weather's going to hold?" I asked Walcott, finishing my coffee.

"C'd be," he remarked.

As I shouldered my next two oxygen tanks, I thought briefly of Anne Putnam: the witch who had sacrificed herself so that I would not feel obliged to let Mictantecutli go free. Well, I thought to myself, I still don't have to make a final decision, not until the copper vessel has been brought ashore; and even then I'll have time to think it over. I believed what old man Evelith had told me, about the malevolent power that Mictantecutli could wreak; but I was still strongly tempted to let the Fleshless One go free, and recover the wife and son-to-be whom I so dearly loved.

Yet how much was I kidding myself? I had already accepted Jane's death more than I would have thought possible. What was making love to Gilly but an acceptance that I would never be making love to Jane again? More than that: what kind of relationship was I going to be able to have with Jane, once and if she was restored to life? What do you say to somebody who's been dead and buried?

I was still thinking about this when Quamus gripped my arm, and said, "Time to go, Mr. Trenton. Second-to-last dive."

Planting the dynamite proved to be the easiest job of all. All we had to do was tumble it end over end until it was perched on the brink of the hole we had excavated, connect the fuses, and let it sink slowly down. When both cases had disappeared into the darkness, Quamus and I packed as much grit and shell and debris as we could into the hole, to make sure that the full force of the explosion would be directed towards the hull of the *David Dark*. As we swam back to the surface, paying out fuse from a small reel, I thought of Edward, and what he would have said if he had known what we were doing. I actually felt sorry for him. In a minute or two, we would be shattering the dream of his life.

And when we broke the surface of the water, and began to splash our way back towards Walcott's lugger, what should appear around the bow of the lugger but the *Diogenes*, with Edward and Forrest and Jimmy standing on the foredeck, and Dan Bass at the wheel.

Quamus glanced at me, and I made a rotating action with my hand to indicate that he should continue to pay out the fuse. We reached the lugger and heaved ourselves up the side. Laurie and Walcott helped us on to the foredeck, and for a moment we lay there like two landed sea lions, gasping for breath; but it was obvious that Edward wasn't going to give us any rest. He beckoned Dan to guide the *Diogenes* right in close to Walcott's lugger, and cupped his hands around his mouth.

"Mr. Walcott!" he shouted. "John! What's going on here? What are you up to?"

"Just showing Quamus the *David Dark,* that's all," I shouted back.

"In a salvage boat? And what's all that waterjet and airlift gear doing on deck?"

"Mind your own business," I told him. "This wreck doesn't belong to anybody. It's unregistered. If we want to do a little excavation of our own, that's up to us."

"The *David Dark* is registered now," Edward shouted. "I just registered her this morning. Gilly called me up from Tewksbury and said that you'd gone off early with a whole lot of equipment."

Thanks, Gilly, I thought to myself. Judas in linen and lace.

"Well, registered or not, we were here before and have a perfect right to stay," I told Edward.

"You want me to prove you wrong?" demanded Edward. "You want me to call the coastguard and have you moved away? This wreck is private property now, and part-owned by the city of Salem. Any vessel suspected of carrying out diving or unauthorized salvage anywhere in the vicinity is liable to be impounded, and the owners fined. So move out."

"Edward," I said, "I thought you and I were friends."

"Apparently we made a mistake," said Edward. And without saying anything else, he turned away, and directed Dan Bass to turn the *Diogenes* about.

"Quamus," I said, without moving. "Light the fuse. Mr. Walcott, start your engines and get us the hell out of here."

Quamus said, "You will not warn your colleagues?"

"My *ex*-colleagues, you mean? Sure I'll warn them. But get that fuse lit first."

Quamus struck a match, cupped his hands over the end of the fuse, and held the flame against the fabric until the explosive core of the fuse ignited. It was a fast-burning fuse, 120 cm a minute, and it quickly sparkled over the side of the lugger and disappeared under the surface of the sea. There was a light cloud of smoke, and a rush of bubbles, and then it was gone.

Walcott gunned the lugger's engines, and it was then that I yelled out to Edward: *"Get going! Move! Fast as you can! Explosives!"*

I saw Edward, Forrest and Jimmy stare across at me, startled. They looked at each other in amazement, and then they looked back at me.

Edward shouted: "What did you say? Explosives?"

"Going off now!" I screamed at him, as the lugger heeled off towards the Granitehead shore. *"Get out of there quick!"*

There was a moment's silence; then the *Diogenes'* engine blared into life, and the little boat began to move away, slowly at first, but quickly building up speed. It had only traveled about fifty yards, however, when there was a curious shaking in the ocean, a sensation quite unlike anything that I had ever felt before. It was like an earthquake, only more vertiginous, as if the world were falling into separate pieces, as if sky were becoming detached from ocean, and ocean were becoming detached from land. I felt as if we were all going to fly weightless into the air, boats, compressors, flags, diving-suits, everything.

Then, the surface of the sea burst apart. With a thunderous roar, an immense cliff of solid water rose into the air, fifty or a hundred feet, and hung there in the morning air. A shock-wave pressed against my ears, suppressing the clatter of tons of brine as it collapsed back into the sea, but my ears cleared again in time to hear the echo coming back from the Granitehead Hills, as clear as a cannon-shot.

The deck of the lugger angled and bucked beneath our feet, and we had to cling to the rails to steady ourselves. But the *Diogenes*, which was much nearer the center of the blast, was swamped first by falling water, and then by a miniature tidal-wave, which broke over her stern and must have gushed into her open hatches unchecked.

Edward didn't seek our help. He must have been too shocked and angry. Instead, I could see him helping the others to bail out, while Dan Bass gently nursed the hiccuping engine, and steered the *Diogenes* back towards Salem Harbor.

There weren't even any shouts of recrimination, or threats of calling the coastguard; but I knew that Edward would immediately report our piratical behavior both to the coastguard and to the Salem police, and that we would be lucky to get back to shore without being arrested.

"What do we do now?" asked Walcott. "The minute that busybody gets back into harbor, the cops are going to be swarming around us like bluefish."

"We must salvage the copper vessel," Quamus insisted. "Disregard the police. The copper vessel is more important."

"As long as your precious Mr. Evelith guarantees to bail me out of jail," snapped Walcott.

"Mr. Evelith will guarantee your complete immunity from prosecution," said Quamus, and the way he looked at Walcott, there wasn't any way that Walcott was going to argue. Walcott was tough, but Quamus was imperious, his expression as stony as the side of a building.

Walcott and his daughter began to unpack the salvage floats which were stowed around the sides of the after-deck. There were twenty of these, and the idea was to attach them to the copper vessel, once we had located it, and then inflate them with compressed air, so that the copper vessel would rise to the surface and could then be towed into harbor like a raft.

By now, the ocean all around us was bubbling and boiling with rising silt and surfacing debris. There were scores of dead fish, floating white-belly upwards, flounder and dabs, mostly, and a few bluefish. There were blackened elm timbers, carlings and deck supports and broken staves, presumably from the ship's supply-barrels, and fragments of masts and rigging-blocks.

"You're not going to dive into the middle of *that*," said Walcott, looking down into the disturbed surface of the sea. "Give it a half-hour to clear up, first. Otherwise you'll never find each other, let alone a copper trunk."

"Half an hour may be too long," said Quamus, narrowing his eyes towards the shore. "The coastguard could be here by then."

"Look," said Walcott, "I don't mind taking risks. I don't even mind a run-in with the coastguard. I'm used to it. But I'm not taking any responsibility for you and your pal diving

into an ocean that's thick with dangerous debris. Just forget
it."

"We assume our own responsibility," said Quamus.

"Maybe you can," Walcott retorted, "but you can't dive
without oxygen, and you're not diving with any of *mine*."

Quamus stared at Walcott with such intense disapproval
that Walcott had to chew on his pipe, and look away. "I'm
sorry," he said. "But if you dive into that mess, anything
could happen."

We watched for another five minutes as more and more
pieces of broken wood rose to the surface. Soon the whole
area around Walcott's lugger was littered with thousands of
pieces of dark timber, the remains of one of the most historic
archeological finds in recent history. It looked as if the dynamite had completely shattered the fragile wreck of the *David
Dark* into flinders. To piece it all together again out of this
floating collection of firewood would be impossible. But I
didn't feel guilty. I knew that I had done what was necessary;
and that sometimes human life has to come before human
culture.

From Salem Harbor, we suddenly heard the distant whoop
of a police-boat siren, and saw its flashing red-and-white
lights. Quamus seized Walcott's arm, and said, "Now we
must dive."

"I'm sorry," protested Walcott, "it's still too risky down
there."

Quamus stared at Walcott with wide-open eyes. Walcott
tried to look somewhere else, but Quamus stared and stared,
the muscles flinching in his cheeks, and Walcott stared back
at him, with an expression on his face of growing horror, like
a man who realizes that his car is out of control and that he's
inevitably going to crash.

"I—" gasped Walcott, but then his nose suddenly sprang
with blood, and he collapsed to his knees on the deck. Laurie
knelt down beside him, and gave him an oily cloth to mop up
the blood, but even though she gave Quamus a frown of
disapproval, she didn't attempt to say anything to him. I don't
think *I* would have, either, after a hypnotic performance like
that.

"Now we must dive," Quamus repeated.

But he was wrong. For, even while the police-boat siren
grew clearer across the water, something rose to the surface

amongst the bobbing raft of broken timbers. Laurie saw it first, and stood up, and said, "Look—look, Mr. Quamus."

We all approached the stern, and stared out at the waters of the bay. Not thirty yards away, wallowing in the waves, was a huge green casket, as long and as broad as a railroad car, but coffin-shaped, with a crucifix marked on the top of it in corroded relief.

Quamus regarded it with a face like ivory. I felt my own blood draining through me; and my heart beating in slow, irregular bumps.

Walcott said, "Is that it? Is that what you've been trying to find?"

And Quamus nodded, and made a sign which I didn't understand, an Indian sign which looked like a blessing, or a sign to ward off evil spirits.

"It is Mictantecutli, the Fleshless One, the Man of Bones," he said. And I watched in growing apprehension as the casket dipped and yawed in the waves, silent and strange, a vessel from a long-dead century, a relic of an antique malevolence which none of us knew if we could even begin to control.

THIRTY-THREE

"Make it fast," ordered Quamus, and Walcott backed up the boat, engines beating slow astern, while Laurie and I leaned over with billhooks and drew the copper vessel closer. The surface of the vessel was heavily corroded, and time had turned it a dark, poisonous green, but all the same it was remarkable how long it had lasted underneath Salem Harbor.

There were copper rings along either side of the casket, which presumably had been used for fastening the ropes to hoist the casket on board the *David Dark*. Some of these rings had been eaten right through, but I managed to hook one that was intact, and then Laurie actually swung herself off the stern-rail, and stood on the floating casket while she ran a rope through it.

"There's no point in heading straight for Salem," I said. "The police will catch us before we've gone half a mile. How about making for the wharf at Granitehead?"

Walcott revved up his diesels. "They'll probably catch us anyway," he said, "but it may be worth a shot. What do we do when we get there? That damn coffin-thing is far too big for anybody to lift."

"There's a ramp there, and a boat-winch. Maybe we can drag it ashore with that."

"And then what? The police will be all over us by then."

"I don't know. Maybe we can borrow a truck. Just give it a try, will you?"

"Sure I'll give it a try. I'll give anything a try. I'm just asking if you had a plan in mind, that's all."

"I'll think of something, all right?"

"You're the boss."

Even before we had covered a quarter of a mile, however, it was clear that the police boat was going to head us off long before we could reach the Granitehead shoreline. Walcott was pressing his lugger to go as fast as it possibly could, but he wasn't keen on burning out his bearings, and the huge green casket that we were towing behind us was nothing but sheer dead weight.

"You must go faster," insisted Quamus, but Walcott shook his head.

Now the police boat was within earshot, and they killed their siren and began to curve around in front of our bows, neat and fast and unavoidable. One of the officers was already balancing his way along the deck with a loud-hailer, and another stood behind him with a carbine.

"Okay, slow down," I told Walcott. "There's no point in getting shot at."

Walcott eased off his engines, and the lugger began to dip and drift towards a slow rendezvous with the waiting police-boat. The copper vessel caught up with us, still propelled by its own inertia, and bumped noisily against our stern.

"Come out on deck with your hands on your heads," ordered the police officer. "I want all of you right where I can see you."

He started to walk back along the deck, but he had scarcely gone three paces when he suddenly gripped his stomach, and collapsed out of sight.

"What's happened?" asked Walcott, standing up on the foredeck to get a better view. "Did you see that? He just kind of fell over."

The second officer, the one who had been carrying the carbine, suddenly ran to the police-boat's cabin. Then their pilot appeared, carrying a towel and a first-aid kit.

"What's happened?" I shouted. "Is everything all right?"

The second officer glanced up at us, and then waved us away. I turned to Walcott and said, "Pull up alongside. Come on, quick!"

"Are you kidding?" said Walcott. "This is our chance to get away."

"Pull up alongside!" I ordered him. He shrugged, spat, and turned over the engines so that we nudged up against the trim hull of the police-boat.

It was only when we actually touched their boat that I saw the blood. It was sprayed all over the deck as if someone had been painting the boat crimson with a firehose. The second officer appeared again, his shirt splashed with gore, his hands bloody.

"What happened?" I asked him, in horrified awe.

"I don't know," the policeman said, in a shocked voice. "It was Kelly. His stomach just blew open. I mean it just *blew open*, and everything came out, all through his shirt."

He stared at me. "You didn't do it, did you? You didn't shoot him or anything?"

"You know damn well we didn't."

"Well . . . go back to Salem . . . you got me? Go back to Salem and report to police headquarters. I have to get Kelly to the hospital."

The pilot came past, his shirt flecked with blood. He was very pale and he didn't say anything; but went straight to the wheelhouse and started up the police-boat's engine. Within a minute, the police-boat had angled away towards the harbor, its siren wailing, leaving the lugger and its attendant casket alone on the incoming tide. I looked at Quamus, and Quamus looked back at me.

"We will continue to make for Granitehead," he decided. "Once they have recovered from their shock, those officers will alert the police at Salem that we are coming, and we will be arrested if we go back there. Let us tow this burden of ours on to the wharf, and I will rent or borrow a car and go back to Salem Harbor to bring the refrigerated truck."

"Do you think Mictantecutli will be safe for all that time, without refrigeration?" I asked him.

Quamus looked astern, at the floating casket. "I do not know," he said solemnly. "For all I am aware, that officer on the police-boat . . . Mictantecutli could well have been responsible for that."

Laurie glanced at her father. "Dad," she said, "let's get this thing to shore, huh?"

Walcott nodded. "It doesn't carry anything catching, does it?" he wanted to know. "It isn't *diseased?*"

"Not in the way you mean it," I told him. "But let's get a move on, shall we? The longer we stay out here, the more dangerous it's going to be."

We passed the Waterside Cemetery and then turned in

towards the boat ramp at Brown's Jetty. It had once been a
fashionable place to launch your pleasure boats, back in the
1930s. There had been a restaurant there, and a cocktail
verandah, and lights strung out along the pier. But these days
the buildings were sagging and deserted, and all that remained of the cocktail verandah was a rotting deck on which
dozens of skeletal beach-chairs lay heaped as if they had been
consigned to a mass grave.

Walcott brought the lugger in as close as he could, and
then we untied the casket and let it drift up to the weed-slimy
boat-ramp on the persistent flow of the tide. With a little
prodding from our billhooks, it lodged itself listlessly against
the lower reaches of the ramp, and then Quamus and I
jumped off the lugger into the sea, and swam and waded
ashore.

I climbed dripping wet to the top of the ramp, and tried out
the winch. Fortunately someone had kept it greased and in
good working order, and it didn't take long to unwind enough
cable to reach down to the casket's rings. As soon as he was
sure that we had the casket secure, Walcott gave us a toot on
his whistle and began to steer his lugger out into the harbor
again. I can't say I blamed him, even though he probably
faced immediate arrest. Even a couple of months in jail is
preferable to having your intestines blown out.

Quamus and I said nothing as we worked the handles of the
winch, gradually edging the huge copper vessel up the concrete ramp. It made a shifting, grating sound as we inched it
upwards, and there was a terrible *hollowness* about it, a slight
rumbling, like very distant thunder. I sweated and gasped at
the winch-handle, and tried not to think what the creature
inside this ponderous vessel was actually like, and what it
might conceivably do to me.

It took us almost a half-hour, but at last the casket had been
dragged right up to the top of the ramp, where we covered it
with two tarpaulin sheets which were usually used for protect-
ing boats during the winter. Quamus looked out across the
harbor, but there was no sign of the police or the coastguard,
or even of Edward and Forrest and the rest of the *David Dark*
fellowship.

"Now," said Quamus, "I will go back to Salem and
collect the refrigerated truck. You must stay here and guard
Mictantecutli."

"Wouldn't it be better if *I* collected the truck? You can't say that you're exactly unnoticeable—six-foot Narragansett in a wet quilted jacket."

"They will not notice me," said Quamus, with quiet confidence. "I have a technique which the Narragansett developed centuries ago to hunt wild animals. It is a way of making oneself invisible to other people, even though one is there. A strange technique, but it can be taught."

"All right, then," I said. I didn't really like the idea of waiting beside this monstrous burial-casket, but I really didn't have a choice. "Just don't be too long, that's all; and if you *do* get arrested, tell the police where I am. I don't intend spending all night out here, with nobody but Mictantecutli for company, not while you're eating steak-and-eggs in the Salem City jail."

"Now you are afraid," smiled Quamus.

He walked off between the derelict restaurant buildings towards West Shore Drive. I sat down on the jetty and looked cautiously at the corroded copper vessel in which David Dark's Aztec demon had been incarcerated for over 290 years. I turned around to tell Quamus to bring me a half-bottle of whiskey while he was away, but he was already gone. He had disappeared. I tried to make myself comfortable, and propped one leg up on the tarpaulins which covered the casket with false casualness, as if it were simply a rather odd-looking boat that I happened to own.

It was only noon, but the sky was strangely gloomy, as if I were looking at it through dark glasses. A wind was rising, too: a wind that hadn't been forecast. It ruffled the gray waves of Salem Harbor, and whipped the dead leaves and collected rubbish on the sagging cocktail verandah. A salt-faded sign above the restaurant still said Harborside Restaurant, Lobster, Clams, Steaks, Cocktails. I could imagine past summer nights, with Dixieland bands and men in straw hats and girls in shimmering flapper dresses.

I tugged up the collar of my jacket. The wind was really cold now, and the sky was so dark that some of the cars on the opposite shoreline were driving with their headlights on. There was probably a storm brewing up, one of those heavy North Atlantic numbers that made you feel as if you were caught in a rain-boat at sea, even though you were sitting in your own living-room.

Then, I heard that singing. High, faint, and eerie. It came from somewhere inside the derelict restaurant, a thin controlled voice that made the hair crawl up the back of my neck as if it were electrified.

> *"O the men they sail from Granitehead*
> *To fish the foreign shores . . .*
> *But the fish they caught were naught but bones*
> *With hearts crush'd in their jaws."*

I stood up, and walked across the decayed cocktail-deck, looking up at the restaurant. I had to jump once or twice across missing planks; and beneath the deck I could see dripping darkness, where crabs scuttled. I approached the restaurant and went right up to the front door. It was locked, and the glass was so thick with years of salt and grime that I could barely see inside.

The song was repeated, louder this time; in the same cold, clear voice. It was definitely coming from inside. I looked around to make sure there was nobody watching, and then I kicked in the door with three or four hefty kicks. The door was held only by a cheap rimlock, which splintered away from the frame; and then it shuddered open and stayed open, almost as if it were inviting me inside. Come in, Mr. Trenton, destiny is served.

I walked carefully inside. The floor was laid with bare splintered boards, dusty and littered with old newspapers and odd fragments of green linoleum. A revolving fan hung from the ceiling, in between two frosted glass lampshades. On the far wall was a wide mirror, spotted and measled with dirt. I could see myself standing in the restaurant like a long-dead man in a stained old photograph. I took two or three steps forward.

"John?" she whispered. I turned slowly around, and she was standing behind me. Her face was almost completely skull-like now, and it was fixed in a grisly grimace. *"John, you must set me free."*

"How can I do that?" I asked. I watched her as she glided around the room, her funeral robes silently flowing. "I've brought you up from the bottom of the sea. What else do I have to do?"

"Break the vessel open," she whispered. *"The vessel is sealed with bonds that I cannot break alone; the bonds of the*

Holy Trinity. You must break the vessel open in the name of the Father, and of the Son, and of the Holy Spirit. Just as it was sealed.''

"I still have no guarantee that I will get Jane back alive, and in one piece.''

"This is a world without guarantees, John. You must trust me.''

"I'm not sure whether I can.''

"Would you trust me to rupture your stomach, like that man who tried to stand in your way? Or to explode you, like David Dark? I may be imprisoned, John, but I still have substantial strength.''

I said, hesitantly, "I just want to *know*, that's all . . . I mean, what you're asking me to do . . .''

Jane glided towards the mirror. Like the classic movie vampire, she made no reflection. But she walked straight *through* the mirror until she was standing in the reflected room, watching me, and there was no image of her on my side of the mirror at all.

"You must believe,'' she said, and then she faded.

I stood in that deserted restaurant for a long time. Now was the moment when I had to make my decision. I had already seen how cruelly and how callously Mictantecutli could destroy people; and how he could raise the dead and send them to slaughter the living. Yet I knew all this time that I wanted Jane back with me with a desperation that had somehow gone beyond love. It had become a matter of proving to myself that miracles could actually happen.

Since Jane had died, I had witnessed some extraordinary and frightening things. But somehow they seemed to me then to have been nothing more than terrifying tricks. It was only when I could hold Jane in my arms again that I would actually *believe* in powers that were far greater than human experience could testify to, or human imagination encompass.

It didn't occur to me, of course, that more than at any other time since Jane had died, I was now very close to a complete emotional collapse. When I think today of the way in which I persuaded myself that Mictantecutli should be released, I still go physically cold.

I left the restaurant and walked back across the cocktail deck. It was so dark outside that I had forgotten it was only just past noon. The corroded green casket was still lying on the boat-ramp, under its draped tarpaulins. On the far side of the ramp was a locked cupboard marked FIREHOSE. I walked around the casket to the cupboard, examined its rusted hinges, and then gave it a good kicking with the heel of my shoe until the left-hand door split, and I was able to wrench it open. Inside was a mildewed hose and just what I had been looking for: a long-handled ax.

I walked back to the casket, and pushed aside the tarpaulins. The casket seemed larger than it had before: green and bulky and silently malevolent. I touched its scaly side with my bare fingers and I felt curiously repelled, almost as if I had unwittingly put my hand on a giant slug in the dark. Then, on impulse, I swung the ax and dealt the side of the casket a tremendous blow with the blade.

There was a deep, reverberating boom, and the casket seemed to shudder. I felt the place where the ax-blade had struck, and I could tell that it had bitten quite deep, and almost penetrated the metal. The copper couldn't have been more than an inch thick to begin with, and the corrosive salt of the sea had reduced it by more than half.

I swung the ax again. "I release you," I panted, as the blade banged into the top of the casket. "I release you in the name of the Father."

I struck again. "I release you," I chanted. I could hear my own voice distantly in my ears, as if I were someone else. "I release you in the name of the Son."

Above me, the sky was threateningly black. The wind began to shriek across the harbor, and the waves rose so high that they were flecked with foam. It was almost impossible to see the farther shore, and on the Granitehead shoreline itself the trees were bending and writhing like tortured souls.

Once more I raised the ax, and once more I brought it down on top of the casket. *"I release you!"* I shouted. *"I release you in the name of the Holy Spirit!"*

There was a screech that could have been the wind or could have been something else altogether: the screech of a despairing world. Before my eyes, the dark green copper casket cracked, and gaped open, and then cracked again, scales of corroded metal dropping to the concrete boat-ramp. A dry, fetid smell arose from the open vessel, the smell of an animal long dead and decayed, a giant rat found between the floorboards of an old house—a baby discovered in a chimney.

In front of my eyes, the Fleshless One was exposed, lying inside its casket; and to my horror it was not simply a giant skeleton, but a giant skeleton made of dozens of human skeletons. Each arm was made of two skeletons connected by a skull, each finger was a whole human arm. Each rib was made of curved and twisted skeletons of children, and its pelvis was a white basin of scores of smaller pelvises. And as it turned and stared at me with eye-sockets that were deep and sightless and infinitely evil, I saw that its head was made of hundreds of human skulls, somehow fused together to form the greatest skull I had ever seen.

"Now," whispered a voice that was as thunderous as a church-organ. *"Now my reign can begin again. Now I can garner all those souls that my spirit has craved for. And you, my friend, you will be my high priest. That is your reward. You will stay with me always, at my right-hand side, interpreting for me my every demand, seeking for me those souls which will fulfill my appetite."*

"Where's Jane?" I shouted at it, even though I was utterly terrified. "You promised me Jane! Just like she was before the accident, unhurt! Alive and unhurt! You promised."

"You are impatient," boomed Mictantecutli. *"There will be time for that; all in good time."*

"You promised me Jane and I want her now! Just like she was before the accident!"

The wind was howling so loudly that I could barely hear what the demon said next. But then I heard a screaming, somewhere close to the old restaurant building. It was high-pitched, terrified, the sound of a woman in total fear. I made my way around the casket, steadying myself against the wind by holding on to the railings beside the boat-ramp, and stared out into the darkness.

She was there. Jane. It was really her. She was standing by the restaurant door, her hands over her face, and she was screaming, on and on and on, screaming and screaming until I couldn't bear to listen to it any longer. I made my way across the cocktail deck again, tearing my socks against a loose board, and went up to her, holding her shoulders, shaking her.

She was real, and she was alive. She was wearing the same clothes that she had been wearing on the night of the accident. But no matter how hard I shook her and shouted at her, I couldn't get her to take her hands away from her face, and I

couldn't get her to stop screaming. In the end, I turned away
from her, and struggled back to the broken casket, where
Mictantecutli still lay, grinning in the fixed grin of all skeletons,
a grin that is neither loving nor humorous, but the expression of death.

"What have you done?" I shouted at it. "Why won't she
answer me? Why is she screaming like that? If you've hurt
her—"

"She isn't hurt," whispered the demon. *"She thinks that
she is about to be hurt, just as she did in the seconds before
her accident. But she is safe, and well, and alive."*

"And terrified!" I yelled at it. "For God's sake, stop her
screaming! How can I live with her when she's like that?"

"You wanted her just as she was before the accident,"
Mictantecutli reminded me. *"That is the way she was; and
that is the way you must have her."*

"What are you trying to tell me? That she'll *always* be
screaming? That she'll always be terrified that she's going to
have a crash?"

"Always and always," grinned Mictantecutli. *"Until the
day she returns to the region of the dead."*

I looked back towards the old restaurant. Jane was still
there, screaming at the top of her voice, her hands pressed
over her eyes. She had been screaming for nearly five minutes now, without stopping, and I knew that Mictantecutli had
tricked me. It had no power to restore the dead as their loved
ones had known them: it had only the power to take them
back to the moment when they were first fatally doomed.
That was the moment when their spirits were first consigned
to the region of the dead, and that was the boundary of
Mictantecutli's kingdom.

I felt tears springing in my eyes. But I was strong enough
and determined enough to pick up the ax which I had dropped
beside the dark green copper vessel, and carry it with me
back to the restaurant. I put it down beside Jane, and took
hold of her again, and begged her to stop screaming, begged
her to take her hands away from her face. But I heard in the
back of my mind the soft coldness of Mictantecutli's laughter,
and I knew that it was hopeless.

"Jane," I said, trying not to listen to the screaming. I held
her tight, trying to reassure her, trying to protect her from the

fate which had already happened to her, and from which I couldn't save her, no matter what I did.

The screaming went on and on.

At last, I stepped away from her, and without looking at her, picked up the ax, and swung it straight down between her hands.

Blood spurted out from between her fingers. One leg jerked uncontrollably. She turned and staggered, and then collapsed. I threw the ax as far away as I could into the wind, and then I walked away from Jane without looking back.

I passed Mictantecutli's casket. I didn't turn to look at Mictantecutli either. I headed for the highway, between the old restaurant buildings, walking at first, and then jogging.

"*You will never escape me,*" whispered the demon. "*I promise you, John, you will never escape me.*"

I reached West Shore Drive, and looked around in the noontime darkness for a car, or a truck, or any sign of Quamus returning. It was then that I saw the pale figures in the distance; figures in rags and tags, like the beggars coming to town. I stared at them for a long time before I realized who they were. There was a whole company of them, shuffling and decaying and blind.

They were the dead of Granitehead, the corpses from the cemetery. The servants of Mictantecutli, searching for fresh blood and human hearts, anything to strengthen their newly-released lord.

I started to run.

THIRTY-FOUR

I had never realized that West Shore Drive was so long. I managed to run about a half-mile, but then I ran out of breath, and I had to slow myself down to a brisk, hurrying walk. Turning around, I could no longer see the company of corpses that had been swarming down the road from the direction of Waterside Cemetery, but I didn't intend to wait and see how long it would take them to catch me up.

I checked my watch, which was still ticking in spite of the sea-water that had gotten into it. It was only 12:30 in the afternoon, but it might just as well have been half after midnight. The wind moaned and whistled all around me, and leaves and sheets of newspaper tumbled past me like fleeing ghosts. There was a feeling of apocalypse in the air: as if this was the end of the world, when the graves would open and the earth would tremble and all beings living and dead would have to stand in judgment. Only this wouldn't be the judgment of the Lord: this would be the ravenous judgment of Mictantecutli, the prince of the region of the dead, the feaster on human hearts, the Fleshless One.

My path ran eventually into Lafayette Street, past the Star of the Sea Cemetery. And when I came panting and limping along Lafayette, my chest bursting and my throat feeling as if it had been scoured with sandpaper, I saw that the graves at the Star of the Sea had opened, too. Scores of the walking dead were there: in yellowed shrouds and rotting robes, flickering with that cold electrical light which had first announced the presence of Jane.

I slowed down. The dead were shambling all across the

highway, and at first I thought they were simply dazed and disoriented. But then I saw that in their midst there was a stationary car. I ducked down, and weaved my way between the roadside trees, trying to get as close as I could without being seen. But I was still twenty-five yards away when I saw the dead had stopped the car, seized the driver, and now he was lying spreadeagled over the hood, his shirt ripped open. The walking dead had torn him, so that his bloody ribs gaped open, and one of them was holding up his glistening heart in a skeletal hand, so that the blood ran down the bare bones of his wrist. Two or three more of them, in varying stages of decay, were feeding on his remains.

I retched, and brought up swallowed seawater. One of the dead raised her head from the car-driver's abdomen, a string of intestine still dangling from between her teeth. She stared at me and screeched, pointing, and the rest of the grisly assembly turned and stared at me, too.

I upped and ran, regardless of the stitch in my side, sprinting along the middle of the highway as fast as I possibly could. I could hear my own breath whining in and out of my lungs, and the flapping of my feet on the pavement. And behind me, far too close behind me, the rushing sound of the dead, rushing and whispering and whooping.

I had almost run back to the intersection with West Shore Drive when the first of the corpses from Waterside Cemetery appeared, and then more, spreading themselves out across the road and cutting off my escape. I turned back, and saw that the corpses of Star of the Sea Cemetery were only a few yards away, their arms triumphantly raised to catch me.

Desperate, I tried to dodge to the side; but one of the corpses clawed at me and caught my sleeve. I punched him hard in the face, and to my horror my fist went right through his half-rotten flesh, breaking his partly-decayed skull. Another corpse, a woman, caught me from behind, and jumped on to my back, tearing with her bony fingernails at my face and neck. Then another grabbed my ankles and my knees. More and more of them clamored around me, scratching and tearing, and for the first time in my life I felt myself dragged down into endless madness and I shrieked.

They dragged me down to my knees by their sheer weight. They whooped and whistled and screeched, their breath whining in and out of ragged lungs, through nostrils that were mere bony caverns. I felt hands ripping at my clothes, scratching at my chest, as the corpses obeyed the blind command from Mictantecutli to bring him hearts. Hearts, he wanted, freshly torn from living humans; hearts to gorge on, so that he could rise again, and stalk the earth.

Suddenly, there was a roaring sound, and the corpses started to shriek and clamor and stumble away. I was down on the pavement with my hands held over my head, rolled up into as much of a ball as I could manage; but I risked a glance to my left, up under my arm, and what I saw was salvation on wheels. It was Quamus, in our refrigerated truck, driving into the corpses with his horn blaring, his engine revving, and his headlights full on. Quamus drove relentlessly through the clamoring tides of resurrected bodies, crushing and smashing them without mercy. Once, they had all been humans, but now they were nothing more than the lifeless puppets of Mictantecutli, the pariah.

Wiping blood away from my mouth, I climbed up on to the truck and knocked on the side door. Quamus saw me, and unlocked it, and I climbed gratefully in. He locked the door again, and immediately pulled away, blinding and killing three or four more living corpses who stood in our path.

"You stink," he said, sharply. "You stink of the grave."

"They were going to tear my heart out," I told him. "They were clawing at my chest, you know that? Clawing at me, like vultures."

There was a long silence between us. Quamus pulled the truck in to the side of the road, and then slowly maneuvered it around, so that we were driving back towards Salem.

"You let Mictantecutli go," he said.

I looked at him. There was no point in denying it. He knew as well as I did that when the graves of Granitehead opened, that meant that the Fleshless One was free.

"Yes," I said.

Quamus kept his eyes on the road ahead, and his foot pressed hard against the floor. In a minute or two we would be passing through that crowd of walking dead for a second time, and he wanted to make sure that we hit them at a good eighty miles an hour, unstoppable, and invincible.

Quamus said, "Mr. Evelith said that you would probably let the Fleshless One go free. He suspected it. So did Enid. Enid said that she had read your fortune in the tea which you drank when you first came to visit us, and she could see uncertainty there, and extravagant promises from a supernatural force. The Fleshless One promised you your wife back, I suppose?''

"Do you blame me for saying yes?''

Quamus shrugged. "We are dealing with a greater force here; a force of magic and terrible malevolence. We cannot talk in terms of blame or recrimination. You did what you felt was right. We know that you are not a bad man.''

At that moment, we collided with a whole congregation of walking corpses, at almost ninety miles an hour. Decayed flesh flew in all directions, and there was a hideous pattering sound on the windshield. Quamus impassively checked his side-mirrors; to make sure that none of the corpses were still clinging to the sides of the truck, and then slowed down, and drove into Salem more sedately.

There was no need to observe the speed limit: the police were already too preoccupied. Salem lay under the midnight-black sky like a vision of Hell. Fires burned all over the city, the Roger Conant Co-operative Bank, Parker Brothers Games factory, One Salem Green, they were all alight, and burning like Satan's ovens. The city was a city of historic cemeteries, and all of them had spewed out their dead: Harmony Grove, Greenlawn, Derby Street, Chestnut Street, Bridge Street, and Swampscott. The dead crowded through the streets savaging the living, and the malls and pavements were splattered with blood and strewn with freshly-killed bodies.

Several times, as we headed out of the city towards Tewksbury, walking corpses clutched at our truck and tried to cling on; but Quamus kept barreling on until they dropped off, and once he swung the side of the truck against a street-sign to dislodge three of them who were holding on to the nearside fender. I glimpsed them in my rear-view mirror, rolling over and over, limbs and skulls tumbling in all directions.

We reached Tewksbury in fifteen minutes, and Quamus blew the airhorns in front of old man Evelith's wrought-iron gates. Enid shooed the dog away, and opened up the gates for us, and Quamus drove speedily inside, jumped down from the cab, and helped Enid to lock up behind us.

Old man Evelith himself was standing on the top of the front steps, leaning on his walking-cane. When he saw me climbing down from the truck's cab, he raised one hand in salute, and said, "You've done it, then? You've brought Mictantecutli back?"

I hesitated, but I could see that Quamus was holding back, so that it would have to be me who explained what had happened. I walked slowly forward across the shingle, and then stopped, and cleared my throat.

"I have a confession to make," I said, hoarsely.

Old man Evelith stared at me for a very long time; fiercely at first, but then more understandingly; and then he turned away to look up at the darkening sky, and the rooks which circled in it like the vultures of hell itself.

"Well," he said, "I guessed this would happen. But you must come in. You look tired, and cold; and you have the smell of death upon you."

THIRTY-FIVE

"I believed it," I said, as we sat in the library over glasses of strong brandy. "It promised to give me my wife back, and I believed it. That's my only excuse."

Duglass Evelith watched me carefully through the half-moon lenses of his spectacles. Then he leaned forward with his elbows on the library table, and said, "Nobody's accusing you, Mr. Trenton. Or perhaps I should call you John. I have been trying for years to rescue my dead ancestor; you have far more justification for trying to rescue your dead wife. Unfortunately, Mictantecutli is not a demon whose word can ever be trusted. It is a demon of death and deception; and you have been deceived, and almost killed."

"What are we going to do?" I asked him. "It's already destroyed half of Salem. How can we stop it?"

Old man Evelith thoughtfully rubbed the back of his wrinkled neck. "I have been giving this matter some considerable thought, while you have been bathing. Quamus believes that Mictantecutli will probably have been fed by now, and will have revived enough to have left the boat-ramp where you landed it. But he doubts if the demon will have gone far. It has awoken after two hundred and ninety years, and it will no doubt wish to acclimatize itself before it attempts to exercise its full power over the local population, and further afield."

"How will it do that?" I asked.

"Well," said old man Evelith, "it is our guess that it will seek out somewhere to conceal itself; somewhere that it remembers from days gone by. Enid has suggested David Dark's old cottage by the Mill Pond. That was where it spent most of its days in Salem; and that is where it will probably retreat now.''

"But that cottage isn't there any more."

"No," said Duglass Evelith. "According to my maps of the 1690s, David Dark's cottage used to stand in a clump of trees just west of what is now Canal Street."

"And what stands there now? Or is it open ground?"

"Oh, no, there's a building there now," said old man Evelith. "The Lynnfield & District Book Warehouse. That, in our opinion, is where Mictantecutli will go to hide for a while; and that, in our opinion, is where we are going to have to go to destroy it."

I took another sip of brandy, and felt it burn down the back of my throat. Then I looked at Quamus, and old man Evelith, and said, "What do you propose to do? How do you go about destroying a living skeleton—especially one as powerful as Mictantecutli?"

Quamus said, "There is only one hope. The Fleshless One must be frozen. Once frozen, it must be attacked with sledgehammers, and dismantled. Each bone must then be buried separately over a wide area, and each grave must be blessed in the name of the great spirit Gitche Manitou and in the name of the Christian Trinity. Then, there will be no escape for Mictantecutli."

"How do you propose to freeze it?" I wanted to know. "Do you think it's going to *let* you? This morning, it blew a police officer's guts out, right in front of me."

"We must take the risk of approaching it," said old man Evelith. "It may kill us outright, but we must take the risk. There is no other way. Once we are close enough, we will spray it with liquid nitrogen. We already have the equipment prepared. We were going to use it to dismantle Mictantecutli once my ancestor Joseph Evelith had been released from his bondage to Tezcatlipoca. But even if that release is not to be, we must still destroy the Fleshless One, and we have the means to do it."

I looked seriously at Duglass Evelith, and then at Quamus. "You're going to have to let me do it, you know that."

Old man Evelith shook his head. "The risk is too great. And, besides, you do not understand these things."

"I released Mictantecutli. I must take the chance of trying to destroy it."

"No," said old man Evelith, adamantly. "Quamus is already prepared."

"But—"

"No," old man Evelith repeated, and this time I knew there was going to be no arguing with him. But he added, more sympathetically, "You can *accompany* him, if you wish. You can be his assistant. He will need somebody to help him to carry the cylinders of liquid nitrogen; and he will need somebody to help him collect the frozen bones of Mictantecutli when it has finally been defeated."

Old man Evelith sounded as if the job had already been done: but I could tell from the stern look on Quamus' face that the danger we were up against was extreme, and that there was every chance that by later this afternoon both of us would be feeding the bony maw of the Man of Bones, the Fleshless One.

"I want you to rest now," said Duglass Evelith. "You will leave for Mill Pond in an hour. I want you to think of nothing else but victory over the influences of darkness, and that you are strong enough to defeat even the most terrible of demons. Consider yourself a warrior, John, who is about to embark on a great adventure. Dragon-slaying, monster-butchering, something mythical and courageous. For after all, destroying Mictantecutli will be exactly that."

In spite of Duglass Evelith's advice, I spent most of the next hour pacing around my sitting-room, drinking whiskey. Outside, the sky grew darker and darker, until I had to switch on my lights. I tried to read, but I didn't feel in the mood for geology, and I couldn't get past the word "Preface." I tried to telephone Gilly, but the lines were down, and all I could get was a distant crackling noise. At last I lay on my bed with hands over my eyes, and thought of nothing at all. Five minutes later, however, when I was just beginning to relax, Quamus came into my room and said somberly, "We are ready to leave now. Please be quick."

I followed him downstairs without saying a word, half-skipping as I went to push my sneaker on to my left foot. The refrigerated truck had been loaded with twenty cylinders of liquid nitrogen, and a device like a firefighter's spray, as well as an insulated suit and gloves to protect Quamus from the sub-zero gas. Enid was to come with us, but Duglass Evelith was going to stay behind. He explained that he was too old to fight demons any more, but all of us knew that if Mictantecutli were to wipe out Quamus, Enid, and me, then somebody who knew how to defeat it would have to remain safe.

Duglass Evelith took my hand between both of his, and squeezed it. "Take care," he said, "and remember that what you are fighting has no moral scruples, no conscience, nothing that even remotely approximates a human conscience. It will kill you if it can. It will expect you to do the same in return."

We drove away into the darkness, the three of us sitting side by side in the cab. We said very little to each other as we headed east towards Salem. We were all afraid, we all knew it, and there wasn't much point in discussing it. The cylinders of nitrogen clanked around in the back, but I wondered whether there was really any future in trying to use them on a creature like Mictantecutli.

All around us, the Massachusetts countryside was like hell by Hieronymous Bosch. Fires leaped up from shopping malls and residential estates; overturned vehicles burned in the roads in grotesque funeral pyres, their tires flaring and dripping like incendiary wreaths.

Enid said, "This is what Salem must have been like in the days when David Dark first brought Mictantecutli back from Mexico. No wonder they tore all references to it out of the history books, and never spoke about it. It must have seemed like a nightmare when they finally got rid of it."

At last we reached the outskirts of Salem, and made a careful detour down Jefferson Avenue to cross the MBTA Commuter tracks quite a way south of the Lynnfield Book Warehouse. As we drove slowly up towards the warehouse, our tires crunched on broken glass, and the highway was splattered with red in places, as if it had been raining blood. I saw a family who had been dragged out of their car and pitifully torn to pieces as if by wild animals. And the dreadful truth of it was that it was my fault, my responsibility. If it hadn't have been for my selfishness and my blindness, Mictantecutli would never have gotten free; and this gory rampage of Salem's dead would never have happened.

All I could possibly do to atone for my stupidity was to destroy the demon I had set free.

The warehouse stood on the intersection of Canal and Roslyn, overlooking the railroad tracks. It was here, 290 years ago, that David Dark had lived, and it was here that David Dark had died. His cottage had stood among a clump of trees that had long since vanished; but for Mictantecutli this was still familiar ground. Demons permeate the ground on which they live with a rank odor, like diseased dogs, or so Duglass Evelith had told me. That was how they knew where to return after hundreds of years; and that was why devil-possessed places like Amityville and Rohrerstown always had a sickening odor.

The warehouse was a gray, rectangular building, with a small brick administration block on one side, and rows of windows high up by the roof. As Quamus drew the truck in to the curb, we knew at once that Duglass Evelith had guessed right: from inside the building, we could see those blue-and-white electric flickers which betrayed the presence of that malevolent energy with which Mictantecutli had been haunting Granitehead. Quamus pulled the truck to a stop across the street, and we all climbed out.

"There can be no delay," said Quamus. "We must go straight in, and spray the creature with liquid nitrogen straight away. Any hesitation and it will destroy us; and you have seen what it is capable of doing to a human body, without even touching it."

I nodded. I was so terrified that I could scarcely speak. I opened the back of the truck, and helped Quamus to unload one of the cylinders of nitrogen, and mount it on a trolley. Quamus then dressed himself in the silvery insulated suit, while Enid strapped the firefighter's hose on his back.

It took us five minutes at least to get ready; but fortunately there were none of the walking dead around, and it didn't seem as if any of Mictantecutli's minions had seen us. We quickly crossed the street, and went into the warehouse yard by a side entrance.

As we approached, the feeling of dread increased; and the stench of that evil demonic presence grew so strong that I felt like retching. I forced open a small back door in the warehouse, and we pushed our way inside, Quamus first, then me with

the trolley of liquid gas, then Enid. We hurried silently
through the corridors of the Lynnfield offices, left, then right,
then left again, until we reached the swing doors which led
directly into the warehouse itself.

Quamus, his insulated helmet held under his arm, beckoned me wordlessly towards the doors. Through the small
windows in them, we could see right across to the far side of
the warehouse; and what we saw there made me freeze in
stark terror. It was a scene from some barbaric representation
of all that was foul.

The skeleton Mictantecutli was sitting cross-legged on a
makeshift throne of crates and packing-cases, its huge skull
bent forward. All around it, in their charnel-house robes,
swarmed the dead of our local cemeteries, from Granitehead
and Salem and Maple Hill. Each of the corpses was bearing
in his hands a torn-out human heart, sometimes two or three,
and waiting his turn to lay his gruesome offering at Mictantecutli's bony feet.

The whole grisly scene was lit by that flickering electrical
light which turned the color of blood to black; and the eye-
sockets of the prince of the region of the dead to dark,
knowing, infinitely malevolent pits.

Quamus said, "This is it. Are you ready?"

"No, but let's do it."

Quamus fitted his helmet over his head, unclipped the
nuzzle of his fire-hose, and then said, "When I shout 'go,'
turn on the gas. Not before. When I shout 'off,' turn it
off."

"I think I can understand that."

"Okay, this is it," said Quamus, and before I knew what
was happening we had pushed open the swing doors and
started jogging as fast as we could across the concrete warehouse floor, thrusting aside corpse after shambling corpse,
dodging away from flailing arms, both of us intent on one
thing only: freezing the Fleshless One before it realized what
we were doing, and blew us both apart.

We slid over blood, and then we were there, right in front
of Mictantecutli, right beneath the immense luminous skull
made up of scores of other skulls. The demon had been
gorging itself on hearts, and its teeth were bloody and tangled
with sinew and arteries. It nodded and turned towards us, its

head overhanging us like the moon, and then Quamus screamed a muffled, "*Go!*" and I yanked the spanner that turned on the liquid nitrogen.

Freezing gas spewed out of the nozzle, and Quamus directed it straight upwards, straight into the creature's skeletal face.

I heard a deep, vibrant, floor-shaking roar, reminiscent of two subway trains at full speed colliding head-first in a tunnel. I was thrown right over on to my side, jarring my left shoulder on the floor; Mictantecutli's corpses flew all around me in a grisly blizzard.

Quamus somehow managed to stay on his feet, spraying the demon's skull in slow, steamy, systematic sweeps. I felt the intense cold of the liquid nitrogen even from ten feet away, and I could see the whiteness of frozen gas forming around Mictantecutli's mouth and eye-sockets.

But the creature was far from defeated. It reached out with one skeletal arm, and before Quamus could duck away, it had seized him around the waist. I heard Quamus yell, and I saw him directing the hissing stream of gas on to the fingers which clutched him; but Mictantecutli squeezed tighter and tighter, and then I heard a terrible crunching noise inside of Quamus' insulated suit. Quamus jerked, sagged, jerked again; and then collapsed to the floor. The gas nozzle fell with him, spraying all around us like a fulminating python.

I scrambled to my feet, and snatched the fire-hose myself. The nozzle was so cold that the skin of my hands stuck to it, and I couldn't peel them free. But I directed the gas at Mictantecutli, streaming it up and down its ribs, from side to side across its face, and shouting at the top of my voice, words that were in no language but those of fear and hatred and hysterical revenge.

Mictantecutli reached out for me, slowly but with terrifying inevitability. I sprayed its fingers, and saw them draw back a little, but then it began to reach out for me with its other arm.

I stepped away; but lost my footing on the decaying body of a corpse. Mictantecutli's huge hand seized my hip, and then my waist, and I felt as if I had been embraced by a Great White shark's jaws.

"*Aaaaaaaahhhhhh!*" I screamed; I knew I was dead. I felt

one of my ribs break, and the crushing pain on my pelvis was unbearable. I sprayed the demon's face again and again, but then I began to lose consciousness. Everything went black-and-white, like a photographic negative, and I felt a creaking sound inside of my body that must have been my hipbone being strained to the utmost.

But quite suddenly, the pressure was relieved, and then released altogether. I dropped to my knees, my eyes tight-closed, trying to keep the stream of liquid gas directed to-wards Mictantecutli, although I hardly knew where the demon was. It was only after I had recovered enough to lift my head and look around me that I realized what had happened.

Standing amidst all of the walking corpses, giving out an unearthly and radiating light of her own, pale but somehow strong and celestial and beautiful, stood Jane. Her hair flowed up about her head as it had before, but now it gave off steady star-like streams of silver radiance.

She was quite naked, but somehow her nakedness was sexless and spiritual. Beside her walked a young boy of four or five years old, as beautiful as she was, also naked, giving off the same calm light.

Mictantecutli unsteadily lifted its ghastly head. Its cheek-bones were thickly rimed with frost, and icicles hung from its collar-bone. It regarded Jane in apparent disbelief, and shook itself like a wounded animal.

I didn't know what was happening or why; but I took my chance. Holding up my liquid nitrogen spray, I climbed on to Mictantecutli's shin, and then on to his massive pelvis. Gritting my teeth against the pain of my own broken rib, I scaled the side of his ribcage, and stood there, pouring out freezing gas until the demon's vertebrae were thick with sparkling white frost.

Jane gradually faded; and the boy with her. But at that moment there was a snapping noise, and one of Mictantecutli's frozen fingers dropped from its hand and clattered on to the floor. Then one of its ribs gave way; then another; and I found myself standing on what felt like a collapsing staircase, as the Fleshless One's entire skeleton began to fall to pieces under me.

Its skull bent forward, and its spine cracked, and then that huge and hideous head rolled to the concrete floor and shat-tered into dozens and dozens of smaller skulls.

All around me, as I scrambled down from the demon's deteriorating skeleton, the dead of Salem and Granitehead were rustling to the floor in ragged heaps; the false life taken out of them; the false breath drawn from their lungs.

Enid came slowly forward, and helped me to turn off the liquid nitrogen. All the skin was frozen from the palms of my hands, and I was severely bruised and lacerated. But I was alive, at least, and that was one blessing that I couldn't question.

"Did you see Jane?" I asked Enid, in a shaky voice. "Did you see her then?"

Enid nodded. "I saw her. I called her myself."

"You called her *yourself*? How?"

Enid rested her hand on my shoulder, and smiled. "Come on," she said, "we still have work to do. All of these bones must be taken away from here, and buried according to the rituals."

"But how did you call Jane? And why did she help us? I thought she was one of Mictantecutli's servants."

"She was," said Enid. "That is, until you killed her a second time, and freed her from Mictantecutli's power. She is at rest now, because of you; and so is your unborn son."

"I still don't understand."

Enid looked around at the carnage in the warehouse, and sadly down at Quamus. "Your wife was a member of the sisterhood, Mr. Trenton. She would never have told you because she was forbidden to tell you; and in any case you would never have believed her."

"The sisterhood?"

Enid nodded. "Your wife was a Salem witch. Not from her mother's side of the family, but from her father's, so her power was not particularly strong. But she was enough of a witch to have been in touch with others of the sisterhood; and enough of a witch, of course, to have been very susceptible to the powers of Mictantecutli."

"What now?" I said, nodding towards the broken skeleton. "Now this monster's dead, are your powers all gone?"

"I don't think so," said Enid. "The power of kindness will always endure. When Mictantecutli saw your wife, Mr. Trenton, it was a reminder that its power is limited; and that there is a greater power which reigns over it, even today.''

I looked up. I felt extremely tired. Through the upper windows of the warehouse, falling in cathedral-like rays, came the pale light of the afternoon, and I realized then that the darkness of Mictantecutli had at last been destroyed. I tried very hard not to cry.

THIRTY-SIX

I left Granitehead in early May, and went to live for a while with my parents in St. Louis. My mother overfed me, and my father took me for long walks in the Missouri Botanical Gardens and talked about life the way he saw it, cut and dried, because he thought it would be good for my head. He made me a beautiful pair of Oxford shoes, hand-stitched, and gave them to me for no particular reason, except to show that he did love me, after all.

I went back to Masachusetts in June to sell Quaker Lane Cottage. I drove up to Tewksbury to see old man Evelith, and to share a sherry with him in his library, and he told me that he believed he had come close to finding the magical bonds which would hold Tezcatlipoca, the Smoking Mirror, and that he would be able to use one of the bones from Mictantecutli's dismembered skeleton in a ritual which would put his ancestor to rest for good. I left after an hour: I didn't want to hear any more of demon talk.

I didn't go to see Edward Wardwell. I had heard from Gilly that Edward had never forgiven me for blowing up the *David Dark,* and I guess he had every right to feel that way. As for Gilly, well . . . I guess she and I weren't destined to remain together. I could have loved her, I suppose, but after the immensity of what I had witnessed, our personalities never quite meshed.

With Walter, I went to Waterside Cemetery and together we laid flowers on the graves of the ones we had once loved; and then we shook hands and said goodbye. I don't know whether Walter forgave me or not, or even if there was anything to forgive. Mictantecutli had hit Salem like a hurricane, and Walter was still busy sorting out legal claims for damages, and helping to identify and rebury the dead.

I said goodbye to Laura; I said goodbye to Keith Reed, and to George Markham's wife. George had never been found, and was listed as "missing, feared dead."

Then, at last, I drove back up to Quaker Lane Cottage, and stood in the overgrown orchard looking out over Granitehead Neck, my hands in my pockets; watching the distant white sails of the boats, and the glitter of summer sunshine on the waters of Salem Harbor.

I pushed the garden-swing, until it began to utter that distinctive *creakkk-squik, creakkk-squik*. Then I left it, and it gradually lost momentum and swung to a standstill.

The wind was warm. I felt as if the world had recently been reborn. I left the cottage, and closed the garden-gate behind me.

THE END